the WRECKAGE of PARADISE

BOOK THREE OF THE TRILOGY OF THE FALLEN

GREG STOLZE

WORLD OF DARKNESS

www.worldofdarkness.com

"Refusing her grand hests, she did confine thee,
By help of her more potent ministers
And in her most unmitigable rage,
Into a cloven pine; within which rift
Imprison'd thou didst painfully remain."

—Shakespeare, *The Tempest*, Act I, Scene 2

Chapter One

The brunette didn't have a gun, but that was okay. She'd never been much of a shot. She was nearsighted, and her prescription hadn't been updated until just a month ago. Now she wore smart, delicate wire-rim spectacles on an unremarkable button nose. Before, it had been mercy glasses collected by the Lions Club, with lenses that weren't exactly right, but close enough to let her drive and read the newspaper. And they'd sat on a blunt, prominent beak that had been (before the plastic surgery) her second most noteworthy feature.

Her most noteworthy one was still her piercing eyes. Even squinted, even behind battered and homely frames, there was — and had always been — some quality about this woman's eyes that made people (and some animals) shy away from her and find business elsewhere.

She didn't have a gun, but that was okay.

Getting into the house was simple. She had a key. She'd taken it from the man of the house, who didn't live there anymore. He wasn't in any condition to notice it missing. She loved him, the brunette did, with more than simple passion. She loved him with religious devotion, which was why she'd driven hundreds of miles to see his wife.

The brunette got into town early, but she spent a few days just watching. Watching the blonde, who lived in the house, who was married to the man. She bit her lip and squinted, even though her new glasses were perfect.

One night she saw the wife drive away with the son and return alone, and the brunette thought, *Ah*. She waited until the lights went off, then she let herself in.

The blonde wasn't asleep.

The blonde hadn't been sleeping much since she'd left her husband camping out in the desert miles away with crazy people all around him and craziness behind his eyes. She was confused and angry, and she felt incredibly guilty. Could she have been more supportive? Listened better? Cared more? But she'd listened and cared and supported for close to twenty *years*. How much more could she do? How much more could she have done?

She lay in bed and wondered these things, and when she heard a noise downstairs, it was almost a relief to have the distraction. Almost, but not quite.

Her eyes popped open, but she didn't get up. She was weary. She'd been looking forward to a night without her son's silent, reproachful glares. Still, she opened her eyes, and then she heard something else.

She heard little chirps coming from a phone somewhere in the house.

The brunette had thought about it and decided to disable the phone when she entered the house, so that the blonde couldn't call 911. The brunette was no electronics expert, but she'd realized during the long drive that all she needed to do was pick up an extension, dial a couple of numbers, and then set it aside. The line would be occupied, and the wife wouldn't be able to hang up and make her call to the police without getting to that extension. Simple. The brunette let herself into the house, found the kitchen phone, and did just that. Then she looked for a knife since she didn't have a gun.

The blonde picked up the bedside phone, tried dialing, tried hanging up and started to get scared. She slipped out of bed and put on her shoes—the pair of sensible black flats she'd worn to work.

The brunette was wearing moccasins. She'd once been told that American Indians moved silently by stepping down with the outside edge of their feet, then transferring their weight inward—a step more stealthy than the white man's "tip toes." So she was stepping, slowly, like that.

The wife crept down the back steps. Two stairways led up, one from the living room and one from the back hall. Like many women, the blonde had thought about what she'd do if an intruder came into her home and she couldn't telephone out. Her plan had always been to sneak down the back stairs and go out the kitchen door.

Unfortunately, that plan was based on the idea that any prowler would be in the living room with the TV and computer and stereo equipment. Thus it was that the blonde crept into the kitchen just in time to hear the brunette rummaging through her junk drawer. She might have been able to sneak up the stairs, down the other way and out the front door if she hadn't involuntarily shrieked.

The brunette flinched and spun toward the sound.

The blonde turned on the lights. Both women briefly shielded their eyes.

"Get the hell out of here!" the blonde shouted, her fear turning into bluster.

The brunette's eyes adapted to the light, and she saw a pile of knives on the counter, waiting to get washed. She seized the longest one—a five-inch slicer—and the blonde's outrage turned right back into fear. The blonde turned and bolted up the staircase.

The blonde was a good fifty pounds heavier than the brunette, and even panicked, she was slower. But she had a head start and a definite home-field advantage, so she passed the top of the stairs before the brunette could close to striking distance. She yanked the first door open, lunged in and almost got it shut before the brunette reached it and slammed her shoulder into it. The two women shoved at the door, and it shimmied back and forth between them. The brunette got her foot in the opening, but that didn't accomplish much except to get that foot crushed when the blonde put her weight on the door again. The brunette howled and shoved once more, and this time there was no resistance. The door flew open and she stumbled into the son's room.

The floor was covered with discarded jeans and underpants, so the brunette didn't recover her balance before the blonde hit her in the face with a baseball bat.

It wasn't a full-sized baseball bat. The blonde's son had used it a few years back in Dad's Club softball and kept it as a souvenir when his team made the semifinals. It was shorter than a normal bat, but it was cast aluminum and more than enough to take the brunette off her feet and slam her onto her back.

For a moment, the blonde just stood there, breathing heavily. Then she switched on the lights.

The brunette was a mess. The blonde dropped the bat, picked up the phone, bit her lip and realized that the kitchen extension was off the hook. She started to tremble as she stepped over her attacker and made for the stairs.

She was halfway down when she heard footsteps behind her. She didn't make the horror movie mistake of turning to look, she just ran. Her weight pulled her down the steps — clump, clump, clump — but the lighter, faster woman had a running start. The knife jabbed the blonde in the ribs, and the ball bat slammed down on her shoulder.

The two women tumbled out into the kitchen.

The blonde had her hands up, trying to shield herself, and she spun to face her attacker. She realized that she'd been stabbed, that she was bleeding, that her shoulder was sore, and then she saw the brunette's face.

The woman's face had changed.

Not only had the instant swelling and bleeding and split skin of a blunt-force bash disappeared, the face had healed into its original configuration—into the shape it'd had before the brunette got all her expensive plastic surgery. It was a face the blonde knew, one of the nut-jobs from the desert. Some southern-fried bitch who'd always looked at the blonde's husband with ill-concealed desire. Joellen something.

"You?" the blonde sputtered. "You still chasing after Teddy?"

"Oh, I've *got* your husband," Joellen replied. "I've come to get your son."

Birdie Mason—that was the blonde's name—once again made the switch from afraid to angry. She'd been terribly frightened by Joellen—who looked even crazier holding a bloody knife in her right hand and a bloody bat in her left—but the threat to her son blew that fright over the top, into rage and right through it into something so dizzying, so intense, so pure that Birdie couldn't have named it. Later, she might have called it "insane" or "berserk," but neither word was really adequate for a place beyond reason, beyond pain or fear, beyond anything but the urge to act. Only it wasn't even an urge, because no barrier stood between thought and action in that wordless place. Mind perfectly empty, Birdie attacked.

She seized a handle, yanked out the drawer and threw it at Joellen's face. It was a heavy drawer, well made and full of silverware. A jangling cloud erupted in front of the intruder for a second and Joellen ducked, the drawer bouncing off her arm with bone-bruising force. Then she staggered off balance as Birdie seized the end of the ball bat and jerked it effortlessly out of Joellen's grip.

Joellen let out a whiny, loud shriek as she lunged in to stab Birdie again, but the bigger woman had reach, and she slammed the bat down on Joellen's arm. The knife (which Birdie had used to cut up tomatoes just that afternoon) clattered to the ground as Joellen's arm broke.

Joellen scuttled backward and started groping on the counter for another knife, and if it had simply been a case of two women, one man, jealousy and violence, that would have been the end of it. Unable to make her fingers clasp, Joellen would have scrabbled fruitlessly for a weapon while Birdie self-righteously beat her brains in like a cavewoman.

But this wasn't a simple case of domestic envy.

There was a demon involved, and that demon had given Joellen the gift of healing. She had other gifts too, but in this instance, healing was the most important. So Joellen's arm healed and straightened itself, and she picked up a three-inch paring knife that still had some apple peel on it. She saw the madness in Birdie's eyes and recognized it. At some level, she welcomed it—*matched* it. She leaped forward, taking another bruising club blow on her left arm—What of it? It was only pain, pain was nothing, Joellen had a goddess on her side—and she stabbed Birdie in the gut. Then the two were entangled, belly to belly, each trying to knock the other down for stomping, but the kitchen was narrow and cramped. Birdie had always wanted a bigger one. They bounced back and forth between the counters, Birdie slamming the base of the bat into Joellen's skull, Joellen stabbing and stabbing into Birdie's broad back. But the knife was better for this. Better for close work. Even crazy, Birdie was slowing down from simple blood loss. She felt herself weakening, falling. She tried to shove the other woman back but could only make a little gap. She got Joellen back enough that she could see her face, and on it Birdie saw vicious triumph. She saw the triumph of the underdog who's always longed for the upper hand, who's always wanted to be a far worse tyrant than her oppressor.

In that moment, Birdie saw herself—blonde, prosperous, well fed—in Joellen's eyes, and she understood Joellen's hate.

The space between their bodies was wide enough that Joellen could finally get the knife between and slash it across Birdie's throat—a good, deep artery cut.

Birdie wasn't angry anymore as she brought the bat up again; she was too tired to strike. The best she could do was wedge it under Joellen's neck. She reached her right hand behind Joellen's back and she felt sad, felt sorry for the other woman, as if all this had been a terrible misunderstanding, a tragedy. But she could not let this woman take her son. No.

Dying, Birdie lurched forward, clutched Joellen, and fell into her hard. Joellen overbalanced, fell backward, and as Birdie had hoped, the back of Joellen's skull hit the kitchen table. Her head rocked forward, the metal bat blocked her chin, and her neck snapped.

Joellen could heal any injury, but this one killed her straight out. She was actually dead before she hit the floor. Birdie died two minutes later, without ever moving.

A recorded voice came on the phone, saying, "If you'd like to make a call, please hang up and dial again." It repeated this until Lance, Birdie's son, found them the next day.

"Humanity's defenders have returned."

Mitch Berger blinked and tried to follow along. The woman speaking had introduced herself as Mukikel and, except for having the alert demeanor of a Navy SEAL deep in enemy territory, she looked like your typical Laura Ashley-clad Southern California hausfrau. Ten minutes ago, she'd been a glorious apparition with radiant wings, claws like daggers and eyes that smoldered with the secrets of blackest space. Right now, she was driving.

Mitch and his old coworker Chuck were in the back seat, and sitting between them was a little girl. Ten years old? Fifteen and skinny? Mitch didn't know from little girls, and until they were bed legal he wasn't much interested. When they'd gotten in the car, he'd reminded her to buckle up and she'd said, "Aren't you sweet?" (She hadn't put on her seat belt, though.) She was called Shadrannat, and she was muttering to herself in some language Mitch had never heard as they drove along. Like Mukikel, she had previously transformed before Mitch's bewildered eyes, growing wings and glowing with grandeur and terror.

Mitch and Chuck were men. The other two were demons.

They were all in a Chevy Tahoe, rumbling along the streets of Los Angeles toward the Pacific Ocean.

Chuck was trying to reassure Mitch that he needn't worry about any of his possessions, all that stuff would get taken care of. Possessions were fleeting anyhow, right?

"I guess I don't... Why do we have to leave?" Mitch asked.

"Los Angeles is occupied territory," Mukikel said crisply, making an illegal right amid a cacophony of honking horns. "Traitors to the cause are entrenched here, and we've got to get you out."

"Buniel's engaged," Shadrannat said tersely. Seeing the red light up ahead, Mukikel turned off the road and rumbled over a well-manicured lawn, making her left-hand turn scant inches in front of oncoming traffic. Mitch felt her gun the engine.

"Buniel! Cut out," Mukikel said. She frowned then said, "That's an order! You've done all the good you're going to..."

"What did she mean by 'humanity's defenders'?"

"Us," Shadrannat said.

"The Elohim," Chuck said. "The angels who built the world."

"And who were the only ones to take humanity's side against a tyrannical master," Mukikel added. The engine was laboring, and Mitch tried to crane his neck to see just how fast they were going. Plenty fast. He could tell from the way the sport-ute rocked and dipped on its heavy-duty shocks when Mukikel wove in and out of traffic.

"Then what I saw was..." Mitch was baffled—his attention split between the road, the muttering girl beside him and the driver's proclamations.

"You saw the Morningstar," Mukikel said. "Our general, and the greatest of our number." Her eyes flicked to the rearview mirror. A moment later, Mitch heard sirens and saw flashing lights. "We seek to restore him to his rightful place." She reached back and put her hand on Shadrannat's knee. "Pinpoint on three..."

"You may want to close your eyes," the young girl told Mitch, but he didn't listen because he was wondering what a "pinpoint" was. She put a hand on his shoulder, and on Chuck's, as if to comfort them.

As Mukikel said "two," she swerved hard, up onto the sidewalk and straight toward a palm tree. Mitch drew in his breath to scream...

"...three."

And then the car was still.

It didn't come to a stop. It didn't rock forward. There was no sudden jarring sensation in Mitch's inner ear. One moment it was going at least fifty, probably more, and then it was at rest—without ever going through the process of slowing down.

Mitch's sense of motion couldn't jibe with what he was seeing.

"I think I'm gonna..." But he didn't finish that sentence either. As the pursuing patrol car shot past, he lurched forward and puked all over his shoes and pants. He heard the screech of tires, but he didn't see what happened to the cops. Mukikel switched gears, backed out, reentered traffic and was soon speeding along again in a different direction.

"Buniel, report," Shadrannat said. Then again, "Report!"

"Sorry about that," Mitch said.

Mukikel barked out one short laugh. "I hope that's the worst thing that happens today!"

"Buniel, *no*, we've got—" Shadrannat stopped mid-sentence, and the roar of an explosion, perhaps a mile away on the waterfront, wafted over the car a beat later.

(Los Angeles had suffered a terrible earthquake the previous year, and many fuel storage depots or other volatile locations had exploded under the strain. But it hadn't happened for months. Things were *supposed* to be getting back to normal.)

"Shit," the little girl said. "He's deincarnated."

"I *told* him to withdraw," Mukikel said, pulling into a small marina and parking at the end of the dock. "Stupid Victory asshole."

"Still, it feels like he bought us some time."

Mukikel opened her door while Shadrannat jumped nimbly over the backseat and started opening the rear cargo hatch.

"Come on," Chuck said, unbuckling his seat belt and opening his door. "We have to hurry."

"Why?" Mitch asked, his voice plaintive.

"You've been watched," Chuck replied. "The traitors knew Lucifer's Army would come for you sooner or later. You're their bait, and we've finally taken it. Now they're closing in."

"Lucifer's Army? Wait, Chuck, you're not... You haven't become some kind of *Satanist*, have you?"

"Hurry up!" Shadrannat said, pulling Mitch by his elbow out to a nondescript power boat. In her other hand, she was dragging a large box that seemed too heavy for such a slight young girl.

Mukikel was in the boat, warming up the engine and untying it from the dock. "Get in," she said, "and get under those." She was pointing at a small mound of peculiar blankets.

"What are they?"

"They're ballistic cloth, so you don't get shot," she replied. "Lie flat."

Mukikel cast off as soon as Mitch hobbled into the boat (he had a bad leg and needed a cane even on level ground). The boat roared out in the harbor seconds later.

"Lucifer's gotten a bad rap," Chuck said, pulling the bulletproof sheet over his head like a hood. "It sounds like he was the only one who was on humanity's side throughout the whole thing."

"The whole thing being…"

"The War on Heaven."

"They're coming," Shadrannat said, peering out over the water.

"I feel them too," Mukikel replied.

Mitch peeked up—he couldn't stop himself, and besides, the smell of his puke on his pants was cloying under the blanket—and saw that their small boat was rocketing along like a racer, bow toward the sky and heading toward open ocean.

He heard a sound like fireworks, and Shadrannat hissed, "Get down!" She'd opened her box and he was shocked to see her slinging a pair of sheathed machetes on belts over her neck and shoulders. They looked bizarre over her *Kim Possible* T-shirt, but no less so than the sub-machinegun she pulled out next.

He ducked his head as he saw her point the gun behind them and open fire.

When she stopped, he cautiously peeked out again. She was reloading.

He looked backward and saw a fast, sleek racer zipping through the water after them. Mitch knew a little about boats—

it wasn't much, but he knew that a cigarette boat like that should have easily outpaced their pleasure craft. Nonetheless, it was barely keeping pace. He saw twinkling lights through the chaser's spray, even by daylight, and realized that someone was shooting at them.

Then Shadrannat jumped out of the boat and started running across the water.

Mitch knew, at some level, that he should put his head down. And he knew that seeing a little girl racing across the waves in a serpentine fashion while shooting a machinegun was simply *not possible*. But he'd seen other impossible things, so what the fuck?

He also noticed that as soon as Shadrannat left the boat, it slowed down considerably—even though the engine was still roaring as fiercely as ever.

She ran back and forth, mostly making for the cigarette boat, and he saw her stumble as she got hit, actually saw chunks of *meat* fly out of her back while a pink mist of blood mixed with the ocean spray, but she didn't even slow down. When her gun was empty, she dropped it, drew a machete in each hand and dove under the waves.

What the fuck? Mitch though. As if she'd been running on stepping stones and had just jumped off…

Regardless, the boat was getting closer fast, he could hear Mukikel shouting something behind him, but he was stunned by what he'd seen and partially deafened by the gunshots, so he couldn't hear her.

He felt the boat slow more, and then a hand shoved his head down hard and pulled the blanket over it. Three seconds of confusing burrowing movements later, Mukikel was lying beside him under the cover. The boat seemed to be adrift, and she hissed in his ear, "Your brains contain important information, so I'll thank you not to catch a bullet with them."

The three of them lay there for what felt like ages, smelling Mitch's puke and feeling the waves of the ocean. Then Mukikel stood up and pushed the blankets aside.

"All clear," she said.

"Huh?"

"It's all right, for now. You can sit up."

Cautiously, he did. He looked around.

The other boat still had its nose pointed to the sky, but it wasn't moving forward. It was sinking, with thick billows of smoke coming from the engine. It was only about fifty feet away, and as he watched, the little girl climbed nimbly to the tip of the prow and jumped toward them.

She landed lightly in the middle of their deck. The boat barely dipped. Her face, arms and chest were splashed and splattered with blood, her twin machetes were slathered with it, but from the way she moved, Mitch was pretty sure that none of it was hers.

"Let's go!" she said brightly.

There was blood on her teeth, too.

Lynn Culver's murderer was back in Oswego. He was in the hospital there, visiting a woman named Glenda Fielding. She was old and had taken ill very suddenly, and the doctors were extra-comforting to her because they were extra-confused.

The killer (whose name was Usiel but who went by Clive Keene) was also extra-confused. He loved Glenda more than he loved anything in the world, except maybe God. Maybe not. God was far away and not talking to him, while Glenda was fragile and grateful and immediately present.

He came into her room, and her face lit up. He felt her love, her trust, her faith.

He'd nearly killed her.

Usiel was... what? He himself wasn't sure. Once he he'd been the Throne of the Sundered. Now he was called the Reaper of Souls.

He was no longer an angel, he had to admit that. He'd been condemned by Michael-Word-of-God and cast into Hell with the rest, but was he a demon? He'd never rebelled. Never *willfully* disobeyed. Even when ordered into confinement with those he'd fought, he went without a struggle.

Now, like the truly fallen, he was free once more. Like them, he could draw on the faith of mortals instead of being sustained by the radiance of the One Above. Like them, he could kill his believers if he needed too much from them.

He'd almost killed Glenda when he was in need.

Usiel had been fighting a demon named Gaviel, and he should have easily won. In any sort of fair fight, the Reaper would triumph. But being, quite literally, a sneaky devil, Gaviel's fight was anything but fair. By throwing mortal after mortal, lie after lie, hard choice after hard choice at his attacker, Gaviel had driven him off.

Usiel had failed, and he had drawn on Glenda's strength in his failure, and as he was drawing out her very life, she'd called on him for help and salvation.

Ironic, but the Reaper of Souls had no taste for irony.

"You've come!" Glenda said. Instinctively, she tried to sit up, but she was too weak. Instead she hit a button and raised the bed to a sitting position.

"Yes." Usiel didn't know what else to say.

"Oh thank God," Glenda replied. "I knew you'd come. I knew you wouldn't abandon me."

He went to her side and brushed back her white hair with his black hand. "No," he said.

"What happened to me? Do you know? Was it... Was it that ghost again?"

"It wasn't. It was me."

Glenda's forehead clouded. "I don't understand."

Usiel had struggled over whether to tell her, but he knew there was only one right choice.

"I was fighting another... fighting a demon. I was hurt. I could draw on you to heal myself, so I did. I'm sorry."

Glenda was quiet a moment.

"So that wasn't... not some evil spirit? You did that to me?"

Mutely, he nodded.

She frowned a little, then said, "If you had to, I guess you had to."

"No, Glenda..."

"If I can help you fight... demons... then I should. Shouldn't I?"

Usiel closed his eyes, wincing. Glenda still thought he was an angel, thought he was still fighting for God against the legions of Hell.

(*And aren't you?* he asked himself.)

She didn't know of his sin, his corruption. She didn't know he'd been condemned like them and imprisoned like them. She didn't know he was adrift in a world with no true angels left. Like them.

(*Don't forget the cannibalism, either*, he thought. *You've stolen the strength of one of your own kind, just like them. And you loved it, just like them.*)

Introspection wasn't common for Usiel, but since his return to the human world, a situation that once seemed straightforward—fight demons, serve God—had become cloudy and confusing. He'd felt pure, heavenly power wielded by the servant of a fiend most foul. He'd been asked why he thought he could repent after Hell, but that the rebel demons could not. He'd been exorcised. He'd murdered men and liked it.

He'd met Lucifer, who had begged his aid in fighting the other demons. When Usiel refused, the Morningstar could have compelled him but did not.

He'd met a demon who reminded him of his lost love, Haniel. He still wasn't sure if he would kill her.

"Glenda, it's not my place to decide who should live or die."

(*But you decided for Gordy Hines, didn't you? You decided for him, and those clods in Florida, and…*)

"Well, the Bible says, 'There is no greater love you can have, than to lay down your life for a friend,' right?"

Now Glenda was offering her life for his crusade. This hurt and baffled him most of all.

"Don't be so sure I'm your friend," he replied.

The scent of Mitch's puke had stung less out in the open air, but now they were enclosed again, and it was dense. Mukikel and Shadrannat had gone off, giving only vague explanations about "making their report" to someone called the "Princess."

The ocean was a flat disc to the horizon all around them, and their small boat was tied alongside a huge cargo ship. Mitch and Chuck had been helped up a rope ladder—Shadrannat had helped them while clinging to the side of the boat like a pubescent spider-girl, smiling encouragement all the while. Her teeth no longer showed blood. She must have licked them clean.

On the deck, the two mortal men had been introduced to Becky and Lawrence, a mismatched pair who'd hustled them belowdecks, out of the wind.

Lawrence was sullen and sallow-faced, dressed in simple and sensible clothes. He'd greeted them with a grunt and offered them a hand as they came down the steps. He'd paused when Mitch reached the bottom to look appraisingly in Mitch's eyes. He'd given a short little puff of air from his nose, but said nothing.

(It took Mitch a few minutes to realize that his mild seasickness had calmed completely. He did not connect it to Lawrence until later.)

While Lawrence said little, Becky spoke enough for two people (or possibly more). As they came below she said, "Oh! Poor darlings! Lawrence, see to them, I'll get them some fresh things. Coffee? Yes, coffee too, and perhaps some cookies for you?" she said, nodding at Chuck. She was a black woman, pudgy, maybe fifty, with white hair and a vividly colored dress. Her expression was open and maternal, but her face showed lines and creases more used to suspicion and bitterness. It was off-putting, but only slightly so.

"That would be great," Chuck said, smiling, but she was already hustling off through one of two doors in the room.

There was a sofa and two bolted-down chairs. With a nod indicating that they could sit, Lawrence flopped down and picked up a copy of *Reader's Digest*.

"This must be the *Longstar*," Chuck said, looking around at the ordinary cabin as if he were in the middle of the Taj Mahal.

"The what?" Mitch asked, taking four cane-steps over to the sofa and perching on its arm. He didn't want to get his vomit on it.

"The floating fortress of Lucifer's Army," Chuck said. He gave an inquiring look to Lawrence, who raised his eyes briefly and nodded. Chuck beamed at this confirmation.

"Yeah," Mitch said, "About this 'Lucifer's Army' business..."

"You take a forty waist, right?" Becky said, bustling back into the room with a pair of khaki slacks slung over one forearm. The other arm held up a tray with waitress-like confidence, and on that were two steaming mugs of coffee and a small plate of Lorna Doone shortbread cookies.

"Is there somewhere I can...?" Mitch gestured at the pants. Becky tittered and said, "I'll turn my back."

While he put on fresh clothes, Chuck dunked a cookie. After a short hesitation, Mitch sipped the coffee.

"This is good," he said. "Just how I like it."

"Two sugars, no cream," Becky said, turning back around.

"Have we... Did we ever meet before?"

"Oh no. I just know what people want."

"Yeah? Can you guess what else I want?"

"Answers."

"You *are* good."

On the couch, Lawrence gave a snort.

"Start asking questions," Becky asked, sticking her tongue out at Lawrence briefly.

Mitch opened his mouth, then shut it. It wasn't that he lacked questions. There were so many that they were forming a logjam.

"Let's start with... Mukikel. And Shadrannat."

"Ooh, you're on a celestial name basis. You should be pleased."

"Huh?"

"You don't know about the name game?"

"Let's... let's set that aside. How did they *do* that stuff?"

"Stuff? You'll have to be more specific."

"How did they *change*? How did they stop that Tahoe on a dime and, and climb up walls and make those huge fucking Morpheus jumps?"

"They're Elohim." Seeing his blank look, Becky added, "Demons, if you prefer."

"So, what, the laws of physics don't apply to them?"

"The so-called laws of physics are really just an agreed-upon set of conventions. If you speak the right language, you can temporarily appeal them."

He just stared. "You're serious."

She giggled and nodded. "It's been a long time and we've all forgotten ever so much, but we remember a few little tricks and shortcuts."

"Why is this so hard to believe?" Chuck asked. "You saw Lucifer perform acts a thousand times less possible."

"I saw that stuff when I was *out of my gourd*."

"You saw the Morningstar?" They were the first words Lawrence had spoken. His voice was raspy, as if from disuse.

"That's why we're here," Chuck said.

"Well, that explains why the knight and the overlord here were assigned to extract you," Becky said.

"Who?"

"The two who got you. You know."

"Mukikel and Shadrannat?"

With a secret smile, Becky nodded. "You may not want to toss those names around. Every time you invoke them, they can hear you."

"Huh?"

"Do you speak pig Latin? Ig-pay atin-lay?"

"Es-yay," Chuck replied. Mitch shook his head.

"You take the first sound of a word, stick it on the end, add 'ay.' Chuck becomes Uck-chay. Mitch is Itch-may."

"I'm lost."

"If you said Ukikel-may's name properly—or Addrannat-shay's—they would be able to listen to your words and even speak back to you. So speaking a demon's celestial name is... unwise. If you don't know what you're doing."

"Is this the name game thing you were talking about?"

"Mm-hm. You remember the old song? 'Let's do Jerry!/Jerry jerry bo-berry/banana-fana fo ferry/me mi mo merry/Jerry!' Remember?"

A vague memory surfaced in Mitch's mind. "I kinda remember that from grade school. The teacher would never do it with my name."

Lawrence gave a dry chuckle. "I bet she wouldn't do Chuck, either."

"Just go easy with any names you learn," Becky said. "Titles are safer."

"Like this Princess I heard about?"

"Mm, the Princess of Majestic Liberation."

"You're kidding."

"Wait 'til you meet her. See if I'm kidding then. The two who brought you in are the Knight of Venom and the Autumn Overlord. The knight is the little girl."

"Why all these titles?"

"Why do officers have ranks in an army?" Chuck asked. "Same reason. Lucifer is 'The Morningstar,' right?"

"Or the King of this World." Becky's smile got a little brittle. "Morningstar gets more use, for reasons you can easily imagine."

"Don't forget host names, either," Lawrence said.

"Oh yes. We use them most often with mortals," Becky said brightly, "but it's still easy to forget. Still, I'm getting very used to being called 'Becky' after all. I believe the Knight of Venom is Tabitha, and the Autumn Overlord is Sally."

"Sally," Mitch said, running his tongue over his teeth and knitting his brows in confusion. "Can they hear it if you use those names? Or their titles?"

"Nope. You can gossip in perfect safety."

There was a pause.

"So what's Lucifer's Army?" Mitch asked at last.

"We are. I'll assume you know nothing about the War on Heaven?"

"That's a safe assumption."

"Well, we lost and history got written by the winners. They claimed we fell because of pride or jealousy or lust for the daughters of Adam, if you can believe that! Our real reasons were concealed."

"And those were?"

"Love," Becky said.

Another pause.

"No, really," he said.

"*Really*. Come *on*, Mitch, you've seen us work miracles with a tiny fraction of our old power. I know fallen who can turn sand into silver or inspire adoration in a crowd with nothing but a hummed tune. They can do that *now*. Back then, we shook the stars in their orbits—or could, if we hadn't hung them there in the first place. What could we envy in humankind—weak, sad, ignorant, bald apes with *so much potential*, and all of it unfulfilled? It wasn't envy. We had everything; you had nothing. Greed? Don't make me laugh. Anger? We didn't know the meaning of anger, only sorrow and pity because we loved you. We couldn't stand to see you abandoned by your Maker, left to your own measly devices, feeling cold and alone and never knowing a multitude of angels adored you!"

"You're blathering," Lawrence muttered, without looking up from his magazine. Becky glared, then composed herself.

"There was war, and we lost. And we were imprisoned, but not destroyed. That would have been too *quick*," she said, and for the first time, bitterness entered her voice, and spite crossed her features. It was like watching some exquisitely specialized tool being fitted to its task, it was miraculous how even a little meanness matched that face so well.

"But now we're out. We're out, the Holy Host is *gone*, and Lucifer is missing as well."

Mitch sat for a moment, just thinking.

"The Holy Host—you mean, God's angels, right?—are gone? So, like no one's minding the store? Why don't you just take over?"

"Well, not every rebel stayed true to rebellion," Becky said. "Most of the escapees are on our side, but there are a few who just couldn't handle their confinement. Mad demons. Mad gods."

"We saw Lucifer kill two of them during the earthquake," Chuck said.

Mitch just put his head in his hands.

The door opened.

"The Princess Nazathor will see you now." The speaker was the Autumn Overlord, Mukikel. Also known as Sally.

Usiel, the Reaper of Souls, sat alone in Glenda's house. She was still in the hospital, and she'd insisted he take the key. "I'd feel better knowing you were there," she said. "Safer."

Like a lot of things she said, it hurt him. Even though she didn't mean it to. Even though he didn't know why.

Before he realized what he was doing, Usiel stretched out with his senses—with one of the senses humans lacked. It was something like smell, and something like hearing, and it let him detect other damaged angels.

Nothing.

He was the only Elohim around.

Idly he poked through Glenda's refrigerator. He heated up some leftover green beans that weren't getting any younger, but that wasn't a concern. He ate food because he had to; different flavors didn't interest him much.

Back in the guest room was a small duffel bag stuffed with tens, twenties and fifties. When he'd left Italy, he'd simply dropped his sack of lira in a bus station. Money wasn't a problem.

He finished his beans and a glass of water. He twisted the ring on his finger and thought of all the demons he'd fought. All the demons he should be fighting? He didn't know.

Gaviel.

Just thinking the name brought a half-snarl to Usiel's lips. Gaviel. That rat bastard. Cold and bright and shiny as a mirror, and like a mirror, he always showed you just what you expected. But when you reached out—in trust, in anger or for whatever reason—you found your hand stopped short and bruised by your own image.

That fucker skates through life like it's one long Mentos commercial. Mentos commercials were from Clive's world, not Usiel's, but the Reaper didn't even notice how his host's ideas had condensed, softly, in his mind.

Part of him wanted to go back and finish the job, but he was tired, too tired and confused and maybe, just a little bit, afraid. Gaviel had gotten the best of him twice. Who's to say what the third time would bring, now that the demon had his measure?

Usiel relaxed for a moment and let the whisper of invocations rustle through his mind.

Usiel you fuck, you shit, you cunt, I'm getting out and I'll fuck you, I'll shit on you, I'll lay my eggs in your eye sockets and watch my maggots hatch...

Usiel the Reaper of Souls is unbound from the Abyss...

Usiel, I can return you to God...

Usiel, I will return you to Hell...

Usiel, angel of night, sweep these phantoms away with your dreadful wings...

The usual shit. Usiel got invoked a lot—mostly demons still in Hell promising to make him pay for putting them there. Sometimes demons who were trying to trick him into helping them, or trap him so that they could destroy him.

He changed his mental frequency.

…Reaper of Souls is trapped in the Soul-Storm, endlessly battling tormented shades…

…Reaper of Souls has the third of the Halaku releasing tools. If only we could seize it—but who can use it more deadly than he?

…Reaper of Souls will rise up to destroy what remains of Stygia, he will polish his bones with our ashes!

He'd been attuned to his title, not just his name, so that he could listen as others spoke of him, even when they thought him unaware. But there was little of interest or value there, either. Just gossip or slander or speculation.

He thought about doing an invocation of his own.

Sabriel.

Thinking about her made him feel as bad as thinking about Gaviel did, just in a different way. Before her, things had been simple. He'd been right, they'd been wrong, he took the pointy stick to them and flensed their damned spirits from their stolen bodies. Maybe it wasn't exactly *easy*, but it wasn't complicated. Good. Evil. Do the math.

But she'd pointed out how much he was like them.

She'd brought him doubt.

She'd made him remember a time before it was Us and Them. Remember it and miss it and maybe hope he could have it again.

She'd baffled him and made him feel good, then he'd found out that she was just jerking him around.

Maybe.

Could he be sure? Someone was playing tricks. Someone was tricking *him*. Something he'd believed had to be a lie, but what? And that meant that something he believed *now* could be a lie, too. How would he know?

He opened his mouth to say her name, but then screwed up his face and shut it. No. Too painful. Too humiliating. And maybe he'd been kicked into Hell for eight thousand years, but he still had enough pride that he wouldn't *choose* lies. He wouldn't be a party to his own deception.

"Lucifer," he said.

Usiel?

"I want answers."

"Give me your questions."

Usiel spun. The Morningstar was right behind him, coming through the door to Glenda's root cellar. Usiel sensed out and there was the Devil, his stink of soot and chime of glory unmistakable.

"Mind if I sit?" Lucifer asked.

"Suit yourself. Coffee?"

"Hot tea, if you've got it."

"Sure."

Usiel, Reaper of Souls, made tea. Then he said, "You think I should kill them."

"The other demons? Yes. I think *we* should kill them."

"How can you be so sure?"

"How can *you* be so puzzled? You saw what Vassago did to his servants, right? To the people who were *loyal* to him, who *loved* him. I'm not even going into what Bow and Coaler and the rest have done to innocent people on Vassago's orders. Ask your friend Sabriel about Nate Kowalski or Brenda Gary. Or if you think humans are beneath your notice…"

The Reaper winced, but the Morningstar continued, "…you could look at how Gaviel treated his *allies*—his *comrades in arms* like Edasul and Joriel."

"I won't deny that the demons are doing evil."

Lucifer laughed.

"But—listen! Men do evil, too. But not every man. Is every demon irretrievably fallen? Of all your thirty million followers, must every single one be corrupt?"

Lucifer sighed and looked down into his tea.

"I don't know," he said.

"And if *you* don't know, how can you say we must fight them all?"

"Because I can't take the chance." Lucifer looked up again. "They call me, Usiel. They speak my name, all the time. Nazriel..." The Devil bit his lip as he spoke that name. "Nazathor, now. Each twilight, for an hour, she invokes me, begging for me to return to her. She does it every night. She has done it every night since the Fall, even when she was in the Abyss. But what can I tell her? That I'm ready to start the fight again? I'm not. That there's a place for her at my side? There's not. That there's a place for her in the *world*? I've spent the ages since the Fall making sure there *isn't*."

He took a sip and looked away out the window. "Remember Malakh? Loyal to a fault. In Los Angeles, I saw him. Rescued him, maybe. Of all of them, I felt I owed him... but no more. He's as bad as the rest, Usiel. He's no angel anymore, just an animal hungry for meat. He's chosen the side of the humans—maybe out of force of habit—but when I saw him, he was a beast, a creature that would chew off its own leg to get at its prey." He sighed. "Grifiel too. I saw him escape, and he's a horror. He was once my best friend, and now he's a murderer, a torturer, an abomination ravening *in my name*. That's the sick joke, that so many of them still think the fight is on, they kill and destroy and rape and claim they're doing it *all for me*."

"Why don't you reveal yourself? Tell them your true will? Become the leader they want? Surely if you pointed your loyal followers at other demons, they would obey."

"Are you so certain? They rebelled against the Ancient of Days when they were perfected beings. Now damaged and damned, what would stop them from turning on me if they didn't like what I told them?"

"What would that be?"

Lucifer was silent for a long time, then said, "What if the Rebellion *was* part of the plan? What if being in this world isn't supposed to be easy or fun or beautiful? What if we were tested, *all* of us, and we *all* failed? Oh, maybe Abel and his tribe passed the test, and maybe your old lover, Haniel, passed the test, and maybe Lailah and the others who stayed loyal to God passed the test. But they're all gone now. Maybe the universe is over, maybe it's *all* Hell and the demons are now just loosed from the lowest part so that they can complete the job of dragging down everything else. How about that? You think they'll like that? You think that will play well in Los Angeles?"

"Is that how it is?"

"I can't say. And that's the one crime my believers would never forgive—ignorance. If I give them no answers, or give them answers they don't want, 'Lucifer's Army' falls apart and we get a second War of Wrath."

They were silent for a moment.

"Isn't that what we're headed toward now?"

Mitch swallowed hard as he was ushered into the Princess's chamber. He wasn't sure what to expect. Sumptuous oriental rugs and pillows, with plank-chested men dancing lewdly before a hookah-smoking degenerate? Skulls and pentagrams and an altar with a screaming naked virgin on it, and this "Princess" in her horned and bat-winged glory about to perform the sacrifice? Or maybe something that was alien like the movie *Aliens* with dripping slime and insectile protrusions and here and there a not-quite-dead victim webbed to the wall?

Inside, it was an office.

Swank, but an office nonetheless. The desk was huge, made of some old dark wood that made you think of fat white bankers, cigars and insider-trading. The bookshelves were glass-fronted, carefully restored antiques, but they were just bookshelves. There were filing cabinets, too, bolted to the floor in case of choppy weather. It was reassuringly normal until the woman behind the (tastefully decorated, slightly cluttered) desk spun the (classy, leather-bound) chair to face them.

She looked normal.

She looked absolutely stunning.

It was a very weird thing, for Mitch. He'd been ready for anything, except for a tastefully coifed woman with light-brown skin, bead jewelry and slender, graceful hands. She looked like a bust of Nefertiti—the kind of classy black dame that insults just roll off of, puddling embarrassingly around the insulter's feet.

But at the same time, he was shaken to the core by awe and wonder. It was hard to put a finger on it, on the exact source of his feelings. It was kind of like when he was a little kid and he saw *Star Wars*. Or there had been a couple of rock concerts—one R.E.M. show in particular—when he'd had that sort of soul-stirring moment of true exhilaration. Maybe when he'd lost his virginity, too.

It was as if he was looking at a masterful painting of an ordinary scene. Michelangelo or Van Gogh could paint something normal in a way that the painting looked luminous, magical, even when the scene it depicted did not. And Nazathor's presence had that same effect. Everything around her was special, was seen as if for the first time, simply because it had the good fortune to be around her.

"Mitchell Berger and Charles Rodriguez," she said, smiling. Her voice was ordinary. Her voice was more moving than any human music.

"Yes ma'am," Chuck said. Mitch nodded.

"Two witnesses to the Morningstar."

Chuck nodded. Mitch shrugged.

"Did you have trouble leaving LA?"

Mitch gave an uneasy chuckle before realizing she'd been talking to Mukikel and Shadrannat.

"Nothing worth mentioning," the little-girl demon replied. She had a small bag of sunflower seeds in her hands, and periodically she'd put a few in her mouth. "Buniel lost his host, though." She tipped her head. "He wants out," she added.

The Princess noticed Mitch's confused look before he even had time to reassess his confusion and try to figure out what Shadrannat—the Knight of Venom? Tabitha?—had meant. "She means he wants out of Hell," she said, her tone helpful.

"Oh," Mitch replied. What else was there to say?

"It's not easy."

"Okay."

"If it was, everyone would do it."

"I told him to pull out," Mukikel said. "He disobeyed my order."

"Mm, and now he's certainly paying," the Princess replied. "Still, one can't fault his courage."

"Only his intelligence."

"Now, now. We'll discuss him later."

"The Victory legion won't be happy. They'll blame us for losing one of their soldiers."

"Leave the Victory legion to me. Right now, I need you to talk to Defiance."

Mukikel grimaced. Whoever "Defiance" was, Mitch decided, Mukikel wasn't eager to talk to him. Or her. Or it.

"What do you need?"

"A blank for our fallen comrade, of course."

Mukikel's eyebrows rose. "You think he's worth one?" she asked bluntly, while Mitch wondered what the fuck a "blank" was.

"It would certainly square things with his overlord, now wouldn't it?"

"Yeah, if his overlord calls him back. Do you really think the Defiance legion is just going to hand us a blank, just like that?"

"They'll provide one for *me*," the Princess said. Mukikel shrugged.

"If you want to just give it away…"

The Princess leaned back and stroked her lips with her right hand's fingertips. "Mm," she said. "I do have a problem with profligacy, don't I? Though I hear there's a lot of good blanks coming on the market lately. A reliable supplier."

"I didn't hear that," Mukikel said.

The Princess smiled. "No reason you would." She seemed to have made a decision as she stood and said, "I suspect the best solution is to have Buniel transferred to our command."

"Especially if you do it now," Shadrannat said, "while he's just one more useless spirit in the Pit." A few more soft crunching sounds came from her mouth.

"My thoughts exactly. Shadrannat, his overlord is… mm, one of the six Proud Walkers, I remember that much."

"I'll find out," Shadrannat said, and her tone of determination sounded odd, coming from little girl lungs.

"Find out, negotiate, drive a hard bargain, but get him reassigned. Mukikel should have a blank ready to go by the time you get that straightened out, right?"

"Yes," Mukikel said.

The three women exchanged glances again, then— wordlessly—the two subordinate demons turned to leave.

"Send in the Star Thorn, please," the Princess said as they retreated.

Then it was just her and the two men. She smiled.

"I envy you," she said.

"Yeah?" Mitch said weakly, looking over his shoulder. The Princess stood and walked around her desk to get a better look at them.

"For a million years I have longed to see, once more, the face you two beheld."

Chuck nodded. The Princess flicked her eyes from him to Mitch.

"You seem strangely unaffected," she said.

Mitch fiddled with his cane, turning it between his hands.

"Well, I..." he said. "You see I... I was not at my best when that whole thing went down."

She raised an inquisitive eyebrow.

"His leg was badly broken," Chuck said. "We'd drugged him up to dull the pain."

"How terrible!" she said. "Which leg?"

Mitch pointed. To his surprise—astonishment, nearly, she knelt before him and put her hands on it.

"Lawrence should have seen to this," she said, and then...

A wave of warmth, soothing sweet warmth, washed over him, flowed *through* him, his entire body, and it was like being a child in winter, coming in from sledding and getting a cup of cocoa from Mom, just right, being warmed and comforted and safe...

And suddenly his leg was straight again.

"How did you do that?" he whispered.

"It's what I do," she said. She stood. "It's what I am." For a moment, those warm, brown eyes held his, and they were sad. "It's what I was," she said.

"Asharu," Chuck said, his tone reverent. "Angel of breath. Angel of healing."

She turned to him. "Someone's taught you well."

"Mukikel," he replied. "She taught me the houses of the Sebettu, so that I'd have some idea what I was up against if... if anything happened."

"And things did happen, didn't they?"

Chuck nodded.

"You had the chance to be her thrall, didn't you?" the Princess asked. "And Shadrannat's, too."

"Yes."

"Why didn't you?"

"My worship is for Lucifer alone," Chuck said, and his tone wasn't defiant or grandiose or even crazy.

(Mitch knew crazy. He and Chuck had met working as orderlies in a madhouse. So Mitch knew that crazy people often sounded perfectly sane and stable and simple and true, just like Charles sounded now. Mitch wasn't sure just what to think. *Oh shit* seemed like the best candidate.)

The door opened, and in walked a rail-thin scarecrow of a man. This guy *did* look crazy.

"Sorry I took so long," he said. "I was examining the strands."

Instinctively, Mitch turned to face this guy, and his hands came up ready, because he *sounded* crazy too. He was dressed in oil-stained jeans and a rumpled Anaheim Angels sweatshirt. His head was shaved clean—a recent job, apparently, because the skin on top was badly sunburned, while his face was tanned and weathered. You could see a clean line of demarcation where his hair had once offered protection.

As he mentally filed away "the strands" with "host," "Defiance" and "blank" in his rapidly growing list of words to get explained, he realized why the newcomer's eyes looked so lemur-big and blank. The sunburned curves over each eye socket showed that he'd shaved off his eyebrows, too.

"Mr. Berger, Mr. Rodriguez, this is the Star Thorn."

"You can call me Dennis," the guy muttered.

"These are the men who saw our leader when he manifested in Los Angeles."

Before, Mitch would have said Dennis the Star Thorn's eyes were lit, but he would have been speaking metaphorically. Now they brightened literally, twin white beams changing the shadows on his face as he fixed his gaze—now terribly blank in its brightness—on both of them.

"These are them? These are the witnesses?" His voice was not just crazy, it was crazy eager, and when he started forward, Mitch's asylum-orderly instincts propelled him to his feet, hands up.

"Hold on," he said.

"Perhaps Mr. Rodriguez would be more comfortable with this," the Princess said.

"Okay," Charles said, also standing—but in his case impatiently, not warily.

"Chuck, man," Mitch said, trying to warn his friend... but of what, he didn't know.

"Mitch. This is okay. This is what I want." He gestured at the unreally splendid Princess and the obviously mad Star Thorn Dennis. "I trust them."

With that, Dennis linked hands with the Princess and reached for Chuck. When they were linked, they closed their eyes.

"Think back," Dennis said, then immediately, "Whoa, *whoa!*"

"It came easy," the Princess said, her voice tight.

"It's all I ever think about," Chuck said, quiet.

"Hold it," the Princess said.

For a moment, the trio was silent. Then, very quietly, the Princess's reserve broke and she started to sob quietly.

"Lucifer," she whispered. "My love." Then she started muttering something else, in some other language. Mitch thought it was Spanish or something at first, but then he felt it on top of hearing it. He felt the light change (though it looked no different), and he felt the sea's swells become melancholy under the deck (though they were neither faster nor slower nor higher nor lower). A shudder of sorrow passed through him, and he wept too, though he didn't know why.

"My Lady?" Dennis said, the question in his voice only a hint.

"We go on," she said.

They were silent for a few more moments, and then she said, "May I see what went before?"

More silence. The three were unchanged, except for the furrows that momentarily appeared in Dennis's brow. The Princess composed herself, and though her eyes did not open, her expression calmed. "A Beast from the earth," she said. "Whose, do you suppose? The Overlord of Hidden Smoke?"

"Maybe," Dennis said. "I don't know."

Silence.

"…and a second," she said. "From an Oceanite?"

"Or one of the Wild."

"Deep Charger, perhaps. Or the Rainbow Hunter."

"The Bright Singing One?"

"Mm, maybe… Too soon to tell, I guess."

"And here's where we came in."

"Stop," she said, and her voice was, perhaps, a bit sharp.

As one, the three of them opened their eyes. Like Mitch, Chuck's were wet, but he smiled, and Mitch had the uneasy feeling that they were tears of joy.

"It's beautiful," Chuck said. "Mitch, you have to remember with them. It's wonderful. It'll… you'll understand *everything*."

"Are you… Do you, um, want to go on?" Dennis said, looking at the Princess.

Mitch was not generally a highly intuitive or empathetic man, but at that moment he realized that the Star Thorn was desperately, hopelessly in love with the Princess—something which probably made him very dangerous to everyone but her. Why he picked up on it, or how, he couldn't say. Perhaps it was just the backlash of the Princess's own plaintive cry. Maybe that woke him up to the broken hearts of others, if just for a moment.

He also saw that she didn't know, and that made him feel just a little bit less intimidated for some reason.

"We'll continue," she said, and Mitch sighed.

I should've known I had no choice, he thought.

"I was clean and sober for over four hundred years, you know," Lucifer said. "Four hundred and twenty-nine, to be exact." He took a sip of tea. "Two more months, and it would be four-thirty. But I needed it."

"Human faith," Usiel said.

The Adversary nodded. "Not just human, either. Do you know... Before I fell off the wagon, I was *used* to it? For four hundred years, I did not exercise my power, for *four hundred years* I used no lore. I dealt with men as a man, using reasoned argument. I built what I needed with my own hands or traded for it with the labors of my mind. I was inconvenienced by wind and rain. I started my fires with tinder or matches. There's a purity to it, Usiel. And I never forgot that I was Elohim, I never thought I was one of them, but being powerless is the only way I've found to ease the burden of power."

"But now..."

Lucifer smiled, and it was a little sly. "Well, power has its attractions as well. As does pure belief, even aside from its usefulness as fuel. I imagine you have had time to learn that, with Widow Fielding, yes?"

Usiel looked away. "You set me up with her."

"You know, 'set me up' has two meanings. A criminal who's been entrapped might accuse the rat-fink stoolie of setting him up. Or a lonesome man who has a friend arrange a date could say his pal did him the favor of setting him up. Which meaning are you using?"

"I'm not even sure," Usiel said. He cleared his throat. "So now you... what? You have churches set up in your name? You sit on a throne and call yourself God to adoring mortals, and they believe you when you show them a flicker of your glory?"

"Ugh, I suppose I'll need to do that sooner or later." The Devil's face was, today, that of a stocky and stolid Midwestern man—a farmer or trucker or factory worker. As he spoke of establishing blasphemous worship, he wore the expression of a husband or dad who knows he's going to have to re-paint the bathroom sometime soon.

"How does that make you better than the fallen?"

"Does having the decency to feel bad about it count?"

"Do you suppose it counts to your victims? Or theirs?"

"Maybe I won't set up a church," Lucifer said. "Actually, I could probably just take over one of those 'Temples of Satan' or 'Baphomet Churches' they have out in California. But mainly I've been Robin Hooding it."

"Meaning?"

"Steal from the rich. Like you with old Vassago."

Usiel realized he was actually blushing, that he was too embarrassed to meet the other's eyes.

"C'mon," the Morningstar said, "there's no shame in it. You were on the right path with him. He stole all that mojo from generations of poor duped suckers, he chewed them up like gum and spat them out when the flavor was gone. The only use he'd make of that power was to victimize others, so what's the harm in taking it from him?"

"You're trying to tempt me."

"I'm trying to get you back in the game! Look, tell me you didn't like it. Tell me you didn't *love* biting off that sweet, juicy chunk of Vassago's soul."

Usiel wouldn't meet his eyes. Lucifer leaned back.

"You won't deny it because you can't. It was fun. Of course it's fun! Punishing evildoers is *fun*. Why do you think God does it so much? And so thoroughly."

"You sound bitter."

"Mm, I suppose I do." Lucifer's eyes glittered. "You want to know how I recovered so much power so fast? I'll show you. I'll *share* it with you."

"No thanks."

"Still cautious? This is the answer to your question, Usiel. I can *show* you how I'm different from them, how *we're* different. I'll do it right now!"

"No…"

But Lucifer was already rummaging in a cabinet, then shaking a canister of salt. "Anyone in particular you'd like to see?" he asked, and Usiel almost said Sabriel. But he held his tongue.

"How about Durnâdin? One of your own, one of the Halaku? He invokes me a lot, you know. He tells me how he's doing my work." As he spoke, the Adversary pushed the table back and spread a thick ring of salt on the floor. Then he drew signs and figures within it. And if his voice had sounded bitter when he spoke of God, it was doubly bitter as he spoke of his own loyal servant.

"Durnâdin! Lucifer, your master, calls!" The Devil paused a moment, and a grin crossed his face. Then he opened his mouth and words came out. The words were Durnâdin's True Name, his true nature and place in the universe. But the tones were discordant, the phrases gnashed at one another and fought.

"Your True Name has changed since we rebelled side by side," Lucifer said, with a wink to Usiel. "What is it now?" He gave Usiel a significant look and tugged his earlobe to show that the Reaper should listen.

Then he spoke again, and this time the True Name sounded brooding and low, and just speaking it aloud seemed to suck the light from the room, making the shadows solid and the air chill.

Lucifer spoke more in the Old Tongue, words of distance and motion and difference, and then Durnâdin the Halaku stood before them, inside the ring of salt.

"It's just that easy," Lucifer whispered to Usiel.

"Master!" Durnâdin was a sorry sight. Called forth in his true form, his raven wings, once shiny sleek, were matted and stank of decay. In the place of hands he had bone hooks, broadly curved but thin, with needle points, lined inside and out with barbs to rend. His skin was mottled, mold white and corpse gray. He was thin, famine thin, with the distended belly common to starvation victims, the only round part of his bone and joint body. Staring at them, he had the face of a dead eight-year-old. That deathly pale visage had a look of hope, awe and reverence. It turned Usiel's stomach.

"I never lost faith!" Durnâdin said, tears crossing his cheeks. "I never gave up your battle!"

"I know," Lucifer said, his voice a soothing balm, warm, caring, compassionate. "I have listened to your pleas, even when I did not respond. But tell me again how you have served my will."

"I sacrifice, in your name," Durnâdin said eagerly. "As often as I can—I try to make it every week. I tell them that you are coming, that you will reign anew, I tell them that your power is real, and then I make them believe."

"How do you do that?" Usiel asked, quietly, dreading the answer.

"At first I just killed them," Durnâdin said, "but it was too quick. They were too fragile, too easy. They didn't *understand*," and his voice had a whining tone as he said it. "They died before it got through to them. But I didn't give up! I learned, and I studied, and I got better. Drowning," he said. "That's the key."

"Drowning."

"Yes, it's much slower, so you can draw it out almost as long as you like," Durnâdin said, the bright glow of love never fading in his eyes. "I dunk them hard, and let them up, and push them under again, and let them up again… They try and fight, but pretty soon they get tired, and I have to hold them up so they can get just a little breath, just a little, before they go under again and feel the water pressing their sides, their face, their lungs… Over and over, until they *see*. One man, I had to do it twelve times, but he believed in the end. In the end, it got through. He *got* it, and he believed only in *you* master!"

"And then the last time."

"Yes," Durnâdin whispered, his voice like a sweaty caress. "The thirteenth time. He said your name with his dying breath."

"I felt it," Lucifer said, his voice thick. He turned to Usiel. "You see? Without demons to conduct the services, 'Satanism' is as hollow as most other worship. People just go through the motions. But with a stalwart follower like Durnâdin, the mortals can be pushed to true belief."

"All for you, master."

"All for me. And I couldn't reject it if I tried." Suddenly, Lucifer was no longer Durnâdin's compassionate commander. Suddenly, he let his contempt show on his face. And suddenly, a burning spear appeared in his hand.

"You believe, too," Lucifer said, and slammed the spear's tip into Durnâdin's chest. The demon in the circle could have cried out but didn't. The heartbreak on his face, the sense of miserable betrayal, was too strong for words.

"Join me!" Lucifer said, looking at Usiel, his eyes lit. "Strike him! Share the kill with me!"

"I don't…"

"Quick! Before it's too late! Strike him and speak his True Name, devour him with me and know his true essence! Only by taking his past, his knowledge, his very *self*, can you see why I have no trust in Sabriel, in Nazathor, in Grifiel and the others who take my name in vain. Raise your scythe and strike!"

And Usiel did.

As he called his deadly releasing tool to hand, he conceded that Durnâdin was going to die in any event, and that was a good thing from any perspective.

As he swung, the temptation to understand the new-come fallen—and with them himself—and most especially to understand Sabriel and learn if he'd been tricked—that temptation added some force to his blow, certainly.

When the blade struck home and he chanted Durnâdin's True Name, the name the demon had so willingly given to his lord, the thought that stealing this strength was wise, would protect Glenda—that thought was balm on the act.

But perhaps what moved him most of all was the urge to feel that sweet rush of power once more. To consume and devour. To unbind and steal an energy that had existed since time's dawn, and to make that energy part of himself.

When he took part of Vassago, Usiel had concentrated only on the sheerest strength, but this time, at Lucifer's urging, he took part of Durnâdin's memories as well. He remembered.

Remembered the sweet relief as the fallen angels descended upon humanity, showing themselves at last, free at last, loved and known at last.

Remembered the fear during the war, but also the joy of courage, the joy of saving a friend, hard joys that Usiel had known in the Holy Host, noble pleasures he'd never ascribed to the rebels.

Remembered the bleakness of defeat, the madness of Hell and the soothing savagery of revenge.

Usiel lived that again as Durnâdin tormented his victims, thinking, *This must be how God feels when he gives a child cancer.* He felt Durnâdin unbound to torture and pervert with no one to stop him.

(There was one ghost, one flicker of conscience: Durnâdin turning aside from an aged woman who looked like Gram Tanenbaum, and that was his host's grandmother who'd spoiled him every Christmas and slipped him candy bars when he was grounded. Durnâdin had dismissed that victim—she'd die soon enough anyway—but grumpy mercy was still mercy.)

And then the last betrayal as Lucifer raised the spear. Somehow, at that moment, Durnâdin felt more sorrow than when Michael pronounced the punishment of the Final House. Somehow, the last betrayal was the worst.

For a moment, the Reaper and the Devil stood silent in Glenda Fielding's kitchen.

"You see what they're like?" Lucifer said.

"I see," Usiel said, "that he could have changed."

"But he didn't."

"But he *could have!*"

"But he *didn't*," Lucifer repeated. "He didn't, he wouldn't, and none of them will. They fought *God*, Usiel! What's going to hold them back now that the angels have retreated and God has hidden His face?"

"They could choose."

"Oh, you're counting on self-control? I don't know if you noticed, but that's not a common characteristic in those who go to war with the Ancient of Days!" He shook his head. "I don't believe that you're afraid of them. I don't believe you're a fool. During the war, you were willing and eager to strike down any rebel who got within the reach of your scythe. What changed?"

"I was cast into Hell for striking blindly," Usiel said. "Maybe now, *just now*, I'm seeing why."

"What's going to happen?" Mitch asked.

"We're going to help you remember," the Princess said.

"Yeah, Chuck said that, but why? I mean, what's the point?"

"Don't you want to see Lucifer's face again?" Chuck asked, as if the answer was obvious.

"Well, I just mean... you guys saw, like, Chuck's memories, right? And, y'know, he was a lot more clearheaded than me. I mean, if you think I'd notice something he didn't..."

"It's not like that," the Princess said. "Everyone experiences Lucifer differently. The human mind isn't built to perceive all the iterations of his glory. Your experience was completely different from Charles's, and completely different from the girl who was with you."

"Huh. So what good is it, then?"

She blinked, and that clear, majestic forehead clouded.

"What *good* is it?"

"Sure. I mean—no disrespect—but if everyone has a different opinion, what's the point?"

"The point," she said gently, "is that by gathering more and more pieces—more and more perspectives—our picture of the Morningstar becomes increasingly clear."

Mitch almost asked what good *that* was, but he felt that would be a bad idea.

Then the Star Thorn took one hand, and the Princess took another, and he was back in the middle of it.

The worst day of Mitch Berger's life started out with seeing a terrifying and mysterious apparition a few hours after midnight. Then a dangerous, murderous lunatic escaped on his watch. He got put on suspension (along with Chuck, who'd been with him). Then a big-ass earthquake hit and his leg got broken. There was other unpleasantness—a guy waved a gun around, and he got jounced around a lot with his leg bone sticking out, and there was yelling and something blew up— but everything was a blur after his leg broke and, frankly, Mitch was perfectly okay with that. He had a vague memory of seeing something huge and... and... something huge, anyway, different huge things, and not remembering them was what he preferred.

When the Star Thorn touched him, he remembered.

"Stop."

That was the Princess's voice, though she wasn't anywhere around. Up above him he could see a figure, but the pain in his leg was so agonizing that only his heavy load of synthetic morphine kept him from going mad.

He was back in the middle of it, and when the Princess said "stop," everything froze. Now it was like *The Matrix* or those Gap khaki commercials, an increasingly cheap digital trick, only this was *his life*, his experience being frozen and manipulated.

"Hm," she said. "Let's get rid of that pain, first off."

And bingo. The searing pain of having his tibia sticking through his skin just vanished—abracadabra, *poof!*—like he was a TV and she'd picked up the remote to turn off the Pain Channel. He could still see the bone sticking out, of course, it was still his memory. But now it was a painless memory.

"And the drug fog. That has to go."

And away it went. In a way, it was even more disorienting than the loss of pain, because nothing visibly or sensibly changed. He just felt his attitude adjust, that dreamy Dilaudid listlessness evaporated, and suddenly he could pay attention to things in his memory again, could *care* about them again.

In his memory, his blurred eyes (and they'd get no clearer, the Star Thorn's power didn't seem to encompass that feat) were pointed down at his splinted leg. He was in the back of his Jeep, with the girl in the flag T-shirt on his left, shielding her eyes. On his right, he could see Charles, but not clearly. And up above him...

"Yes," whispered the Princess. "In his glory..."

The figure he beheld didn't make sense, even in his partial vision. Lucifer was fire, a pillar of white flame. But at the same time, he was sound. A song. A glorious symphony, at once as crooning and warm as the smoothest make-out jazz, as loud and triumphant and strong as a rock guitar solo can only be in front of a live audience, angry as hardcore, sad as a ballad. Lucifer was, to Mitch, music visible, and the concept made his mind twist.

"Roll it back," the Princess said, and Mitch was along for the ride, helpless, as his mind rewound. It was blurry and incoherent, even with Dennis's tweaking, but he was aware as Lucifer fought two... what? Two songs, one stately and grim and atonal, one whisper-quick and full of dissonant venom? Or two elements, a vast but crumbling pillar of stone and a shuddering rainstorm?

Mitch had never taken LSD, but he'd heard people talking about how they could "see" music under its influence. He wondered if this was what they meant. He didn't think so: If it was, he couldn't imagine anyone wanting to do it again. Except...

Except that Lucifer was glorious.

Even without unnatural clarity, that was clear. Even drugged and drunk and destroyed by pain, he had sensed that pull, and he had wanted it. He'd wanted to look. It was the kind of tug you feel on the roof of a building, that perverse urge to jump. It was the desire a moth has for a flame, or a junkie for a needle. Mitch (somehow) knew this, and even though he wanted Lucifer more than anything, he looked away. He felt (or heard, or experienced) the Morningstar's destruction of the two opponents, and he wanted to see Lucifer in triumph, even knowing it would mark him forever, scald his sanity, reinvent his life...

But somehow he pulled his head away.

"Ah," said Dennis.

And then the fugue was over, and the Princess looked at him with pitying eyes. "That was very helpful," she said.

The message from Dennis's face was clearer: contempt for Mitch's cowardice.

Chapter Two

G abriel McKenzie suddenly had a lot more work.

If Gabe had been a small businessman, that would probably have been a good thing. Or if he'd been a typical wage slave who got paid just as much when things were slow, it would have been a bad thing. But Gabe McKenzie was an FBI agent, and he was interested in a lot more than the bottom line.

This month, Gabe was interested in May Carter.

May was in her twenties, a dental hygienist, black, active in her church, 5'6", 140 pounds, no criminal history, lived alone, no known criminal confederates, no arrests. And no sign of how or why she'd disappeared from the face of the Earth.

No ransom demand. No suicide note. No sign of a struggle.

Gabe had started by scouring her apartment (finding nothing immediately important), her car (abandoned in Maryland Heights with the key in the ignition, no meaningful prints) and her workplace (a forensic nightmare—hundreds of people through it in the course of a week, so finding anything significant would be total needle in a haystack).

Primarily, he was focused on the boyfriend, Noah Wallace.

Good-looking guy, Noah. Straight-arrow type. Knew May in high school, rekindled their acquaintance on a bus trip to help earthquake victims in Los Angeles.

Gabe had copies of the video tapes of that trip. It had been recorded and broadcast in cable syndication, because May and

Noah's minister was Matthew Wallace, a televangelist and host of *The Hour of Jesus' Power*.

Matthew was also Noah's father.

On the surface, Noah seemed A-okay. Obviously smart, also well educated (the two not always being synonymous), poised, confident and charming. He reminded Gabe of a joke, that Will Smith was "the black man everyone at work can agree on." Noah was the same. And Noah was clearly devastated by the thought that anything might have happened to May. Especially upset by the thought that it might, somehow, be due to him.

Because strange things had been happening to Noah ever since he moved back to St. Louis and returned to his father's fold. He'd been on the scene when a Catholic church in nearby Mulesboro caught fire—in fact, he'd run in and rescued a woman who worked there.

A man named George Lasalle had confessed to the arson, turned himself in and the church priest spoke on his behalf. A local judge, affected perhaps by Lasalle's age and admission, had suspended his sentence, and apparently Lasalle had become a regular churchgoer.

It was a tenuous connection, but as his other leads dried up, Gabe started thinking about Lasalle. Especially when a few other facts about Noah popped up. Most prominently, the fact that two men had broken into Noah's home and thrown him out a window.

In addition to being handsome and intelligent, Noah also seemed to be lucky. Gabe knew of people who'd done twenty-foot drops onto concrete and *died*. Noah didn't even seriously break any bones, just got a few cracked ribs and some bad bruises.

And then, scant days after Noah was attacked, the Reverend Matthew Wallace broadcast May's picture on his TV show with a plea for information.

Suddenly, hundreds of people had (apparently) seen her. The FBI office was flooded with calls. She'd been spotted in Dogtown with two burly white men. She'd been seen in East St. Louis, running through a vacant lot. She'd been seen at the Anheuser Busch plant, taking the factory tour.

Gabe had requested more secretarial staff to help deal with the influx of calls. He'd reminded his superiors that time was of the essence, that finding her alive would be a tremendous coup. But money was tight, there was all the new Homeland Security red tape, he really ought to go through the local police forces…

The next day, there was some sort of commotion at Matthew Wallace's church. It left a window shattered, pews burned and walls bullet-holed. It prompted an editorial in the *Post Dispatch*. Once the print media mentioned the case, Gabe had all the support he needed.

But at a price.

Where, before, Gabe had been the sole Agent in Charge for the Carter kidnapping, he was now folded into the larger Hate Crimes Task Force. The AIC for that was Charles Davidson, who was okay as long as you didn't call him "Charlie." The HCTF was looking into the connections between the Jesus Power church, the Mulesboro burning, the attack on Noah Wallace and (now) the disappearance of a Jesus Power parishioner. It was confusing, and having eight agents trying to straighten it out sometimes didn't help much.

The morning he got the report on Cal Jordan, Gabe was already tired and cranky. He had a baby at home teething, this was his first case since paternity leave, and it had turned into a huge *thing*.

"Morning, Gabe."

"Morning, Juanita. Coffee fresh?"

"Fresh as a diaper rash." Juanita was the task force data analyst, and she had two kids of her own. She was always ready with a sympathetic ear, and her perpetual gratitude that she no longer had to do field work was sometimes comforting to those who did it. She had a knack for listening to complaints with good grace and making people feel that they were justified and not whining (even when they were). Plus, she was detail-oriented and made good coffee. All in all, a tremendous asset to any police effort.

"Remember Lynn Culver?"

"Wait, wait…" Gabe got coffee and, to give himself time to think, looked for milk in the bureau's small fridge. They were out. He sighed and used nondairy creamer. "She's the woman Noah pulled out of the burning church, right?"

"Was. She's dead."

"What?"

"Died exactly twelve days ago. Keeled over in the parking lot on her way home from work. Coroner called it a heart attack and said there was no evidence of foul play, but Davidson wants to exhume the body."

"Didn't she move to Illinois?"

"Oswego, yeah. So now it's a turf battle."

"Ay caramba." He pronounced it badly on purpose. Juanita gave him a sour little smile. "Any new May sightings?"

"Only about a dozen."

When people called the hotline, a secretary took the call and got down the principal information. Each call was recorded and transcribed by computer. Then the secretary typed up a summary and, based on his or her personal judgment, rated the call for apparent usefulness on a scale of one to ten. Most calls were fives. Obvious cranks and nutcases were ranked one. Sober calls with a lot of hard data would get a ten, if such a call ever came in.

Cal Jordan's call was a five. The summary sat on Gabe's desk with ten other summaries. Gabe sipped coffee, read through them and made a few notes. For a few calls, he pulled up the transcripts on his PC, grimacing at homonym spelling errors committed by the computer and missed by the secretaries—they were supposed to read over the transcripts and catch such things. For a few of those, he picked up his phone a couple of times, poked buttons until he was in the St. Louis FBI's vast phone mail message bank, and listened to the recorded phone calls. He did that for Cal Jordan.

There was something about Jordan's call that intrigued him. He frowned at the transcription, followed along on it while listening to the phone, then smiled.

It was the phrase "old guy, white hair, but big. Like a bodybuilder."

More key taps and mouse clicks, and he had Noah Wallace's description of one of his attackers: "Older, blond hair turning white, about six feet tall and quite muscular."

He switched from computer to phone and called Cal Jordan for an interview.

The demoness Sabriel was worried, and she took it out on her one surviving worshipper. She often did this when she was worried. But sometimes, for whatever bizarre reason, she felt bad for mistreating poor Thomas Ramone (that was the worshipper's name), so she would reward him immediately after (or perhaps just before) abusing and tormenting him. She really couldn't explain it. There was just something about him.

She was worried because she hadn't heard from Usiel in weeks. He'd intended to kill her, and she'd talked him out of it by playing on their shared history with Haniel (Usiel's lover and Sabriel's close friend, back in the Oldest Days). She'd figured he was under control. She'd *counted* on him being under control. But he wasn't responding to her invocations, and that didn't sound much like control at all.

She'd lambasted Thomas and threatened to kill him and threatened to have him thrown in jail and threatened to kill his entire family or drive them insane. She'd made him cry. Then she'd told him he could make it up to her if he did a simple thing—if he got her some more money. But to help him steal it, she'd taught him how to turn into a cloud.

Now Thomas was off, presumably robbing a home in Ladue. She'd picked it out for him, the woman who lived there had a lot of expensive jewelry, historical stuff that they could easily ransom back at a fraction of its value and still come out way ahead. Shit, the old snob would probably get her money's worth in the long run by boasting about how her collection was notorious enough to get burgled by a professional.

Thomas was not, of course, a professional. But a man who can turn into vapor by giggling doesn't really need to be a professional.

Sabriel had planned the whole thing out and now, sitting in a loft with a glass of wine waiting for a local rock drummer to come back, she wished she'd gone and done the damn thing herself. But then Thomas wouldn't have done it, and it was important to keep the little monkey busy; important to remind him of his station.

Sabriel worried that Thomas might forget to be afraid of her. That would be bad for her, but very much worse for him.

So now she was seducing a musician again. Ho hum, she'd break his heart and break his will and maybe make him her thrall or maybe make him self-destruct somehow, but she was distracted and irritated the whole time he made his predictable "moves." She cooed and gasped with feigned delight, while inside she was bored and antsy and most of all worried.

She was worried about the demon Gaviel. What was he up to?

She was worried about the demon Avitu. Had she really been put in check?

Most of all, she was worried about Usiel. Had he changed his mind?

Was he in trouble?

Had she hurt him?

It all came down to TiVo and good luck.

Cal Jordan worked at a BP gas station during the day and was going to night school to become an x-ray technician. He shared an apartment with four students and one of them had TiVo—a sort of digital VCR.

"Yeah, we all kind of portioned out the time on the hard drive," Cal told Gabe McKenzie, who nodded and pretended to make a note on his pad. "Stewie got the sixteen-hour one and he called half the hard drive, but I didn't much care, I don't watch a lot of TV, but I do watch *The Hour of Jesus' Power* because my sister's in the choir there."

"Mm hm."

"And anyhow, I didn't see the show live—I mean, at its normal time—this week because I was sleeping in an' all, so I didn't watch it until after I saw her."

And that was how TiVo fit in.

"You say you saw her on the fifteenth?" That was the day May Carter had vanished.

"Yeah, I was working the night shift, and they came in 'round seven thirty or eight."

"You sure of the time?" May had left her apartment before six-thirty. Her last outgoing call was at three o'clock.

"Mm…" Cal shrugged, looked embarrassed. "Not that sure. It was dark."

"What caught your attention?"

"Well, she looked a lot like my cousin Emmaline. I mean, a *lot* like her. I thought it *was* her for a second, but she's in Pennsylvania plus pregnant, y'know?"

And that was the good luck.

"Gotcha."

"And the guy who was gassing up the car, he was..." Cal shrugged. "I mean, you don't see a lot of guys with that build and white hair, know what I'm saying?"

"Yeah." Gabe opened the catch on his briefcase. "Seen one of these?"

"Uh uh."

Gabe had an irritated thought that the local cops had dropped the ball with this guy, then realized that this was probably the first interview. *He called us, not them, after all.* He made a note on his pad to call the police and share.

It was a composite sketch of the white-haired man who attacked Noah Wallace. Cal eyed it with interest.

"Your bodybuilder look much like that?"

"A lot like, yeah."

Bingo.

"So when you saw the notice on TV..."

Cal gave a small, shy smile. "I thought, 'Dang, that girl looks like Emmaline too.'"

"Remember what the big guy was driving?"

Cal shrugged and looked helpless. "A lot of cars come through here."

"That's okay." Gabe took a deep breath and relaxed into his chair. He watched Cal do the same.

Soothing blue ocean, Gabe thought at Cal, working to keep his own excitement off his face. *Soothing blue ocean. Relax. Let the memory come. Don't worry that you may be the key to her living or dying.*

"What was the big guy wearing?"

"Just... clothes. Y'know."

"So no ball gown or tuxedo?"

Cal smiled. "Jeans, I guess. No coat. I thought that was weird."

"An old giant with no coat in the snow. Yeah, that *is* weird."

"Maybe he left it in the car and had the heater on."

"Very possible," Gabe said. "What did the guy look like, standing next to the car?"

"What do you mean?"

"I mean, did the car seem the right size for him? Low down? Really big?"

"Hey, you know, it was up to his head."

"Yeah?"

"So it was a sport-ute!" Cal grinned again. "I remember now, a big one. Like a Bronco or a Tahoe or something."

"What does Emmaline drive?"

"She drives a 4Runner, I think."

"What color?"

"Hers is a sort of purple blue, which is another way I knew this wasn't her."

"What color was it?"

Cal opened his mouth, then closed it again, shaking his head.

"Try this," Gabe said. "Imagine you're not seeing it from here." The two of them were in the cashier's area, looking out at the gas pump. "Imagine that you're... mm, over there by the vacuum thing, looking at it sideways."

"All right." Cal closed his eyes.

"It's not blue," Gabe said.

"No."

"Green?"

"Nuh uh."

"The woman, she's in the passenger seat?"

"Yeah."

"What's she wearing?"

"A cloth coat. Dark, like navy blue or black or something."

"Is the car black?"

"No."

"White?"

"No…"

"It's not red, you'd remember that."

"Not red." Gabe saw Cal screw up his face, concentrating, and he bit his lip.

"Was the car dirty or clean?"

"Dirty, I think."

"You think?"

"Hard to tell."

"Was the car brown?"

"It was gold." Cal's eyes popped open. "It was, like, a dark gold color, so it was hard to see dirt on it."

"Cal, you are a genius."

"And there was a sticker on the back. A red sticker, a little red shape."

Gabe's heart gave a hard thump.

It can't be this easy. He flipped to a new page in his notebook and drew a tiny sketch.

"Like this?"

"Uh huh."

I don't believe it. The bodybuilder must be senile. He did his crime in a rental car.

Later that day, Special Agent Gabe McKenzie tapped his pen on his pad and wondered what the hell was up with George Lasalle.

The old man seemed beat down, and that was all right. Not like Gabe wanted him to be depressed because George was a wicked old racist. Gabe was well past the point of feeling gleeful about unhappy scumbags. It was all right because it fit. Crook gets nabbed, gets depressed: check and double-check. Even if his sentence gets suspended and he winds up with practically a second family at the church he torched.

"I'm lucky," Lasalle said, voice leaden. "I'm a lucky man. I'm a lucky, lucky man. Y'all happy now? They forgave me, I got Christ's forgiveness an' everything and I'm blessed an', an' lucky. Why do we need to go over this again?"

For a lucky guy, you sure whine a lot, Gabe thought.

Maybe that was it.

"So you only met Noah Wallace once?"

"That's right."

"Came to talk to you about the error of your sinful ways."

"He made me see that being a racist was wrong, that I was hurting myself as much as anyone else." Lasalle said the words like they were blocks of stone he was dragging uphill. "Letting go of my hatred opened me up to a new life in Jesus Christ."

Right. I'm not buying that line, and you're not even selling it very hard.

On a hunch, Gabe decided to go back to the fire.

"Tell me about the arson."

"What's to tell? I set the church on fire and… and they came and put it out before it could spread too far. Thank the Lord. And lucky no one was hurt."

"Did you use an accelerant? Like, gas or kerosene or something?"

"Yeah. Uh, gasoline."

"Leaded or unleaded?"

George looked helpless. "Unleaded, I g—… Unleaded."

"Uh huh, and did you use some kind of timer mechanism or did you just light it?"

Lasalle was silent.

"Mr. Lasalle?"

"I just lit it."

He looks pissed, Gabe thought with wonder.

"And where'd you light this fire?"

"In the church kitchen. By that back door there."

"Uh huh. Just a second here," Gabe popped open his briefcase and got out the file with the fire report. He paged through it. "I just want to check something," he said. The other man looked impatient. "So, okay, yeah. The fire started in the back and spread up the wall to the roof. You splashed gas way up high, right? And over to the east, toward the choir practice area? I guess that would be to your right as you were facing the back of the building, right?"

"Yeah."

"You entered through the kitchen door and left the same way."

"Yes."

"You're sure about that?"

Lasalle shrugged. Gabe opened his mouth and then shut it.

Because the accelerant wasn't splashed up on the ceiling, and the kitchen door was dead-bolted, and the choir room is to the south, to the left.

Gabe kept his face carefully neutral, but it wasn't easy. He couldn't believe no one had grilled Lasalle before. His story matched up on the surface, but it hadn't taken Gabe much prodding to poke a hole in it.

Is it really that implausible? he thought, and he hated himself, hated being cynical, but it made sense. Hate crime gets committed, there's loads of pressure to find the arsonist, and this guy comes forth of his own volition to confess and beg forgiveness. Loner, white male, Klan history, why dig into it? It's perfect.

It's too perfect.

"Who are you protecting?"

"No one!"

He answered that way too quick, too angry. He was expecting it.

"It's Wallace, isn't it?"

"...no..."

"Why are you covering up for him? Why'd he do it? Was it all so he could rescue that woman?" *That's crazy. No one starts a fire just to look like a hero, there are too many things to go wrong.*

"I did it! Can't you... Look, I did it, me and no one else, and that's my story! That's my story, and I'm sticking to it!" Lasalle's lower lip quivered, and regardless of how big a bastard he'd been as a young thug, Gabe felt sorry for him.

"Get the hell outta my house!" Lasalle said, and Gabe realized he'd let his pity show on his face.

Poor old guy, no friends, no family, just a church that thinks he set 'em on fire, and he didn't even do it.

"I'll come back some other time," Gabriel said, rising.

"I got rights, y'know!" Lasalle sounded like he was about to cry.

Out in his car, Gabe paused to call in.

"Hey Tish? Gabe. You might want to tell Charles that Lasalle didn't torch that church. Yeah. Really." He listened, and when he spoke again he let a little exasperation into his voice. "Really. I talked to him and he didn't know enough about how the fire started. He was not on the scene, I'm sure of it. I think he's covering up for someone, and I think it's Noah Wallace. No, no idea why, but can you call him and set up another interview?" His eyes widened. "What? Wow. You have it on tape? Yeah, I'll be right in."

The Reverend Matthew Wallace stood before his congregation and said, "We are a troubled people."

There were a few little murmurs.

"Everyone agrees with that? I'm not surprised. We are a troubled people. America, the American people are troubled. We have troubles at home and abroad, we have economic problems and education inequalities and tax debates and political scandals. So any American would agree that, yes, we're a troubled people.

"But I didn't mean Americans."

He frowned.

"Some of you here, and some of you watching at home, may think I mean blacks. American blacks, blacks worldwide. And we're a troubled people too. We've got a disproportionate number of our young men in jail, a vastly unfair number of them on death row, we have crises of faith and conflicts within our conflicts. Blacks are a troubled people, but I'm not talking about blacks, either.

"Christians?"

"Amen!" called a parishioner.

"You're right Christians are troubled. It's hard to live a Godly life in America, in a culture where your choice of Coke or Pepsi gets more attention than your choice of Godly or Godless. We've got church vs. state, and we've got declining church membership and, we've got some scandals and some people who call themselves Christian but seem more concerned about pointing fingers, at other Christians, and saying, 'You ain't being Christian right!'"

"Tell it, preacher!"

"But I'm not talking about Christian troubles either." He paused to let his listeners calm down.

"I could talk about our congregation right here. Lord knows we're troubled. One member of the church kidnapped, stolen right out from under our noses. Our building, here, burned, shot up." He gestured at the bullet holes, visibly scattered around the altar.

He took a deep breath and sighed, and he looked pained.

"But when I say we're troubled, I mean my family."

This provoked some muttering.

"You, you listening to me preach, you're like a family to me. I've told you everything about my son leaving, my son coming back… That's what you think, anyhow."

In the front row, Noah Wallace sat up straighter. There was no expression on his face at all, just a posture of alertness.

"But I haven't told you everything. I've done you a… a great, grievous wrong, and I'm here to beg your forgiveness."

The muttering through the crowd was louder.

"I have…" The Reverend looked straight down at his feet, his mouth was pointed away from the microphone and his voice was quiet, but they could still hear his confession.

"I have been unfaithful to my wife."

Thereafter followed about thirty seconds of shocked gasps and horrified babbling.

"I'm… I'm not going to say who with," the reverend continued, but his words were lost in the sounds of the crowd's dismay. He raised his head and raised his voice. "I'm not going to say who with," he repeated, "but I feel compelled to say this. I'm… I have to get this out, I have to show my sin…"

"For shame!"

The cry was so loud, so shrill that it cut through Matthew's words like a knife.

"For shame, stepping out on a fine kind woman like your wife! Shame on you!"

"I deserve that," Matthew said. "I'm a shame to my family and a shame to my congregation. My throat has been an open sepulcher. I've been a hypocrite, I've lied to you and deceived you… but I'm up here, confessing, giving it up, because I need to be free of this! I need to get free of this sin!"

"Boo!" cried some in the audience, as if he'd fumbled a touchdown pass, but others stood and shouted for understanding, saying the congregation should hear him out. But as his wife shot to her feet, it was her words that silenced the room.

"How dare you condemn him?" she asked.

Zola Wallace didn't have her husband's voice. When she spoke, it was high and a little breathy, but this time she had the force of anger behind her.

"For years he's listened to your sins and forgiven you, and now you condemn him? If you're blameless, why don't you get on up and start preaching? Why don't you let people call you, all hours of the night, hearing, 'Oh Rev'ren', my son's in jail,' 'Oh Rev'ren', my wife's stepping out on me,' 'Oh Rev'ren', I don' know what to do!'" She turned to the pulpit. "I am so mad I could spit right now, and if anyone's gonna condemn this man it's me. But if y'all can't forgive him the way he's always been forgiving you, you're as bad as he is."

Then she turned her back and stalked down the aisle toward the doors.

For a moment, Matthew looked after her and leaned, just a little, forward, as if to follow.

"Go after her," Noah urged, and there was no microphone on him, just the low power of his voice. People watching at home, glued to the set, turned to spouses and asked, "What'd he say?" But Matthew's words were loud and clear.

"You'd like that, wouldn't you?"

Noah said nothing, but his eyes were hard, his face set like flint.

"You'd like me to back down from you again, wouldn't you?" Matthew asked.

Noah said something—maybe "Don't do this thing"?—but the microphone was off him, only Matthew's voice could be heard.

"You would like me to leave this congregation in your hands. You'd like it if I was too weak to refuse you, again. You'd like it if I backed off, backed down, walked away and stayed asleep, wouldn't you? But I confessed for a reason. I confessed to make myself clean. Maybe I'm ruining my TV show, maybe I'm losing my congregation, but it's worth it!"

Noah stood, and his stony expression was changing, glacially, into one of absolute fury.

"I'm taking the board from my eye," Matthew said, "so that I can remove a speck, and you're that speck. You're the unclean influence here. You're the pollution in the middle of God's church, and I cast you out!"

The gasps from the congregation were almost as loud, almost as shocked, as when he admitted adultery.

The camera switched briefly to Noah, who stood there with fists clenched, teeth grinding, but when Matthew spoke, it turned back to him and his face was just as angry.

"By the power of our Lord Jesus Christ, get out! By the power of the Holy Spirit, begone! By the power of God Almighty I cast you forth!"

"I'll destroy you for this!" Even without a microphone, Noah's cry was audible. Then the cameras turned to him as he sprinted up the aisle, out of the church.

They were still pointed at his retreating back as Matthew responded.

"Bring it on."

Special agent Gabe McKenzie watched the end of the tape with his eyes wide and his jaw slightly open. Then he rewound it and watched the whole thing again.

"Holy frijoles," he muttered. He tapped his pen on his pad, but he couldn't think exactly what to note down. After the second viewing he drew a line across the page and started capturing thoughts. The top half was labeled "MATTHEW" and it read:

Nutjob? Puts an exorcism on his own <u>son</u>? Burns churches himself to… what? Raise ratings? Get attention for his show? Kidnaps May for…? Is she his mistress? Maybe she's his mistress, he's uninvolved with kidnapping but thinks he'll get outed during investigation, so beats it to the punch. But why kick Noah out? Matthew was present when the Mulesboro church burned. He was <u>on site</u>, phoned in the 911 call before anyone. May trusted him (even if she wasn't his mistress), he could easily have lured her away without a struggle. Did he shoot up his own church? Where was he when that happened? Alibi?

Below the line, he scrawled "NOAH" and wrote:

On site with Mulesboro. Lasalle maybe covering for him. Rescued Culver who later died. Knew May who later disappeared. What's <u>his</u> story for the night the church got shot up? Maybe Noah's crazy, burned the church, threatened Culver into silence, threatened Lasalle into the cover up, kidnapped May? His dad knows? Matthew covers it up, then can't go through with it? But if that's so, why does Matthew confess to adultery? Or maybe Matthew's the madman, Noah's covering up, trying to minimize the damage—saves Culver, gets Lasalle to admit to Matthew's arson, but draws the line when May gets grabbed? Noah's going to go to the cops, Matthew disowns him in an attempt to discredit his accusations? But he hasn't made them. And who threw him out the window?

For almost a minute, Gabe just stared at his notes, tapping his pen against his teeth. Then he opened the conference room door and leaned out.

"Juanita? Is there any coffee left?"

It was time to call Noah Wallace again.

"Yeah, I ran the engine and sprayed it with some water, like from a plant mister? And I could see sparks arcing all over the place," the mechanic said. He was also trying to casually look down Sabriel's top, but the angle wasn't good. He couldn't do it without being obvious. Almost instinctively, she shifted to make it easier for him.

"Can you fix it?" she asked, and of course he could. He quoted a price and she sighed but, hell, you need a car to get around.

Sabriel the Defiler had shitty luck with cars. She wondered—really, it was more Christina, the woman whose body Sabriel used, *she* wondered—if this guy was cheating her. She thought he probably was, and it made her angry, furious really. Christina hoped Sabriel would kill the guy or at least fuck him up so that he spent the rest of his life in deranged, sexually impotent misery.

But Sabriel didn't really care if the guy was dishonest. She figured he was, but she almost *preferred* it. Fraudulent humans didn't bother her. She expected it. What really made her see red was when humans thought they could be better than cheaters, better than crooks, better than sleazy car mechanics. When they thought they could create and communicate and build something real—those were the sins she punished.

So her car had broken down when she was driving home from the wannabe rock-star's place, and she was going get hosed on the fix. It didn't bother her much.

Sabriel.

It was Gaviel's voice, sounding in her head.

"Excuse me, can I use your phone?" she asked. The mechanic nodded and pointed, then checked out her ass as she walked away.

She mimed dialing and then said, "Gaviel. What good luck. You can give me a ride home."

Oh, can I?

"Pretty please?"

Sure, he said, and she suddenly suspected she'd pay for his largesse.

(Gaviel was in a bad mood. Going to see the Reverend Wallace's mistress had cheered him a little, not much. She'd been hysterical, of course, terrified that Matthew was abandoning her, terrified that he wasn't, afraid that everything would change, afraid that nothing would change. Gaviel had pointed out, so helpfully, that everyone would instantly guess she was the mystery paramour if she ran away. But, of course, if she stayed with the show, she'd have to carry the secret around all the time without even the comfort of adulterous love. "What's so terrible?" he'd asked. "You're only getting his second best." "His second best was still better than any other man's," she'd replied, and he'd looked sympathetic but felt a vicious pleasure. This would work out just fine. He'd consoled and expressed his concerns and shook his head at her problems, and when he left, he was hopeful that she'd kill herself before morning.)

Where are you? he asked, and she told him.

He took his time getting there, and by then she was getting along with the mechanic like they were old sewing-circle buddies.

"So," Gaviel said as she got in the car, "I'd like a new face, please."

"Yes?"

"Yes. This one's getting a little too hot. An FBI agent left a message on my answering machine, and I'm pretty much fed up."

"An FBI agent? So what? Just tell him to fuck off."

(For demons, this was actually a feasible plan.)

"It's more than him. The past on this body has gotten to be more trouble than it's worth. Matthew exorcised me this morning."

"Really?"

"On live TV." Gaviel ground out his cigarette in the car's ash tray with a little more aggression than was needed for the task.

"My goodness." Sabriel smirked. Seeing Gaviel, Mr. Slick, get pissed and pushed around—that was a rare treat. "Did you spin your head around and puke pea soup? That's in the script, isn't it?"

"Do you want to know *why* he exorcised me? Because yesterday he saw me duking it out with your fucking ophanim *boyfriend*."

"The Reaper?"

"Him, yes. Unless you're flat-backing for the Angel of Pain, too."

She opened her mouth, then closed it, genuinely surprised. She left the question of how the hell he'd survived unsaid, asking instead, "Did he say anything?"

"The Reaper? Usual 'To Hell Returneth' bullshit. Nothing useful. Just enough to turn Matthew against me."

"I'm really sorry to hear that," she said. She meant it—mostly because she was worried that she was the next target.

Gaviel shrugged. "Maybe the Noah Wallace persona was played out anyhow. Maybe I was getting too comfortable." Already he was putting his frustration behind him. She could nearly *smell* him doing it.

"Always looking on the bright side, aren't you?"

"I don't like pessimism. I don't like anything that makes being wrong more attractive. Now, how about a new look?"

"Sure," she said. She'd promised to protect him from Usiel and clearly failed to deliver. A little bodywork was certainly a reasonable request. "What did you have in mind? Want to stay black?"

"Yes. Actually, I wouldn't mind being a little darker."

"As you wish." She put her hand on his as he changed lanes on the highway.

"How about something more butch, too? Not too far, just... mm, 10% more Wesley Snipes."

"Okay."

When they pulled onto the off ramp, he checked himself in the rearview mirror. "Not bad but... uh, a little more warmth."

"Just a touch of Denzel?"

"Excellent suggestion."

When they pulled up in front of her apartment, Gaviel was satisfied with his look.

"Thanks," he said.

"Yeah, well, don't get it hit hard. If it deforms and you heal it, it's going to go back to its original configuration."

"Good to know. What about the skin tone?"

"Yeah, that might fade with rapid healing too."

"Leaving me blotchy? Great. I guess we'd better put it back the way it was."

"You're the boss," she said, with a little glare. She started to open her door.

"Where are you going?"

"Up to my apartment."

"Without fixing me?"

"I thought you were coming up."

"Sorry, I've got business to attend to."

"Oh." With a touch, she removed her coloring from him.

"Thanks." He slammed her door.

"Gaviel, are you... I mean, are we okay?"

"I'm not angry, if that's what you mean. You made a promise, you couldn't pull through, I'm not eager to jump into work with you again, but I'm willing to call it a wash. Now don't say I never did anything for you."

As he drove off, she said his name again, but she could feel him ignoring her.

When she opened her apartment door, Thomas Ramone was sprawled on her couch, naked. The air was redolent with marijuana fumes and classical music was playing softly in the background.

"Hi!" he said, obviously stoned like a rock star. "I'm working on being more comfortable with my body!"

"Charming," she said.

"You'll never guess what that chick in Ladue had in her house. Besides those jewels you wanted, I mean."

"Let me guess. Was it reefer?"

(It was, in fact, genetically engineered marijuana that cost ten times what Thomas was used to spending on grass because it had roughly twice as much THC per ounce. Plus, she'd dusted it with a chemical compound that, in 1998, had been pulled off the US market as a heart medicine for horses, but which was still legal in Spain. The reason it was outlawed in the US was not because the FDA was worried about sick horses, but because certain connoisseurs liked the way it made you feel alert and clever and invulnerable when smoked. It had some off-putting side-effects like nausea and jitters, but astute drug users had noticed that good pot would take care of almost all of them. Thomas had smoked plenty of herb in his time, but he'd had no idea this particular bud was spiked. That was what had made nudity seem like such an inspired joke.)

He chuckled mindlessly for a moment then said, "That's not all. Whaddaya think of the music?"

"It's certainly a switch from Foghat."

"Check the CD case. On top of the stereo."

She looked at the cover and felt an icy shock run through her.

It wasn't a particularly impressive cover—a nicely composed picture of a piano, taken from an unusual angle, a little self-consciously edgy. The Sony Classics logo. And the title: *Nathaniel Kowalski Plays the Brandenburg Concertos*.

"That fucker," she hissed. Behind her, Thomas chortled again. She spun.

"You think it's funny?"

"That's the guy, right?"

"You think it's funny?"

"No," he said, and he put up a good struggle, trying to keep his giggles in. But they bubbled out, beyond his power to still.

Sabriel picked up the CD case and mashed its flat front right into Thomas's nose. Mind dulled by Mary Jane, he couldn't get his hands up in time. He flinched, turning his head, but she bored on in, forcing him to tip back deeper into the sofa. He finally got his hands coordinated enough to knock her arms aside.

"Hey," he said, and the giggles were gone now. "Don't blame *me* if he's tougher than you think. He's the guy you tried to ruin, right? The guy you thought would go off himself 'cause you stepped out on him. Isn't that right?"

"And you *love* seeing me wrong, don't you?"

"You're the one who keeps going on about how you're not my friend."

"There's a big comfort zone between 'non-friend' and 'enemy.' Don't cross it."

"Or what? You'll kill me like all your other, other, whaddaya call 'em, 'thralls'? I'm your last one. Your last meal ticket, right? You wanna punch your last ticket, is that it?"

Sabriel punched him.

She wasn't terribly strong, but he wasn't terribly coordinated. She didn't spill blood or loosen teeth, but he'd have a fat lip to show for his insolence.

But Tom, acting on instinct, shoved her back hard and stood up, and he was amazed to see her wince when the back of her calf clipped the edge of a coffee table. He had a moment to wonder if he could beat her up and if he even wanted to before she charged him. They struggled, briefly, before he got both her wrists caught. She tried to knee his groin, but he turned his hip toward her—he'd seen that one coming. He'd made up his mind to slug her if she bit him when she said, "You think I won't punish you for this? You think I *need* you?"

And he started to get dizzy.

"I can get all the mortals I need. I can eat you fuckers like candy. Every day is Halloween for me."

He struggled to keep his grip, but she was doing something to him, and he could see his hands changing before his eyes. He could feel his *face* changing.

"I'm going to drain you, Thomas. I'm going to hurt you by draining you to give me the strength to hurt you by *changing* you."

His hands had broken out in boils, scars, gross red patches of dry eczema, and suddenly he wasn't holding her, suddenly she had him by his arm and was holding him up, he was so weak and wobbly…

"Maybe if you're a good boy, I'll give you your face back. Or at least something *human looking*."

She jerked him over in front of a mirror, and he screamed. At least, he tried to. His jaw was swollen, bulbous, offsetting the warty bubbles that clouded his forehead and cheeks, they were almost growing over his eyes and he was hideous, a monster, an Elephant Man.

"You go think about what you've done and figure out how to apologize," she said. Then she jerked the apartment door open and shoved him, naked and gruesome, out into the hall.

There was a moment of silence after she slammed the door, a momentary pause before he started banging on the door, begging her to let him back in, to at least let him get his clothes.

Sabriel sighed and sank to the floor, her back to the door, feeling Thomas thumping it. The changes she'd worked on him would come undone as soon as he changed into water or mist, she knew that. And he could get his clothes just by flowing under the door. But to change he had to laugh. She didn't think he'd be laughing very soon.

She was surprised when she started to cry.

It took Reverend Matthew Wallace some time to find his wife. He tried her mother's house first, then her sister's.

Matthew's mother-in-law said Zola had been there, but had left. She had reproachful words for him, but she'd always liked him and he could tell that, deep down, she felt that boys would always be boys, even when they were men. She compared him to Jesse Jackson before he left.

Zola's sister, on the other hand, wouldn't tell him if Zola was there or not. When he turned on the charm, she threatened to call the police.

He finally found her when he knocked on the door of her old college room-mate. He was in luck—Zola was alone and she answered the door.

"I'm sorry," he said.

She slapped him. His eyes popped wide with surprise. Then she slammed the door in his face.

He knocked again.

"I, I deserved that," he began, as she opened it once more. This time, she had a bowl in her hands, and she cracked it down hard on the top of his head.

He saw stars and yelped like an animal. The pain was intense, all the more so for being unexpected. He'd seen her raise the bowl, seen it descend, but the concept that his wife was going to hit him—again—with more force than was appropriate for a purely symbolic gesture... well, that just didn't fit in his brain.

Perhaps the hard clay impact made room for it.

He dropped to his knees, clutched his head as if to shield it (far too late) and took a deep breath so he could yell some more.

"You deserved that too," Zola said, glaring down at him. The bowl was still in her hands, uncracked, unbroken. She gave it an uncertain look.

"Can... we talk?" Matthew gasped, wincing.

"I think we all know *you* can," she retorted, but seeing him kneeling there in obvious pain softened her expression. "C'mon in," she said. "I'll get you some ice."

"Much obliged."

By the time she returned, he was sitting on the sofa. A substantial lump was already visible on his scalp. He was relieved to see that she'd left the bowl in the kitchen.

"I'm sorry," he said again. "I mean it. You know I do, I just... I'm sorry. I'll say it as many times as you like."

"Once was too many." She handed him a plastic bag of frozen peas, which he put on his head with a wince.

"Damn," he whispered.

For a moment, they were quiet. He sighed.

"Can you forgive me?" he asked.

She rolled her eyes.

"I... I know this comes as a shock..."

"A shock? You really think I'm dumb as a turkey, don't you?"

He blinked.

"You think I didn't *know*?" she asked, her high voice piping with indignation. "I knew when and who and how often! But I kept my mouth shut because I didn't want to ruin you, and shame our children, and look the fool in public!"

"Wait, you *knew?*"

She just shook her head in disbelief.

"Why didn't you say something?" he asked.

"Because I didn't want the children to find out." She looked like she was trying not to look at him, but she did anyway. "I guess I figured... I thought you'd get bored eventually." With each word, her voice seemed to get smaller and sadder. "And then, when the kids were away at college it... it seemed too late. It had just gone on too long and I was... I don't know." Her lower lip trembled. "People can get used to anything, I guess."

When she started to cry, Matthew moved in to hold her. Instantly, she was alert, and he flinched back when she raised her hand.

He went back to the couch and they both deflated.

"Why'd you do it?"

"Oh Zola..."

"No, not... that. Why'd you tell everyone?"

"I had to."

"How come you *had to* this morning and you didn't have to for the past five years?"

"I had to come clean," he whispered.

This answer enraged her.

"*You* had to get clean. *You* had to ease your conscience, huh? Well let the *heavens fall* as long as Pastor Wallace got himself cleaned up!"

"You'd feel better if we were still living a lie? I did this for you too, Zola!"

"Oh, you thought I'd *like* a surprise humiliation? Damn, even your generosity is selfish! I hope you at least get *good ratings* out of this!"

"The ratings don't matter!"

"Sure."

"They *don't matter!*" Zola shifted back in her seat, because her husband was bellowing. She'd heard him shout before—he'd shout during sermons, he had a good shout—but really roaring, straining his precious voice, with the words leading him instead of him leading them... she hadn't seen that from him more than once or twice. It was serious.

"The ratings don't matter, and the church doesn't matter, and *I don't matter!*" he yelled. He paused, and he was hyperventilating. He looked down at his hands in his lap and spoke again.

"Zola, I love you. I always have, through everything. If you don't want to see me again, it will break my heart, and that's the truth before Jesus Christ our Lord. But if that's what you want, I'll go that way. If you send me out, I'll stay away, and I'll be miserable, but I'll at least be satisfied that you're *safe.*"

"What do you mean?"

"Zola... there was an unclean, unholy influence in our church. An influence over all of us, and maybe over me most of all. I had to cast it out. I *had to.* And as long as I was... impure... I couldn't do it. I had to get clean, to save you, to save every parishioner we have. And if they leave me, go to someone else, someone who never fell... well, fine. Better that than they stay in danger. And if I had to ruin myself in this world and... and be hated and despised and jeered at... fine. Maybe that's what I deserve. Better I fall now than lead them into temptation."

"Matthew, you're not making any sense."

The reverend took a deep breath. He raised his head and looked her in the eye.

"Zola, our son Noah is possessed by the Devil."

There was a moment of silence. Then she said, "Get out."

"Zola, I—"

"Get *out!*" she screamed, pointing at the door.

Matthew stood up and opened his mouth, but nothing came out.

His mighty voice had failed him.

Chapter Three

Out at the compound, Black Hawk O'Hanlon was the first one to hear about his mother's death. He was not the first of Avitu's worshippers to hear. That was actually Pamela Creed, who heard about it on NPR but didn't attach any particular significance to the news. She'd met the O'Hanlons, but didn't know their real names or their past. To her, they were just others who also served the Keeper of the Twin Winds. Since she felt that following grisly true crime news stories (such as the O'Hanlon case or, as one tabloid dubbed them "the Hillbilly Death Duo") was beneath her, she quickly put the news out of her mind.

The bearer of the tidings was known as Gwynafra Doakes, and she wasn't human. She looked human. She looked (in fact) like a porn star. She had a vaguely defined but well-paid job at a casino in Las Vegas, she screwed her boss, and she'd been created out of desert dirt by the animating will of Avitu the Tree of Ignorance. She knew Blackie and Joellen's true identities very well—she'd been the one who arranged their makeovers and paid for their new wardrobes and scheduled their facial reconstruction surgeries.

She found the last surviving O'Hanlon in the compound's single finished building—a small cabin used by Avitu's high priest. Blackie was there because it had air-conditioning.

"Black Hawk," she said. "I've got some bad news."

"It's mom, isn't it?" he asked.

She nodded. He slumped his shoulders.

"Aw shit," he muttered.

Blackie had gotten stuck with the unenviable task of watching over May Carter, which was why he was at the compound instead of wandering around Las Vegas. While Gabe McKenzie had speculated about her being raped or murdered or chained up in a basement somewhere, her real fate had never crossed his mind. (This is perhaps, not surprising: The FBI deals with lots of murders and hostages and kidnappings, but very few unlicensed lobotomies.) Now, as Gwyn brought her tidings, May was crouched in a corner of the cabin, muttering softly to herself and poking her fingers into her nose and ear holes.

"She's been arrested, hasn't she?" Blackie asked, dread on his features. "She was *soooo* sure the FBI would never find her."

"It's worse than that."

"Oh no."

"She's dead, Blackie."

Slowly, Blackie sat down on the cabin's single bed.

"Oh," he said. Slowly, his large frame seemed to deflate and crumple inward. "Oh."

"Blackie..."

"Oh mama..."

May chose that moment to emit an unusually loud bleat.

"*Shut up!*" Blackie shrieked at her. Then he started sobbing into his hands.

"If there's anything I can do..." Gwyn said.

"Find someone to watch the fuckin' *gimp* here," he said, with a savage gesture at May. "And then find out who killed my mother, and get me a gun!"

"That won't be necessary." Gwyn explained that Joellen's murderer was, in fact, the High Priest's wife and that she'd died in the fight.

Black Hawk couldn't exactly feel worse, but he found his misery becoming far more tiresomely complicated.

Teddy Mason was with God.

That's how he felt, anyhow.

Teddy Mason—Birdie Mason's husband and Joellen's lover, but Avitu's High Priest first and foremost—was with his Goddess and everything made sense.

He was not on Earth, not anywhere above or beneath it. He was Somewhere Else. Somewhere with no space and with alien time, somewhere where the laws of matter and causality and this-follows-that were looser, cloudier.

He thought of it as "Godspace" or "the Blue" because when he left it, he always remembered it as being blue, a deep luminous blue something like a summer sky, and something like the heart of a sapphire, and something like looking up at the sun through deep ocean water. Though when he was there, there was no color, there were other things instead of color. But he remembered it as blue.

In the Blue, all his thoughts split apart, like an exploded diagram of a complicated machine, and though this was confusing at first, he was learning to use it, to pick through his thoughts more carefully and choose only to think the best (the most loyal one, the most confident one, the most reasonable one) instead of the thrashing, rattling feeling he had outside the Blue, when all his thoughts shook him this way and that simultaneously.

"JOELLEN IS DEAD," Avitu told him.

A variety of responses formed around Teddy, rushing toward him, as if to condense on him like humid summer air on a cold glass. He could respond selfishly, mourning the loss of the woman who shared his bed. Or there was shameful relief, for he still was unwillingly loyal to Birdie, the mother of his son Lance. There was a thin possibility that he could feel sorry for Blackie, but that potential was brief and flickering. Blackie was Teddy's son too, but he barely knew Blackie and had made little attempt to do so.

He considered anger, but that was pointless, and he considered some oath of vengeance, but he knew Avitu was no revenging spirit. Like a radio signal coming clearer, the best response grew stronger and he said, "How does this loss impact your plans?"

"IT IS A BLOW. OF MY GREATER PRIESTHOOD, ONLY YOU AND TIM GRADY REMAIN, AND HE IS A WEAK TOOL WHEN I DO NOT GUIDE HIM DIRECTLY."

His next set of responses was smaller, and he was quicker to choose. "What of Black Hawk? He's a priest of the blood, and he's taken your oath."

"BLACK HAWK HAS YET TO MAKE A SACRIFICE, AND HIS FAITH LACKS THE STRENGTH YOU AND GRADY POSSESS. HE IS UNRIPE. HE MIGHT BE READY TO BE A FULL PRIEST IN TIME, BUT NOT NOW."

"And Gwynafra?"

"SHE HAS NO SOUL. SHE CANNOT CHOOSE TO PERFORM MY RITES. SHE CAN ONLY OBEY."

"What of the others, then? The sheriff and the other lesser priests?"

"THOSE OF THE LESSER PRIESTHOOD ARE BARELY FIT TO PERFORM MY SERVICES, THOUGH THEY COULD GROW MATURE. I SHALL TRY THEM ELSEWHERE, FAR FROM THE GROVE. THE LOSS OF SUCH AS THEM IS LITTLE TO ME — THEY ARE NOT OF THE BLOOD."

"Would you seek more servants? Men and women who are better fit and more faithful?"

"FOUR PRIESTS WOULD SUFFICE, IF THEY WERE TRULY MINE. IF THE BLOOD OF MY SERVICE RAN IN THEIR VEINS."

A great number of responses flew around Teddy, but none of them pleased him deep down. Ultimately, he picked the simplest one. The inevitable one.

"My son Lance."

"YOU MUST TRAIN HIM. HE MUST LEARN HIS DESTINY."

"How am I to get him from his mother?"

"SHE IS NO LONGER AN OBSTACLE."

In the Blue he had no body, but just as he later remembered seeing when he had no eyes, he would later remember a bitter taste flooding the mouth he did not have.

"RETURN. DRAW YOUR SON TO YOU, OR FETCH HIM IF YOU MUST. IT IS TIME TO BEGIN HIS INITIATION."

There were dozens of denials, defiances, pleas, but they were ephemeral possibilities next to Teddy's leaden, "As you wish."

"BEFORE YOU TEND TO HIM, THERE IS ANOTHER MATTER. THE TIME HAS COME FOR ME TO MAKE A SIGN."

Rosemary Nevins' ghost watched. She was watching Tim Grady. Her killer. She'd watched him since she died in 1957.

She'd watched him and shadowed him and frightened him until he got sloppy, got careless, got caught. She watched him in jail and in court, watched him get convicted for the brutal slayings of herself and four other pretty young women. She read the headlines about the capture of the Hollywood Ice Pick, she saw him get judged Not Guilty by Reason of Insanity, she saw the anger and public outcry. But she kept watching, even when the outrage died down and he became a punch line for jokes, and then later, when they made a B-movie based on his crimes, and when a cartoonist did a speculative comic book about him and his five lovely victims, each woman drawn carefully, beautifully, and their deaths—each restrained and killed by an ice pick through the eye—depicted with equal attention.

Rosemary watched.

She watched as he was largely forgotten, left in an institution to be drugged, to get electroshock "therapy," and to eventually be dismissed as a hopeless case, a human husk fit only to be warehoused.

She watched it all.

When she had the opportunity, she made things worse for him.

And then one day she helped him escape.

She felt like she didn't have much choice. Ironically, he had become one of the few things tying her to the living lands, and even after decades as a spirit she wasn't ready to let them go. Being remembered kept her active, let her siphon off just a little of that world's radiant, sunlit heat, it gave her a way to continue even in the dim and the dark and the chill of death.

As long as the Hollywood Ice Pick was remembered, she'd be remembered. As long as she was remembered, she could go on.

When she felt he was too close to being forgotten, she helped him get out. She figured that his escape—the escape of a seventy-year old maniac!—from a high-security asylum would get some attention. And when she helped him kill again and again, that would be even better.

That was the plan. And the first part, the getting him out part, had worked just fine.

The very next day, a massive earthquake hit Los Angeles. His asylum cracked open like a rotten egg, spilling its rank contents out into a city already bedeviled by fire and riot and fear. One woman reported it when Grady attacked her, but the news was lost in the general alarm of the quake.

Then he got into the desert and there was something there. Something ancient and powerful, something that existed outside the worlds of life and death. Something Other.

It was something that could frighten even a woman who remembered her own murder.

Now Rosemary knew that the Other—the tree in the desert—was named Avitu. She knew it had gathered followers. She knew that Gwynafra Doakes was its agent, and that Gwyn was not properly alive, no matter how much she faked it. She'd gathered that Teddy Mason was crucial, no matter how depressed and despondent he'd become. Mostly, though, she watched Tim.

Tim had come to the Tree shattered and aged, and now he was vital and strong (if visibly still old). Avitu hadn't fixed his mind—maybe nothing could—but it was clear that the Tree was protecting and healing him, even as he went about doing its business.

Interestingly, its business seemed to involve shoving ice picks through people's eyes, up into their brains.

Rosemary Nevins had a lot to think about. While she made her plans, she continued to watch.

Some of them had come from a long way away, but not many. Most were local to Las Vegas and the small towns around it.

Rumors were going around Vegas, as they always did, but these weren't rumors about Siegfried and Roy having substance abuse problems, or rumors that such-and-such a restaurant was a mob front. These stories were about a new religion.

As yet, this new faith had no name. It got started (they said) out in the desert, like so many of the old beliefs. But this one supposedly had the real goods—a true hotline connection to

God (or a god, or a goddess, depending on whether you talked to an ex-Christian or a disenchanted New-Ager or a fallen Hindu).

The central tenet of this faith? That human existence is torment, that we were never meant to be higher than the animals, that modern man's state of mind was monstrous, perverse.

Like Christianity, this new religion promised relief. Like Buddhism, it said that true bliss lies in the annihilation of the ego. But unlike them, unlike any traditional church, it promised a quick fix. One simple ceremony, one self sacrifice... and all that unhealthy thought, all that confusion and doubt, all the burdens of knowledge, could be swept away forever.

Granted, there aren't that many people for whom total oblivion sounds appealing. But there are some.

Gwynafra Doakes found them in Alcoholics Anonymous meetings, in support groups for terminal illnesses, in the many 12-step programs promising recovery and health throughout Las Vegas. She attended and watched, she picked the weakest and offered them a program that had only one step, a program that would give them the release they craved.

Pamela Creed followed Gwynafra's lead. There were plenty of groups to go around. She was not as successful, though: In the months since she'd acquiesced to Avitu, Pamela had shriveled into a shadow of her former self. Sickly thin, with haunted eyes, she did not look like a woman with answers. She looked like someone who needed solace herself.

Joeesha Murfee had more success in Reno. Her sax playing was still mediocre at best, but she'd developed a strange sort of stage presence. In between blasting fierce discord from her instrument, she barked out blank verse poetry of despair and surrender. There wasn't a huge audience for nihilist jazz fusion in Reno, but the people who liked it, liked it a *lot*. And they were the kind of people who were receptive to exterminating all rational thought.

Stuart Flaubert did the best—better than Gwynafra, in fact—because he was the most daring. He didn't stay in Nevada. Instead he went to Los Angeles, which was still a dangerous town, still a place where the police always had too much to do and the charities never had enough to give. With human misery so thick on the ground, he found many who were eager to forget. Orphans, widows, the bankrupted and maimed... they followed him, and he drove them out to the desert to sacrifice their minds on Avitu's wooden altar.

But while many were ready—impatient, even!—some were less ripe. And this was, of course, understandable. The most prominent symptom of the illness of consciousness was indecision. Avitu understood, and for those who were almost sure, but *not quite*... those who wanted the void but who lacked the courage to take a permanent step... she had prepared a demonstration.

Twenty-four people were there. Twenty-four, plus Gwynafra. They had gathered from Las Vegas and Los Angeles and Reno and smaller towns in between. They had come out to the compound and slept in tents, and they had seen the Tree and touched her, but Avitu had not spoken to them, had not drawn them into her secret realms. That was hard, opening the paths. It wasn't natural to her—that power was stolen, false. Instead, she would give them a miracle from her heart.

Teddy Mason, the High Priest of Avitu, was present. It was through him that this wonder would happen. He was an ordinary man, unassuming, wearing a black shirt with a minister's collar.

Creed, Murfee and Flaubert were there, looking out over their flocks. Flaubert kept his face carefully immobile. Creed looked ready to cry or collapse. Murfee had an expression of barely concealed disgust—over the past months, it had rarely left her face.

Black Hawk O'Hanlon was there. So was Tim Grady.

The rest of them were the wafflers, the fence-sitters, the maybe-maybe-not sacrifices, there for a sign from the goddess.

It was four in the afternoon, and they were the only people in the cemetery.

It wasn't a spooky, atmospheric, gothic old graveyard. It was modern and irrigated and had the level green grass of a golf course. The monuments were low, flat plaques set in the ground, made of some rustproof metal. There were no actual tombstones. Nothing stuck up to interrupt the ground's gentle rolling swells, except here and there a tasteful, appropriate statue. The closest one was a bronze faun, curled up asleep.

They'd driven out in three minivans and four full vans—big ones, the kind that can seat a dozen people. Black Hawk wondered why. It seemed wasteful. They could have carpooled.

Gwyn, Teddy and Avitu's other ministers knew the reason. None of the passengers bothered to think about it.

When all the vehicles had arrived, looking very much like a funeral, Teddy stepped forward and raised his arms.

"Good day," he said. He cleared his throat.

"I'm not much of a public speaker," he said, "but I hope I can... y'know, show you people what I believe and why. I think it's important that you all understand what you're getting into. What you're being offered."

There were a few coughs, but people were listening.

"First off, let me say this: I envy you. I... I know you all have had trouble. Some of you have told me, or Stuart or Gwyn... I know. All of you know pain. You know this life *is* pain." He frowned and looked down at the ground.

"I know that pain too. I've lost my wife... recently... and..."

His listeners frowned, craned forward to hear. He took a deep breath and raised his head again.

"Avitu... the great goddess... she offers you freedom. A freedom she can't offer to me. I have to... stay. I have to stay bound, enslaved to a mind I wasn't meant to endure, I have to, to tolerate that so that I can free you. It's not... not a burden I necessarily want, but I've agreed to it. I understand that it's necessary. I have to... stay back, so that you can go forward.

"But some of you hesitate. That's understandable. You're addicted to thinking, and you can't give it up, even when it's poisoning you. You're attached to material things, attached to people you know and love. And you're afraid. Afraid of losing out. Maybe afraid of death, too. Right?

"I'm here to tell you there's nothing to fear. Your attachments—your loves and hates and hopes and fears... they're all illusion. They're all in your head! Avitu can remove those, pull them up by the roots, take away their power to torment you.

"That's hard to admit. It's hard to own up to how much of our love is just *lies*—just, just air, nothing real, intangible. Like a ghost. Fantasies. The people you love are loved only as images in your mind. That's when love hurts, isn't it? When your image is false? When reality doesn't follow the script? The, the man you thought was honest turns out to be a liar. Or the child who was, was going to be a doctor grows up and he's just... I don't know, a criminal or something. The disappointment that things aren't how you think they *should* be, they're as they *are*. It's not reality that's hurting you then. It's that *should*, that damnable expectation. That's what sets you up.

"My wife died recently, but she's still alive in my mind. When I think of her, I... I see her..."

His voice broke. People looked away, embarrassed, as his tears fell.

"My wife died and I couldn't go to her funeral. But in my mind, my lying mind, she's still alive. It's a lie! And you're all clinging to that lie, all those lies... you're doing it too. It's destroying you. Destroying us all. But Avitu has the truth."

He gave a hard snort, trying to clear his nose of mucus, he got out his handkerchief and gave it a hard blow.

"Avitu has the truth," he repeated, his voice still thick but stronger.

He put his hankie away and stood up straight. Then he opened his arms wide, like a yawn, and the people with him jumped back, startled, as the ground gaped wide.

"Avitu *is* the truth," he said, and like mouths in the soil, holes opened by headstones.

"The death you fear is nothing," he said quietly, and every ear strained to hear him. "Living and dying are just the same. Only the lie of consciousness thinks different. What is movement or stillness compared to the truth?"

There was perfect silence as he drew in a deep breath.

"Arise!" he said.

Another moment of quiet.

Then they all heard the sounds, the thuds and thumps, as the coffins in the ground were struck from within.

The ghost of Rosemary Nevins had never seen corpses rise. When she heard Teddy telling Pamela about it, she hadn't known what to think, but she'd followed Tim out to the graveyard. And now, sure enough, the dead rose.

The priesthood—Pam and Tim, Stuart and the rest of them—got hammers and crowbars from the vans and set to work opening the coffins. With much hesitation, the others did as well.

When the first casket opened, the people around jerked back, appalled by the stench.

The creature that emerged was bones and skin stretched tight, the embalming fluid long since dried out. The nails and hair were long and unruly, seeming to have continued to grow for some time after death. The teeth weren't actually bigger, but they looked longer because the gums had drawn back and the lips were shriveled away from them. Their skin was ashy gray or dirt brown, except on the faces. There, the morticians had used heavy-duty makeup—more like paint, really—and the bright flesh tones remained, unnatural, out-of-context and grotesque on shriveled lips and worm-gnawed cheeks.

Women and men, the corpses looked the same. The only way to tell was by clothes, and by the eyeliner that remained on some bodies' eyeless sockets.

Rosemary counted as the living reeled back. Fifteen corpses had arisen, widely scattered across the cemetery. If forced to guess, she'd judge by the decay of their clothes and estimate that they were the most recently dead.

Examining them with the eyes of a ghost, Rosemary could tell they weren't really living. They moved, but only in the way a sock puppet does when you jam a hand up it. They were, in a word, possessed.

This wasn't entirely new to Rosemary. In fact, she could do the same thing, though heretofore she'd been restricted to overwhelming the living. But now that this "Avitu" had gone to the trouble of offering her an option...

Rosemary drifted toward the zombies—they were now stumbling, barefoot, toward the big vans. The priests were shifting the seats out of the way so that the walking dead could lie down under tarps, stacked like cords of firewood.

The likeliest-looking was a woman (probably) whose loose, leathery skin indicated great flab in life. She was big-boned and (unlike some others, who must have died in falls, car crashes or industrial accidents) she was complete. Rosemary enveloped her like fog and exerted her will…

It was different. She could slip in and ride passively—that was easy enough—but this dead thing had only rudimentary senses, mostly touch, poor hearing, no sight… but Rosemary's own vision still worked fine even through rotted-out eyes.

When she tried to control its muscles, she ran into resistance. *Something* was already there—Avitu, she presumed—and it was something *tough*.

Rosemary slipped out of the corpse, hoping that the— What? Goddess?—wasn't focused on her.

It's got to be distracted, she thought. *Guiding multiple bodies? And she hasn't seemed to perceive me before.* But she was whistling past the graveyard and she knew it. Really, she had no idea what this thing's true capacities were. Whether it was just watching and waiting. What it could do to her if it knew.

But still. With a real good effort, she might be able to seize one of those zombies. That would be worth something.

Ruby Fowler sat in the lobby and wept. It wasn't a complicated, bittersweet weeping. These weren't the conflicted tears of a jilted wife or jealous lover, nor were they the thoughtless, purely selfish tears of a miserable child. They were tears backed by mature sorrow, by a mind old enough to understand the fullness of loss.

Mothers cry like that for lost sons. Ruby cried and her nose got clogged with snot. It blocked out the antiseptic smell of a hospital emergency room and she missed Rob already. She was shocked to find herself missing his flaws. She'd miss him skipping school and sneaking booze with his no-good friends while she was at work. She'd miss his no-good friends. She'd miss him skateboarding without a helmet, and she'd miss nagging him and fighting with him and the way his music was too loud and crude. The way he always left the bathroom in a mess…

Without him, their house was going to be as dead and silent and empty as her heart.

"Are you okay?"

She looked up and saw a man in a priest's collar, holding out a tissue.

"Yeah," she muttered and took it. She gave a good blow. He offered her another one.

"I don't think you are. Okay, I mean," he said.

She gave a rattling sigh. "My son just died."

He nodded. "Yeah."

"Are you a minister?"

He nodded again. "Yours was Robert? The traffic accident?"

His words restarted her hitching sobs. She nodded.

"Why are you crying for him?" he asked.

"Oh Father," she said, "Look. Look I, I know you mean well and all, but if you start in on how he's gone to a better place, I think I'm going to scream." Her voice was leaden. She sounded ground down and flattened, like she couldn't scream if you branded her.

"I don't know where he's gone. I don't know what's happened to him. But I know that *you're* here and *you're* in terrible, terrible pain. That's what I care about."

"My son just died. That hurts, you know? Or maybe you don't."

"I know what it means to lose a son. I know how much it hurts when your child gets taken away."

She squinted at him. "You're not Catholic?"

"No."

She shrugged. Guessed he was some protestant minister who was allowed to marry.

"I just wish…"

"What?"

"I wish I could see him again. Just once. To, you know…"

"What good would that do?"

"I could tell him I loved him and… you know. All that stuff."

"If he didn't know when he died, there'd be no point in telling him now."

"Look, do you have to be so *reasonable*?" Her voice rose and, on the last word, cracked.

He just looked at her with his chin in his hand.

"I can help you," he said.

She groaned. "Father, what's the point? I mean, I know you mean well, but *what is the point*? All you have to offer is, is words. Words and gestures and, and Bible verses and just a lot of *noise*. I lost something *real*. Someone I could *hold in my arms*. All your talk about Jesus and God and everything, they're just words, how can I believe in something that's just, just made out of air?"

"If I could bring him back, would you listen to me?"

"Oh Lord…"

"No. I'm serious. If I can make him walk and move and speak again, would you listen to me? Would you consider letting me help you?"

"But you can't."

"Come with me." He stood and held out a hand, and there was something in his posture that made her obey. "He's in there, right?" he asked.

Ruby chewed her lower lip and nodded. The minister pushed open the door.

Seeing the figure under the sheet was like a punch to Ruby's gut. They'd covered up all the bloody parts. He was there, just waiting.

With no hesitation, the man walked to the head of the gurney and pulled the sheet off. Ruby thought she'd look away, but it just numbed her. Seeing her son's dead face just made her numb.

The man raised his left hand over the corpse and sprinkled it with something. Sand? It looked like sand.

And then Robbie's eyes popped open.

"Ma?"

The voice was rough and scratchy, propelled by lungs in broken ribs and coming through a throat thick with blood. He sat up, face blank as the gaze of a maggot.

"Robbie?" she whispered.

With glazed eyes and no expression, Rob began getting up. One of his legs was broken, shattered really, and with gentle pressure the minister convinced him to sit on the edge of what had, recently, been his deathbed.

"Robbie," she said, and it was hard, very hard, to repress a hysterical giggle. Surely she was mad. Yes? Yes. This must be exactly what going crazy felt like.

"You'll listen now?" the minister said.

"Oh... oh, I..." Ruby had eyes only for her boy. He was looking around listlessly.

"We have to get him out of here." The miracle-worker's voice was sane and calm. Together, they put Robbie under the sheet again and kept him still while they went out to Ruby's car. The man in black explained, clearly and concisely, that Ruby would have to go on the run, that there would be questions from nonbelievers and that people would think she'd stolen Rob's body, that they couldn't afford to let people know, to let them see the miracle.

They drove to her house and collected as many valuables as they could, and they emptied as much of her bank account as the ATM would permit, and as they drove around she came to understand that Robbie wasn't really all back. He was moving and looking but he was barely talking and he wasn't really thinking.

It was all so unreal, so unsettling, so alien to her everyday life (Ruby was a land surveyor) that she started leaning more and more on the minister's words. Like a drowning woman who will clutch any straw, her drowning mind grabbed onto his claims and explanations. He talked about consciousness, and how it was poison, and how Robbie was now the way he should be—free of pain and uncertainty, free from the many pitfalls of foresight and expectation and regret and rational analysis. Ruby, overwhelmed, just nodded and nodded and tried to grasp what was happening, but she couldn't get much farther than a vague sense that the minister wanted to help her. He was kind and could take her pain away.

When they arrived out by the tree, he led her to its trunk and showed her more miracles. Then he asked her if she wanted to accept Avitu's gift. She did.

The minister's name was Teddy Mason.

It took about two weeks to get the zombies from Las Vegas to southern Illinois. The actual driving was two days, but Teddy thought it wise to clean up the creatures and try to get the stink off them before that. It was a more involved process than expected. Furthermore, since several of them were incomplete, Teddy, Gwyn and Stuart wound up making crude prostheses for them—stuff on the level of peg legs, club arms with hooks, and a ceramic plate to return one skull to a more human profile. (Stuart had been a painter before he became a demonic minister, and he'd dabbled in pottery at art school.)

Tim Grady drove the truck, and he didn't have any trouble. He had to get fuel several times, but he paid at the pump with one of Pamela Creed's credit cards each time. He mostly gassed up at night or during the middle of the afternoon when fewer people were around to see, fewer to smell the ghastly scent from the corpses (which, while much milder, was still perceptibly present) in the back of his panel van. Even if the tank was half full, he'd stop and refill at stations that looked particularly empty. He wasn't impatient.

He slept in the driver's seat. The smell didn't bother him. He had no dreams.

Sheriff Grant Dagley spent those weeks scrambling. He'd gotten his orders from Avitu—her voice had echoed through his head in the middle of the night, waking him gasping—and he had no choice but to carry them out.

Well, I guess I could choose to fight her, and get all sickened and killed, he thought, *but that ain't much of an option.*

The demon in the desert had commanded him to launch a police raid. Which, to the uninitiated, might sound simple, right? He's a cop, he should be able to go arrest a bunch of crooks, right?

Wrong.

First off, the crooks Avitu wanted him to get were in East St. Louis—miles outside of his jurisdiction. As far as the law was concerned, he was an ordinary citizen there. No, worse, he was a cop off his turf, with *more* legal constraints on his behavior than a regular civilian.

Even if he could find some legal way to do it—cobble together some sort of State Police task force and get on it, some bullshit like that—he had not one jot of evidence. No probable cause. Without that, even the most rabid anti-drug judge wouldn't authorize a no-knock bust. "A goddess told me to," was not going to play in court.

And finally, the biggest problem: Avitu said she'd send him "soldiers" to assist him. Deputizing them would be an immense bureaucratic hassle, and even then any *legit* cops with him would certainly twig to it fast.

No way. It was the bureaucratic equivalent of parting the Red Sea.

So—as he'd done so often in his life—Grant decided to fake it and cheat.

Luke and Dean, his most trusted assistants, could cover for him when he took a day off to go rumble East St. Louis. Hell, his entire office had evolved a number of plans and excuses and contingencies for cases when he was unexpectedly absent over the years. Between his drinking and his extracurricular activities, he was AWOL so often they simply had to. When he gave warning, it was actually much easier.

Getting uniforms for fifteen people was going to be a hell of a trick, and of course Avitu hadn't told him their sizes. (He just assumed they were all men.) But in the long course of his dirty career, he'd helped other dirty birds get on the perch, and one such dirty official was Mavis Redfern. Mavis was the bureaucrat who kept track of county law enforcement property. Having lost a great deal of such property over the years (what with one thing and another), he'd cultivated her and put her on his payroll. When he explained what he needed, she gave him the number for a guy in Springfield.

"He's a stone-cold nut," she explained. "You tell him this is a black-bag DEA vigilante thing and he'll give you a truck, uniforms—he'll probably blow a load all over your face from sheer excitement. Just don't get him started on the Bill of Rights. He thinks it's a Communist plot."

Grant chuckled.

"I'm not kidding," Mavis insisted.

So Grant talked to the stone-cold nut, who agreed to get him fifteen sets of riot gear—on the condition that Dagley get it back within twenty-four hours so it wouldn't be missed. "I can get it out for that long," he said, "but after that—nuh uh."

"That won't be a problem at all," Grant said, with no idea whether he was lying or not. "I'll get you the measurements for the team as soon as I know, 'kay?"

"Right on," the nut said back, eyes gleaming.

It was after that talk that Grant heard from Avitu, telling him that Tim had almost arrived. Grant had a few more questions about what she wanted, and while she was very patient, she was not fully able to explain to him what he was up against. But he was (eventually) satisfied that the way he was doing things would work.

Dagley suggested that Tim meet him out by an old, abandoned barn on some property the sheriff owned.

It was just as well, when Dagley discovered the type of "soldiers" Avitu had sent.

"Fuck," he said, backing away. "Fuck. No. Fuck no. No. Just... no. Uh uh. No fucking way."

"Yes," Tim said.

Dagley's back hit the rail on the pigpen. He was standing right where he'd sexually assaulted Joellen O'Hanlon, so many months ago.

How did the fact that her "soldiers" were goddamn corpses slip through a goddess' mind? Grant thought.

He sighed.

"Fuck," he said one more time. "They'll need riot helmets."

Tim said nothing. Even his face was blank.

"Don't think I'm gonna arm them," he warned. "I got some guns, but not that many."

"They don't need guns," Tim said.

Measuring the zombies for their uniforms was no picnic, but eventually, after much breath-holding and swallowing-back of rising gorge, Grant and Tim called in size requests for riot gear.

"So *all* of these are slims?" the stone-cold nut asked.

"You could say that."

"That's kind of weird, there's... Y'know, most of the guys who go for SWAT training are pretty pumped up."

"Look, just... just get me something, okay? And the helmets. Don't forget helmets and gloves."

"Avitu can work through me," Tim told him. "If things become desperate, she can work through you as well, but it's better if it's me."

"You're the boss," Grant said, trying to keep the sourness out of his voice. It galled him, being someone else's bitch, but at the same time, shit, Avitu wasn't like that cock-biting state attorney who was gunning for him. Avitu had *real* power, and knowing that he was completely outclassed made taking orders a *lot* easier.

That and the threat of instant death, of course.

"You drive," Tim said, and Grant drove. The fifteen stinking riot cops sat in the back of an unmarked truck, clutching batons. Tim sat in the passenger seat with a large backpack on the floor between his feet.

"So we just drive up and... and go nuts? Just waste everyone?"

"There is only one creature that *must* die, but many humans will try to protect it. It does not matter if they live or not."

"How many?"

"Many," Tim said.

Grant cursed under his breath.

"Can you tell me where we're going?"

"I'll sense the place when we get close."

"So, and I just want to get clear, here, we don't know where we're going, or who we're going to run into there, but they'll fight us, and then we're going to kill some... some *critter* that you can't even explain what it is?"

Tim cocked his head for a moment, as if he was listening to something distant and quiet.

"Right," he said.

One more f-word crossed Dagley's lips. It didn't help, but he kept saying it.

As they crossed the city limits into East St. Louis, Tim said, "Turn right."

"Where?"

"Anywhere. It's that direction. I feel it."

"That's great, Timmy. That's terrific."

They drove a couple of miles, got through some traffic, Grant just taking it easy, when Tim said, "They're coming."

"Who?"

"The slaves of our enemy." He bent down, unzipped his backpack, and pulled out a sawed-off shotgun.

"Hey!" Dagley said. "Whoa there! Y'can't just open up in broad daylight, not even in East—"

But he didn't finish his sentence because he needed to concentrate on driving.

There were two cars, well coordinated—he'd guess they were on two-ways or hands-free cells—trying to corral his van like a pair of cowboys. The one in front was big, an old rebuilt steel-body sedan. It wasn't as heavy as the truck, but heavy enough. It had stopping power.

The chase car was some flashy rice rocket, three inches off the pavement with spoilers and a fly magenta paint job. It had the speed and the turn radius, it could orbit the truck if it had to.

Grant realized that the chaser probably had gunmen in it, at the very least. Its job would be to close off his options, get him behind the sedan so that they could roadblock him down, hold him in place until the cavalry arrived. Or just encircle him and mow him like a lawn, for that matter.

No way.

The chaser was coming in from the left, they were on a fat four-lane main road—two lanes northbound, two lanes south. Grant gunned it and lunged over into the left lane—if they had a shooter in the passenger seat, he'd have a tougher shot over the hood of his own car. If they had one in the back seat too, he'd have a hard angle without blowing out their own windshield. Either way, the thick back wall of the truck would be between Dagley and any bullets.

He felt, or rather heard, the first bullet's impact on the back of the truck. No problem.

The blocker sedan was in the right lane in front of him, that was his real problem right now, it was trying to close in, but there was traffic.

He heard a pistol crack, saw a muzzle flash from the blocker, but they missed him, Tim was waving the shotgun and that kept the sedan at distance. Grant heard a chorus of horns and glanced in the rearview mirror. Damn. The chaser was in the oncoming lane, heading against the flow of traffic to give their passenger a shot at driver Dagley.

"Fool," he muttered, looking—ah, the timing wasn't exactly right, he wouldn't be able to knock the little bastard in front of some oncoming car, but as the Jap crap pimpmobile pulled alongside he turned into them, not too hard, just a tap.

A Jap crap tap? the sheriff thought, smiling slightly.

It was like a linebacker hip-checking a cheerleader. The truck rebounded about a foot, right back into his proper place. The car swerved a whole lane over, steam rose from skid marks, but my, my, the driver was good. He swerved back, fishtailed a little but he had fat, grippy tires, he got back in the lane behind the truck before he could lose control and go into a lamp post or mailbox.

Tim's gun was deafening in the truck's cab. While Grant was pushing the chaser around, the blocker made his move. Tim had shot out a side window and, from the red spatters on the windshield, it looked like the passenger got tagged. But the driver was still intact, he had the hammer down, pulling in front of the truck—didn't want to stay alongside, knowing the trucker had a taste for sideswipes. He was racing to get in front free and clear.

Dagley turned the wheel—just a little—and slammed on the brakes, grateful that the truck didn't have airbags. The sheriff was braced against the steering wheel, but he still felt a shock as the seatbelts engaged. Grady whipped forward, the shotgun clattering against the dashboard and popping open, and then the pursuit car rear-ended them.

Both men in the front seat snapped back, their heads hitting the cushions between them and the back section. No whiplash, no problem. From the rear, Dagley heard a series of thumps as the zombies clattered over. He wondered if they could be hurt.

Looking back, Dagley saw that the chaser had hit the truck's bumper at an angle, as he'd hoped, bouncing into the oncoming lane once more. And that car was wrecked—the front end looked like an accordion, its bumper must have been far too low to offer any protection. They were going nowhere.

The blocker had stopped too, the driver started to lean out the window to aim just as Grant plopped a heavy foot down on the accelerator. He'd been watching traffic, there was a red light up ahead and no traffic oncoming, he swerved into the oncoming lane and aimed inches from the car before he remembered that he was in a truck with lousy pickup instead of his cherried-out pursuit vehicle.

He had time to think, *Oh shit*. Time to perceive that the guy had a big old black steel revolver and it was pointed straight at his face. Time to piss his pants in true, abject terror.

And then the truck's left side made gentle, scraping contact with the car and he smeared the driver, tore off his arm and pinched off his head. The two vehicles ground together like the blades on scissors and the guy never even took his shot.

He must have been too scared to move, Dagley thought.

He pulled around the blood-smeared car, went straight, hung a left and was free.

Sheriff Grant Dagley had unconsciously expected to head into East St. Louis's deep downtown—that was the area he associated with bad trouble, though he'd never gone. But Grady was leading him along the periphery instead, south toward the river. They set a brisk pace, and Tim assured him that they were outrunning other servants... for the time being.

Grant smelled something that was cutting through even the zombie funk, and then they were pulling up by a pumping station.

"Here?" he asked, incredulous.

"Here," Tim said, opening his door. "You can stay or come with us."

Grant weighed his options. Stay in the car when a bunch more violent goofballs were on the way? Or head into the heart of darkness with one geriatric demonic nutjob and fifteen ersatz-SWAT-team zombies?

It was a tough call, but Dagley decided to go forward rather than wait. Really, he wasn't a patient man.

The thing in the treatment station had no name. Gaviel the devil called it "the Foe," and that would do as well as anything.

What was it? Where did it come from? No one knew. The bastard child of a demon and a human, forgotten under some prehistoric rock for millennia? Maybe. Some crazed, ancient ghost, so bloated and deformed by power and hatred that it didn't need to be remembered by name, didn't even need to remember itself, now buoyed up by the ancestral fear of the generations it had poisoned and tormented? Could be. Or was it, perhaps, some psychic cess-creature, the collected bad vibes of an impoverished, wretched, despised and unlucky town given shape and volition by the impotent rage and nightmares of twenty years of neglect?

Did it really matter?

The Foe was real, and it had no need to remember its past or ruminate on its origins. It was *there* and it *hated* and it had *power*. The power to punish and hurt and control. That was all it needed and all it knew.

When it felt other powers—the bright spark of Gaviel's malicious curiosity, the chill wind of Avitu's self-righteousness—it resisted, instinctively.

But Dagley and Grady had caught it off guard. It was no pushover on its home turf, but for the first time, it had to defend itself. Not its interests, not its pawns, not its power base.

For the first time, the Foe was in danger of being destroyed.

All the workers there were infected. Tim told him and Dagley believed, not that it mattered much. He wanted to get in, get out, get home and get a shower. Whether the blue-jumpsuited figure screaming into a telephone was an innocent bystander or the servant of mystic weirdness, he didn't give a shit. He just shot the guy and moved on.

The living dead were a definite plus, Dagley could see that now. Some of the workers were just bonkers, they'd charge forward screaming and waving a wrench or a pipe or a broken-off mop handle. He put a bullet in one skinny chick and she just kept coming, hollering like a banshee until a dead riot cop clotheslined her left-handed. Blood came out of her throat, and

Grant realized that it was that one zombie with no left arm, just a stump and a pole with a sharp hook on the end. Cool.

Other psycho employees jumped on the corpses and waled on them, but the zombies didn't care. Blows from a pipe didn't faze them a bit, they just swung back, dished out as good as they got. It was crazy, the workers and zombies weren't even properly fighting, there was no attempt at defense, no dodging, not even any flinching—just blow after blow after blow until one fell down. Usually the humans. Clearly they were more fragile.

The security guys for the place weren't as reckless—they were sane enough to use guns, but the SWAT zombies treated bullets like bee-stings. Or, better, like mosquito bites. If they even paid attention enough to turn at the shooters, the gunmen often freaked and ran. Those who didn't got clubbed and clawed.

"Down," Grady said. "This way."

"Uh huh," Dagley replied, watching behind him and listening on his police scanner. It was bad. East St. Louis had crap police, as badly under-funded as the rest of the city, but they were closing in fast. At least twenty units, which meant a cordon soon.

It wasn't until Grady opened a big steel door in the basement—a door with one of those spinning hatches like you see on a submarine—that Dagley wondered why a pumping station would smell so foul. After all, this was supposed to be drinking water, right?

Fuck, maybe I'm just confused, he thought, and then something icy and wet and incredibly strong wrapped up both ankles and slammed him to the ground.

Rosemary the ghost had watched the whole car chase and gunfight with a great deal of interest. She only interfered once — possessing a man in a car long enough to hold him still and make him die, long enough to save Grant Dagley's life. She didn't care about Dagley, but she couldn't afford to see Tim Grady gunned down in the street.

When she saw sewage and ice water lunge out of a hole in the floor and knock the sheriff on his back, she wasn't particularly alarmed. Dagley was nothing to her. But when Tim and the zombies grabbed the tentacle (or whatever the hell it was) and it turned its attention on her murderer, she became involved.

The pseudopod slammed a load of shit right into Grady's mouth and nose, but he was scrambling for the backpack. He wasn't trying to live. He was as bad as the psycho sewage workers who'd died by zombie. He was willing — eager! — to die, as long as he killed Avitu's enemy.

The prick.

Rosemary decided it was time. She claimed the body of a zombie, and it took all her effort. It was like pulling a coat around her in a hundred-mile-an-hour wind, but Rosemary was used to fighting wind, and when she had the corpse she grabbed Tim and pulled him away, pulled him free of the tentacle. Her withered hands pumped his chest and her rotted lips closed on his, sucking the feces right out of his mouth, spitting it aside. What did she care? She had no tongue, no taste.

When she heard him cough and sputter she looked. The tentacle had one zombie wrapped up and was using it as a club to batter the others, the sheriff had stumbled back to the wall and was pushing himself to a standing position.

"Get out," Rosemary told Grady. Tried to, anyhow. This rancid tongue and lacy lungs could only produce a thin wheeze, she pointed but he was looking at the backpack again and she knew what was in it.

It took an inhuman effort, but Rosemary was inhuman. She called on the strength that let her fight free of death and she showed her killer, once more, her human visage.

Rosemary's hateful face overlaid the zombie's rotted one and that did it. Grady's eyes grew wide with fear. He was seeing the only thing he *could* fear, and he fled. Dagley blinked, muttered a swear word and followed.

Rosemary, still possessing the zombie, grabbed the backpack and made for the hole.

Moving through the tentacle was hard, much harder than swimming, even against a stiff current, but her muscles were dead and felt no weariness. They were fired, not by some chemical reaction, but by her will alone.

She swam down deep toward the Foe, and then she was with it, *in* it, inside a dark pool of living ice water and refuse and hate. It started to claw at her and that was fine. It tore the body to pieces and that was okay. In its fury it ripped apart the backpack and the large, bulky, watertight plastic bag inside.

The bag was filled with pure, powdered sodium.

When sodium touches water, it burns. And explodes.

Grant Dagley stumbled when he felt the floor twitch beneath him. He heard a muffled thump but didn't think much of it. He had to catch up with Tim.

He caught up abruptly, when Grady went from full speed flight to standing stock still.

"It's done," Grady said, and suddenly he was calm again, like he was asking for a second helping of pecan pie.

"Great!" the sheriff said. "Now let's run!"

"We can't leave through a door. We are surrounded by police."

Dagley, predictably, swore.

"There's another way," Tim said, after once more cocking his head, listening to nothing. "This way."

When Tim opened a hatch on a big, thick pipe, Grant said, "Oh Jesus, no."

"Swim forty feet down in this and you'll emerge in a storm sewer access tunnel," he said.

Dagley grimaced—but at least the water was clean.

"Shit," he said, but he took off his shoes and tied them on his belt, pulled out his baton and hit Tim in the back of the head as hard as he could.

But it wasn't really Dagley that did that. It was Rosemary. Similarly, it was Rosemary who cuffed Tim to a convenient stair-rail and threw the handcuff key deep into the water. And then Dagley was himself again, just in time to hear footsteps above him. He looked at Tim and tried to think up a plan but, shit, the best he could come up with was "Let the big dummy take the fall." He dove into the water and swam for freedom.

Chapter Four

Sweet Pete's gold teeth flashed as he said, "I will pay a million dollars to the sonofabitch who kacks that whore."

(He got his nickname from his fondness for sweets, not his disposition.)

"You got a million dollars?" Sal Macellaio asked.

Sweet Pete sighed.

The conversation took place before Grady's raid on the Foe, before Avitu and Teddy had even raised the zombie troops. Sal didn't know about any of that. He'd just heard there was demon bullshit in Vegas, and he was interested.

Pete was behind glass, dressed in prison orange, his wrists chained together even to speak to a visitor through a short-cord telephone. His handcuffs made it look like he was holding the receiver with both hands, like he was that weak.

"Ahh, all my assets are frozen, all my stuff, it's impounded. That rat-bitch bit me good. I was stupid. I ain't proud—I was stupid an' I admit it. *Cherchez la femme*, right?"

"Uh huh," Sal said. "So this woman. What's her name? Gwiddy... Gwen..."

"Gwynafra," Pete replied, and those three syllables held a dissertation's worth of hatred and spite and still, underneath, longing.

"You two weren't together all that long, right?"

"Yeah, 'fore her I had Chelsea, who was no brain surgeon but, shit, at least she didn't Jew me out for the cops."

Sal, whose maternal grandmother was vividly Jewish, said, "Uh huh?"

"But Gwyn, hell, I lost my head. I mean, you can see how it would happen, right? You've seen the pictures?"

"She's got a hell of a rack, I gotta admit."

"The boobs, fuggeddaboudit. She was a hose monster, you hear what I'm saying? Like one of those nymphy-maniacs. Could—not—get—enough. *Capisce?*"

"I gotcha."

Pete shook his head, rueful. "And now, here I am in the can like a sucker. Jacking off in my jail cell. I ain't had to beat off since I was fourteen, but here I am."

"How'd she get you so bad?"

"I dunno. I mean, it's not like I was alla time telling her my bidness, y'know? But she, I dunno, I guess she had access. I dunno. She couldn'a hit my operation harder if she'd been a frigging cop."

"An undercover cop, I guess."

"Huh?"

"Get it? Undercover? Like, under the covers?"

"Oh." Pete laughed. "That's good. I'm gonna use that."

"You ever get the feeling that there was anything, I dunno, *weird* about her?"

Pete opened his mouth, then closed it. "Weird?"

"Yeah, weird."

Sal could feel Pete nearly trusting him, but the gangster's pride or his pragmatism or maybe his shame interfered. "Nah," he said.

"Nah?"

"Fuggeddaboudit."

Hasmed the demon—also known as Harvey Ciullo, once titled Knight of the Hated Lash, and often called Mr. Fortune—sat on a bench next to Roscoe Paum. Being only a man, Roscoe only had one name.

"Mm," Roscoe said, nudging Hasmed as a woman walked by. "Check that out. Aw, I wouldn't mind having two scoops of that, know what I mean?" He was referring to the woman's buttocks, which were of the large size he fancied.

The demon turned a flat stare on the mortal. Since one of Hasmed's eyes was a wreck of blood and stale pus, his stares were exceptionally potent.

"You know that some day, some guy is going to talk about Tina that way?" Tina was Harvey's daughter, but Roscoe had been watching over her during the recent troubles—troubles that seemed to be at an end, though you never knew.

"Yeah, but..." Ros looked up at him, looked over at the retreating woman (who was utterly oblivious), then looked back and sighed.

"You take the fun outta everything," he complained.

"Just watch for that Brinks truck and keep y'r mind outta the gutter," Hasmed said. "We pull this off, and you can hire all the fat-assed whores you want."

"Cheez, Hawv, you know I'm not one a' those guys who has to be going to pros alla time..."

At that moment, the truck turned the corner.

"Time," Hasmed said quietly.

"Eight twenty."

"*Meraviglioso*," Hasmed replied, making a note.

He'd been clocking the truck route for a couple of weeks now, sometimes alone, sometimes with Roscoe, sometimes with one of his other "business partners."

Hasmed wasn't in the armored car business, unless you considered armored cars to fall under the gangster rubric, along with loan sharking and racketeering and general heisting and hijacking.

For Hasmed was a Made Man, pledged to Rico Pudoto from Atlantic City, and he'd bought his way into Rico's graces with other people's blood. Rico's war with Johnny "Bronco" Vuoto was over—a decisive victory for the Atlantic City crews, and only Rico and his closest advisors knew just how critical "Harvey Ciullo" had been to that win.

But now the war was done, and Mr. Fortune was expected to go to work. Kacking rivals and torching the other guy's businesses was a good way to bring wild dogs to heel, but it didn't exactly pay the bills.

So, like many before him, Mr. Fortune had decided to go where the money was: Armored cars. It sounded easier than working for a living.

(There had been talk about giving Mr. Fortune his pick of the remnants of Johnny Bronco's grifts and grafts, but Rico's other lieutenants hadn't liked that. To them, he was still the new guy. Plus a Judas on Bronco was a Judas however much Bronco deserved the cross, *capisce*? They wanted this new punk to prove himself, and Hasmed was really fine with that. He figured it would be good to be a stringer, make a few big hauls now and then. The last thing he wanted was to get stuck holding the hands of a bunch of pimps and bookies every time they had to pee. Fuggeddaboudit.)

"...really skinnied up, huh?"

Hasmed turned to Paum and realized he'd been woolgathering. The man had an expectant expression.

"Yeah," Hasmed said, "Those free weights are really tightening me up." He ran a hand under his jawbone, where the loose skin of a second chin had drawn back. He'd never be baby-butt smooth, but he wasn't sagging and jiggling when he walked anymore.

"I betcha feel a lot better too, huh?"

"At least I look better," Hasmed said. "C'mon. Let's go see 'bout that Chrysler."

Sal had gotten a job at the big-ass Disney casino. He might be on the lam, maybe Rico from Atlantic City had a price on his head (or maybe Rico figured he wasn't dangerous anymore), but he still had friends in Vegas who could get him a lousy job — even in a casino that wasn't mobbed up.

It wasn't literally a Disney casino — there weren't Little Mermaid slot machines, the guys dealing Caribbean Stud weren't wearing pirate costumes or Mickey Mouse ears, but it was owned by a company that Disney owned, or something. Dealing with the management, there was a humorless uptightness that Sal didn't remember from Mafia casinos. They weren't any *nicer*, he didn't think, they weren't any less focused on squeezing out every last gambling dime. But they were Nazis about the staff *acting* nice and *seeming* nice.

Screw it. He was here to watch Gwynafra Doakes, and he figured he'd learned about all he could. He'd quit soon — might not even bother with his last chump-change check.

He'd timed things. Timed her, mostly. He stopped in at the security station after his shift, on his way from changing out of his monkey suit. He chatted up one of the camera watchers there, a gal named Janet. Told her some gossip, laughed at her jokes, but all the while kept one eye on the newest surveillance camera, the one pointing at Gwynafra's office.

When he saw Sweet Pete's bitterly hated ex emerge, he started to extricate himself from Janet's conversation. He suggested that he call her some time to go out, maybe catch Cirque, but he had to get home and let the dog out, see ya, bye.

Therefore, it seemed entirely natural that he got on the elevator with Gwyn, a skinny guy and a man who resembled a be-suited side of beef. There were a couple other folks on the lift, but they didn't matter.

The big no-neck was the obvious bodyguard—the bullet catcher. He didn't look too sharp, but Sal knew better. The best bulls always cultivated a dumb look. It gave them an excuse to shut up, listen and watch. Still, he'd stand his ground, absorb some flak in his bulletproof vest and cover her escape. That was his job. He'd be predictable, and to Sal, someone predictable was someone you could always get around.

The little guy was something else, a troubleshooter. (Or, from Sal's perspective, the trouble that shoots you.) He'd go ahead, scout the path, blend in and probably neutralize threats before they threatened. With that haircut, he was probably ex-Special Forces, a Green Beret or a Navy SEAL or some Force Recon bullshit. Like Vietnam Ham, only a couple decades younger and without the sense of humor.

By gossiping, Sal had learned that the big guy was Freddie and the little one was Phil. Freddie was an official bodyguard. Phil was supposed to be an executive assistant to Ms. Doakes, who was Vice President in Charge of Competitive Standards. Ms. Doakes also had a secretary—a squirrelly piece of work named Pamela Creed who always looked like she'd just gotten a forehand slap and was waiting for the backhand to hit.

From what the other staff members could tell, Ms. Doakes did exactly Jack and Shit. Oh, and maybe she was also doing Jerry Bogart, the guy who ran the joint.

"Hey," Sal said, all smiles, getting on the elevator. "Hot enough fer ya?"

No expression from Freddie. A hard little glance from Phil—Sal worried for a second that he'd been made, but no, Phil looked like that at everyone. Gwyn gave him a patronizing smile, but no response.

As he turned to face the doors, following elevator etiquette, Sal stole a peek at Gwyn's obvious, copious physical charms. Not that he was genuinely hot for her—when he was on a job, his mind was All Business—but he knew that the kind of guy he was pretending to be would visually grope. And to be honest, the view wasn't bad.

By the time they reached the parking garage level, he'd gotten into a discussion with an off-duty blackjack dealer over whether the Cubs were due or if they were just too damn jinxed to ever recover.

The Cubs, he thought. *Ciullo's favorites.*

He kept the dealer in conversation for a while, traded some opinions, while Phil went off to get Gwyn's limo. About the time that Freddie shifted from one foot to the other—he didn't change expression, too much of a pro, but Sal guessed that he was kicking an expression of concern downstairs for his knees to deal with—Sal excused himself and went to see what was taking Phil so long.

He arrived just in time to witness the bluffed threat of a pistol-whipping. Phil held a gun in one hand and a scruffy guy's trench coat lapels in the other. The man was cowering. Phil was hissing.

"You come near her again, you *spy* on her again, you fucking *think* about her while jacking off, and I will knock your ass out, drag you into the desert, shoot you in the cock and leave you for the scorpions. Are we clear on this?"

From the man's blubbering, Sal was unable to determine if he was clear on what day it was or which planet he was on, but Phil seemed satisfied to spin Trench Coat toward the door and plant a solid foot in his ass.

Sal, who was standing between two vast sport-utes, stood perfectly still. Phil looked around.

Someone with less experience would have tried to hide: That is, would have ducked down low or darted right or left, so that his feet would be behind the tires of a vehicle. But Sal was good at not being seen, and he knew that movement caught eyes that would overlook a man in a dark suit standing in shadows inside a car park—especially with bright light coming in from outside. If he darted for cover, there were a multitude of reflective surfaces in which the motion could be betrayed. A smart cookie like Phil would pay attention to even the ghost of movement, something subliminal. Sal didn't even give him that.

Sal waited until Phil was in the limo, then he made his unhurried way to the doorway outside. Sal didn't leave. The metal door had a panel of chicken-wire-reinforced glass, through which he could see Trench Coat sitting on the sidewalk, bawling. Instinctively, Sal's lip curled.

Wassamatter, ya big baby? he thought. *Yer pussy hurt or something?* But then, unbidden, another thought crossed his mind.

My son cried like that. Before Ciullo killed him.

Luckily, before his mind could follow that path too far, the limousine pulled out right by Trench Coat. He gave it a fearful look and started to scuttle away, he was trying to stand but he was so scared, so hurried that he lurched and stumbled, and the back door opened.

Sal didn't hear what Gwyn said to Trench Coat, but her gesture was clear: She beckoned.

Trench Coat stood up, and for a moment froze. Then he turned and ran.

Gwyn watched him go, no expression on her luscious full fox face, then pulled her door shut. The big white car drove off.

It turned the corner before Trench Coat reached Sal's door. Sal opened it and yanked the guy in.

"Don't hurt me!"

"Shh, it's okay. Hey, it's a'right."

Close up, Trench Coat smelled like shit. Usually, when Sal said someone smelled like shit he meant they stank in a generic way. But in this guy's case, he literally smelled like he'd mistaken his boxers for an extra capacity diaper.

Staring through spread fingers on raised hands, Trench Coat got his back to a corner and slumped down, still crying.

Sal watched for a moment and clinically realized that his son *hadn't* cried like this. Even at the end, he'd been embarrassed by his misery, embarrassed by the show of pain. But this guy clearly existed in a Shame-Free Zone, he was weeping openly like a child.

"C'mon. You like booze?"

Like a toddler promised candy, Trench Coat's wild sobs died down.

"I'll get you some booze. Come with me."

With a sigh, Sal realized that the shit stink was going to get in his car, but he let the guy in.

"What's your name?" Sal asked.

"Bartholomew," the man replied, still hunched away from Sal on the other side of the front seat.

"You go by Bart?"

"Barney."

"Uh huh. Isn't that usually a short form of 'Barnabas'?"

"My brother. When he was a kid. Couldn't say 'Bart.'"

"Yeah? You got any family to call?"

"No! No, they can't, can't know! I have to stay away!" With each sentence his voice got louder, and then he tried to open the car door. Since they were cruising along at fifty miles an hour, Sal was glad he'd used the electric locks.

"Hey, hey, take it easy!"

"My family cannot know," Barney said. He licked cracked lips and his mad eyes bounced back and forth like a seismometer during an earthquake. "I've been polluted. Corrupted. I can't spread my contagion to them."

Huh, Sal thought. *Crazy old freak's got some honor.* For a moment he frowned, thinking about contagions spreading to families. His son. Ciullo's half-sister, and old Mother Ciullo down in Florida. He wondered about his niece.

"That sounds pretty harsh," he said.

Bartholomew's answer was a moan. They were silent until they reached Sal's rental bungalow. Sal gave the man a single shot of single malt and then asked if Barney wanted to use his shower. Shyly, the nut agreed—once he cautiously established that Sal's intentions weren't homosexual.

(If Barney had been sane, Sal would have taken offense. But coming from an obvious kook, he could laugh it off.)

While Barney was scrubbing down, Sal threw the soiled clothes in the washer and opened a couple beers on the kitchen table. Eventually, the bum emerged clean, wrapped in a bathrobe. He looked considerably saner, but Sal still thought *Shit. Johnny L gave me that bathrobe, and now I'm gonna have to throw it away.* He smiled, gestured at the beer, and got a squint in return.

"Why are you helping me?" Bartholomew asked. "Crying men can't be that uncommon near casinos."

Sal considered lying but decided against it. *Why waste his lucidity?* he thought. *Better to just get to the point.*

"Gwynafra Doakes," he said. "What's your interest in her? What did she say to you?"

Bartholomew gave Sal a long, thoughtful glance. Then he cracked the beer open.

"My interest," he said, "is that she's got the taint of Hell on her." He paused, waiting for Sal's reaction, and when Sal didn't laugh or get uncomfortable, Barney's eyes brightened. "You've seen one too, haven't you? You've seen a demon."

"Maybe."

"Hah! You saw one, like I did, and she seduced you. She coated you with her intoxicating vaginal poisons!"

Oh here we go, Sal thought. Bartholomew put both hands on the table and leaned in, eagerly. "Was it Makiko?" he whispered.

Over the next hour, pausing only to make coffee and put Barney's clothes in the dryer, Sal got the whole story.

Bartholomew Hightower was an insurance salesman who'd won a lot of money on a business trip in Vegas. He'd also met a girl named Makiko who had done something to him, or with him, or something. Hightower couldn't talk about it without getting agitated and going into weird details that Sal didn't really need or want to hear. Clearly some sex business was involved, and afterward Barney gradually fell apart. Lost his wife. Got fired. Started drinking. Returned to Vegas to search for Makiko, couldn't find her, ran out of money, got rolled at the homeless shelter and lost all but one set of clothes, but he'd seen *her.*

"Her Makiko or her Gwyn?" Sal asked.

"Gwyn," Hightower said dismissively. "She's not the one. She's not *one of them,* can't you tell? Can't you sense it?"

"I guess not."

"Perhaps it's because you didn't experience the carnal abandon of—"

"Yeah," Sal said hurriedly. "I didn't. But Gwyn, she's... what, she's like you?"

"No," Barney said, sounding hurt. "I'm a victim. She's... I don't know. Something else. Like that Creed woman."

"Pamela Creed? Doakes' secretary?"

"She's one too. I almost got her to talk to me once." He frowned. "I was a little more... together... back then. But that doesn't matter. She's... they're both tied in, somehow. Others... I've seen others with them who have the same pollution."

"Yeah? So how'd you figure out they were... um, demons?"

"Isn't it *obvious?*"

Thinking back on what he'd seen Ciullo do, Sal had to admit the guy had a point.

"Does anyone else know about this?"

"I don't know," Hightower said, biting an already bitten fingernail. "I haven't met any other victims, though there have to be lots of them… hundreds, maybe thousands! Then there's Roark."

"Roark? Who's that?"

"Dr. Roark, Dr. Emily Roark. She knows *something*. She feels nothing, but she's studied. She's a history professor. She knows *things*, but she doesn't believe. No one could study it like she has who really believed. I tried to talk to her about this, to see if she *knew*, but she only has facts. Texts. Documents and study. She could have helped me if she wanted to, but she wouldn't. She threw me out. Wouldn't talk to me."

"She might talk to me," Sal said, eyes narrow. "What about Gwyn? What did she say to you from the car?"

"Gwynafra, the one you know, she… she offered me consolation."

"Oh yeah? You mean… like, uh, carnal…"

"I don't think so. I think she meant something else. She said she could take my pain away." Hightower put a hand over his mouth, rubbed his bum-fluff beard and whispered, "I don't know if I can resist that for long."

"Now Barney, you don't… you don't wanna do that. You don't wanna get infected again, do you?"

"Of course I do. More than anything in the world."

Hasmed's armored car job went down bad.

It started out according to plan. They'd gotten this young punk named Tony to drive the Chrysler. He had a clean record, and he slammed the car into the tunnel wall at the right spot. He hit his mark and blocked the lane... but some jagoff in an old El Camino had gotten between him and the Brinks car, so the armored car didn't get stuck. The plan was for it to be right behind the Chrysler and be trapped as the traffic in the left lane kept breezing past it. Hasmed and "Milkman" Lee Boyer Jr. were in a Ford Windstar behind the target, they were there to pinch it in place and empty it out. Thanks to the El Camino, however, the Brinks truck didn't have to fully stop. It slowed, but it was still able to switch lanes and get around the crash.

The second step in the *plan*, after the truck got stuck, was for a Ford Excursion in front of the Chrysler to suddenly disgorge four guys with AR-15 rifles and stockings over their faces. They'd neutralize the two guards in the front of the truck while the back got gutted. The whole thing was timed to go down in less than four minutes without a shot fired.

But that damn El Camino.

The driver in the Excursion was solid, a Made guy who'd driven successfully at a couple of bank jobs, but the guy riding shotgun pulled rank and ordered him to ram the armored car off the road. The driver thought it was stupid, but he knew his passenger was a twitchy bastard, and he wasn't going to antagonize the guy when he had a rifle to hand, fuggeddaboudit. So the Excursion knocked the Brinks car into oncoming traffic, tearing up its bumper in the process, and the guards weren't surprised when shit started to get kinky.

The secret part of the plan—the part Hasmed had only told his thrall Boyer, because none of the others would believe it— was that, with the truck stopped and its driver and front guard immobilized, he would turn invisible and hop out. Then he'd use a little trick he'd pirated from another demon to open the locks on the back of the truck. He'd permit the guards in the back to see him only when he had a gun on each of them, they'd give up, all the other locks in the back would surrender to his preternatural command and everyone would live happily ever after.

Instead, the Excursion had to block in the armored car itself, putting itself at point-blank range for the guards inside. Those guards, naturally enough, opened fire as soon as they spotted the rifles.

Those mob riflemen were supposed to have their own truck and the Chrysler as cover. Instead, the driver and one man in the rear seat had nothing. The guy in back caught a slug in the arm and the driver took it in the neck.

"Stupid fucks!" Hasmed hissed, but he cloaked himself from sight and jumped out. Boyer was hunched down behind the door on the driver's side, a manic grin on his face. Hasmed could feel how much the ol' Milkman wanted to be throwing down the death, but he was smart, a good soldier, following orders and trying to salvage the plan.

Unseen, Hasmed raced to the back of the truck, a .45 semiautomatic in each hand. He lay down behind the back bumper, reached up and rapped on the door with the butt of one gun. The door popped open. Hasmed waited a moment (during which he heard those stupid cowboy *fucks* firing away, what were they trying to do?) then pulled the door wide open.

As expected, at least one of the guards spun toward the mysteriously open portal and fired out, jumpy. He kept it covered as Hasmed, unseen, climbed up inside. The other was looking out a rifle slit in the side, taking her time and shooting carefully at the gangsters. Now and then her eyes would flick sideways to the door, making sure (she thought) that no one was approaching.

Fuck this, Hasmed thought as he got behind the pair of them. Unseen, his gun barrels approached their necks...

Nah.

Instead he pistol-whipped the guy, hard as he could on the back of the neck.

"Owww!" the guy shouted, stumbling forward and up. "What the…"

Hasmed's other gun-butt smashed into the man's temple, but he *still* didn't drop, lousy luck. Now both of them were peering around for an enemy they couldn't see, so Hasmed just shot them both.

So much for mercy, he thought. He looked out the gun slit and saw the interior of the Excursion. It looked like someone had slaughtered a cow inside and the cow had thrashed. If anyone from that crew was still alive, they weren't in there.

Which was their only escape vehicle. Classic.

Hasmed holstered his weapons, started kicking and slapping at the lockboxes, popping them open with abandon.

"What's going on back there?"

There was no door from the front seat to the back, but there was a radio/intercom, now squawking.

"All secure," Hasmed said.

"We've got a ton of open lights here," the voice said, and the demon realized it wasn't the driver. He was talking to their home base.

"Armitage, is that you?" asked the voice, suddenly suspicious. Hasmed squinted at the dead male guard and saw that his nametag said *Meier*.

"This is Meier," Hasmed said, hoisting up money sacks in both arms.

"Bull*shit*!" said the voice in the radio, and Hasmed just cursed. He was fine, they couldn't see him, what were they going to do? He hauled the money to the van and saw that Boyer had done a three-point, facing the van the other direction.

Good idea, he thought, dumping his load in the back door. He went back for another and decided to quit when he heard sirens coming.

They were out of the tunnel before he realized that one of the four guys from the Explorer was in the back too, panting and spattered with blood. Remarkably, none of it was his own. He told them that no one else from the Ford survived.

Well, at least there's no one to squeal, Hasmed thought. Tony seemed like a stand-up kid—if he survived he could stick to the story that the Explorer had rammed him over in front of the Brinks truck. Even if he ratted out the crew, he'd been recruited blind. He couldn't lead anyone back to them.

"Damn it!" Hasmed hissed, grinding his teeth. "What a fuckup!"

"Take it easy," Boyer said, rolling his neck and shoulders as he got on the highway.

"We left half the take on the truck!"

"Well, yeah, but look on the bright side. We only have to split it four ways."

"You're Dr. Roark? It's a real pleasure."

"Oh, the pleasure's mine, Mr. Turner." Emily Roark was a little overweight and plain in the face. She had straight, limp, graying hair the color of some well-camouflaged woodland creature. She had wire-rim glasses and didn't wear makeup because of her politics. Reading romance novels was a shameful secret, and there was something about John Turner that gave her a little flutter.

It wasn't that Turner was particularly handsome. He had an *interesting* face, eyes that were hard but intelligent, a strong mouth and the kind of weathering and scars and bronzed color that you didn't see much on academics. When they shook hands, he gripped her hand with both of his and his palms were rough and strong.

He was, in a word, *rugged*, and it thrilled her. Just a little.

She showed him into her office and said, "Now, you said you're a reporter?"

"Yeah, I did an article for the *Seattle Intelligencer* recently, on the upswing of Satanic interest since that whole LA thing. Did you read it?"

"No," she said, "but I'll have to look for it."

Good luck, he thought, *since it doesn't exist.*

He wasn't really John Turner, of course. He was Sal Macellaio. In the course of his criminal life, he'd often gone to talk to academic types—it was a surprisingly easy way to find out about metallurgy, say, or cutting-edge counter-surveillance measures or the legal ramifications of credit fraud. He'd even had a John Turner driver's license and press card made up for just such occasions.

"I found a lot of material, and I've pitched a longer article to a guy I know. Edits a magazine in Toronto called *Fleur de Lis*?"

"I'm sorry, I've never heard of it."

"That's okay, it's got a pretty small circulation." Sal didn't act modest very often, but he could put on a good fake of it when he needed to. "Anyhow, I'm trying to get a good overview of, you know... diabolism, I guess, through the centuries. And your name keeps popping up."

Her laugh was surprisingly girlish. He let her catch him checking her hand for a wedding band. There was one, which didn't really matter since he wasn't *really* planning a move. And if he had, the marriage wouldn't have stopped him. But that look changed things, nonetheless. She was flustered now, overthinking, and far less likely to question his credentials.

"You flatter me."

"I was wondering... well, I mean, what's it all about?"

"Do you mean Satanism, or devil-worship, or the whole thing?" Seeing his puzzled look she said "One so-called devil-worshipper may be as different from another as a Ph.D. in

Christian Theology is from a snake-handling folk Christian in the Black Hills, or from a Haitian Voodoo Christian."

"That makes sense, I guess. On the low end, you get teenagers knocking over tombstones and spray-painting them with pentagrams."

"Right—the 'do-it-yourself' Satanists who are really just acting out against their parents or the status quo or whatever, and who get their guidance from movies or comic books or cheap, lurid paperbacks. One major strain of Satanism is what I call 'reactionary Satanism'—people who declare themselves Satanists primarily as reaction to something else. They want to, you know, 'piss off the squares,'" she said with a titter. "So they put on a pentagram and make it up as they go along."

"That's the kind of thing that's been on the upswing since LA and Devil's Night, yeah?"

"Exactly. There's been a *big* surge, though smaller than you might think. With the media coverage, there's a perception among some that being a Satanist is almost *normal*, and these rebel-types resist normalcy above all else."

Right, Sal thought. *The Marilyn Manson family. They aren't gonna help. If they know anything about this demon shit, it's just how to get into trouble.*

"Is there a more... serious strain of devil-worship?"

"Oh yes. There is, and always has been, a small hard core of people who genuinely revere the diabolical, in the same way that Muslims worship Allah. I call it—"

"'Reverent Satanism,' yeah, I read your article on that."

She smiled. "I wish my students paid as much attention. Anyway, there are more of them than people think—Anton LaVey and the Temple of Set and such, those are just the tip of the iceberg, the public face of the reverent Satanists. Have you read any of the stuff from the Blood Cult Awareness Network? A lot of it's hysterical and overblown, but you can find some good research in there on the confluence of sanguinary fetishism and reverent demon-worship."

"Well, see, that's what I was hoping you could help me with. I don't know that I can tell good research from bad. I mean, there's a *lot* of stuff available, sure, but my gut tells me most of it's crap."

"Your gut tells you right. Anything you find in a Barnes and Noble is probably 'crap' as you so succinctly put it—a quick-buck lure for the gullible, slapped together by some hack after a month and a half of research. Here's the worst offender I've found," she said, pulling a paperback off her shelf and passing it over. "*Dies Ignam.* They didn't even get the Latin right."

He thumbed through it. "What is it?"

"Wish-fulfillment—like those New Age Christian books that say the Gospels contain coded instructions for winning the lottery. There's a persistent myth that the Devil himself wrote a text called *Days of Fire* that tells all about Armageddon, the truth about the past and future of the world. Usual rigmarole, only with horns and pitchforks instead of harps and halos."

"You're not religious, are you?"

She stiffened. "I don't see where that's relevant."

"It's not, it's not, I'm sorry. I just..." He looked down and shook his head.

"No, it's okay. I guess I'm a little touchy. It seems like every class I teach there's some overwrought Christian telling me I'm going to Hell. I've gotten a little defensive. As it happens, I'm agnostic."

"Me too," Sal lied. "But anyhow, back to business. People are really using this as a Bible?"

"Well, if we've learned anything from Heaven's Gate and Aum Shinryko, it's that people can believe anything. Reverent Satanists are no different. Some groups are founded on genuine, historically accurate documents, rites and principles. Others think they have a thousand-year history that actually dates back to the 1960s."

"Which ones are the 'accurate' ones?"

"In the Special Collections here they've got a hand-copied book dating back to the thirteenth century — the *Wormwood Text*, if you've heard of it. It's pretty 'correct,' if you want to use that word."

"Could I get in and see that?"

"Sure, I think I can arrange that." She fluttered her eyelashes. "If you're nice, I might even talk you through it. It's in archaic German."

"Oh."

"*Wormwood*'s been a real... it's given a big boost to my research on the sociology of Satanism," she continued. "The thing's like a magnet for infernalists."

He knew she'd left him a hole and, dutifully, he plugged in a question. "Infernalists? Are they different from the reverent Satanists?"

"Oh yes. They're a very rare breed. An infernalist doesn't necessarily revere the profane. Some do, but some worship devils about as much as a motorist worships cars. They're the ones who believe that they can *use* demons, make pacts for specific powers and prerogatives. They want to contact Hell, draw a devil out and trade their souls (or whatever) for infernal powers — I've heard some of them use the term 'investments.'"

"Like stock brokers."

"Naturally it's all just hooey, but you'd be shocked — really shocked! — to find out how many intelligent, well-educated women and men want nothing more than to summon, bind and control a demon."

"I'm sure," Sal said.

Hasmed of the Hated Lash was grocery shopping when the demon overlord Vodantu invoked him from the depths of the Abyss.

HASMED. YOUR MASTER CALLS.

Just what I need, Hasmed thought. Tina was with him, running up and down the cereal aisle. He beckoned her back. She didn't come. He reached for his cell phone, intending to do his usual dumbshow, then realized it wasn't there.

Crap. Musta fallen outta my pocket in the car.

"What do you want?" he asked politely.

"Fruity Pebbles!" Tina yelled, pulling a box off the shelf and shaking it.

I WISH TO KNOW THE PROGRESS OF YOUR INVESTIGATION INTO RABBADÜN'S FATE.

Hasmed shook his head at Tina and switched to antique Sumerian for Vodantu.

"(I must regretfully inform you that I have made no progress.)" He made a silly face as he spoke and Tina giggled.

I AM SERIOUS ABOUT MY INTEREST IN THIS MATTER. YOU HEAL ONE OF MY MOST FAITHFUL SERVANTS, AND SOON AFTER YOU DO, HE IS ERADICATED—NOT MERELY EXPELLED FROM HIS HOST, BUT TORN APART UTTERLY.

"What?" Hasmed worked hard at selling shock and confusion.

"Can we get Trix?"

YOU DID NOT KNOW OF YOUR COMRADE'S FATE?

"Absolutely not."

"But there's a prize!" she whined.

WHY DID YOU NOT REMAIN WITH RABBADÜN?

"(He didn't want me there. He seemed embarrassed by the defeat, anxious to get far away, and I had to return to my...)" Hasmed bit his tongue—he'd nearly said "duties," meaning duties to human beings, and that was not something Vodantu would hear with good grace. "(...my thralls, lest they become restive and rebellious.)" He held up a box of Rice Chex in one hand and Cheerios in the other. Tina made a face and stomped her foot.

"Awwwwww…"

YOUR THRALLS, YES. THAT SEEMS TO BE YOUR MOTIVATION, YOUR EXCUSE, WHENEVER I ISSUE A COMMAND.

"One of them," he said, pointing his face at each box, then cleared his throat and continued in Sumerian. "(One of them was directly responsible for Rabbadün's liberation. Do not underestimate their value. Rabbadün seemed to think his captors were vassals of someone or something, or had been. It's possible that they were the ones who found him and finished the job after I left.)"

I DO NOT LIKE HEARING THAT MERE MORTALS HAVE DESTROYED ONE OF MY BEST SERVANTS. YOU, HASMED, ARE TO FIND HIS KILLERS AND DELIVER THEM UNTO ME.

Hasmed felt a surge of relief. "(I swear to you that by the end of the year, Rabbadün's destroyer or destroyers will be in your power.)" He got a funny look from a young couple buying oatmeal, but he didn't care. This was an oath he could easily keep: He was *already* in Vodantu's power. "(I swear it on my Name.)"

SEE THAT YOU COMPLY, LEST YOU SUFFER THE SAME DESTRUCTION. I HOLD YOU RESPONSIBLE FOR HIS LOSS, HASMED. THIS IS YOUR FAILURE, AND PUNISHING THOSE WHO DID IT CANNOT BEGIN TO PAY FOR THE LOSS OF MY HOUSE BROTHER.

Hasmed was about to reply, but he felt Vodantu break contact. Just in time to avert a major Tina tantrum.

She sniveled and whined through the frozen foods section, he had to cave in on ice cream, they came close to the brink during the checkout, but things didn't really explode until the parking lot.

Hasmed heard squealing tires as he went through the sliding doors, but it wasn't a human sense that told him someone was hurt.

Not my problem, he thought, even as the woman started to make an ugly "Ugh uh, uuunnng," sound.

"Daddy, what's wrong with that lady?"

"Don't look sweetheart, let's just get inna car…"

"She's a *mommy!*" Tina had looked, of course.

"My baby!" the woman gasped, and with a grimace of disgust, Hasmed forced his head to turn.

There was the child, in the car seat. Young enough to still be facing backward. Mom—a fatso in her twenties or thirties—had been loading the groceries in the trunk when someone backed into her. Now she was sitting, legs splayed out, on the wet black asphalt, a grocery bag spilled all over her and blood dripping out of her mouth onto her American-flag leather jacket. She wasn't really screaming because she couldn't. She was hurt bad.

"Daddy…"

"It's okay, kitten."

Someone tried the back door, but it was locked. The child inside looked on curiously.

"What's going to happen to that baby?"

"Look, it's—"

"Daddy, you go *help her!*"

He sighed.

"Fine." He strode over. "Stan' back, everybody. Back! C'mon, give her some air f'r Christ's sake."

He bent down over her and she looked up with wide, frightened eyes.

"It hurts," she whispered.

"Calm down," he said. "You're okay, I saw the whole thing." He brushed frozen peas and a box of muffin mix off her chest. He exhaled, squinted. Made her whole.

Damn, Vodantu would blow his top if he knew about this. One of his servants healing a mortal instead of killing her, on the say-so of a thrall. This is so fucked up.

"Oh… Oh God I'm *bleeding!*" Now that he'd fixed her lungs and diaphragm, she had enough air to really start bleating and getting hysterical.

Hasmed wiped a big dab of blood off her jacket, sniffed it and sucked it off his finger.

"It's tomato sauce, ya dummy," he said. "Now c'mon. Get on up. You're fine."

Hesitantly, she did. Then she started to cry, and scrabble at the door to get her son, and her hands were shaking too hard to get the car alarm remote out of her pocket. Seeing his mommy distressed, the baby started to howl and the store manager came running awkwardly out. But by that time Hasmed was back in his car with Tina.

"You saved that lady," she said, smug.

"There was nothing wrong with her!" he barked.

This sucks, he thought. With a grimace, he contemplated.

Okay, I helped her, and it's stupid and depressing. Or, I could have hurt her, which is stupid and vindictive and depressing. I guess I could do nothing, but that's just stupid and depressing and lazy. Crap.

He didn't want to admit it, even to himself, but later he would recognize that parking lot as the place where he decided to turn against Vodantu.

Chapter Five

Three dead women were defending their home, and it wasn't going well.

One of them had died over a century ago. She'd been in a wagon train, and she'd fired at the Indians alongside her husband. She shot one brave's horse in the neck and watched the savage die when his mount rolled on him. That had made her pause for just a split-second. Then another—Apache? Navajo? Choctaw? No one had ever found out their tribe—had sent a bullet through the wood wall of her covered wagon, which had hit a nail and deflected upward through the roof of her eye socket, killing her.

Her husband and three daughters had gone on, made it to Oregon, and now the rifle she'd used was a treasured family heirloom. Her story had been told (sometimes with embellishments, sometimes without) hundreds of times. Her name was Minerva, but she'd been going by Minnie.

The Contessa Helga von Keudell (who had never really been a contessa, but was remembered as one) died of cholera decades before Minnie was even born. She died with unfinished business and was remembered, even in the twenty-first century, because she had seduced (or been seduced by, depending on her mood when she told the story) a faithless soldier, mediocre libertine, dreadful poet and compulsive diarist named Giardi Camparanelli. While neither as successful as Casanova nor as amusing as Pepys, students of history still read the Camparanelli diaries—and the lengthy description of the Contessa's charms often got particular attention on long winter nights in cold dormitories.

The third woman was both the oldest and the youngest. She was oldest because she'd made it to the ripe age of forty before dying at the hands of an ultra-top-secret government science project run by doctors with more money than sense and more curiosity than morality. She was the youngest because she'd only died in 1961—all the while being promised that she was saving her country from the communists. Her name was Elizabeth, and she went by Liz.

The house they fought to defend was eternally unfinished, the overblown, broken baroque wreck of a mansion built by a man named Kurt Stroeder. Stroeder became an overnight millionaire some time in the 1920s, and his ruination required years, bathtubs of gin and three separate conniving wives. The house was almost-made for the third, youngest, prettiest and least-successful gold-digger. She left him when he went bankrupt, and he killed himself. His flawed Valhalla sat in half-baked solitude for years, nestled in the Montana wilderness and gawked at by tourists, until it caught a lightning-strike in 1977 and burned to ash. But it still existed in faded scrapbooks and a few treasured postcards, and the story of a man who loved neither wisely nor well but expensively was told again and again. Thus, even though the real house was nothing but dust, the shape of it remained in the lands of death and memory.

The three lady ghosts had been thrown together by fate, and they'd stuck together by choice. Minnie had heard about "Stroeder's Folly" years ago and, when the lands of the dead went violently insane, the three of them holed up there.

Outside was the storm, and worse things rode it. Inside were three women with the ghosts of guns. Minnie had the ghost of her Winchester, since her descendents always pictured her holding it. The Contessa had scavenged a brace of pistols that a Baronet's widow had burned after her husband died in a duel. Liz had an old Navy revolver that had rusted away to nothing in a Chinese river, years before she was born. They were firing at the specters in the storm, greedy mad ghosts covetous of the mansion's realness, even false realness... but they were running low on ammo, they knew the end was near. As they watched, they saw dark shapes massing.

"Let's group," the Contessa called out. "One last stand in the ballroom."

"Naw," Minnie said. "The master bedroom. There's only one way in."

"Something's happening," Liz said.

Looking out, they saw their enemies scatter.

"What in tarnation?" Minnie whispered. "I ain't never seen nothing like..."

The figure in the middle was coming clearer, and now they could see the scythe, now the wings.

The dead have their myths too—stories about strange rescues from things even the dead fear, stories about the Ferrymen and the Trench-Diggers and the great Gaston Belladotti (who will rise from the depths of despair when the dead need a hero again) but this figure matched one of the newest stories, which was a retelling of one of the oldest.

The last of their assaulters fled, screaming into the wind, while the gaunt and skeletal figure drifted closer to the mansion.

"The Reaper of Souls," Liz whispered. They were all thinking it.

They were somewhat surprised when he bothered to knock. The Contessa was the best at false imperiousness, so she opened the door.

"Who comes?" she demanded, nose in the air.

"ONCE AN ANGEL OF DEATH," the figure before them said. "MAY I ENTER?"

"Of course," the Contessa said, and to her credit she sounded gracious and not afraid.

"You will forgive our martial air," she said.

"NATURALLY."

"We're much obliged, sir," Minnie said.

Then she blinked. For as the fearsome Reaper left the winds of madness outside, he changed. He took a deep breath, and then a small black man with not a hair on his scalp stood before them.

He looked around.

"This will do," he said, in human tones.

"Do for what?" Liz asked. She would have been suspicious, but to be suspicious one needs some feeling, however slight, that something bad *might not* happen. Instead she just sounded resigned.

"I feel the need for an abode in this realm, and this would serve admirably. However, I don't want to expel you from your home. Are you three the only residents?"

"Perhaps we can work something out," the Contessa said.

"Yes," he replied. "Those storm-riders won't stay away forever. I can give you the means to call me in case of attack. They hold little terror for me."

This seemed too good to be true, and Liz asked, "And in return?"

"I reside here. You allow no one else within its confines, except by my word."

"That seems reasonable," Minnie said. She knew she was caving in easy, but she knew that the house would have been torn to pieces without him, and them with it. It was hard to say no to someone—anyone—who spared them that fate.

"And one more thing," he said. "I may bring guests. They are not to be harmed, of course… and never, ever are they to be released."

"Why weren't you at mom's funeral?" Lance Mason asked.

"This isn't the time to talk about it," Teddy Mason replied.

"Please make sure your tray tables are in an upright position," the flight attendant said.

"When *will* we talk about it?" Lance asked, and the eyes he turned on his father were terrible. They were red rimmed, they had bags and they were bleak. Those old eyes in that young face, it was shocking. It was like his tears had washed his youth away.

"When we get to Nevada," Teddy said.

"Why are we going to Nevada? Why do we have to move? Why does it have to be so sudden? And *why weren't you there when Mom got killed?*"

The last one was a shriek, a genuine scream that everyone in Coach class could hear, even over the engines' whine.

To his credit, Teddy didn't look around, didn't pay attention to anyone but his son. He leaned over and gripped Lance's shoulders.

"Son, I know you're hurting. I'm sorry you lost your mother. I lost her too, and I'm hurting too. I'm sure you're scared and angry and... and feeling lost. It's a terrible thing, a... a *stupid* thing, senseless, it *didn't have to happen.*"

"Dad!" Lance was starting to twist uncomfortably in his father's grip.

"I'm sorry." Consciously, Teddy relaxed, eased his grasp, but he didn't let go.

It had been a lousy week for him. He'd seen Tim and his reanimated gang off, and he'd made sure things were under control at the site, made sure the construction crews were on task... and then he'd flown back home. He returned to phone messages of condolence, and then confusion, and at the very end *suspicion* as he didn't call back, didn't pick up, didn't respond to anyone from his old life. He'd gone to court and answered a lot of questions—why he separated from his wife, where he'd been, what he'd been doing, did he have any idea how this could happen… and all the time he lied, lied, lied.

He didn't tell them he was the high priest to a goddess awakened. He did not tell them he'd performed close to fifty unauthorized lobotomies. He did not say his wife had left because she feared for his sanity, and he did not admit that his wife's killer had been his lover.

He did make one final trip to his old psychologist, Dr. Ng, and he hid the effect her very slight resemblance to Joellen had on him. He played it right—guilty and confused and miserable, none of which he had to fake. He asked for a referral and hoped against hope that she wouldn't talk to the police.

He told his story over and over again and, in the end, they'd given him custody of his son. What else could they do? He wasn't a suspect—the crime was clearly committed by Joellen O'Hanlon, a wanted murderess and fugitive who was found dead on the scene with the murder weapon in her hand. Open and shut. Sure, the timing of it was a little strange, but he was still the boy's father and the law was very, very clear.

"Why didn't you come get me right away?" Lance whispered, looking down into his father's chest.

"I couldn't, son," Teddy replied, only then realizing he'd put it off, he'd delayed fetching his son out of selfish fear. Tears started to drip down his cheeks. "You'll understand everything soon," he promised. "When we get home."

But when Lance looked at him, Teddy knew that the boy was not going home. He was leaving it.

YOU HAVE FAILED ME, said the voice in Grant Dagley's head. He tried to ignore it, tried to drown it out with drink, but it didn't work.

YOU HAVE FAILED ME. He got home. He'd lived alone since his wife died. He didn't even bother changing out of his pants, which were stiff and pee-stained even after he swam in them. He just made a beeline for the medicine cabinet and the isopropyl bottle and its sweet, soothing fumes.

YOU... FAILED... but it was dull, distant, meaningless noise, yes, the fumes, filling his head with a warm buzz, like friendly bees making sweet honey in his mind, the fumes, they'd save him from his goddess.

Then he was wrenched forward by pain, convulsed, and the booze was streaming out, splashing out of his anus in a diarrhea torrent, coming up his throat like scalding lava, and the soft gas numbness was gone. He could feel it coming out his tear ducts and sweat glands. His body was inflating as Avitu swelled into him, pushing out every distraction, making him a hollow drum that reverberated with her voice...

YOU HAVE FAILED ME!

Grant Dagley wept and begged forgiveness.

"I'm sorry, I, I dunno what happened, I didn't mean to hit him, I didn't mean to run off, I'm a brave man, I... I'm... you gotta believe me..."

I do believe you, Grant. Your weakness is not your fault. You were not meant for such things.

"R-really?"

I forgive you.

"Thank you!" he sobbed, and blubbering there on the floor he meant it, he knelt and clutched his hands and prayed his gratitude. He'd seen people do this to him, in his barn, usually between torture and death, but he'd always figured they were faking. He didn't know the real feeling. He didn't know how profound it is, to pray for mercy from a force you cannot stop.

But Grant, that doesn't mean there is no problem.

"I'll make this right. I swear it! I'll get him out if it's the last thing I do!"

At that moment, covered in his own filth, he was utterly sincere.

Sal popped another stick of nicotine gum and rang the doorbell. Ever since seeing Harvey Ciullo—or, he guessed, Hasmed the demon—make people sick just, *bam!* like that, he'd quit smoking. Johnny Bronco had smoked for years, and he got lung cancer at a really convenient time for Ciullo. Maybe Hasmed could have done it anyhow, but Sal wasn't going to give him a head start.

Talking to Dr. Roark had helped him some. Not a lot, but some. She'd given him some book titles, and most of them were in her school's regular collection—she'd made sure of that. She'd told him that "supposedly," speaking a demon's name could call its attention to you. She called that "invocation" and went on and on about how it was a subconscious reaction to the omnipresence of clerical authority in feudal Europe. He'd smiled and nodded and figured that she'd never spoken a demon's name and actually had it *answer*.

Speak of the devil, fuggeddaboudit, he thought.

She'd shown him passages in the *Wormwood Text* that described how to call up and control a demon—"evocation" and "binding"—but the catch was that the whole damn book was only good for that *one demon*. And that demon's name wasn't even in the book, it was referred to throughout as "Wormwood." Dr. Roark thought the last page had revealed the name, but it was torn out—presumably stolen by some antique librarian who didn't want another infernalist to poach his spirit.

It was all good background, he'd particularly been interested in a translation of the *Code of Diabolical Loyalty*—an old Greek text that was apparently a "how-to" book full of advice on demon summoning. It had been, after all the other crap, refreshingly straightforward and common-sensical. *The first term of your bargain should always be, "Never Harm Me."* Sal could appreciate that.

Perhaps most importantly, he had—after overcoming her reluctance with some drinks and promises of anonymity—gotten the names of some "serious infernalists" for his "article."

"They've done good scholarship," she said, "and most of the guys I'm telling you about won't mind talking." As she'd said that, a nervous look had creased her brow, just for a moment. He'd called her on it.

"Oh, I'm just thinking about... aw, never mind."

"What?"

"Well there was this one man..." She frowned, took a drink. "I think he was seriously dangerous. I mean, most people who want to call up a demon and bargain for power are somewhat... intense? But he was really something else. He wanted to see the *Wormwood Text* and he *threatened* me when I told him no. Since that time..."

"What's his name?"

"I won't tell you."

"Look, I'm serious about my job," Sal said, "but I'm not about to go poking a stick in a beehive just to see what happens. If you tell me this guy is nuts, okay, I won't go shake the nut tree. But is it possible these other infernalists know him?"

Reluctantly, Dr. Roark had nodded.

"In that case, I'd like the name so that I don't wind up talking to him on accident."

The name was innocuous: Marvin Morris. After talking to the other infernalists (most of whom seemed like put-on artists to Sal), he'd come to Marvin's apartment.

It wasn't an impressive place on the outside. Just another gruesome '70s building with bad lines and an ugly crushed-rock diamond design on the front wall.

He frowned, pushed the doorbell button again. There was no sound.

Broke? He wondered. *Or disconnected?* He balled up a fist and pounded on the door. Then he paused, pushed his ear to the wood and listened.

Someone was definitely moving in there.

He started pounding again and didn't stop until a voice said, "Go away!"

"I'm selling *Wormwood Texts* door to door," he shouted.

That got it open a crack with a chain on it. One bloodshot eye looked at him from under a curtain of dark hair.

"Fuck off," Marvin Morris said.

"C'mon, be polite."

"What do you know about the *Text*?"

"I know you want it and can't get it."

"And you can?"

He held up a piece of paper.

He'd asked Dr. Roark if he could take pictures of the book and some of its diagrams, and she'd said no, the flash might damage it. So, as they pored over it, he'd kept her there until she had to go to the bathroom. Then he'd gotten out his digital camera and taken the pictures anyhow. The picture he showed Morris was the biggest illustration, printed out.

Morris squinted, then opened the door.

Inside, the apartment was completely black.

Not only was it black, it was edgeless. The ceiling and the floor were covered in billowing drapes of cloth, the furniture was a series of vague mounds under dark coverings, the windows were totally covered. There was not a hard edge anywhere to be seen. The only light came from a single, heavily shaded bulb.

"I love what you've done with the place," Sal said.

"The Glinting Devil," Morris replied, "I angered it. It sees through reflections, through the shapes of corners."

"Uh huh," Sal said, and then he spun around. You don't get to be a crew chief without a good sense for danger, and he'd seen Marvin's sudden move. The guy was no gunslick—he was still trying to get the safety off when Sal got his hands on the pistol too. Morris wasn't much of a fighter, either. The struggle was brief and ended with the infernalist on the floor, clutching his testicles and howling, while Sal pointed the gun right up his nose.

"I was gonna deal ya straight," Sal said, "but you hadda go put on the bitch act."

Five minutes later, Sal was cursing the fact that there was no firm furniture to tie the guy to. Ten minutes after that, he was planning to start smoking again—nicotine gum was okay, but just didn't make the same impression when rubbed on someone's forehead.

It took close to two hours of interrogation (eventually performed in the bathtub) and some light scalding before Sal was satisfied that Morris had told him everything he knew. It wasn't much.

Marvin Morris swore up, down and sideways that each demon needed a special, hand-crafted ceremony before you could control it. It wasn't like buying a suit off the rack: Everything had to be perfectly tailored, or the whole thing would unravel. Worse, you might succeed at summoning the thing, but have no way to control it.

Sal didn't tell or show Morris the names "Vodantu" or "Hasmed"—he satisfied himself that this putz wouldn't know anything about them. But Morris did provide one thing that was very damn useful indeed: the Rebluhé Ritual.

"What the hell language is this?" Sal asked, transcribing the text as Morris spelled it out.

"It's Enochian," the infernalist replied... and some ember of enthusiasm for the topic showed through still, even though he was tied up in his bathtub and under duress.

Fuck, Sal thought, *This guy's so hard up for someone to talk to about this shit that he's actually* relieved *I tortured it outta him.*

"What's Ee-nocky-un?"

"The wordless words spoken by the stars! It's the mute language of Creation itself! Enochian, the primal tongue, is—"

"Right, demon language, got it. Make with the ritual."

Once he blazed a trail through Morris's meandering cosmic claptrap, Sal got the lowdown. If you had gotten a demon's attention—through an invocation, probably—the Rebluhé Ritual could break it off. Otherwise, apparently, the demon could continue to speak to you and hear your words as long as it cared to pay attention.

Sal was dubious about anything that long-haired weirdo told him, but it was better than nothing. Maybe he'd try it with Hasmed.

Or maybe I should be careful about using mumbo jumbo dictated by a demonologist I kicked in the crotch, he thought as he drove away.

The demoness Mukikel, Autumn Overlord, was a member of the Legion of Majestic Liberation. Ruled by Princess Nazathor, her goal was to find and free Lucifer, their great leader. Her current mission involved protecting Chuck Rodriguez and Mitch Berger until they could make themselves useful. Fine, she didn't mind. She was a loyal soldier. She would face enemy troops without flinching and carry out her duties obediently — no matter how unpleasant.

What really frosted her panties was getting backchat and bullcrap from her *own allies*.

The Legion of Stark Defiance was charged with defense, supply, recovery, infrastructure... all the necessary but unglamorous tasks that the other two legions needed in order to fight the good fight and carry out their search. And it was a Defiance fell knight in Taos who was making Mukikel grit her teeth.

"I just need a blank," the Autumn Overlord repeated. "It's on the orders of the Princess."

"You need a blank, she needs a blank, the Blade of Flowers up in San Francisco needs a blank, a Malefactor in North Dakota wants me to ship her a blank... Everybody needs a blank, everyone cites higher authority, and everyone seems to forget that bodies without souls are *rare*." The fell knight had possessed a fat roofing contractor named Hugh Jeffries, and he retained Hugh's truculent style of negotiating.

"Look. I don't give a shit about any of that," Mukikel said sweetly. "I'm from the *Princess*. You remember her?"

"Why don't you just invoke her and get confirmation? Then I'll happily give you the *one and only* blank I've got available now, and when the *duke* I promised it to comes—a frigging Rabisu with a temper, who could eat me for breakfast without belching... well, then I can point him her way for an explanation."

There was a pause.

"I'm not about to—"

"—bother her with little stuff, sure," Hugh said. "I understand perfectly. But there's fierce, *fierce* competition for limited supplies, and I have to obey the ranking Elohim. I'm sorry, but..."

"Yeah, you're all heart."

("Blanks"—people with no consciousness left—could, of course, be made fairly easily, but doing so contradicted a standing order for all legions. Since human consciousness was a gift from Lucifer and the initial cause of the rebellion, Lucifer's followers weren't about to start stripping it out of people, no matter how convenient.)

Hugh bit his lip. "Look," he said. "I may be able to help you after all."

Mukikel narrowed her eyes. "Really."

"Sure. I help you, you help me, everyone's happy."

"Peace, love and harmony," she said sourly. He shrugged.

"You want a blank or not?"

"I thought you only had one."

"I do. But I know where there are more." He leaned in. "We've bought a few from this operation in Nevada called Rothschild Laboratories."

"Who runs it?"

"Humans, I guess." Seeing her look, he threw up his hands. "Seriously! I don't know where they're getting blanks—I heard it was an insane asylum trying to cut down on overhead. Anyhow, they use 'em for drug trials or something, and a couple that were too sickly for that got put on the open market. You're an overlord—you could put a squad together, raid the place, carry off the blanks. It's perfect, see? The mortals aren't going to complain. I haven't checked, but I'm pretty sure using catatonics for involuntary drug trials is illegal in Nevada. If some other demon is behind this, you've got the clout and the power to back him off."

"If it's such an easy task, why don't you do it?"

"I have responsibilities. It wouldn't be a cakewalk for *me*, but you're pals with the Knight of Venom, right? She'd go through this place like termites through weathered pine."

"Then why shouldn't I just take all these blanks for myself?"

"Go ahead. I can't stop you. Consider the tip a gift from me to you. *Or*, you could give me the blanks after you nab them, and then you don't have to worry about feeding or hiding or taking care of them until you need them."

"And you'll owe me."

"Yeah, plenty. That's always a good thing, right?"

Mukikel scowled. "Fine," she said at last. "You'll owe me. But I'll decide when the debt is discharged."

The demon Gaviel kept most of his money in cash, and it added up to a little over sixty-thousand dollars. He had a Lexus, and he'd be sorry to see that go, but it was a link to Noah Wallace. That link, like the apartment and the face and the bank account, had to be broken. The cell phone was abandoned in a gas station rest room, and he'd emptied as much money as he reasonably could from ATMs before putting in a bad code three times to get the card confiscated. His credit cards were sheared in half and discarded, and now he was in line for a new drivers' license. He was tempted to just head to the front of the line, but it wasn't worth the effort. He could wait. He'd already waited forever.

"Hi," he said to the woman behind the counter. "I'm Malcolm Jones, and I lost my license. Well, I didn't *lose* it, it was in my wallet when I got robbed."

He smiled and charmed and talked his way through the bureaucracy, and when she asked for documents he just looked her in the eye and said, "MY DOCUMENTS ARE IN ORDER."

That took care of that.

Checking his watch, he figured it was too late to get a new bank account with his new license (which was based on the stolen Social Security number of a black man who'd be about Noah's age, had he survived pulmonary complications arising from AIDS), but selling his car on the black market and getting another legally might be feasible if he stepped lively.

As he turned on an AM news station, he became uneasy at the story of multiple deaths and major damage to an East St. Louis water-pumping station. Could it be related to his Foe?

Sucking on his teeth, he decided to investigate it later. Today, housekeeping.

While Mukikel was in Taos looking for a body, Shadrannat was in Burbank, bargaining for a soul.

"You picked a bad time to request a transfer." The speaker was a red-haired woman, passably pretty but past her prime. She was also Dûminor, the Silver Duchess, and the demon Buniel's commanding officer. She was in charge of all offensive actions in the state of California, and she had detached Buniel to work for Princess Nazathor with reluctance.

"Is it such a big matter?" Shadrannat asked. "The re-positioning of one soul in Hell? One of the myriad?"

"One of *mine*." Dûminor turned a speculative glance on the underweight teenager before her. "Now, if the Princess wants him in particular, I'd be happy to swap him for you."

Shadrannat just laughed.

"Seriously. What are you doing in her legion anyhow? You're a front fighter. That's your nature. You can't deny that."

The young girl slipped a few more sunflower seeds between her teeth and cracked them. She smiled. "Natures change. Change is the nature of nature."

"Very philosophical. You sound like one of the oracles, now."

"Nah. But some truths are true, no matter how philosophical they sound."

Dûminor sighed. "We could really use you. I know the official line is that Los Angeles is ours, but you know the score. There are two Old Ones in there, and we don't even know enough to invoke them. Buniel knows the city. He retains that from his host, even if the body is lost. He's an experienced fighter in that terrain, and that counts for a lot."

"You speak his name and speak well of him," Shadrannat said, "but the Knight of Embers disobeyed direct orders, and that's why he's back in the Pit. If it was up to me, I'd let him stay there, but the Princess wants him out. Worse than you, I'd wager. If you had a body to house him, would he be your first choice? When the Bear King remains imprisoned? Or the Wave Strider? Or the Lady of the Crimson Throne?"

The Duchess shrugged. "Maybe you're right. I guess. Very well. But you owe me!" She cleared her throat. "Buniel, Knight of Embers, is hereby reassigned into the Legion of Majestic Liberation and is under their full orders."

"And is under the command of Mukikel, the Autumn Overlord."

"...and is under the command of the Autumn Overlord."

"*Mukikel* the Autumn Overlord."

"All right, all right! Buniel the Knight of Embers is under the command of Mukikel the Autumn Overlord. Happy now? Is every I dotted and every T crossed?"

"Observing the formalities is important. It ensures discipline."

"You've been with Liberation too long. Come over to Victory. We'll show you a good time."

Shadrannat tilted her head. "How about this? Once the Morningstar is found, I'll put in a request to transfer—to your command specifically. Does that promise negate our debt?"

"Very much so!" Dûminor smiled. "You still have the lust for battle in you."

"Oh yes. But until I know I'm fighting for the right reasons, the search is more important than the struggle."

"The money does not, of course, go to *us*," Gwynafra said in a lecturing tone.

"Uh huh," Blackie said, craning his neck to the back of the van. The latest group of sacrifices—including Ruby Fowler and several from the graveyard experience—sat slackly back, mouths lax, staring at nothing or maybe at each other.

"On paper, the money is a donation from Rothschild Pharmaceuticals to the Drusse Foundation, a nonprofit charity. Some of the other priests are on the board of Drusse, but Oscar Black is the listed chairman."

"Oscar Black" was the phony name Black Hawk had received to go along with his phony face and phony job. He was glad that "Blackie" still made sense.

"Did Drusse pay for the land?"

"No," Gwyn said, flipping on her turn signal. "That purchase was made in my name alone. Should anything happen to me, the High Priest inherits."

"So your job paid for it." Her mysterious job. He had no idea what she did at the casino.

"My signing bonus paid for the land, and my salary pays for the improvements," she said crisply. Someone honked hard as she cut into the lane, accelerating.

"So… processing… the sacrifices. That's a separate thing entirely?"

"Yes."

That was what they were doing. That was where they were going. And thanks to an unexpected visit from a fire safety inspector at the compound, they were going at seven at night instead of four in the afternoon. That was why they were hurrying.

"On paper, there's no way to trace it to me. And on paper, there's no way to connect you or Drusse to the property *or* to me."

"Very tidy."

"I'm glad you approve. You'll need to take more and more responsibility for Drusse. I've been operating as treasurer with another assumed identity."

"Phyllis Inglewood, right?"

"Yes." There was a pause. Phyllis Inglewood had been created as a new name for his mother, for Joellen, but now... "Soon Ms. Inglewood will have a fatal car wreck and Oscar Black will reorganize the Foundation, placing control of the budget directly with the chair."

"Swell. Just how big is the budget?"

"Currently, the Drusse investments are worth $1.1 million."

"No shit?"

"Straight up, word to your mother," Gwyn said dryly. "Not much of that is liquid, of course..."

"But where'd it all come from? Surely..." He took another look in back. "They can't be worth *that* much."

"No, initially it was a real estate investment, with seed money from an anonymous donor—myself, through several removes. The real estate was near the old town of Serro Gordo, and a stockpile of bar silver was found buried there not long after the Drusse purchase."

"What?"

"Serro Gordo was a mining town. One of your ancestors lived there during the silver boom." Gwyn shook her head. "During the height of the boom, there was one murder a *week* in Serro Gordo. So much consciousness..."

"But where'd all the silver come from?"

"Serro Gordo was a very rich strike. For a while, people actually lived in shacks with walls made of the silver bars that were awaiting shipment out. It was easier to just use the silver than to buy wood, and when each load went they simply built more. They were mining and smelting it faster than they could haul it away."

"And this ancestor of mine?"

"He hid some silver for a rainy day. Now, his descendents use it to further the great work." She pushed the brakes and shifted into Park. "Here we are."

Rothschild Pharmaceuticals was on the outskirts of Las Vegas. The area was zoned Industrial for miles around, and featureless buildings made of sheet metal or poured concrete hugged the ground like beetles. Behind their chain link fences they were anonymous, except for small, plain signs that announced their names—*Morgan Processing* or *Keliel Industries* or *Schawmm Manufacturing, Ltd.*—as grudgingly as prisoners holding up their ID numbers for the jailhouse photographer.

The van's destination was even more forbidding than its neighbors. The place's fence was twice as high, soaring to twenty feet and crowned with glinting concertina wire. At each corner of the fence, a video camera rotated, unblinking, back and forth. Other cameras moved in concert at the corners of the one-story building within. Lights on the fence and the building filled the parking lot between them with a harsh yellow glare.

Gwyn pulled up by the front gate and waved to the camera affixed there. She said nothing, nothing came from the speaker next to it, but the gate clanged and rolled open.

"I'll introduce you," she said. "Then they'll know to open up for you as well."

Instead of going to the front door (which, Blackie noticed, had another camera over it—making a total of six he'd seen so far) they drove around to the side, passing more cameras on the fence (seven, eight) and more on the building (nine, ten) before arriving at a loading dock which was, of course, monitored (eleven). The fence in back and on the sides had opaque strips of plastic woven through the links, and there was an overhang between the sky and the loading door.

After Gwynafra verified her identity again, the metal door clanked its way upward.

"It's simple," she said. "We unload them here, they wheel them away, and they hand us a check."

Blackie still felt uneasy as he left the van and opened its back doors. The men and women inside—the sacrifices—groaned softly. A few looked wildly around, mostly upward. One started to cry.

"Come on," Gwyn said, unbuckling one from his seat and pulling him to his feet.

Inside the building was a man in the bland uniform of a security guard, holding a very fancy and compact machine gun.

"Hi," Blackie said, starting to unbuckle another.

The guard grunted. He looked pale, sweaty... unclean, maybe. But he held the gun with great assurance.

"So, uh, here at last?" Another pale man came out of the building's dim recesses. He was wearing a lab coat and looked, if anything, even more wan and played-out than the guard. He also seemed jumpy—he kept looking over his shoulder. Blackie found himself wondering just what illnesses Rothschild Pharmaceuticals was researching, and how contagious they were.

"We got held up," Blackie said.

"Yeah, well, see that it doesn't, y'know, happen again."

"Mr. Black, this is Dr. Clark," Gwyn said. Both men nodded, and instead of shaking hands Blackie pushed one of the nonconscious walkers toward him.

"I, uh, I had to stay late to take this delivery," Dr. Clark said, glancing back toward the interior door, then restraining his new "patient" on a gurney. "I had tickets to see, uh, Penn and Teller."

"Sorry. We were detained." Blackie said it without a lot of sincerity. He didn't like Dr. Clark, didn't like his looks or his attitude or the rough way he handled the sacrifices.

From the dim recesses of the building, they heard a cry. Maybe a scream, quickly muffled.

"What sort of research it is you do, again?" Blackie asked. He was unbuckling a woman now. Ruby Fowler, though he didn't know her name. She struggled weakly, but he was able to calm her and get her off the van.

Dr. Clark paused in the middle of strapping someone down. "Medical research," he finally said.

"Got it," Blackie replied.

"In the future, come when you're scheduled."

"We'll do that," Gwyn promised.

The next night, Gabe McKenzie said, "Sorry I'm late," as soon as he walked in the door. He could hear the baby crying.

"It's okay," his wife said, and she smiled even though her eyes were tired. "Can you take him?"

"Do you mind if I change into sweats first?"

"I've been waiting to go to the bathroom for the last half hour."

"Oh." Gabe reached out for the child, hoping it wouldn't urk on his suit. His wife draped a receiving blanket over his shoulder.

"I think he's teething," she said as she went into the restroom. "He's been drooling up a storm."

"Huh." Gabe carried the baby to their bedroom and carefully set the child in the middle of the unmade, queen-sized bed. The boy continued to cry and wave his tiny arms, he was red as a lobster, but there was no way he could roll off the bed. He couldn't even roll over on his own. Still, Gabe worried about it.

He stripped rapidly, putting his suit coat and pants on their hangar and draping his empty shoulder holster over a chair. Ever since his son had been born, Gabe had gotten in the habit of leaving his gun at work.

As he put on his old sweats from Quantico and picked the baby up, he heard the toilet flush and the sink start running.

"My hands are so chapped." His wife came through the doorway, rubbing on lotion. "I must be washing them twenty times a day."

"What do you want to do for dinner?"

"I dunno. Throw in a frozen pizza?"

"Brilliant."

"Here you go, my little buddy buck," she said, reaching for the baby. She hoisted up her shirt and started nursing him. Instantly, he quieted.

"That gives me an idea," Gabe said, heading for the kitchen to get a beer from the fridge.

"Wish I could join you," she said, trailing behind him with the baby still attached.

"Sorry. You want me to make you some tea or something?"

"I've got water."

For a little while, the three of them just sat on the couch. Eventually, Gabe sighed, stood and started fixing dinner.

"So how was work?"

"Weird. Just really, really weird."

"Yeah? Did you finally talk to that Noah Wallace character?"

"Oh no. Not only is he not returning my calls, Noah Wallace has disappeared."

"Disappeared?"

"Mm hm. Someone hit about eight ATMs yesterday, taking the max cash out at each one. He's not answering his phone, the stakeout at his apartment turns up nothing, and nobody's seen him at his usual haunts. We're going to run the pattern on the ATMs and check their video, but I don't expect much."

"So he's your man."

"I dunno. If he's rabbiting, that looks mighty bad for him. We're getting a search warrant, that could turn up something. Or maybe the old bodybuilder grabbed him and extorted his PIN number out of him. Or perhaps he's fleeing in fear. There's a lot of circumstantial evidence but…" He frowned. "I'd hate to think he could do it. You know? He seemed like such a good guy."

"You never can tell."

"Heh. Anyhow, it gets even weirder. Remember the stolen rental truck?" Seeing her blank look he said "May. She was spotted in a gold colored sport-ute, a rental? Turned out to be stolen. Some woman named Bridget Mason reported it stolen out in Nevada. I call her number to ask questions, and she's been murdered."

"What?"

"Murdered in her home. But it's okay. They know who did it: Joellen O'Hanlon."

"No way." The O'Hanlon murder and flight had been big news on the tabloid shows, so Mrs. McKenzie was familiar with it. "So the woman who rented the truck killed Joellen O'Hanlon?"

"They killed each other."

"But I thought that was way up in Montana."

"Bingo."

There was a pause. Gabe sipped his beer. The baby made a little raunching noise as his mother put him over her shoulder and started to pat his back.

"Wait, I'm confused."

"It goes something like this: Joellen O'Hanlon and her son kill the old woman down South and disappear from view for months. The Masons—Bridget, Theodore and their son Lance—rent a Bronco on a vacation in Nevada. The sport-ute gets stolen, maybe by the old bodybuilder. In any event, the old bodybuilder shows up here in St. Louis. Throws Noah Wallace out a window, then presumably kidnaps May Carter in the stolen Bronco. Meanwhile, Bridget goes back to Montana. O'Hanlon shows up and whacks Bridget."

"This makes no sense."

"You're not the only one who thinks so. Shall we turn on the news? I'm curious how they're going to cover the next part."

"Next part?"

"Yeah. You heard about the water plant thing in East St. Louis? Well, guess who was found, handcuffed and unconscious on the premises?"

"Noah Wallace?"

"No. A very large, muscular man with white hair. And when we ran his prints, the name Timothy Grady popped out."

She blinked, frowned. "Should that name mean something to me?"

"He murdered five women, back in the 1950s. He went missing from an asylum in Los Angeles during the big Devil's Night quake, and everyone assumed he was dead. But now he turns up alive, well and apparently dangerous in St. Louis."

"You think he could be *your* old bodybuilder?"

He shrugged. "We're bringing the gas station guy in tomorrow." He shook his head. "And that's without tying in Lynn Culver up in Illinois. I swear, this case just keeps getting bigger and weirder. Next thing you know, it's going to tie in to those prostitutes who were getting mangled on the East Coast."

"Yeah, or that guy they found down South with his arms and legs chopped off."

The timer dinged. Dinner was served.

Kevin, the drummer for a rock-and-roll band, was nailing a beautiful woman. He was particularly excited by the thought, *I'm nailing a beautiful woman because I'm the drummer for a rock band.*

They were at his place, he was stretched out on his back on the bed, and she was on top, stark naked and just, wow, fantastic. She had big boobs and long thick hair and was, on top of everything else, a gymnast. It seemed too good to be true.

And, of course, it was. The woman on top of him was not a true woman. It was Sabriel, who could truthfully be called "false" in any number of ways. The body was not her body. It wasn't even Christina's body, except in the grossest material sense. The breasts were real flesh, but any natural woman would have sagged at that size. Not her though. What was the point of being a demon of desire if you couldn't bend the rules on tit-sag?

One thing that wasn't fake was her enjoyment.

"I'm trying to decide how to do it," she said, voice low, fingernails lightly scratching down his chest. "I could just kneel on you like this, and pump away…" She gave him an example.

"Whoa," he said. He could feel her slippery little *yoni* on his prick. Christ, it was like getting lightly kissed…

"That's pretty pedestrian, though," she said. "How about a nice split?" One hand settled next to his hip, another behind her back and she did a perfect split, it was like she was *floating* there just inches above him, toes pointed. He'd never seen any woman look this good unless it was an airbrushed photo.

"Oh, baby…"

He was desperate for her, and Sabriel liked that. Christina absolutely despised Kevin the drummer, and Sabriel liked that too.

"Or I could just flatten out on you." With a delicious, velvet smooth turn she did, they were belly to belly and those fabulous tits were within reach of his mouth if he craned his neck really hard, her muscular, perfect thighs enveloped him, and he bridged his back up, trying to work his cock into her pussy.

"C'mon," he grunted, "I gotta give it to ya…"

She giggled and let him burrow…

"Oooh, it's so BIG!"

…and she knew he'd screwed his ex-girlfriend Cindi just two days earlier and had lied to her about it, she knew he was talentless and not too bright, she knew their band was going to succeed wildly, and soon, and that it would all be because of her burnishing the talents of their guitarist and their singer…

"Oh, it's so hard, ah, it's like a *tree!*"

…she was polishing them bright and their dreams would be just within reach when each of them would find out she'd been screwing them all. She planned for Kevin to be the one who found out, the one who ratted out the other two. Their boyhood dream would be so close, and they'd all fail. The band would break up because they couldn't share.

Kevin was the most arrogant of them all, with the least reason. His faltering sense of rhythm was a real problem, and not just in the bedroom. But he'd never admit that he'd done anything wrong, never believe it, never permit himself to think it. He was pathetic.

"Baby, you're the angel on my Christmas tree." He slopped the words into her ear, and then it all went wrong.

Sabriel felt it first and she didn't even freeze, she just pushed him back and got her legs under her, trying to stand, to run.

Kevin saw it first, because it was behind Sabriel's back. A gray line, but more than gray. It wasn't only gray, it was grayness itself. It was shadow. It was something that sucked the color out of everything around it, and then it got wider. It was like a rip in a movie screen with the film still playing, only the film was his apartment.

He screamed when the thing came through, but not loud enough to drown out its words.

"I HAVE COME FOR YOU ONCE MORE, DEFILER."

Something more hideous than any Iron Maiden album cover, more gruesome than Marilyn Manson's wettest nightmare, something that was bones and ash and fire and death came through the hole and grabbed the girl and pulled her back with it. It pulled her right out of Kevin's bedroom, out of the world and out of his sight. Then the grayness disappeared and he was by himself.

Kevin the rock drummer screamed and screamed.

Chapter Six

"So," Gabe McKenzie asked Matthew Wallace, "Do you believe your son is possessed?"

"Is this relevant to your investigation?" There was just a bit of defiance in the reverend's voice. Simultaneously, Wallace's lawyer was saying, "You don't have to answer that."

"I think it's relevant." Gabe shrugged. "It's not a difficult question."

"Maybe not to you." The minister sighed. "I believe Noah is in bondage to sin, certainly."

"Maybe I'm just Catholic, but aren't all of us in bondage to sin?"

"Yes."

There was another pause.

"Why did you kick him out of your church?" Gabe asked.

Matthew said nothing.

"Know where he is now?"

"I have no idea."

"Ever hear of Timothy Grady?"

Matthew thought. "I don't believe so. I have a pretty good head for names."

"How about the Hollywood Ice Pick?"

The minister's eyes widened. "I heard they arrested him in East St. Louis."

Gabe waited.

"You think there's a connection?"

The minister was quiet, his face blank, and Gabe realized the older man was shaking. "Dear Lord," Wallace whispered.

Gabe waited. A lot interrogation was just knowing when to be quiet.

"Listen," Matthew said. "There are children who are in great danger. Leotis Grant, Renee DeVries, Chasney Shaw…"

"Wait, all those… Your son mentored them, right?"

"I do not know what…" The minister's face twisted. "I was so blind," he said. "I was a *damned fool!*"

"Matthew, I'm recommending that you quiet down," the lawyer said.

"He played me the *whole time.* I don't know what his connection to, to Grady is, or what he was doing out in California, I don't know."

"Matthew, everything you say is admissible, please just take a minute—"

"I know so little. Lord! It could be that, that George Lasalle didn't burn that church and Gaviel coerced him into admitting it."

"Who?" Gabe asked. But Matthew didn't seem to be listening to him any more. He'd started shaking again, and Gabe knew the signs of genuine no-shit fear. He'd seen people with guns to their heads and people with gaping holes in their bellies. He knew the signs of terror and the minister was exhibiting every single one.

And then his expression switched to anger.

"*Damn* you! Damn you back to *Hell!* May Christ and His angels smite you into nothing! May the Lord Almighty expunge your foul influence! May the Host of Heaven—"

"This interview is over!" the lawyer said, jumping to his feet and pulling Matthew up after him. The preacher continued to rant.

"Don't leave town," Gabe said as the two men left.

For a while, he just sat. He made a few notes. He got a cup of coffee. Then he asked Zola Wallace to please come in.

"I realize this has been very hard on you," he told her.

"It's fine," she said. "Anything I can do to help you. Anything to find my boy, or that poor Carter girl."

"I appreciate that." He cleared his throat, pitched her a few softballs. He asked her about Grady, noted that her confusion seemed genuine, asked her about Lasalle, she didn't seem to know more than she should. He sighed.

"This next part," he said. "Let me apologize in advance..."

"This is going to be about my husband, isn't it?"

"Yeah."

"It's all right. After what he... After that TV show, I don't think I can be much more embarrassed than I am."

Gabe almost told her that he liked interrogating criminals better than talking to victims, or that he disliked it less at least. But he didn't. He just asked, "Do you think May Carter could have been your husband's mistress?"

"Absolutely not."

"Okay."

"His mistress was Gina Parris, and I'd have known if he'd made room for a *third* woman." Her voice was quite bitter.

"All right... then..."

"Ms. Parris was our choir director for the past twelve years. She has quite a lovely voice."

"Mrs. Wallace... I'm, again, I'm sorry..."

"It's all right. Let me be perfectly clear: May Carter would not have gotten involved with a married man. Full stop. Particularly not my husband. She was a good girl." Her voice broke up a little on the last sentence.

"Okay."

"Do you think you'll find her?"

"I think we'll find her, eventually."

"Alive?"

He opened his mouth and then closed it. This woman had been lied to enough. "With Tim Grady involved, it doesn't look good."

Sabriel struggled at first as Usiel pulled her out of the world she knew and into another. But when she saw where she wasn't—when she realized where he had taken her—she went limp. And as the winds of death and loss picked up, she had to turn to him and cling tight.

"If you wanted to see me," she said, "you could have just called."

He said nothing, simply beat the wind down with his ragged wings. Presently, a building—a sprawling baroque mansion, half-finished, with the look of a classic haunted house—materialized in the fog. One more swoop, and they were through the front door.

She released him just as he shoved her back. Naked, she sprawled in the corner of the foyer.

"Now you kill me, right?" She could have kept her balance, but decided that falling was better, that being clumsy and weak was better.

"Don't tempt me." He shed his angel shape and seemed human once more. But as he spoke, his releasing tool formed in his hand, a mute threat of woven shadow.

Hesitating, she stood. "Can I get some clothes?"

"I'd have thought nakedness was your preferred state."

"Oh, I get it." She raised her chin and glared. "You're going to rape me first."

"Don't be absurd!" He spun away and she could tell he was angry, but it was good, the anger worked for her. He stepped into another room and returned with a patterned blanket. "Here!" He flung it at her and she caught it.

"I *should* kill you," he muttered as she fashioned it into a crude sarong.

"Then do it already. Shit, the suspense is killing me, even if you aren't."

He laughed. It was the first time she'd heard him laugh as a human. There was a sad, bitter edge to it. His scythe disappeared, and he shook his head. With a gesture, he led her into a living room whose magnificent marble fireplace was vandalized and empty, and whose sofas and chairs were rat-nested and torn. They sat.

"L—... Someone I've met tells me not to trust you," Usiel began. "But I don't trust him."

"Ugh. Is this the way it's always going to be? What you just said seems to sum up every single encounter between three or more... of us." She'd almost said three or more demons, but caught herself in time. "There are variations—endless, boring, tiresome variations—but 'X tells Y not to trust Z, but Y doesn't trust X,' that's the central theme."

"Why would I trust you?"

"We've been over this."

"But you were different before the war. You might as well be a stranger, now."

"I could say the same for you. If you're so uncertain, why not just *leave me alone*? It's not like there's no middle ground between my death and your trust."

He shrugged and looked away, and Sabriel knew she could capitalize on his loneliness.

"You miss what we once had, don't you?"

"Of course I do!" He turned back and his eyes flashed. "I miss Paradise! I miss the unsundered world! I miss the warm regard of the Almighty, and I miss a harmonious existence!"

"Do you miss the ban?"

He was still. She asked again. "Do you miss that? Do you miss the command to hide from mankind? Was that better than your unbroken Eden?"

"Perhaps it's foolish to look to the past," he muttered.

"Perhaps it's foolish to assume that everything is lost! Perhaps it was foolish of me to think that my old friend, the Throne of the Sundered, might still exist in the black heart of the Reaper of Souls! Perhaps there's *nothing left* but war. War without end, demon against demon, man against man, and God against us all..."

"The Lord is nobody's enemy."

"Oh no? Who was it that struck the world? Whose all-powerful hand crushed dimensions with its mere light touch? Whose punishment cursed men with death and weakness and brought decay to the whole cosmos? Whose hand, Usiel?"

The Reaper of Souls just looked at her for a moment. "Can you really believe that of Him?"

"What else?"

"Did you ever, did *any* of you never think that God's touch upon the world was not to strike it, but to catch it as it fell?"

Gabe sat at his desk with a cup of Juanita's excellent coffee and looked at his watch. It wasn't even 11:00 yet, and already the day had been exhausting. He'd spent what he felt was an unconscionable amount of time getting permission to talk to Tim Grady that afternoon. It was like trying to get face-time with the President—everyone wanted a piece of the Ice Pick. If it wasn't the journalists, it was the East St. Louis cops; and if it wasn't them, it was the St. Louis police with theories about cold cases; and if it wasn't *them*, it was his court-appointed lawyer or the district attorney or the gal doing the psych evaluation to see if he was fit to stand trial or the physician someone had asked to figure out how a seventy-year-old man could gain fifty pounds of muscle in under a year. Gabe was just glad that no cops from Nevada were horning in. Yet.

After many attempts and a lot of swearing at, over and about LA's phone system (which was still screwed up, even months after the earthquake), he spoke with a Dr. Gould, who had treated Grady for years. Gould wasn't encouraging. He made the Hollywood Ice Pick sound like a combination of Ed Gein and Harry Houdini, with a dash of Mike Tyson's fight skills for flavor.

"If he kidnapped that woman, she's dead," Gould said bluntly. "Grady may have once been cunning enough to use guile, but even in his heyday he wasted very little time between victim acquisition and victim elimination. I have *watched* him degenerate over the decades — to the point that the sight of any woman would send him into a violent frenzy. He was, at one time, a clever and even charming man. Now, it's not unfair to call him sub-human."

"How'd he escape, then?"

"Well, we were planning an inquiry into that very matter when the asylum's foundations collapsed. We were, apparently, on a previously undetected fault line. During the quake, the institution effectively ceased to exist. FEMA has cordoned off and condemned the site, and we've salvaged what records we could… I believe they're being warehoused in Sacramento. In any event, the staff are scattered. Many have left the state entirely."

"I see." Gabe frowned and tapped his pen. "So, wait, you said you were *planning* an inquiry when the quake hit?"

"Correct."

"So he escaped before that?"

There was a pause that, even over a static-ridden long distance line, sounded uncomfortable. "Yes," Dr. Gould finally admitted. "We've never really resolved what happened to our satisfaction. Grady was in the sick bay under the care of two orderlies when he escaped and, later, attacked a woman near a train yard. The police believe he jumped a train and left the city then."

"They believe that now, you mean."

"Yes." Dr. Gould gave a nervous little cough. "The two orderlies were Charles Rodriguez and Mitch Berger. I could give you their contact info if you wish. Though I can't promise how current it is."

"I'd appreciate that."

After hanging up, Gabe went to the bathroom, then came back to make more notes.

GRADY: Old man kills 5 women in 1950s—all white, all "starlet" types. Gets imprisoned. "Degenerates into subhuman." Escape attempts. Electroshock. Finally escapes again at age 70+. Gets past two orderlies, Rodriguez and Berger. Assaults woman. Hops train. Steals Bronco. Drives to St. Louis. Kidnaps May. Blows up water station. Turns into muscle-bound giant at some point.

He tapped his pen on his teeth and frowned. He stared down at his notes like a tough Sunday crossword.

Months pass between escape and May's kidnapping. Where was he? What was he doing? What's the connection to the water station? He was gassing up going west. Where did he take her? How did he escape? Did Berger and Rodriguez help him?

He shook his head, picked up the phone and called Las Vegas.

Thomas was at Rocket Bar, nursing a noontime beer when he heard Sabriel's voice in his head. He jumped.

Thomas.

"Hey boss," he said, "I just wanted you to know I'm sorry, I mean, yeah, I screwed up, but it was the drugs, y'know?"

Yeah, fine...

"That woman had some kind of kooky dope and, y'know, I was outta line, I got you a new car to, like, make up for it."

Thomas, that doesn't matter now.

"I mean, not a *new* car but a used one, it's kind of cool, it's an old El Dorado, and the guy said it's in terrific shape."

The waitress walked by and was completely unfazed by the sight of a young man talking to himself about a car. She assumed he was on a hands-free cell phone.

Thomas! Shut the fuck up!

"Okay. Um. What's up?"

I've been kidnapped is what's up. I don't know how long I can talk, either.

"What? Who... I mean, who *could*..."

The Reaper of Souls, he grabbed me and pulled me away into the afterlife.

"Huh?"

The afterlife! The, the place where spirits go, ghosts, dead people! I'm trapped, and I can't get out!

"But... what should I—"

I don't know! Call other demons, see if they can... oh shit, he heard me, he's coming back!

"Other demons?"

I can't say their names, he'll hear... You know the ones! You know the names!

"Sabriel? Sabriel?!?"

There was no response.

"Oh fuck," he whispered. He bit his lip and stood, then sat down again, then took a long drink from his beer, and then stared down at the table. "Trapped in the afterlife," he muttered. "What the hell does that mean?"

He got up and made for the door and there was a brief scene when the bartender thought he was trying to bolt without paying. He paid and overtipped the waitress and went out to the car and lit up a joint to help him think. It didn't help.

Okay. I gotta rescue her. Immediately, he frowned. *Wait, why do I have to rescue her? She turned me into a twisted sideshow freak and kicked me out into her hallway buck naked!*

Another toke and he settled back into his seat, eyes hooded in contemplation.

Maybe I should just let her rot. "Afterlife," hell, what am I supposed to do anyway? Serves her right. She just kept bitching up everyone she met until someone bitched back.

As the smooth, mellow THC seeped from his lungs into his veins, he realized that this was actually funny. He giggled.

She must be really hard up. I mean, she must be really hard up if I'm the one she calls. If the only friend she's got to call is the guy she tied up and starved in her basement...

But even as he thought that, he had a flash of guilt. After all, he had broken into her house. Her reaction was totally uncool, way out of proportion, but still...

It was goofy, but when he'd heard her in his head, he'd been a little bit relieved. Also scared, but... it was weird. He was used to her. She was a part of his life. A big part, actually. She'd gotten him out of his lousy job and, sure, she could be bossy as hell, but... but...

But he couldn't help remembering the one time she showed him her true face, her true form, and the glory of it. It had been the most magnificent, magnetic, magical thing in his life, and maybe it was almost worth it. Maybe it was almost worth all the abuse and yelling and random mean bullshit to know that something like that was real.

He sighed. If he left her in some dead people's jail, what did that make him? Maybe she'd be nicer to him if he saved her ass.

Plus, if I don't do anything, she could kill me.

Oh yeah. That. She'd already knocked him out once, when she needed juice and he was a long ways away. If she was in trouble, in real danger, she might suck him dry again. Why not? Damn.

Okay, so if I rescue her I'm a decent guy, a white knight, shining armor, all that shit. And if I don't, she'll probably kill me. He sighed. It's not much of a decision, is it?

"Gaviel?" he said.

Who speaks?

"Gaviel, it's me, Tom. Thomas Ramone."

Oho? How you doing? Your boss lady treating you okay?

"Well actually, I'm calling about her. Someone kinda came and grabbed her."

I'm not in the least surprised. Grabbing, coming, groping, fondling… It's all in a day's work, right?

"No, I mean someone took her. Like, kidnapped her. Took her to, uh, she said the afterlife."

What?

"Someone, like, grabbed her and took her to some ghost world, some place where ghosts go. That's what she said."

One of the Halaku, then. And the smart money says it was the Reaper of Souls.

"Yeah! Yeah, that's the guy, she said he took her and… and that I should call you for help."

That's rich. There's not a goddamn thing I can do for her.

"But…"

Not a god… damn… thing. Sorry Thomas, but that's the way it is.

"Dude, if she doesn't get out, it could be my ass!"

Well too bad, but that doesn't suddenly give me the power to breach the walls of life and reach the lands beyond, now does it? I'm sorry, genuinely sorry, but I can't do diddly for her, and she should know it. But hey, give me your cell phone number, and I'll call you if I think of something.

Thomas sighed and did it. Then he said, "Uh... Hasmed?"

What? Who is this? Sal?

The voice inside Thomas's head was distinctly different, less smooth and with a heavy Jersey accent. It was still in his head, though. The fact that that didn't fucking terrify him anymore was just one more part of the freak show his life had become over the last few months.

"No it's... it's me, Thomas. From Florida?"

Oh yeah, you. Well? Whaddaya want?

"Sabriel needs your help."

And people in Hell need ice-water pajamas. Why should I help her?

"Uh... I dunno. I mean, she could... uh... you know she's got powers an' stuff..."

Big fucking deal. May I remind you that the last time she offered me her "powers and stuff" she flapped her chicken wings and ran the first time the heat came on?

"I didn't... I mean..."

So now she's in the fire again and squawking for me as soon as her little cunny hairs get singed. Well tough tits. I got problems of my own.

Grasping wildly at straws, Thomas said, "Gaviel said you'd help, though."

He did, did he?

I said what, now?

This last was Gaviel's voice, overlapping Hasmed's in Thomas's mind. That scared him, and he started to panic. There were too many voices in his head.

Hasmed: *Well, he's wrong. I don't know what he's thinking, but I ain't in the "helping people who ain't worth it" business anymore.*

Gaviel: *If you're taking my name in vain, Thomas, I will be very disappointed. Disappointed and angry.*

"Look, I'm... I'm sorry, but one of you guys has to help me, I mean, c'mon, I can't go up against this Reaper of Souls guy on my own, can I?"

Hasmed: *Who? The Reaper's got her? Boy, you better just start the grieving process.*

Gaviel: *To whom are you speaking, Thomas? If you're trying to enlist help against the Reaper, you've probably got a serious uphill fight.*

"Can you guys at least tell me how to, I dunno, get to this ghost place she's in?"

Gaviel: *One of the Halaku could take you, if he was strong enough, but Thomas... it's hopeless. None of the Slayers are going to face off against the Reaper just on your say-so, especially on his home turf where he can smack them down like overeager puppies. You have nothing to offer them—not even your soul. Since you're already Sabriel's thrall, you're spoiled goods to other demons. Give up.*

Hasmed: *I'll tell you how to get to the lands of the dead. Die. Eating shit first is optional. And if you want a really quick way to die, start fucking around with the Reaper of Souls. I'll even give you a name to conjure him with. He's called Usiel. You hear me, Usiel? This is the sound of me staying the fuck out of it!*

Hasmed wasn't in a good mood when Thomas invoked him, and the news didn't cheer him up. He was a little surprised, actually. The thought of treacherous Sabriel in peril should have brought a smile to his face. Instead, he just felt disgust.

He felt a lot of disgust, these days.

He wasn't terribly active. The armored car job had done him fine financially, Rico wasn't beating his door down for money...

but still, it was his first real string, and it had gone seriously wrong. He knew it wasn't his fault, those morons in the other car hadn't played the script. Nevertheless. They had friends, friends talked, and if Rico wasn't holding it completely against him, he wasn't totally forgiving him either.

Plus, no one was real anxious to sign up with a stringer whose last job had fifty percent fatalities.

He had time to himself, and at first it was great, but soon inactivity weighed on him. Like today, sitting around the apartment reading, still fighting Harvey Ciullo's cigarette instincts. The invocation had almost been a welcome distraction, at first.

The down time was okay, really, he'd had some time to find patsies, crusading priests and deliverance ministers down south that he could frame up for Rabbadün's death before sending them home to Jesus (or whatever). Vodantu was off his back, for now. Apparently things were going okay for the Stone of Despair, Vodantu's new favorite, and that didn't make Hasmed feel terribly good.

But the armored car investigation was cold, the cash was laundered well, Tina was okay at her fancy-schmancy new preschool, Boyer was under control, Roscoe was doing fine. Everything was fine, fine and good. And it wasn't enough.

That was it, really. It just wasn't enough.

What the hell do I want? Hasmed asked himself. *To help people? Ros and Boyer got no complaints, that's for sure. Or do I wanna hurt people? Nah, I don't. Fuggeddaboudit. Look at those poor bastards in the Brinks job, or that dumb bitch in the parking lot. Shit. What do I want? I want not to want anything. Whoa, profound.*

What really bothered him was the thought of Gaviel helping her. Or more precisely, what bothered him was the thought that Gaviel was disappointed—disappointed that he, Hasmed, wasn't signing right up for the fool's crusade.

It's just like him. Loyal. Brave. Noble. Shit.

Hasmed frowned harder, and he almost felt tears welling up.

Hasn't changed a bit since the War on Heaven.

Why did I have to change so much?

Hasmed drummed his fingers, instinctively reached for a smoke and a lighter. Then he almost stood to get a rice cake, but no. He was not hungry. He was not going to eat just to pander to Ciullo's leftover oral habits.

Demon, mobster, single father. No wonder I got an identity crisis.

It was at that moment that he felt the day's second invocation.

Hasmed?

"Who is it now?"

Has—... Hasmed of the Hated Lash?

"You're gonna feel that lash up your ass if you don't identify yourself."

Instead of giving a name, the unknown invoker started saying something, something that was almost the language of angels, but not quite. Hasmed sat up straight in his chair and cast his mind out, reaching for his caller....

The words flowed on, Hasmed could almost follow the drift, something about barring the unwanted, being unseen and unheard....

But the demon was focusing in, this guy was far away, thousands of miles to the south and the west, he was zeroing in, someplace hot, sandy....

And then nothing.

"Who is it? Damn it, who is this?" But there was no answer. The caller had severed the invocation.

"Call him a pussy," Sal Macellaio said. Barney looked at him with frightened eyes.

"G'wan," Sal said. "This guy hates me already and hasn't done nothing, so it stands to reason he can't. And if he can't get at me, who killed his sister, it stands to reason he can't get at you."

"You're... you're a pussy," Barney said, tentatively, eyes screwed shut.

Nothing happened.

"Do you feel him at all?"

"No," Barney said, and the word came out all in a rush. He'd been holding his breath.

"You sure?"

"I'm sure." Barney opened his eyes. "It worked. It really worked."

"Okay. Good news." Sal frowned down at the notepad with the spell's words on it.

Incantations. Jesus Christ forgive me.

"You killed his... his sister?"

"Half sister, fuggeddaboudit." Sal cleared his throat and felt like an ass. "I'll try the next one." He looked down at the notes one more time. Then he said "Vodantu?"

"Hey," Black Hawk O'Hanlon—or "Oscar Black"—said.

"Hey," Lance Mason replied. He didn't look up, though.

"You mind if I sit?"

"Whatever."

Blackie sat.

"So, you're one of the investors here?" Lance asked.

"I guess you could say that."

"Can I ask you a question?"

"Sure."

"What... What is all this stuff?" He gestured.

Lance had been shocked, genuinely baffled, when he saw what had happened to his campsite from not too long ago. On his last visit, it had just been dunes and bristlecones and a few parked cars. Now, there were three little cabins, a larger building like a mess hall or barracks, an actual toilet, a water tank, a generator... and fences. Everywhere, fences. The outmost was low, barbed wire, but then there was a cyclone fence inside that, all around the cabins, with a padlocked front gate and poles set in concrete. It enclosed all the trees and the houses and it didn't look friendly or decorative.

"What do you mean?" Blackie asked.

"I mean... Come on, I was out here a few months ago when there was nothing out here. Now, there's all these houses and... and you've run out power lines and telephones? What's it for?"

"What do you think it's for?"

"My dad won't tell me!"

"If you're dad won't say, do you really think it's right for me to say?"

Lance turned to face him and scowled.

"What's your name again?"

"Oscar Black."

"And we never met?"

"I don't know. I don't think so."

"You just sound like... I dunno. I can't remember."

"Maybe I've just got a similar accent or something."

"I hate it here." He said it so low, Blackie could hardly understand it.

"Maybe you'll come around."

"Come around to what? Dad says he's going to home school me. Out here. In the middle of nowhere with no other kids and just a bunch of smelly weirdoes coming and going. What kind of life is that?"

"It won't be so bad," Blackie said. "Look, there's a reason for all the privacy. I mean, the people you've seen, they're in bad shape, right? They wouldn't want a bunch of people to know about, you know, how messed up they are. Would they?"

Lance scratched his head. "I guess not."

"We're helping them. Your dad really believes in that, it's... he's really good at... and, so, yeah. It's not easy. But it's important. It's gotta be done."

"You don't sound so sure of that."

"Of course I'm sure," Black Hawk said, but his voice sounded uncertain and even his borrowed, blandly handsome face looked troubled.

Gaviel drove through East St. Louis, expressionless, but inwardly he was uneasy.

Nothing.

He drove by crack warrens and hookers and gangbanger hangouts.

Still nothing.

Previously, he'd been unable to visit the city without the scent of his enemy touching almost everything, embracing the streets like a cloud of stink. Now? There was no sign of the Foe, not even in places where its influence once was strong.

Gaviel had his senses wide open, but for now, the city seemed almost clear of the supernatural. Maybe a ghost here and there, nothing you wouldn't expect.

With a small effort, he changed his mental channels. Instead of casting about for what *existed*, he opened himself to what *had been* and what *might be*.

What he detected didn't surprise him, but he was displeased enough that his brow briefly furrowed. He put on

THE WRECKAGE OF PARADISE / 177

his turn signal and followed his senses to a corner where Grant Dagley was browbeating a trio of teen toughs.

"I don't much care," Dagley was saying. "There's a new boss in town, so y'all better just get used to it. That or write out a will so your dumb-ass friends don't shoot each other over your damn M.O.P. albums."

"Sheriff. What a surprise," Gaviel called.

Dagley turned, narrowed his eyes. Then he turned back to the street kids and said, "We're done. Scoot."

As they grudgingly complied, he moseyed over to Gaviel's new car. "Don't seem to recall you."

"Last time we spoke, you threw me out a window. Oh, but I looked different then." Seeing the reaction the sheriff tried to hide, Gaviel smiled gently. "We can do that, you know."

"You don't say."

"Where's your big buddy?"

"Ain't read the newspapers? Or is reading something you *can't* do?"

Gaviel's smile imperceptibly widened to a grin. "So you're all by yourself. Walking these dangerous streets. A man could get hurt."

"I'm protected. And don't you have some kinda non-aggression pact with my boss?"

"I thought we did, before she started moving in on East St. Louis."

"Beg your pardon?"

"I'll explain. And as a favor to you, I'll use small words and speak slowly." The grin dropped as he said, "You... stole... my... kill."

Dagley shrugged.

"Some of my fellows can imagine no greater insult."

"Whoops. Sorry." Dagley was patently insincere. "I didn't see your name on it."

"Your keeper is being awfully aggressive."

"Hey, maybe you should piss more clearly on your territory. Seems to me, you're just mad 'cause she did what you couldn't."

"That's a very dangerous assumption, Sheriff."

"Oh, I apologize. Again. It's just that I didn't exactly see *you* going into that crazy shit-hole with a backpack of explosives. Or were you planning to wait until it died of old age?"

"This is a warning…"

"No, *I'm* warning *you*. Avitu wants this and she's gonna get it. Your options are to get crushed, get on board or get the hell out of her way."

With that, Dagley turned his back and walked away.

Gaviel's expression didn't change. But a nearby shopkeeper singed his fingers lighting a cigarette, and a car driving past had a violent backfire, and the stove burner in an upstairs apartment flared up tall and white before settling back down to blue.

Gaviel was livid. It enraged him that Grant could so impudently dismiss him. It angered him more that the man was right.

As for Grant, his show of confidence was just that—all show.

Avitu had ordered him to free Tim Grady as soon as possible, but he had no idea how to do it. He'd talked to his (few) contacts at the lockup where Grady was held, and they told him the guy was being guarded as close as an oil sheik's wife. He was considered a maximum escape risk, he was under constant surveillance and was kept out of the general population due to the danger they posed him—and the danger he posed them. When Dagley sent up a trial balloon about having Grady transferred to his jail for safekeeping, they laughed out loud.

"Look," one watch commander told him, "I don't care how many cases of whiskey you send the superintendent or how many votes it would get you to keep the Hollywood Ice Pick locked up, it *ain't gonna happen*. Come on. The Federales are on this guy, it's not just us. And no one's gonna transfer him after what he did. And if they were, they wouldn't send him out to you. Especially not with all the heat you're getting from Springfield."

"What about when he comes to trial? Maybe a change of venue?"

The man just shook his head.

Dagley had reported his failure—he was more concerned about the repercussions of concealing it—and Avitu had given him a patch of boils on the underside of his scrotum. They itched and leaked every time he walked or sat.

While Grady's imprisonment was hell for Grant Dagley, it was close to heaven for Rosemary Nevins.

The bizarre story captivated the American tabloid-news public, even to the point of kicking Joellen O'Hanlon off the cover of the Enquirer. With the angle of a threat to public safety, even the legitimate newspapers were giving it more than cursory coverage. In at least half the articles, the Ice Pick's victims from the '50s were listed.

Rosemary was remembered. It was bliss. She thought this might be, almost, what fame felt like. Or being alive.

(It wasn't a thing like being alive—not even close—but Rosemary had forgotten the real feeling of living.)

She drifted unseen through the newspaper offices. She found the man she was looking for, and it was hard to influence him—hard to slip inside and give him a nudge—but she had strength now. She had a thousand eyes seeing her picture and a thousand voices speaking her name. It gave her power, the power to get stronger still.

His office was bright and cheerful, and it was hard to even think of ghosts there, let alone be one, but Rosemary was strong. She pushed, and he decided to use a picture of her on the front page of the Perspective section for Sunday. He decided it would be a poignant statement to counterpoint an article about the issues of incarcerating the murderously insane.

In fact, even without encouragement he decided on two pictures, side by side. One, a publicity still of Rosemary in glamorous clothes, giving the camera a sultry stare. The other, a crime scene photo of her body.

It thrilled her, but she couldn't stay and watch. She had to get back to the jail in time for Tim's next interview. If she had her way, it would be a good one.

"So," Gabe McKenzie said. "May Carter. Where'd you take her?"

Tim Grady said nothing.

"Maybe you don't remember her." Gabe slapped a photo down on the table between them.

Tim didn't even look.

"I've got an eyewitness who places her, with you, in a gold Bronco the day she disappeared."

No response.

"Playing it tough, huh? I don't blame you. Jail can be pretty tough and, wow, I bet an insane asylum can be even worse. Under the right circumstances, I mean. Like, if we gave you back to Dr. Gould, say." Gabe squinted at the silent hulk on the other side of the table. The FBI agent stood and started to pace.

"You should hear Gould's voice when he's talking about you. Man. I bet a fun time for him would be to pack a picnic lunch and watch you twitch *all day*. You think? I heard electroshock therapy has been discredited, but a guy whose leg's all messed up might just bring it back for a special case like you."

The prisoner didn't even change expression. Gabe watched Grady's eyes as he paced, and wasn't surprised when they stayed still.

Is he even listening? Gabe wondered. But it had been a chore and a half to get this interview, and damned if he was going to waste it.

"Look. Grady. I can grease the skids for you. The water station? I don't give a shit. Those women back in the '50s? Hell, if you'd been sane you probably would have been paroled by now anyway. What I care about is May Carter. If I have to step on some local flatfoot's toes for her, well, too bad. You help me find her, and I can make things easier for you. You cooperate, and the FBI is going to throw its weight around. Tell people you're too dangerous to move, for one thing. Uh huh. If you've got a brain cell left sparking, you don't want to go back to California. Back to Gould. You throw me a bone about Carter, and we're friends. Got me?"

There was still no reaction. Gabe fought an urge to shine his penlight in Grady's eyes, just to make sure the man's pupils would contract.

And then he thought he heard something.

Gabe twitched, looked behind him. He couldn't help it. But there was nobody there.

Grady reacted too. His head jerked up and his lips started to twitch.

Gabe's head swiveled back to face him. "You finally starting to wake up and smell the coffee? Tell me something. Rodriguez and Berger—they in on it? Did they help you out? Trust me, they won't stay silent for you. Or what about Joellen O'Hanlon? How does she link in?"

Grady started to puff and pant, and Gabe frowned. He'd suddenly started thinking of the Reverend Wallace. A moment passed, and he realized why. Grady was showing the same signs of terror.

"O'Hanlon? Is that what scares you? What about her son, Black Hawk? Talk to me, Grady! Help me find Carter, and I can protect you! Whatever it is, *I can protect you.*"

"Ughhhh…" Grady started to make a low moaning sound. McKenzie kept silent, waiting. Waiting for the other man to speak. But Grady didn't speak. He just kept groaning, and now he was whipping his head back and forth, gazing around wildly.

"What about the Masons? Theodore, Bridget and Lance? What's their connection?"

Grady raised his hands, as if to swat a fly or shield his face, but only his left hand came up. The right was chained too tightly. Blindly, like an animal, he tugged at the restraint.

"…*sssay my naaame…*"

This time, Gabe didn't spin around—he wasn't going to turn his back on the Hollywood Ice Pick, even when the giant was chained. But he did glance back, looking for that voice, still seeing nothing.

"Awww! Aw awwww!"

"The Masons. The O'Hanlons. The water station. May Carter. How does it all tie in, Grady? What's the connection? What's the connection?"

"…*ssaay iit…*"

"Rosemary!" Grady screamed. "*Rosemary! Rosemary!*"

He lunged off his chair, his arm jerked cruelly against his bonds, but Tim Grady didn't notice. He just crawled under the table and kept screaming.

"*Rosemary! ROSEMAAAARY!*"

"So where do you go when you leave?" Sabriel asked.

"None of your business," Usiel replied.

"Looking for Heaven and God's loyal angels?"

"Maybe watching Hell for more like you."

She shrugged. "I've met your three housekeepers. The Contessa seems interesting. The other two I can take or leave."

"I'm afraid you'll have to take them. Or haven't you looked at what's outside?"

"Oh, I've seen. But I might take my chances eventually. If I get bored enough."

"You'd never return to the physical world. Not in a million years. Your House doesn't have even the rudiments needed to understand those transitions."

She sighed. "You're boring, do you know that? You're boring me."

For a while, they sat. Then he said, "Here. I brought you this."

It was a carryout bag from Subway. The incongruity of it made her laugh.

"Thanks a ton," she said. The food revolted her—the whole eating process did, really—but at the same time, she knew she needed it.

"I think I understand you better, now," he said at last.

"You understand me? Or us?"

"All of you. Demons. The fallen."

"That's swell."

"I understand how you could come to take worship from mankind."

She raised an eyebrow. "Oh? So you've... partaken? Next you'll start slaying demons to gobble up their souls." Seeing his expression, she laughed again—a musical peal of delight. "You already have! Haven't you?"

He said nothing.

"How wonderful! Step by step you're becoming more and more debauched. Did you do this all on your own? Or did you have a professor of desire?"

"I don't know why I even talk to you," he said, standing.

Her laughter followed him out the door and into the storm. He shrugged his wings, twisted space, and then he was a mortal man, walking through the woods in northern Montana.

"Lucifer," he said.

What?

He paused. He stood still, framed in green-dappled sunlight.

"How am I different from them?"

You never disobeyed. Remember that. When all seems darkest, you can at least take solace knowing that you never meant to transgress.

"But is that enough? There were those in your army who never fought, weren't there? Defenders who never raised arms against angels or men. How am I better than them?"

You're better because they are now twisted and mad. Those kindly protectors would poison humankind in an instant if they were free to take the chance.

"How can you know this?"

Oh, I know.

"But I've suffered the same tortures as they. How can I know that they don't..."

Don't feel regret like you do? You can't. But you can judge by actions, and the actions of my former followers are universally vile. They are a plague upon the Earth, Usiel! Watch them if you don't believe me. Watch your friend Sabriel. She'll betray you within a year if you give her the chance.

"And all who cry out for your guidance? They're all contemptible? All, without reservation?"

There was a pause.

I shall watch my followers, Lucifer said at last. My so-called "Army." For a year, let us say. And if, in my name, they are just and merciful and a blessing to mortals, I shall reveal myself and rally them. But if they are cruel and selfish and a curse upon humankind, I shall remain hidden with every wile at my disposal. How about that? That a fair bet?

"You would condemn the few who might repent along with the many who cannot."

I have no other choice. I can't let thousands wreak havoc because one might repent. I'm faced with a downpour. I cannot evaluate every drop.

"I think you're wrong about Sabriel. Wrong... or you could be wrong."

You think you can save her? Try. It's noble; it's a risk. But I'd be a hypocrite if I condemned a risky kindness. Know this though: Even now she calls her allies.

"Gaviel!" Sabriel whispered. "I think I've figured him out."

And that concerns me why, exactly?

"Because after he devours me, you're next on the plate?"

Surely no minister of the One Above would sink into a sordid habit like that?

"He already has, Gaviel! And why else would he capture me but not kill me immediately? He's going to try to find my True Name so that he can consume me!"

My my... that does explain his actions rather neatly.

"Exactly! He's got his spies in this house listening, watching. He probably hopes I'll tell one of my thralls my True Name so that I can get summoned out of here."

And when you do... chomp chomp chomp.

"I can't even use any power here! He might piece things together by the traces..."

That is a conundrum. But if you think a summoning would free you, why not have it done without your full Name?

"The only thrall I have is Thomas. Do you really think he's got the mental chops for that? If he's going to call me, he's going to have to have every advantage he can get."

Yeah, a few months working at a New Age bookstore wouldn't give him the background. I still don't understand what you expect me to do.

"Look, I hate to admit this. I really, *really* hate to say it, but you're smarter than me. Can't you think of something?"

Flattery will get you nowhere. But appeals to self-interest are something else again. I'll think about it. Right now, that's all I can do.

Gabe knew, of course, that Rosemary was the name of Tim Grady's final victim. But what was the connection between a woman dead for nearly fifty years—a white glamour queen—and a black dental hygienist of the twenty-first century?

Unless there was another Rosemary involved?

Playing a hunch, Gabe rifled through his files on Rosemary Nevins, pulling a picture and taking it down the hall to compare with a posted image of Joellen O'Hanlon.

"No way," he muttered. There was no comparison. Okay, two eyes, one nose and mouth apiece, but after that... Rosemary was gorgeous, curly red hair and sculpted features and a cupid-bow mouth. Joellen was on the ugly end of plain, flat features, coarse straight bangs setting off the sort of suspicious, deep-set eyes you expect to see peering at you from inside a dumpster.

"Gabe? You were looking for a guy called Mitch Berger, right?"

"Yeah. What's the scoop?"

"He's vanished."

"Vanished?"

"Well, no one's seen him for a couple weeks anyhow. He's skipped his physical therapy appointments, he hasn't paid his rent, landlord says the mail's piling up—including disability and relief checks."

"Swell. Just swell. What about Rodriguez?"

"Oh, *he* disappeared months ago."

Gabe grimaced and briefly contemplated banging his head against the wall. "Anything else I should know?"

"Well, the autopsy on Lynn Culver got the green light yesterday. Local coroner pulled an all-nighter with a bureau guy, and they agreed on a verdict of 'inconclusive.' The grapevine thinks Reverend Wallace's mistress was Gina Parris, who put her head in the oven and died. Zola Wallace keeps calling, wanting to know if we've found out anything. And apparently, despite the scandal, *The Hour of Jesus' Power* is posting its highest ratings ever."

Gaviel sat in his new apartment. He was perfectly motionless. His mind was wordless, but busy. He visualized Sabriel, Dagley, Usiel... them and Matthew and Thomas, and others besides.

The forms in his mind were not simply images, no more than Gaviel was constrained to mere visual perception. Each mind shape contained his evaluations of their power, their weaknesses, their prides and errors and their positions on one another.

He contemplated silently, and when he was done he spoke.

"Hasmed."

Gaviel.

"You've heard of Sabriel's imprisonment?"

Yeah. Pisser, ain't it?

"I could be next." His voice was perfectly tranquil.

It could be any of us.

"I have a plan. A good plan, I think."

Oh Gaviel, I... I can't. I wish... but I got responsibilities. You know? I got obligations.

"And are you happy about that?"

The sound of his old friend's sigh echoed through his mind. Hasmed's sorrow was exquisite.

I can't lie to you. I ain't happy at all with it. But I'm not sure what I can do.

"Who do you serve, and why?"

You know my master of old. He possesses my True Name.

"Is he still in the Pit?"

Yes.

"Then that's not an insurmountable difficulty."

There was a long pause.

You think you can free me from him?

"I think that if he stays imprisoned, he'll be unable to compel you."

Another pause.

You've got a plan, huh?

"Better than a plan. A strategy."

If it was anybody else...

"It's not anybody else. It's me. Gaviel. Lord of the Summer Sun and hero of Needleblack Woods. You know me, Hasmed. Are you with me?"

What the hell. Yes. I'm with you. I got nothing here I can't bring or leave behind. But Gaviel... One thing...

"Yes?"

Promise me that... that you won't be too disappointed.

"Disappointed?"

I've changed a lot.
"Haven't we all?"

Black Hawk and Gwynafra didn't talk much as they made another run to Rothschild Pharmaceuticals. What was there to talk about?

"Do you think it would be a good idea if I screwed Lance?" Gwyn asked, apropos of nothing.

"What?"

"He's unhappy. It might go a long way toward cheering him up."

There was so much wrong with the idea of an animate statue of a mature stripper putting out for a confused and lonely fourteen-year-old that Blackie just didn't know where to start.

"No," he finally said.

"Why not?"

"It's just a terrible idea. Trust me."

They drove on for a few more miles.

"Teddy would freak out if you did it," Blackie added as the gates opened.

Neither of them had felt a thing when the demon Shadrannat latched on to their van. They'd pulled up at a stoplight and she'd put her hands, then her feet, on the back doors. As they started moving, she skittered down to the undercarriage and clung there.

Mukikel wasn't far away. She'd left Mitch and Chuck at a hotel with strict instructions not to go far. She didn't think any demonic forces were seriously hunting them. Even if they were pursued, being far from the Venom Knight and the Autumn Overlord would only make them harder to find. Nevertheless, she was uneasy. She wasn't disobeying her Princess, but she was following her orders very loosely.

MUKIKEL. I'M PAST THE GATE.

"Good," the demon said to her friend. "Call me if anything goes wrong."

Shadrannat dropped off the bottom of the truck as it turned the corner. As she hit the dust, she changed. Now her skin was dust-colored, and her hair, and her Levis Silver Tab T-shirt. She was perfectly camouflaged. So were her machetes.

The corner cameras were at a tilt, aimed at the fence and the ground before it more than at the base of the building directly below them. Shifting to corrosion red and industrial gray as she climbed the dingy walls, Shadrannat felt moderately confident that she was unobserved. That fat bastard from Defiance had given her a hair comb which he promised would make her invisible to video cameras (and mirrors), but she wasn't going to take chances—particularly when it was so easy to play it safe.

She scampered over the edge with a gecko's agility and got behind the camera.

The roof was all blind spot. She'd spoken with the flies and the hornets and knew there was no camera up there. The roof access door was locked, of course, but she'd never planned to use that anyway.

Despite what Hollywood tends to show, heating vents are neither wide enough nor strong enough to support a beefy action hero. It was a tight fit for Shadrannat, and she was in the body of a small-boned and underfed teen. Even her weight would have been enough to bring the vent crashing down, had she not adjusted it down to the point that she could have skipped across a swimming pool and left only ripples.

The guards knew that invading the vents wasn't practical, which was why they ignored them. But those who hired those guards…

Gwyn and Blackie had a problem with one of their sacrifices. Pamela had done this one (reluctantly), and she'd damaged its eye before completing the ceremony. The Tree could heal its injury, of course, but the sacrifice still remembered the pain and had been loud and unmanageable ever since its purification. Blackie had suggested drugging it, but Gwyn said that Rothschild insisted on clean examination subjects.

While the sacrifice made a break for it and had to be restrained, Shadrannat encountered a ghost.

She'd felt something unusual coming but hadn't been sure what until the phantom materialized.

"Are you a person?" the ghost asked.

Her weapons had risen to the surface of Shadrannat's skin as soon as she felt the presence, but she suspected they would avail her little against a spirit. "What do you mean?" she said, quietly, her voice cautious.

"Well, I've been summoned and compelled to guard this building," the spirit said. "My specific orders were, 'Don't let any unauthorized person enter this building without alerting the guards.' Initially, they told me, 'Don't let anyone in,' but then I asked for clarification and gave the examples of rodents, employees, other incorporeal spirits and so forth, until they became more particular."

As he spoke, the ghost became more solid, taking on the form of a fat man in a powdered periwig and black robes. "You were a lawyer, weren't you?" Shadrannat asked.

"In life, I was a judge."

"And you're being forced to guard against your will."

"Indeed."

"So if I can convince you that I'm not a person, you'll do nothing?"

"I take issue with 'convince.' My 'handlers' have been quite clear about their disdain for my opinions. If you can provide a sufficient argument, then I should feel no compunction about allowing you to continue on your way without alerting the nine guards and two doctors."

"Okaaaay… What's a person?"

"An individual human."

"Then we're golden. Surely no human could move through these flimsy vents without collapsing them?"

"No living human, no, but a ghostly person like myself—obviously I can."

"But I wouldn't have a body if I was a ghost."

"Ghosts can possess bodies."

"Mm. But if I'm living I can't be a ghost, can I?"

"True, certainly true." He looked her over. "You seem more alive than most people." There were tones of envy and sorrow in his voice.

"So if I'm not a ghost and not a human, I must not be a person. Right?"

"Well, it's not quite QED, but I'll take it. You're going to kill all the guards, right?"

"It wasn't necessarily my plan. I was thinking I'd overpower any who got in my way, though."

"It would make me happy if you killed them."

"I'll see what I can do."

"If you crawl forward, take a left and then a right, you'll come up on the vent to the video monitoring room. There are usually three men inside, but if you hurry you might get there before the third returns from the vending machine."

She did, indeed, make it before the third guard returned. Normally, taking out two humans silently wouldn't have been much of a problem, but she had to get out of the vent before they could take action, so she had to rush. It was almost a challenge.

Thinking of the helpful dead judge, she broke their necks. Then she set their heads back forward and positioned them in their chairs. She heard footsteps coming down the hall as she climbed the wall and clung to the ceiling above the door. Her machetes were still sheathed, but her other weapons were out.

"This is a pretty thin load," Dr. Clark said. "Remember, we can take as many as you can supply."

"Hey, we brought these guys in as a *favor*," Blackie said. "You were the one who wanted another delivery so quick. Finding people who—"

"Mr. Black? Are you just about ready?" Gwyn interrupted. Blackie caught himself.

"We're working as fast as we can," he said to Dr. Clark, his lip curled. Clark sneered right back.

The demon Shadrannat had four stingers, one on the inside of each wrist and one on the back of each calf. As the third guard entered, her girlish leg swung down and caught him in the throat.

The venom she picked this time wasn't necessarily a poison per se. It was the vasoactive protein mosquitoes used to keep blood flowing during a puncture. Only instead of the minute quantity you'd get from a mosquito bite, Shadrannat pumped in about half a cup. It hit the guard's bloodstream in a wave, opening every vessel wide. His face turned bright red, then white as all the blood pooled down in his feet, and then he passed out.

Shadrannat considered killing him, but she just took his pistol, tucking it into her fanny pack next to the other two guards' guns, and her package of seeds. Then she poked around until she found the gate release. She pressed it.

"Mukikel, it's heavier than we thought," she whispered. "There's a ghost-binder at work. Luckily, he's a dumb-ass."

She was silent for a second, then said, "Nah, I'm still operating black. Just keep an eye out for spooks."

Silent as a crawling gnat, she sped down the hall.

194 / GREG STOLZE

What she found in the building surprised her. For one thing, there was nothing in the way of medical research gear. Not even enough to run a decent crystal meth lab. Furthermore, there weren't any *people*—other than the guards.

Nine guards and two doctors, he said. What the hell kind of research lab is this?

She did meet one more sentry, but she leapt the twenty feet down the hall at him while he was still drawing breath to shout. If she'd wanted, she could have slammed into him with rib-cracking force, but she still preferred silence, so she crossed her arms in front of her like an X and took him in the throat with both stingers. Her feet had touched—gently as a fly landing—on the opposite walls of the corridor, and like a fly's feet they held her up as she pumped a different insect's venom into his neck. This time the effect was to swell the affected tissue, giving him instant buboes in his neck the size of two softballs. They closed off his windpipe, silencing him and then smothering him as she lowered him to the floor.

There wasn't room in her fanny pack for a fourth pistol, so she scampered back to a bathroom and left it in the toilet.

She found the stairs after that and went down to the ground floor. That was where she found the people.

They were in a long, low room with a locked door. (A serious lock, too. If she'd had to pick it or force it by brute strength, it would have given her pause.)

The people were on gurneys. They were strapped down. They were naked save for cheap blankets. When she entered, there was a burly male nurse staring at the forced door and running for a dusty red button on the wall.

Damn, Shadrannat thought. *I should have used the vents again. I suppose that's an alarm.*

She pulled out a gun, emptied it at the nurse and dropped it when she felt the dry-fire click. Some of the bullets hit, some missed, some struck the bedridden prisoners. They screamed.

The nurse didn't hit the alarm, but it didn't really matter. There was certainly plenty of noise.

"Mukikel dear, I'm not operating black anymore." There was a nice grinding metal sound as she pulled out her machetes. "I'm switching to red."

I'LL BE THERE SOON.

Her blades flashed and the blanks screamed (for these were blanks, she could feel it), but she was only cutting their straps. They stumbled up and many crashed immediately to their knees. Glances showed her saline drips, bedsores... no monitors, no charts, nothing to indicate that these patients were being observed. They were clearly weakened by their ordeal, though.

Was that guy one of the two "doctors"? she wondered.

Then a guard came through the door, and she stopped worrying about it.

Her right hand machete flashed through the air, and as she released it, she gifted it with a little extra momentum. Not speed: She could have made it faster, but instead she chose to make it hit like it weighed fifty pounds. It tore him nearly in half as she leapt up to the ceiling.

The men who came after were careful—they just ducked their heads in and out, quick, made cautious by the bloody pile that was their former co-worker. They didn't pay particular attention to the ceiling, and even if they had, they wouldn't have looked for a perfectly camouflaged young girl. One guard took a few panicky shots at the patients, who were stumbling around hollering. That did it.

Damn me again, *she thought*, if I go through all this bullshit to let two slope-browed rent-a-cops shoot up the goodies.

Machete #2 went between her teeth, and she juggled a gun into each hand. The next time they peeked in, she was dangling from the ceiling, aiming. Once more she was generous with ammo, once more she hit with about a third of her shots, and once more, it was abundantly sufficient to put mortals down.

With a deft flip, she dropped to the floor, transferring blade to hand as she went.

"C'mon," she said, pointing at the door. "Up and at 'em. Let's move out."

The blanks ignored her.

"I mean it! Let's go! Boots and saddles, people!"

They just cowered away from her.

"Mukikel, where you at?"

Coming through the front gate.

"Keep your eyes peeled for hostiles, though I think I've drawn their attention." Shadrannat sheathed the clean machete as she picked up the bloody one. The handle was sticky with gore. It felt good.

"The blanks are in a room on the east side of the building... 'bout a hundred feet back from the front door. I counted eight blanks, but three are shot and probably not worth the effort." She scavenged a new pistol and put it into her fanny pack — this guard had his own piece, slightly bigger and shinier than the others. Then she picked up and racked a pistol-grip shotgun.

"The blanks are like sheep. They aren't responding to me."

I'll take care of it.

"I'm sealing the door," she said, doing it as she spoke, "But not in any serious fashion. I'm heading south looking for more. There should be two guards and one or two doctors left."

She was running along the wall, up by the ceiling, colored the same putty gray and off-white as the corridor. She reached the back loading bay and that's when things started to go wrong. She came to a pair of double doors, clenched the machete between her teeth and pulled one gently inward. Then she snatched her hand back as a shotgun blast hit the door, denting its metal surface and flinging it sharply back.

Someone inside is jumpy, she thought, waving her stinging hands. Then she saw a shadow.

One of the guards—probably the shooter—was creeping cautiously to the door, checking for a kill. She could see the silhouette of his shotgun, the same type as the one she held.

Her eyes flicked across the hall to a heating vent. Easy peasy.

The guard's plan was obviously to peek around the door and duck back, but he just didn't have the speed. He got to the peeking part and then caught her left ankle stinger in the side of the head. Spider venom this time—more than enough to kill.

"Mukikel. One guard remains," she whispered.

I'm getting into the blank room now. Do you want to just fall back?

"Might as well make a clean sweep," she said, eeling her way into the ventilator duct.

Okay. Be careful.

In the next room, Shadrannat peeked through a grating to see a man in a uniform, a man in a suit and a man in a doctor's coat. There was also a busty woman in business attire, along with three more tied-down blanks.

(She was seeing the last guard, Blackie, Dr. Clark and Gwyn, though she didn't know those names.)

She hugged the shotgun close to her in order to move it through the shaft without rattling, and it took a great deal of contortion to draw the pistol without clunking loudly. But the people there were (she assumed) still partially deafened by the dead man's blast. She took her aim at the last guard, braced herself well, and then reached out with her senses just to double-check.

An eyebrow rose. As expected, the people in restraints were empties. But the suit man was demon-touched, one way or another. And the woman wasn't alive at all, just a walking repository of infernal power. Even the doctor had an unnatural vibe coming off him. The only ordinary one was the guy with the machinegun. Swell.

From far off, Shadrannat heard Mukikel's voice of command. She contemplated withdrawing, but three more blanks would get her in very tight with Defiance. And besides, if she was going to leave supernatural enemies behind, she wanted them dead and cooling.

She decided to kill the guard first, and as she shot him through the grate, all hell broke loose.

The woman spun to face her as she fired—and Shadrannat had expected at least a moment of confusion as they tried to find her. The woman appeared unarmed, but she balled up a fist, drew it back and then *threw her hand across the room.*

Shadrannat had seen some weird stuff in the war, but this was a new one. Furthermore, it was a new one that punched through the grate and hit her in the face with the force of a hundred-mile-an-hour rock. Shadrannat was a tough spirit, but her flesh was only flesh, and she blacked out under the impact. It was only a moment's unconsciousness, but it was enough to break her spell on gravity and send her crashing through the bottom of the vent and down onto the floor of the room.

"Blackie! Get out of here!" the woman screamed, and from the Doppler sound, Shadrannat could tell she was getting closer. She forced her eyes open in time to see the woman growing another hand out of her mud-brown stump as she charged. Shadrannat tried to leap aside, but Gwyn weighed close to a ton and had a lot of momentum. The girl's small frame was crushed against the wall, and Shadrannat groaned as she forced bones and blood back into place.

The woman grabbed the girl by the shoulders and hauled her upright into a bear hug, the shotgun pinned between them, barrel down and useless. Bear-hugging the Knight of Venom would have been a big mistake, for a human. Shadrannat flicked up both legs and scissored them around the woman's thighs, driving in both ankle stingers...

But they ground against stony toughness. They did nothing but shred the woman's tasteful earth-tone office wear.

Shadrannat switched to Plan B. Using the same power that let her stick to walls, she made her shoulders unnaturally slippery, and squirted out of the woman's grasp. As she dropped toward the floor, she unlaced her left leg but made sure to keep contact with the right. She also spotted her dropped pistol and picked it up.

As she hoped, the bigger woman tried to stomp her while she was down, but Shadrannat easily twisted out of her way. That was elementary infernal combat. Advanced demon fighting taught Shadrannat to ramp up the force behind the stomp, tripling it, to the point that the concrete floor shattered on impact—and so did Gwyn's stony foot.

Shadrannat then noticed that Lab Coat had picked up the dead guard's machinegun and was running toward the wall, jockeying for a good shot. She shifted her foot on the other woman and pushed hard. Slippery as wet soap on shower tile, she slid away along the wall, firing her shotgun as she did. The pellets did little to the woman, but the doctor cried out. He didn't fall or anything, but she hoped he'd at least become cautious.

Tilting her head back, Shadrannat saw Suit—"Blackie," apparently—pause while getting into his van. He was looking at the stone gal, his face a mask of uncertainty.

"Gwyn?" he called.

Arching her back and firing upside-down, Shadrannat nailed him with a load of buckshot. She only watched for half a moment as he fell, registering that it had hit groin, belly, both thighs—a nice center-of-mass scatter pattern. Even if he was devilish, it would stop him for a while.

But shooting Blackie elicited a scream from the woman. Not a scream of rage, but of pure primal horror. Flipping up so that she was standing, a gun in either hand, Shadrannat saw the alarmed look on Gwyn's face. She had just enough time to contemplate threatening the man for leverage when the woman pulled off her left forearm and hurled it like a juggler's club.

The Venom Knight dove sideways and the arm crumpled the van's side where it struck. Then it was a spray of five fingers from the statue's right hand, flung like stones but with murderous force. Three struck—shoulder, shin and thigh—as Shadrannat pulled the shotgun trigger on an empty chamber.

Maybe I should have counted that gun's ammo before starting this, she thought as she flung the weapon like a boomerang. She put extra weight on it, and she could see the stone gal crack as it hit her. The woman was still charging and re-growing her flung parts. She was maybe just a little bit smaller, but that really didn't matter because the doctor was shooting too, and Shadrannat was about ready to be done with both of them. She reached into her fanny pack. Right hand: the slightly nicer pistol. Left hand: a seed from her cellophane snack packet.

Her plan was to jump up over "Gwyn" as the woman charged and wedge the seed in the moving statue's ear-hole. While doing this, she would shoot the doctor.

To understand why a seed in an auditory canal is an effective attack, it's necessary to understand Shadrannat's onetime position in the celestial hierarchy.

Having been an angel of nature, Shadrannat had command over the beasts of the field (insects in particular) and the plants of the soil. With an effort of will, she could make a seed sprout, grow and attain unnaturally large size—all in a matter of seconds. Such a seed would grow with its usual strength, a strength easy to ignore when it's patiently pushing up a sidewalk block an eighth of an inch a year, or cracking a stone cliff over the course of centuries. But that earth-breaking power is in every seed. That was what she'd used to open the door to the blanks and then, by weaving a thicket, seal it again.

So when she got the seed in and ordered it to grow, she split Gwyn's head like a ripe melon. The roots dug deep into the mud-woman's chest and belly, hollowing her out and crumbling her to useless dust. That part worked perfectly.

But Shadrannat didn't get quite high enough on her jump, so Gwyn's last clutch broke both her legs. And when she pointed the gun at the doctor, she realized he must be unusually resilient, because he was standing and aiming the assault rifle at her.

He opened up, full auto, as she pulled her trigger once. Both shots hit. Hers went right through the neck. His shredded her torso.

As the smoke cleared, the only sound was Blackie's voice gasping, "Avitu... Avitu please..."

Chapter Seven

Langdon Hagen didn't expect anything when the phone rang. For weeks, he'd been jumpy—every time the phone rang or the doorbell, every time someone came to see him at work. For weeks, he'd been terrified that it was the police or worse. He'd been afraid someone knew about the Thing.

That was what Hagen called it in his head. "The Thing." He didn't like to make it any more specific, even in his own mind, because that would mean thinking about it, and he didn't like to think about the Thing.

The Thing was—had been—a group, six of them, and no one sensible would have thought they had anything in common. But they had demons in common. That was what they couldn't tell their wives or their children or their parents. They got together to deal with it, and that was the Thing—the silent thing, the unspoken thing, the unthinkable Thing between them all.

Now there were four. Three really—Jill didn't count since she was in jail. They'd caught that creature—that monster, Rabbadün—and then everything had gone to hell. Somehow the cops found out, and somehow there was a shootout, and somehow Manny and Ross got killed. The police connected Jill to the farmhouse (somehow), but she hadn't talked.

(They'd all taken an oath not to talk about the Thing. It had seemed reasonable, easy enough. Particularly to Langdon, who didn't even want to think about it.)

And the day the phone call came, he'd almost gotten used to it. He could almost think that the Thing was over, like it had never happened.

"Gilly's Café," the voice on the line said. It didn't sound like someone calling to confirm an order or something. It was a harsh, growly voice that sounded like it should be saying phrases like "hell to pay" or "come alone."

"Excuse me?"

"This Langdon Hagen?" The voice mispronounced his last name and put a sneering drawl on his first.

"Who's this?"

"None of your business. Go to Gilly's Café, noon sharp. Sit at the booth by the pay phone."

"Look—"

"Come alone." There it was.

"I think you'd better—"

"Rabbadün."

"What?"

Click.

Langdon glanced at the corner of his computer screen. It was 11:40.

"Sherry? I'm going to lunch."

"Yes, Mr. Hagen."

Gilly's wasn't far. He ate there often, which made him think that his caller knew him and his habits; knew about the Thing.

As he walked in at 11:58, the pay phone started to ring. He had to jog to get to it.

"Hello?"

"Langdon?" Same voice, same drawl.

"Who are you? What do you want?"

"You're in big-ass trouble, ain'tcha?"

"I don't know what you're talking about."

"Rabbadün. Don't worry, he's gone for good, thanks to you. Someone wanted him dealt with, right? You and your five buddies got tapped for the job."

Five. Oh shit. Langdon stuck a fingernail in his mouth and bit it. The voice continued.

"I don't particularly care who your patron is or what you're after. But since you seem to know the score about demon-killing, I got another one for you."

"Look, I don't—"

"She's called, um, 'The Savior of the Falling Stars'—wow, that's poetical, ain't it? She's in Argentina, which is where you're going."

"Ar... what?"

"Unless you'd rather I help those grab-ass cops you got down here put three and three together. It makes six, y'know?"

"I think you're bluffing."

"Let yer fingers do the walking."

Langdon glanced down at the booth's phone book. There was a Manila envelope stuck in the yellow pages.

Inside he found pictures of him, Jill, the rest of them. Going into the farmhouse and coming out. The pictures had dates on them. They weren't terribly clear, but... clear enough. There was also a key.

"The key opens a locker at the bus station. Locker 666, as it happens. Heh, get it?"

"Yeah, I *get* it," Langdon said, frustration and wrath starting to leak into his voice. "What am I going to find there?"

"Three tickets on the late Greyhound to Miami. An introduction to Harudo down there—he'll get you to Argentina. When you get to Argentina, you'll find money, guns, other shit you'll need to deal with Miss Falling Star."

"Just how do you expect me to 'deal' with her? I don't even speak Spanish!"

"You musta gotten *something* for your soul, right?"

"I think you've got the wrong impression of my 'patron,'" Langdon said bitterly. He switched the phone to his other hand, turning his face away from other diners. "What if I refuse?"

"Eh, prison ain't so bad. Either way, it's no skin offa me. I'll be watching, so I guess I'll know soon enough which way you jump."

Click.

Miles away, Lee Boyer Jr. smiled as he hung up the phone and cracked a can of Enfamil. This chump would do it. He could tell.

He took a long, satisfying slurp, then invoked his master.

"It's going," Hasmed told Gaviel. His voice was very soft—Tina was sleeping in the airplane seat next to him. She'd been on a real roller coaster, emotionally. She'd hated the idea of leaving Atlantic City, but since she'd been there less than a year, she wasn't quite as hysterical as when they'd hastily arrived. Last night had been one extended tantrum, and being told that Mr. Paum was coming too only partially mollified her. But today, she'd been delighted and excited about flying in an airplane for the first time. And once they'd gotten above the clouds, once the view below them was flat and white and featureless instead of a fascinating vista of miniature farms and lakes and cities, she'd fallen asleep.

I'm glad to hear it. Can you give me details?

"I've assembled a crew of losers—someone's thralls or something. I dunno, half the group that nailed Rabbadün. My best guy is going to run them down in Argentina."

Where the Savior of the Falling Stars is?

"Yeah. She's had a hell of a time adapting—money trouble since day one. Mostly she's been running around living hand to mouth, y'know?"

Do you really think these three vassals can handle her?

"My guess is they'll soften her up so my man can close in for the kill. I'm not all that worried about it. As long as she's not coming up for me, I'm happy." Hasmed cracked his knuckles. "The one I'm worried about is the Stone."

You said he was in Guam, right?

"Last I heard."

Invoke him and find out.

"Eh… I dunno what my master has told him about me. He could be real suspicious."

You don't have a master anymore, remember?

"But I'll have a mistress."

Don't think of it that way. Think of it as… being cradled safely in the bosom of your old comrade.

"Yeah. Whatever. See you in Las Vegas."

"Gabe, are you okay?"

"I'm fine," he said, rubbing his eyes. "It's the baby. Damn. Colic. You know what colic is?"

"I seem to recall something like that from my own kids."

"Sorry, sorry…"

"Hey, no need to apologize, Juanita. You aren't the one who was screaming all night, right?"

"Yeah. Cup a coffee and I'll be all right."

"For about fifteen minutes," Juanita said, rising to get him one.

"You're an angel."

Coffee in hand and desk chair under his seat, Gabe looked at his notes and decided it was late enough to make his day's first call.

"Desert Experience, can I help you?"

"Yeah, I'm... uh, is this 555-4220?"

"Yeah."

"Who is this, please?"

"Who's *this*?"

"Special Agent Gabe McKenzie with the Federal Bureau of Investigation."

That got him a long pause.

"And you are?" he prompted.

"Pete... Mortenson."

Gabe narrowed his eyes and checked his internal bullshit detector. He decided the pause was suspicious, but inconclusive.

"Well Mr. Mortenson, I'd like to speak to Theodore Mason, please."

"Okay, um... I mean, sure, I'll... uh, can I tell him who's calling?"

"Gabe. McKenzie. From the FBI, remember?"

"Right, I'm, sorry, I'm really spaced out. I'll, um, I'll go get him."

Gabe frowned as he waited. Some people got freaked by the FBI—probably people who'd once shoplifted some tube socks or smoked pot in college—but still. This guy didn't sound like a receptionist, and "Desert Experience" apparently didn't have a phone network that could transfer.

"Hello?"

"Is this Mr. Mason?"

"Yes. You're from the FBI?" Mason sounded cautious. Really cautious. Very polite too—like a stonewalling lawyer. Gabe found himself glad that his BS-o-scope was already warmed up.

"That's correct."

"Can I ask what this is about?"

Your wife was recently murdered, and you want to know why the FBI is calling? Oh, Mr. Mason. Gooseflesh popped on Gabe's arms but he kept his voice tightly controlled.

"You signed for a gold Chevrolet Suburban, license number VOR 4893..."

"Yes. It got stolen. My wife..." There was a sound, and Gabe didn't think it was the phone line. "My wife reported it, I thought."

Gabe's instincts were prowling that last sentence like dogs trying to find a fox's scent but... no, it seemed clean. The guy genuinely *did* seem wrecked by his wife's demise, his voice hit all the right notes.

"Right. Well, it turns out that vehicle may have been used in a federal crime."

"You mean... You mean after it was stolen from us?"

"Exactly."

"What would we know about that?"

"Do you know a man named Timothy Grady?"

Long pause.

"...I don't think so?"

Twang! went Gabe's mental crap meter.

"Do you know who Tim Grady is?"

"Um..."

"Do you read the newspapers, Mr. Mason?"

"Oh! The, the guy in, uh... was it Louisiana? Did he... was that the guy who stole our car?"

"You know, Mr. Mason, on her police report Mrs. Mason stated that you were the only one who'd seen or spoken to a

'Fred Allston,' the man who supposedly made off with your car. Is that correct?"

"Um, well I... Birdie, she... that is, Bridget, my wife, my... she never saw Fred Allston, I don't think we were... uh, we were camping and... Uh, could you repeat the question?"

The needle was buried in the red on Gabe's gauge. *I don't know what color mud*, he thought, *but this guy is dirty.*

"Tell me about Fred Allston." Nice open-ended question. It gave Mason a nicely made bed on which to screw himself.

"Fred Allston... um, I don't know if that was his name, his *real* name, you know. He, his car broke down near our campsite when we were out in the desert and, he said he'd gotten a call that his daughter was very sick and could he please borrow our car to get to her."

"And you lent it to him?"

"Well I mean it was... it was late at night and I wasn't, you know, my mind wasn't at its clearest..."

"And you were camping out in the *desert?*"

"It's really beautiful out here. Very primal."

"Primal. Uh huh. So you just let this stranger take off with your rental car?"

"Um, yeah."

"Which contained your wife's identification and traveler's checks?"

"At the time I didn't know they were in there." Mason seemed to be getting a grip on himself, rallying. Gabe pressed again.

"You let him take it when it was your *only vehicle out of the desert?* You willingly stranded yourself, your son and your wife in the middle of nowhere on the say so of a complete stranger?"

There was a long pause.

"Maybe I'm not a very smart man," Mason finally said.

"Uh huh. So any idea why a federal fugitive would pop up to kill your wife in particular?"

"Maybe it was a random crime. Certainly I don't... I mean, I'd never met Joellen before. Joellen O'Hanlon. Neither had my wife."

Liar, liar, liar.

"Okay then. I'm going to try and have someone in the Vegas bureau come out to get a description of Fred Allston from you."

"Actually, why don't I just come in? We're... we're kind of out in the sticks."

"That's very accommodating."

"Look, I... I know you may think I'm... well, I don't know what you think. But if someone else was involved with my wife's death..."

(There it was again, that pain, that raw and present sorrow.)

"...then I promise you, I want them found. Caught. You know. Whether it's this Fred Allston or Tim Grady or... or whoever."

"I appreciate that sentiment. One last thing. The name May Carter ring a bell?"

"No." Flat, quick, decisive... honest?

You sure had to think hard about Grady.

"Okay then. Have a nice day."

"You too."

In the desert, in the tree, the spirit of Avitu was coming ever more awake. As it woke, its power grew, spreading roots under the ground, branching up through the winds. When her High Priest was frightened, she felt his fear. When Blackie, the heir apparent, was harmed, she could immediately reach out and heal him. When Gwynafra, her finest tool, was unexpectedly shattered, she felt that too.

Her power was waxing—with each sacrifice, it grew. But even as buildings and fences and machines were put into and upon sands that were almost her own flesh, she found herself hedged in by setback after setback. Her priestess of the blood, killed. Another minister from her holy line imprisoned. Her weapons wrested from her grip before she even woke fully to use them...

It was as she took stock of her losses (Tim, Joellen, Gwynafra) that she heard once more the mosquito buzz of Gaviel of the Summer Sun.

Avitu, Keeper of the Twin Winds and Tree of Ignorance, I commend you.

She had no tongue with which to reply, but she still made her words felt.

WHAT LEADS YOU TO SUCH KIND WORDS?

Naught but simple honesty. You've accomplished many of my goals in East Saint Louis even before I could. I can be a good sport about it.

GAVIEL, I FIND IT HARD TO BELIEVE THAT AFTER OUR STRUGGLES, YOU INVOKE ME SOLELY IN A SPIRIT OF CAMARADERIE.

Is that so difficult to grasp? Refusal to face facts is a human trait. I know when I'm beaten, as I've shown you before.

WHAT IS IT YOU WANT?

Very astute. This call is not, as you surmise, purely social. What I want is, quite simply, to get on the right side.

MY SIDE IS NOW THE RIGHT SIDE?

Your side is the winning side.

NOW YOUR TRUE PREJUDICE APPEARS. YOU DON'T CARE FOR MORALITY—ONLY NAKED POWER.

Let us say, rather, that I recognize the reality of naked power. That's much more polite, don't you think?

DO THOSE WITH POWER NEED COURTESY?

Touché. Nonetheless, my offer of fealty remains. Trying to go it alone in a world as strange and dangerous as this one is rankly foolish, no matter how powerful one might be. I recognize that now.

WILL YOU SUBMIT YOUR TRUE NAME TO ME?

No.

There was a pause.

LACKING THAT GUARANTEE, WHY SHOULD I EXCHANGE MY PROTECTION FOR YOUR SERVICE?

I have things you want.

I DOUBT THAT.

Really? How about one of the Defilers, bound and helpless, obedient to your will? I know I've found great use for her power to mold flesh. Given your vassals' predilection for murder, I imagine you could also find it handy.

OF WHOM DO YOU SPEAK?

One for whom you took Vejovis's blow, Gaviel said. Ages ago, in the War on Heaven, Avitu and Gaviel had cooperated in a grand battle against the archangel Vejovis. They'd been joined by many of their kind, including the Scourge Hasmed and the Defiler Sabriel.

AND SHE IS UNDER YOUR COMMAND?

Not yet. But she is imprisoned. Her sole chance of escape lies in being summoned. And as you know, what can be summoned can also be constrained.

YOU WOULD SELL YOUR OLD COMRADE INTO SLAVERY, THEN?

I think it's pretty clear that I would. Gaviel's tone was slightly impatient. *You get her service in full, my voluntary cooperation and the capable assistance of my old friend the Knight of the Hated Lash. Three demonic servitors. How's that for a deal?*

I DON'T THINK SO.

Why not? It's not like we haven't done business before. Didn't May please you?

YOU DO NOT UNDERSTAND ME IN THE LEAST, DO YOU GAVIEL? DO YOU THINK I ACCEPTED MAY'S SACRIFICE OUT OF SOME

SELFISH GREED? I DID IT TO SAVE HER FROM *YOU*! I REPAIRED HER SOUL, RATHER THAN LET YOU BEFOUL AND CORRUPT IT FOR EVEN A DAY LONGER!

And you're content that you did right?

I AM.

Then perhaps you'd do well to keep me on a closer leash, lest my amoral excesses continue.

IF I BECOME A PARTY TO YOUR DEGRADED ACTIONS, I DEGRADE MYSELF.

So spare the world my evil. Or dishonor your vow and fight me. Or ignore me and let me spread like cancer.

Again, there was silence as both demons ruminated.

In fact, I'll sweeten the deal. Accept my terms, and I'll rescue your man Grady.

Outside ordinary space, Usiel the Reaper watched.

Zisithras the Asharu—the demon Usiel had under observation—could feel it. He knew he was being observed, but he did not know how, from where or by whom.

Usiel did not know the mortal name of Zisithras's place, nor did he care. The Asharu was in a hospital, and it was a poor one. Zisithras had found a despairing child, one too young for his sorrows, and had possessed him. Now the demon went to the source of that despair, his vessel's dying uncle. The child's parents were already dead. Now the man who had raised him had the same illness, the same sickness that was so common in their region—common among the poor, anyhow.

Usiel watched and wondered what Zisithras would do.

The Asharu were angels of healing. Had been, anyhow. If this returned rebel could master his powers, could escape his own misery long enough to feel the pain of another... *if* the demon could do that, could feel empathy... then the healing would be trivial, an act as challenging as a human striking a match. But if the demon could not, if he failed to set aside his own pain for someone else, then no degree of power would give him the skill to heal. Corrupted, the Asharu could only harm.

Perhaps Zisithras would kill the uncle. It made a certain amount of sense. Host souls stuck around, and they could be trouble if they got too strong. Killing the man would be the final nail in the host's coffin, the final blow of misery to leave that young spirit helpless and weak.

(If Usiel thought that would happen, he ought to appear, raise his scythe, defend humanity, smite the demon. But could he afford to pre-empt the crime? If he acted too rashly, might that not be the greater evil? Could he afford to give the demon the benefit of the doubt? Did he dare assume it was evil? Did he dare deny it?)

Or perhaps the demon would heal the uncle and make him a thrall. That was another clever play, acting the angel it once was to fuel the demon it could become. Usiel appreciated, now, what a balancing act that was. Love them enough to help them, but not so much that you couldn't use them, couldn't feed from them, couldn't steal their souls. He understood that mix of love and selfishness too well.

(If that was Zisithras's course, what was Usiel's best response? To kill the demon who saved a life? Or to let him go, having stolen a soul from God? Action? Or inaction? Each had its perils.)

His hope—barely a hope—was that the demon would heal the man and leave. That he would take nothing and give. That he would be, if even for a moment, the healing spirit he once had been.

(This was the smallest chance, but if the demon took it, Usiel would rejoice. And yet some part of him, something vindictive and selfish and weak, hoped the demon would choose ill, that

Lucifer was right and that there was no hope. Part of him hoped the fallen were truly beyond redemption, and that his choices would be simple once more.)

Zisithras neared the bed. Usiel watched.

"I don't expect you to believe me, but we weren't asked to spy on you."

"I don't believe you." Sabriel said it with a smile. The Contessa was fun. The other two, well, whatever, but the Contessa's attitude appealed to Sabriel, while her life and history appealed to Christina.

"Are you flattered?" the dead woman asked.

"Flattered that he kidnapped me? Hardly."

"You should be."

"It's kinda romantic, don't you think?" This was Minnie, the settler—or in Sabriel's mind, "The Hayseed Queen."

"Don't be ridiculous," Liz replied. "We've been over this before. A woman doesn't need a man to be happy!"

"Though, to be sure, it is a great help," the Contessa said, smiling briefly.

"A woman doesn't need a man to define her!"

"But without one, you can only define yourself as a few things," Minnie objected. "There's only so much you can do on your own."

"In your day, yes, but now a woman can be a doctor or a soldier or even a mother without needing a man's help."

"How wonderful," the Contessa said. "You could scoop phlegm from fever victims or march through filthy ditches with a rifle, just like a man. Truly you've come a long way, baby."

"Maybe you can be a mother without a man," Minnie said, "but you can't be a wife. And that was one of the best things I ever was. I'm sorry you missed out on that, Lizzie, but—"

"Ladies? Please?" Sabriel said. "Listening to you reinvent the wheel of feminism is mildly diverting, but I have a few other concerns. Like, why did this demon kidnap me?"

"You really consider him a demon?" Jennifer said.

"As much as I'm one. He transgressed the laws of God and was cast down into Hell."

"You seem so worldly," the Contessa said. "I'm surprised you can't guess his motives."

"You think he's in love with me?" Sabriel asked.

"Men do every kind of fool thing for love," Minnie said, shrugging.

"He's not a man!"

"He looks like a man. Sometimes. Acts like one."

"Minnie, I don't think this is a case of 'if it quacks like a duck,'" Liz said. "We've all dealt with things that seemed human but weren't. Remember?"

Minnie looked away at that comment and nodded. Sabriel felt her heart speed up and wondered if she could get them on her side.

"I can understand your position," she said. "I mean, he swooped in and rescued you. Or that's what it looked like, anyhow."

"Are you accusing him of setting that up?"

"I know he can call and command spirits," Sabriel said, shrugging. "I don't know if he orchestrated events one way or another. He probably didn't. Why would he? If you'd resisted, he could have just compelled you."

"He could have tried," Minnie said, nostrils flaring.

"Of course, this is only your view of things," the Contessa said.

"He warned us that you'd try to turn us against him," Elizabeth said.

"You do what you have to do," Sabriel said. "If I was in your shoes, I wouldn't be in any hurry to cross something so dangerous, powerful and unpredictable."

"Unpredictable?"

"Sure! I mean, running out and seizing me like that—it's not exactly the mark of a stable mind, is it? Elizabeth? Do you think? He could easily decide one day to just chop me up and scatter my pieces to the wind, and I'd have no way to stop him. Neither would any of you, I'm sure."

She could feel their rising apprehension—the Contessa least of all, she had a cool head on her shoulders—when the front door slammed open.

"Ah," Sabriel said. "Our hell-harrowed Heathcliff returns to Wuthering Heights."

She rose from the sofa and went into the entryway.

"Ward," she said, "I'm worried about the Beaver."

"Cute," he replied. "I brought supper."

"Joy. Burger King or McDonald's?"

"Actually, it's Lebanese. You like falafel?"

"Better than nothing," she said, while Christina's stomach growled with anticipation.

As they ate, she said, "So, what's my role?"

"I beg your pardon?"

"You've obviously got some plan for me—hence your ham-fisted abduction. I've been here long enough to get bored and start wondering what fate has in store."

"Fate."

"Or, I suppose, *you*. C'mon, spill it! What do you want from me?" She couldn't help but shift her posture to give him a little cleavage on that last question.

He looked away. "You don't get it, do you? You think I just want to, to use you? Manipulate you?"

"Oh, you seized me as a favor?"

"Sabriel, could you drop the act for a minute?"

"The act?"

"Could you stop being... being provocative and ironic and defensive and fake-playful and flirty and..."

"Stop being a succubus, you mean."

He sighed. "I remember the way you were."

They were silent for a moment.

"I remember the way I was, too," she said at last, and he looked up. It was the first time in eons that he'd heard her voice free of artifice. She spoke in those same tones of sorrow and puzzlement that crept out in front of Thomas and made him feel pity, despite her cruelty. Usiel looked, and she was slouching, looking down at her chickpeas with a numb expression.

"Don't you want that back?"

"That me is *dead!* The war killed it, Usiel! You, Michael and the ophanim and the malhim, and the whole Holy Host! Ten thousand years of torture and suffering and watching the world blacken—that killed me!"

"Oh, and Lucifer's Army had no part in it?"

"I *don't care!* I don't care if we were wrong or not! It doesn't even matter anymore! What matters is I can't forget what I've seen and done, and what I've *been*. I can't forget what humans used to be, and seeing them now just... It's horrifying! It's the most disgusting, repellent thing, and *I'm one of them now!* I'm nauseated by my own skin! I'm stuck in what I hate, and I can't get out! So don't talk to me about being the old Sabriel again, please. I'd love to turn back the clock, get back to Eden, but Eden is gone, Sabriel is gone, and humankind is fallen!"

There was a brief quiet—if not total silence. The moan of the wind outside and the rattle of loose shutters shuddering still undergirded their dinner. Then a third small sound joined those two.

"Are you crying?" Usiel asked softly.

"No I'm not!" she shrieked, clearly lying, oblivious to it as her pretty face reddened and tears splashed down. She bolted to her feet and fled the room. He rose as well.

"Leave her go," Minnie whispered in his ear. "Just let her be for a moment."

As he waffled, he felt the stirrings of an invocation.

"Who is it?" he snapped. His expression went from concern to a sour sneer. "Oh, it's *you*. What do you want?"

Minnie asked who he was talking to, but he shushed her.

"You must be joking," he said. But he still listened to whatever voice it was, silence to Minnie, and she saw the certainty eroding from his face, bit by bit.

"You know a lot less than you think," he said.

"I am not your ally, and you're a fool to think I could be," he said, and this time his tone was angry, defensive.

He narrowed his eyes, silent for a while, then said, "Maybe I should kill her first." His voice was cool and snide, but Minnie could see on his face how much he dreaded the action he'd described.

"You think you can trick me," he said. Then he listened some more. His eyes widened with surprise, and concern.

"Who told you that?" Now he was definitely uneasy.

"Now you're trying to tempt me, too. It won't work." But something in his voice told Minnie it had already.

His posture relaxed soon after that, and he frowned.

"Are you... done?" she asked. He grunted.

"Who was it?"

"Never mind. Leave me."

"Do you want—"

"I want you to leave me."

"Right." She crept away, silent as only a ghost can be.

Mitch Berger had been through some wicked unpleasant experiences. In his old job as an asylum guard, he'd heard paranoids rave about the conspiracies that controlled not only the government, but people's very ideas about reality. He'd heard serial rapists discuss their crimes in minute detail, sounding bored. He'd heard muscle-bound murderers scream at him that they'd kill him, kill his family, kill the man who dug his grave. Creepy stuff.

He'd survived the Devil's Night Quake in LA, and he'd seen Satan himself. Every day, he secretly gave thanks for that screen of drugs that had protected him, and every day he secretly cursed the demons who'd stripped that screen out of his memory.

What he was seeing now was maybe even worse.

It didn't have Lucifer's sense of crushing unreality—which was a relief in one way—but by the same token, it made it harder to just trance out, let his mind boggle and fail and wait for it to go away. He could comprehend what was happening, even though he didn't want to. His mind could grasp it, but not let it go.

"This is going to take a long time, and it's going to be hard, but you can do it," Mukikel said. "I have faith in you," she added, with a narrow-eyed look over at Mitch.

(She'd offered Mitch a chance to get in on this action, but he must have let his fear and revulsion show on his face.)

"I'm ready," Chuck replied.

That was what made it all so horrible. Chuck. Chuck and the knowledge that all this stuff was *real*. Without knowing that, it would have been fuckin' *hilarious*—uptight Charles Rodriguez, the stiffest stiff on the guard staff, dressed up in a cape made of ten gazillion dragonfly wings, making this crazy pattern of sugar in the desert, way the hell out in nowhere, and piling a couple hundred bucks' worth of cut flowers in the center of it. Charles Rodriguez leading a black goat and a white goat forward as sacrifices. Charles Rodriguez clearing his throat and chanting all this crazy crap from some language no one ever heard of.

It looked like a scene from a bad B horror flick. Except Mitch knew it was all real, all true.

And *Chuck*. That was the worst part, worse than the reality even. Chuck. Stand-up guy Chuck, whose clear thinking and courage and all that good stuff had saved Mitch's life during the worst day of his life. Chuck, the decent man. His savior.

Chuck was summoning a demon.

He started the chant that went on and on and *on*, and Mitch's nervousness was finally starting to wane. Then it changed. For the longest time, it had been just noise, just blah blah, but now he could feel… something. Meaning in it, woven through it, pushing up under it. This language was more than words, it wasn't right going through a mere human voice, but the power was there. Mitch couldn't follow it, and later he couldn't even remember the sounds. But he sensed that, next to this, human language was as random and pointless as the buzzing of crickets.

He listened, and his mind went numb. He listened because he could only listen; the sun crept down and vanished without him noticing. He couldn't think. He could still feel the dread and terror, but he couldn't think.

"That's it. You're doing great. Keep going," Mukikel said, standing back by Mitch but staring so intently at Chuck.

Desert insects had started to speak in tandem with the chant.

"YES. FEEL THE POWER. BRING HER, CHUCK. BRING HER BACK."

She had changed into her other form, in the darkness, her form of red leaf wings and hard shiny surfaces, and Mitch hadn't even noticed. Even that couldn't penetrate the ritual's spell.

(Hours ago, Mitch had asked why Mukikel couldn't simply do this herself. She'd explained that only humans could summon a demon from Hell. No one knew why.)

The sugar lines were crawling with ants and flies and spiders when Chuck pulled forth a perfectly ordinary hunting knife and slit the black goat's throat. The blood spilled forth as the buzzing increased.

"IT'S TIME," Mukikel said. She wasn't talking to Mitch or to Chuck. She'd turned to the open back of her van, and she was talking to the naked woman inside. She was blonde and plain and pale and thin. Her eyes were dull and vacant. She'd been at Rothschild: She was one of the blanks.

"GO INTO THE CIRCLES AND LIE DOWN ON THE FLOWERS," Mukikel said, and even someone with a mind would have felt that compulsion. The blank sleepwalked forward obediently, leaving footprints in goat's blood after stepping in the cooling pool.

Chuck slit the white goat's throat, and instead of blood, maggots poured out. The woman lay down, and Mitch threw up.

He saw a second shape over the blank woman, a shape with glowing hands and butterfly wings, a shape he'd seen once before. Then it flowed down like melting wax, and the woman sat up.

"Iiii reeeeturn," she said, her tones droning and nasal, but human.

"Welcome back, Shadrannat," Mukikel said.

Chuck collapsed. The two demonesses went forward to help him, and Mitch snapped out of his trance to go tend his friend.

"Is he going to be okay?"

"He's just exhausted," Mukikel replied, now just a woman once more. She gave him another hard look. "Are you sure you don't want to do the summoning tomorrow? I'll walk you through it. Not just the evocation, either—Buniel I want bound. He would be your servant, Mitch, unable to disobey."

The thought wasn't tempting. It was terrifying. Mitch just shook his head. And as he tried to bring his friend back to consciousness, he just shook.

Blackie was uncomfortable. He had a stomachache, and that wasn't right. The goddess had cured him—zap, just like that, and he should feel perfect. But still his stomach hurt, because he couldn't forget that he'd been shot.

"Are you okay?" Teddy asked, for maybe the fifth time.

That was another thing. His... dad. Blackie wasn't used to having a dad, and Teddy had ignored him, pretty much, since day one. He'd thought (kind of hopefully, kind of fearfully) that that might change after Lance came to the compound, but Teddy stayed distant.

I guess he's still mad that my mom killed his wife, he thought, gingerly poking at his perfectly healthy sore belly.

"I'm fine," he said.

"You look like it still hurts."

Blackie nodded. "Yeah. It still hurts."

"It's psychosomatic."

Blackie had no idea what that meant. "I guess," he said.

"Have you ever heard about amputees with phantom pains?"

"Ummm..."

"People who lose an arm or a leg often hallucinate that they feel pain there. In the missing limb. You see? They imagine pain in a body part they don't even have anymore."

"Whoa."

"It's the curse of consciousness. We feel pain even where we *cannot*, because we think we ought to."

"You think this stomach thing is like that? It's a phantom pain?"

"I think so."

Blackie digested that for a moment. "Then there's nothing we can do, is there? You can't get rid of a pain that's not... not a real pain."

"Exactly right." Teddy was looking out the window, and he sounded sad. He turned back to his son. "That's our dilemma, Black Hawk. We have to stay conscious, it's our fate. We have to endure all its phantom pains. I hate to see it, hate to see my..."

He trailed off.

"How's Lance doing?" Blackie asked.

Teddy looked surprised.

"He's... he's okay, I guess. He still misses his mother a lot."

"Teddy, I... um."

"Maybe I should go."

"It's hard to lose someone, I know. Even someone who... Look, my mom was bad, okay? I guess I know that, but... I mean, she was my mom. I loved her, y'know? She wasn't ever bad to me. I'm sorry about what she did, and if I could go back, I..."

"She thought it was for the best," Teddy said, his voice leaden.

"I know that doesn't excuse nothing," Blackie said, "but she... she did it for Lance too, y'know. And it's wrong, it's all twisted up and wrong, but she thought... She really believed, y'know? In Avitu. She believed that bringing Lance here was important, that... that it would help him. And everything."

"But it won't help him," Teddy said, and although his eyes were pointed in Blackie's direction, they were staring off somewhere a million miles away. Someplace distant where sad things were happening, things he could never change. "He's doomed to be conscious, like you and me. He's a priest of the blood. He's destined for imprisonment."

They were silent for a moment.

"There are some new sacrifices from Fresno," Teddy said. His eyes were focused again, locked on the here and now.

"What are we supposed to do with them after? I mean, we can't... without Rothschild we can't... process them."

"That's not important. We'll figure something out. We'll find a way." He lowered his eyes, and then put a hand on Blackie's shoulder. "What matters is this: They haven't been purified. And I think *you* should do the ritual this time."

Blackie's dismay was so sudden and strong that, for a moment, he completely forgot to have a stomachache.

"Wow," Shadrannat said, sitting on the hotel room bed and tuning a cheap acoustic guitar. "This one's really different." She picked out a credible intro to the song "Imagine."

"Yeah?" Mitch asked. "Different how?"

"Well, she's a musician for one thing. That's pretty cool."

"And you... get all that?"

"I can remember parts. Lot of it's muscle memory."

"Cool." He scratched his arm. This new version of Shadrannat was giving him the creeps.

It was midmorning, and Mukikel had gone out into the desert with Chuck at dawn. They'd taken another blank, a man this time, and they were going to conjure Buniel using flames and prisms and a knife made of gold. They'd been gone when Mitch woke up. Shadrannat had been doing a handstand up against the wall next to the TV. Slowly, she'd lowered herself until the top of her head touched the floor, and then—red, grunting, her muscles trembling—she'd pushed her arms straight again. A Chinese push-up—Mitch had seen guys do them at the gym, but never a woman as scrawny and sick-looking as the one Shadrannat had become.

"Plus, this body is sexually mature. That's a *real* change in perspective."

"You don't say," Mitch replied. He didn't think about it, but he edged a little farther from her. He cleared his throat. "So, uh, how come she wound up as a... what you call it? A blank?"

"They lobotomized her."

"No shit? She's a frontal?" Mitch knew about full frontal lobotomies from his asylum work.

"Not anymore."

"How come they did that? I mean, she doesn't look old enough for it to have been therapeutic."

"A demon did it to her."

"I should've guessed. So, let me see—a demon frontalized her to make it easy for other demons to take over?"

"That's a good guess, but it's wrong. A demon 'frontalized' her because that demon—a creature called the Tree of Ignorance—believed it was the right thing to do. The ethical thing."

"Huh?"

"It's a long story." Shadrannat cracked her knuckles and started plinking on the guitar again. "The Tree would be appalled if it knew there was a demon occupying its sacrifice. And this woman would be delighted to appall that demon. What goes around, comes around. Or something."

"What was her name?"

"Jennifer Arliss. Hey, you want to get some brunch?"

Sal lit a cigarette, took two puffs and ground it out. He was at an impasse.

He'd never considered himself an impatient man. There was a word for impatient criminals: "jailbird." He could be cool as the tides while he was watching, waiting, gathering information, getting ready for the right time. All that stuff, fuggeddaboudit, he did crossword puzzles.

What really bugged him was cooling his heels waiting for some guy to make up his mind. Or, in this case, some demon.

Sal got a very bad vibe off this "Vodantu" character, but that was okay. He was used to ignoring bad vibes from people. Doing it with demons was the same kind of thing, just ten times more intense. Every time he did it, he needed a shower afterward, and he felt like going to church.

But when you got down to it, talking to a demon in Hell was kind of like communicating with a mob boss in the big house. Not *exactly* like, but it was a framework to go on. Like an imprisoned boss, the demon's power was limited, but it still had a lot of influence. Like a jailed don, its missing luxuries were a real sore point. And like every boss, in jail or out, it tried to push him around.

He had the Rebluhé Ritual for that. He didn't kid himself that hanging up the phone on demon lords—especially those who had freaks like Hasmed running around doing shit in the world—was the safest way to play, but he figured Vodantu wasn't going to grease him for disrespect when there was still a chance Sal could get him something he wanted. He just had to keep playing that card—as long as he held out a promise, being a little pushy would make Vodantu respect him, not hate him.

Assuming, that is, that Vodantu was not actually insane.

"Look, worship, it ain't gonna happen. Got me? That's off the table."

YOU DARE DEFY ME?

"C'mon. Maybe you got alla time in the world, but can we please cut past the posturing and get to some quid pro quo?"

I AM NOT A MERCHANT, MORTAL! DO NOT PRESUME TO HAGGLE WITH ME!

"All I'm saying is, I can help you, you can help me, or neither one of us can help the other and we're both worse off. Is it so crazy for me to think we could work something out?"

MY POWER IS INCALCULABLE BY YOUR STANDARDS, MORTAL. ANY DESIRE YOUR MIND CAN ENCOMPASS IS MINE TO BESTOW UPON MY LOYAL THRALLS AND SERVANTS.

Sal decided to let it slide. "Any desire, huh? Well I'll tell you what I desire. I want revenge on the asswipes who killed my boy."

PLEDGE ME YOUR FEALTY, AND I WILL SWEEP YOUR ENEMIES BEFORE YOU.

"Even when those enemies are your own soldiers?"

There was a pause.

OF WHOM DO YOU SPEAK?

"I got one name I don't wanna say. You understand. The other guy, I dunno his name, but he's one of yours. The two of 'em kinda ganged up on my son, Scott. Sacrificed him to *you*, in fact."

I REMEMBER.

Sal swallowed hard, and that was almost it, he almost quit, did the Rebluhé. He thought about turning himself in, handing state's evidence on that shit bag Pudoto, maybe finding religion in jail before the Family kacked him for a rat... but Hasmed. He had to get Hasmed. And if that meant damning himself to damn another, well, that was the Mafia way. His way.

"So I guess you remember the two bastards who did it?"

I DO.

"And you'd Judas them for my help?"

BOTH ARE WORTHY FOLLOWERS. THEY HAVE BOTH MADE MANY LAUDABLE SACRIFICES IN MY HONOR.

"Yeah, no shit—but so what? Are you there for them, or are they there for you?"

THEY ARE LESSER SERVANTS, BUT THEY CAN BEND TIME, TORMENT SPACE, HEAL AND HARM MORTALS WITH A BREATH, DRIVE MEN MAD WITH A WORD. WHAT DO YOU OFFER OF GREATER VALUE?

Sal took a deep breath and hoped he was right. The *Code of Diabolical Loyalty* had said it. Marvin Morris and *Wormwood* had said it. Dr. Roark said most of the traditions agreed. But if they were all wrong, he'd pissed this thing off for nothing.

"I can summon you outta Hell."

There was some unpleasantness as Mukikel drove Buniel and Chuck back from the desert. Buniel had come back angry—angry that his new body was scrawny and weak and pill-addled, angry that he'd once more been in Hell, angry that he'd needed a mortal to call him forth. More than that, he was absolutely livid that Charles had the effrontery to *bind* him—him, a Devil of the First House, enslaved to this mortal tub of guts! Perhaps his greatest wrath, however, was reserved for Mukikel, his new superior, who had ordered him to relinquish his True Name to her *and* to Chuck as a condition of his freedom. She'd justified it, saying he disobeyed orders in Los Angeles, but that didn't salve his hurt. If anything, her mealy mouthed words were only fuel to his fire.

She doesn't understand, he thought, glowering silent in the back seat. *Her and the other weaklings from the Liberation legion, the hangers-on who don't have the guts for the real work, for the battles of Victory. They're as bad as Defiance. She needs to contain me because I'm her better, and she knows it.*

As he sat, fuming and clenching his fists, a slow smell of hot metal and drying paper began to fill the van.

"Buniel," Mukikel said, her voice starched with the light authority of a grade school teacher, "please stop it."

"I don't know what you mean."

"Perhaps it's an accident," she said, "but I believe you're upsetting the fire."

He realized it was true, and it startled him. If she hadn't noticed, the papers in the glove compartment and the stuffing in their seats might have spontaneously ignited. She was right, and that only made him angrier.

They met the Devourer Shadrannat and the other meat-bag at an International House of Pancakes. Her, at least, Buniel could respect. He'd fought at her side in the war, during the first battle of Shenrizar, and he trusted her ferocity.

"Is it good to be free again?" she asked.

"If you call this freedom."

Shadrannat nodded sympathetically and leaned in toward him. Mukikel had gone to the bathroom, and when Shadrannat spoke again, it was in ancient Akkadian.

"(You resent your binding,)" she said.

"Um... beg your pardon?" Mitch asked.

"It's private," Shadrannat told him. He frowned hard and gave Chuck a dig in the ribs. Chuck shrugged and kept looking at the menu, his face serene.

"(Wouldn't you resent it?)" Buniel replied. "(I mean, look at him!)"

"(Isn't it better to be bound to a mortal than to be imprisoned by the Almighty?)"

Buniel still frowned, but admitted she might have a point.

"(I know it galls you, but this human is crucial. Our great general has revealed himself to this man, a distinction none of the rest of us can boast! Our enemies, the slavers in Los Angeles, they knew his importance.)"

"(You needn't talk to me about the LA slavers.)"

Mitch was frowning, having picked "LA" and "Los Angeles" out of their foreign words. Buniel glared at him until Mitch looked away.

"(I know,)" Shadrannat said. "(You fought them well. You fought them unto your *death*, and that is the reason we wanted you to guard Rodriguez.)"

At that name, Mitch's eyes once again flicked to them, then down again.

"(He's a great treasure,)" Shadrannat continued, "(and we needed someone who would risk returning to Hell for him. You alone showed that loyalty.)"

"(I'm loyal to the Army, not to one mortal.)"

"(And that's why Mukikel bound you. But don't hold it against her. She had to decide between your dignity and the safety of the operation, and she chose. You may not like her choice, but she's your overlord now. Furthermore, if you fall again, he has the knowledge to call you forth once more—and the binding gives him a reason to do so without fear. Yes, giving your Name is a sacrifice, but it is for the larger good.)"

"(I've already sacrificed much, Shadrannat.)"

"(Then what's a little more? We have all given many times over, but isn't it worth it? Now we're free! Now we can find our leader once more! Now we can continue the fight!)"

"I admire your sentiments, but you might want to lower your voice," Mukikel said, sliding in next to Chuck.

Shadrannat looked up and saw that people in other booths were starting to give her curious looks.

"What were you talking about?" Mitch demanded.

"Matters difficult for humans," Mukikel said, voice smooth, as if she knew everything and wasn't just blowing smoke. "You don't need to worry about it."

Shadrannat and Buniel both felt it, their leader's subtle call to Mitch's blood, calming his heart rate, tweaking his endorphin level, giving a gentle prod to the pleasure centers in his brain... nothing overt, nothing dramatic, just enough to incline him to obey. Enough to train him for future compliance.

"Buniel," Shadrannat said, "who is your host? How did he come to be blank?"

"Bailey Sanger," Buniel said, his mouth compressed with distaste. "A drunk. He was lured in by promises of nihilistic oblivion and thereby persuaded to surrender his sovereignty. He was weak. He was weary. He was contemptible." He nearly spat on the table as he spoke. "I assume yours is the same?"

"Oh no. Jennifer Arliss... she was coerced. I believe she saw this demoness at its weakest, saw it when it was just waking up."

"It is one of the Earthbound, then?" Mukikel asked, her eyes sharp.

"One of the..." Mitch asked. Chuck shushed him.

"I'm not sure," Shadrannat said. "Most Earthbound lie in tombs of stone or metal, but this one is bound in a living thing... even as we are," she said, eyes switching to Buniel and Mukikel. "But there's no humanity in her. She is tied to a tree in the desert, an ancient pine, its roots sunk deep in the earth, its branches clawing the sky and its heart bound tight to ages past. She is alive like us, but still like them. I do not know what she is."

"She is a threat," Buniel said. "That much is clear. You have not yet told the Victory legion?"

"You two are the first to know," Shadrannat replied.

"Call Victory, and we shall sweep her from the sky and uproot her from the earth."

"Are you sure that's wise?" Mukikel said.

"All other things being equal," Shadrannat said, "Jennifer Arliss wouldn't mind seeing her burn."

"But are all other things equal?" Mukikel asked.

"Do you doubt our power?" Buniel asked.

"I do," she said. Buniel drew breath for a heated reply, but at that moment their meals arrived. By the time the waitress was gone, Mukikel had a reply prepared. "Even a mighty lion can be dragged down by a team of hyenas. Victory has the best part of our best warriors, but you are beset in Los Angeles, in Tibet, in Brazil. Do we need yet another front in our war?"

"You said she was weak, Sha—... 'Jennifer.' If we delay our strike, we may only give her time to compound her strength."

"Perhaps the wise choice is to refer this to your old comrades," Mukikel said. "Our mission, now, is to protect Mitch and Chuck, and our duty is to find the Morningstar. This creature has no connection to either task. Let Victory decide whom to fight."

"That might be complicated." Shadrannat said.

"Oh?"

"Defiance," Buniel said, his voice sour. "You think they'd interfere?"

"They are short-sighed. They're most likely to see this... thing... only as a resource. A factory for blanks."

"Why can't they make their own?" Mitch asked. Mukikel laughed.

"My friend, this Tree's acts are anathema to our cause. We threw down the gauntlet by making man know himself. What Defiance lord, even their archduchess, would betray Lucifer by taking that gift away?" Mukikel shook her head. "No, we cannot duplicate this creature's crimes, no matter how convenient."

"But you think they would... let it slide. Ignore it. Be silently complicit," Buniel said.

"To supply themselves?" She shrugged. "Who can say? And they can always say that it is not their job to battle the Earthbound."

"Then let Victory do it!"

"Yes, Victory without the aid of Defiance. Without backup and supply and support and protection. What a splendid notion," Mukikel said.

"We all know what happens to Victory cadres who antagonize the Defiant," Shadrannat said, her voice gloomy.

"If this thing's so dangerous," Mitch asked, "why are we even staying nearby it?"

Mukikel smiled at him. "A very good question," she said. "The answer is, we aren't. Not for long. Once I get confirmation from Durdiel that he has the blanks in hand..." She paused, listened, smiled. "Yes... now we can drive to Lake Meade, where there's a Master of the Paths. He can take us to Canada, where we have a better stronghold." She glanced at her watch. "In fact, we should get going."

"I'll pay," Shadrannat said.

"Okay. I'm going to go gas up the van. You guys want snacks? There's a convenience store."

"Yeah, and I'm gonna see a man about a dog," Chuck said, heading for the bathroom.

Mitch looked around as the group stood, but Shadrannat seemed to have one eye on him even as she settled their bill. With a grimace, he trudged toward the van. He was about ten feet away when he heard Buniel, behind him, shouting in that peculiar language. He'd just about decided to turn when he felt the skinny frame of Bailey Sanger slam into his back. Before he could even wonder why, their van exploded—with Mukikel inside.

After a busy day of quiet, secret invocations, Sabriel and Usiel had a nice dinner. He'd found a place that would, for merely a princely sum, pack you a delicious picnic for two with wine and china and real silver forks—smaller than a normal service, and everything fit in the basket so cleverly, fresh bread and crisp fruit and a bottle of superb wine.

They had unpacked it on the mansion's vast oak dinner table, and the Contessa flitted here and there, clearing dishes and filling glasses as they spoke. Liz played Vivaldi, softly, in a corner. She played upon a remembered cello, with a bow made from her own ghost-flesh, transformed.

"How do you defend mortality?" Sabriel asked, but without her usual anger, without pain. She looked at Usiel closely, and unless her expression was false, she was genuinely interested in his perspective—the view from the other side of the war.

"How can you *condemn* it?" he said in response, lifting his wineglass.

"Mankind was made for immortality."

"Mankind was also made for self-knowledge. And yet, when it was given it instead of taking it, *earning* it... well, it became an impure blessing at best, yes?"

"But what is the good side of death?"

"How can you look at a fallen world and ask that? Yes, the living fear death, and you among the... fallen... fear that unknown..."

"'The undiscovered country,'" she said, smiling lightly, toying with the stem of her wineglass. He frowned, a little.

"Wasn't that a Star Trek movie?" he asked.

"It was also a Shakespeare quote," she said softly. "But forgive my interruption."

"Right, right... well, I mean, look at the world. It's become so limited, so dirty and gray. What worse fate for humankind than to be trapped there, undying, forever? What could be worse than never knowing something *more*?"

"And you're so sure there *is* more?"

"You knew Eden! You know the world can be so much more than it is, because it *was*!"

"So when we wrecked the world, God made a door out of it?"

"A door through our realm."

She took a deep, thoughtful drink, then patted her perfect lips. He'd bought her a dress, too, a lovely evening gown made of red velvet. He'd gotten her size all wrong, but she'd fixed that easily.

"I should have known a Slayer would have a good defense of death."

He winced a little at the title Slayer but didn't correct her. "Well, if it wasn't for death we'd all be out of work." He gave a little smile.

"So why were you condemned, then? If death is so wonderful, the gate out of a ruined realm?"

He looked down at his plate, and she wondered if she'd gone too far. "Perhaps," he said at last, "if we've learned anything… it's that the greatest goods can be the most vicious evils, when they're taken too soon."

In Greece, many months ago, she'd seduced a 15-year old virgin. His name was Janos. She thought about Janos, nodded and raised her glass. "I'll drink to that."

After dinner, they danced. He walked her to her bedroom and said, "Whatever happens, I want you to know: I'm sorry I've hurt you."

Her reply was very quiet. "Whatever happens, I'm sorry if I hurt you, as well."

She put her hands on either side of his face and kissed him on the cheek.

Later that night, after she'd been freed from the deadlands, he realized that while his statement had clearly referred to the past, hers could have encompassed the present… and the future.

"Just relax, read the words, follow the pattern. You're doing fine." Gaviel was pulling the oars on the rowboat, but he still spared a smile for Thomas.

Tom was at the back of the boat with a bunch of ice bags from a gas station, and can after can of iodized salt from a grocery store.

"Do I do one of the rings here?" Tom asked. Gaviel nodded.

There was a pattern, Gaviel had drawn it carefully on graph paper. It was beautiful. There was a big circle with three other circles inside it, and in those circles all these extra lines and figures and squiggles. They were making the big circle on the surface of the water with ice cubes and salt. The little circles were drawn in salt only. Next to each little circle was a jumble of letters—phonetically spelled words that meant absolutely nothing to Thomas, but he had to read them as he made the circles, and he had to make the circles right, or Sabriel would stay trapped.

He made the circle and muttered the mumbo jumbo, and he found himself thinking about the drive out to this murky little waterhole—a swampy Missouri pond and park miles from nowhere with a secluded lagoon. The perfect place to do this kind of weird hoodoo at midnight.

The drive had been a blast. It was a clear, warm day, a little hot—perfect weather for Gaviel's new car, which was a convertible. They'd jammed along the highway with the top down, the wind too loud for the radio. Gaviel didn't like the radio; he'd ragged on jazz at great length.

"Every race of humanity has invented something useless and complicated," he said. "Like jazz. Listen to Mingus or Parker or Coltrane—there's no point to it except to be difficult.

Like a crossword puzzle. Believe me Thomas, the only purpose for jazz is to occupy the minds of brilliant young men who would otherwise cause trouble. In Europe, it's chess—same thing, same pointless thing."

"Yeah? What about in Asia?"

"Manners and philosophy."

For a moment, Tom looked at him, trying to figure out if he was serious or joking. Of course he couldn't tell.

"So wait," Thomas finally said. "Jazz isn't nearly as old as chess."

"Your point?"

"So how come the blacks haven't, like, achieved a whole bunch of stuff? Like, 'cause their best brains didn't have jazz to distract 'em?"

"You wanna know why? 'Cause *the Man* be keepin' us down!"

Gaviel glared over at him for a second, and then they both burst out laughing.

What else had they talked about? Thomas had told him a bunch of stuff, all about his life and robbing houses and concerts and smoking pot. He'd told Gaviel about how he met Sabriel, too (though the demon had cautioned him against speaking her name, had warned him about eavesdropping). Thomas actually told it funny, told about being imprisoned and tortured, and it was *funny*. They both laughed out loud, and Gaviel had brought along some foreign drink called "Shy" or "Chai" or something. It was really good with these gourmet ginger-infused kettle chips; they'd eaten the whole bag. When they were done, Gaviel had just tossed the empty bag aside.

"Dude! Litter!" Thomas had shouted, instinctively, over the hiss of the highway wind.

Gaviel had just laughed and laughed, shaking his head. After a moment, Tom had started laughing too. But when he ate the last of their Powdered Donettes, he stuffed the box under the seat so he could trashcan it later.

"Okay, Thomas. The last circle."

Tom swallowed and started forming the final pattern. His lips were dry, but he knew he couldn't stumble over these words, couldn't stammer—shit, this was like handling plutonium; who knew what a screw-up with *demon-calling* would do? His heart was tap-dancing, but Gaviel was looking at him, and he got every word right.

"Great. Hard part's done. Now for the cakewalk." Gaviel started sculling toward shore, and Thomas felt an intense surge of gratitude. No one had ever believed in him this much before.

For the last part, Thomas had to get naked, but it wasn't weird in front of Gaviel. Well, maybe it was, but that particular weirdness was just swallowed up in the general weirdness of the whole crazy thing—so he stripped and stood and read the page and a half of gibberish that meant nothing to him. It was just goo goo gaa gaa, like baby babble, but halfway through, the lagoon started to freeze.

It didn't freeze along the edges, as in a natural winter. It froze where Thomas had dropped the cubes, a warty and irregular ring of ice rising to the surface and shining in the leaf-broken moonlight. The salt arose, too. It floated and cohered, and there was thin glinting circle inside the ice, like frost on a window, only this frost had three whorls of intricate tracings, like fingerprints or circuit diagrams.

"Keep going," Gaviel urged him, and Tom did.

At the end of the chant, she was there, in the middle of the ring. Not as Christina with her tats and freckles, not as Angela or Penthesila or any of the other names she'd used. She was there as Sabriel, the angel with rainbow wings and waterfall hair, and Thomas just stared.

"The binding," Gaviel said.

Thomas just stared.

"The *binding!*" Gaviel hissed.

"WHAT?" The apparition on the water bellowed. It was the crash of a tidal wave striking stone, and Thomas's pale naked skin shriveled into goose bumps.

"Bind her Thomas! Do it now! This is your only chance!"

"IF YOU DARE LAY BONDS UPON ME, YOU SHALL SUFFER TO YOUR SOUL'S LAST WHIMPER!"

"She's bluffing!"

This was it. They'd talked about it last night, and Gaviel had made it all sound so reasonable. Tom had nodded and frowned and thought, *Yeah, why shouldn't I? Why should I be her toy for the rest of my life? Why should I let her be the boss and rag me out and treat me like her fucking house-nigger?*

Last night, it made perfect sense. Seeing her now, the idea of trying to contain her... it was like trying to put the ocean in a cage.

"Snap out of it, Thomas! This is your last chance! You can do it! *Trust me!*"

And Thomas started reading the next page, the one labeled "Binding" in Gaviel's tidy printing.

In the ring of ice, the demon Sabriel flung up her wings and howled.

Chapter Eight

Buniel had never seen Mukikel really pissed. He found himself liking her a lot better.

"This Sanger," she snapped. "How much does he remember about her defenses?"

"He remembers fences, people and dogs, but he didn't see a single gun."

"Is that good or bad?" Mukikel turned to Shadrannat. The Devourer shrugged.

"Could be good, could be bad. Maybe she's weak, has no firepower, is too primitive to understand the white men and their boom-sticks. Or maybe her supernatural defenses are strong enough that guns would just gild the lily."

The car bomb had been crude, but effective. Whoever had planted it had raised no alarm to the demons' senses, so it had to be someone normal. That bespoke a powerful organization, but in the final analysis, men were only men.

If Buniel hadn't heard the bomb's explosives murmuring in their sleep, their potential heat and light wound tight and ready to spring, it would have been far worse. He couldn't stop them from waking, but he confused them, frightened them, robbed them of their greatest power. Thanks to him, Mukikel was only burned, not incinerated. Thanks to him, Mitch was only hurt, not killed. Thanks to him, the gas pumps at the station had not joined in the chorus of flames.

"Buniel, you've talked me around. The time to strike is now."

"Now? You mean, *right* now?"

"When better?"

Mukikel was badly wounded. The bomb hadn't had a lot of force, so she hadn't been shredded; it had broken no bones, but her skin was seared and split. Her hair was burned off, her shirt and skirt were singed away, and the plastic and nylon of her bra and shoes had melted, carving hot runnels down her cooking, puffing flesh.

Buniel had dragged her from the burning van while Shadrannat hauled Mitch and Chuck back. Now, staring at glaring eyes in a blackened face, he remembered the fall of Kâsdejâ, the mad and brutal resistance mounted by the Devils' House when all hope was lost.

"We'll counterstrike immediately," she said. "They can't know of Buniel, or they'd never have hit us with flame. They'll believe me gone and expect, at worst, Shadrannat's lone retaliation."

"Mukikel... You yourself said this wasn't our mission. Our mission is to protect the witnesses."

"And if Chuck had been with me? If Mitch had been ten feet nearer? No, this is a clear and present danger to our charges, and it must be settled without delay."

"We don't even know where our charges *are*," Buniel said. He had the skill of passing unseen by mortals, he'd taken his wounded overlord to the other vehiclee, but Mitch had been out in the open, had been bundled into an ambulance and motored in toward the city. Chuck was with him.

"Chuck will invoke us soon enough," Mukikel said. "And I have favors to call in on his behalf. X'Dorvu! Attend me!"

While Mukikel made her invocations, Buniel drew Shadrannat aside and said, "Is she serious?"

"Oh yes."

"But, to just assail one of the Earthbound? With no plan, no strategy, no rear-guard? This is… It's the very madness she said I—"

"Our overlord likes her plans and her schemes and her determinations," Shadrannat said, "until things go wrong. And then… Well, you'll see. She has a flair for improvisation. It frightens her, I think. She can always think of what might have gone wrong, even after she's pulled it off. And so she always tries to predict and offset and rely, so that she won't have to wing it again. Until things snap, and she snaps back." She smiled. "It's really kind of cute, once you get used to it."

"Chuck has invoked me," Mukikel announced. "The pair of them are at University Medical Center, and I have dispatched X'Dorvu to fetch Toctagan there."

"Ouch," Shadrannat said.

"They know I'm good for 'repayment,'" Mukikel sneered. She looked out the tinted window of the car and narrowed her eyes. "Now bring me a policeman."

The state trooper's name was Brenda Eisling, and she wasn't thinking clearly. Mukikel had that effect on a lot of people. Officer Eisling wasn't thinking straight, but she knew she had to go to… to… well, she didn't know the name of the place, but she knew the *place*. She had to go there and… and… it had something to do with the burning truck, the car that blew up at the gas station, and it was okay that she'd left, the local cops had shown up. It was okay, that was all… it wasn't… none of that was a problem, the problem was the place. The place she had to go to. Yes.

The place with the tree.

While Officer Eisling was headed north on the highway, off toward the rutted dirt track that would lead (in time) to Avitu and Blackie and the rest of the Tree's compound, the three demons from Lucifer's Army were bouncing off-road, headed east. Shadrannat laid hands upon the dashboard and the truck's speed jumped—even on the sandy scree-strewn ground. If they started to skid or tip, she destroyed their momentum, they rebalanced, they moved again. Momentum was a little thing, to her. They averaged about 120 miles an hour.

They ran straight and fast until they spied the compound's fence creeping over the horizon. They were the only thinking things for miles, and that gave them the freedom of shape. Mukikel opened the sunroof and emerged, still singed and sooty but unbowed and magnificent. Spreading her wings wide, she caught the air and soared.

Shadrannat was the next to leave, but not until they'd hit the eastern bend where the fence turned north. They weren't close enough to feel the Tree yet, but that was okay. It wasn't a terribly complicated plan. Mukikel from the south, Shadrannat from the southeast, Buniel from due east. Buniel had lost his wings in the war, but the car was as fast as Mukikel. Between the Devil's head start and the Devourer's speed, they ought to arrive at roughly the same time, with him closing in shortly after. He was their secret weapon. That was the plan, anyhow.

Brenda Eisling stopped her truck at the gate and looked for a phone or an intercom. There wasn't one. She honked her horn. Nothing happened. She honked again. Nothing. Finally she clicked on her loudspeaker and announced herself.

Mukikel was hurt—hurt beyond her ability to paper over it with sheer will, hurt enough that even her true form showed wounds. But she'd had worse, and she was determined to *do* worse as she drove herself on, claws twitching, a black and red shadow in a cloudless blue sky.

Shadrannat's butterfly wings seemed fragile, but she made her agreement with velocity and plunged forward with reckless speed. She was the first to encounter resistance—a form rising up from the ground and this one made no pretense of being human, it was no animal shape, just rock moving like mud, surging up to seize her. It was like a hand and a tentacle and a wave, but she stopped on a dime, stopped dead, and it turned slowly for another swipe at her. Her speed was dazzling and her control impeccable. Like a mosquito darting effortlessly away from a drunk man's flyswatter, she buzzed up and down, and, when it had overextended itself and fallen—*splat*, spread across the desert floor—she darted on past it without a backward look.

It gathered itself up, formed a ball and rolled after her, but its pursuit was slow.

The dogs came for Mukikel, but she was above them. They barked and leaped, but they were nothing to her.

A nervous-looking white man opened the gate for Officer Eisling. "Sorry this took so long," he said. "We don't get many... well, anyway. Can I help you?"

"Do you mind if I take a look around?"

"Um... do you mind if I ask why?"

Buniel had poor aim. It took him several bullets, even at close range, to shoot through the mountings on the electric fence. But presently he was rewarded with a shower of sparks. Hesitantly, he reached for the steel links. He sighed, relieved, when he touched them without pain. Then he got back in the car and tried to ram the fence down.

The next obstacle to Mukikel was not part of Avitu's planned defenses. It was a young man. He'd been playing with the dogs when they all ran off, and he was utterly unprepared for the grotesque beauty that swept up from behind a dune. He just gaped.

"GO EAST," Mukikel commanded. "DIG UNDER THE FENCE AND CONTINUE WALKING."

Those hammer-words scoured conscious thought from Lance's mind as quickly as one of his father's ice-pick lobotomies. Stupefied, he turned and obeyed.

At the gate, Teddy heard his Goddess's voice in his mind. She told him they were under attack—but more than that, she told him his son was in danger.

"C'mon in," he said to the trooper, turning to run for his own vehicle. "I... uh... gotta go!"

Driving a car through a tall chain-link fence proved to be harder than Buniel expected. It was like trying to body-slam a trampoline—it just bounced the car back. If the traction had been better, maybe, but it wasn't better, it was absolutely shitty on the desert dust. With a curse he got bolt-cutters from the back and invoked his colleagues to warn them he might be a while.

"NO PROBLEMMM," Shadrannat said, right before she saw the first hand claw its way out of the ground. In Jennifer's body she'd have needed to squint, but her true form had flawless vision and could instantly see that this was no stone mimic, this was human bone preserved in desert sand and animated by demonic will. Her multi-faceted eyes could watch them emerge, watch the sky darkening with rare rain clouds, and see the rolling mud behind her all at the same time.

She didn't think much of zombies until the first one stumbled its way under her and exploded.

Blackie hadn't seen Mukikel when she came to get Shadrannat at the Rothschild fight. Even if he had, he wouldn't have recognized her with her true nature revealed. But he'd been commanded to attack, and he felt he had little choice. His father had radioed him, told him that even if he couldn't hear the Goddess's voice, she would be able to act through his priestly blood—and that Blackie would only have to hold off the intruder until Teddy could get there.

Blackie was still dubious until Teddy told him that Lance was in danger.

Seeing him, Mukikel pegged him for a thrall and gave him the same command she'd used on Lance. But unlike Lance, Blackie only heard words and felt no impulse to obey.

I hope this works, he thought. He bit his lip and fanned his hands downward violently.

The apparition before him was seized by a sudden gust of wind and pancaked down into the desert floor. Blackie could barely believe it. Hesitantly, he crept closer.

Mukikel raised her ruined face and stared at him, sand crusted on her blood. "WOULDN'T OBEY? THEN I'LL HAVE TO TELL YOU A STORY."

Blackie drew up his hands, ready to sweep her back and pummel her, but her words were faster. This time they weren't merely words. This time, each syllable held years of her pain. In just a half-second, she told him of the Fall and the War of Wrath and the vengeance of maddened angels.

He cried out and fell back and threw his hands over his eyes, so he did not see the dogs crest the hill and fall upon her.

Buniel got through the fence and floored the gas.

When the zombie exploded, it wasn't just fire or pressure or anything ordinary like that. It was celestial energy. It wasn't pure by a long shot—it was coarse and corrupted and diabolical—but it was the real thing, the unrefined power that had been spun down into everything in the universe.

Shadrannat was hurt and stunned, and she couldn't keep herself aloft. She barely recovered enough to slay her downward momentum and fall like a feather. She could see more corpses stumbling forward, even as she figured it out.

The Earthbound is putting power in them until they can't contain it. Ten gallons in a one-gallon water balloon. Pop. Not efficient, but there it is.

She sculled her wings back from them just as the living boulder breasted a dune and started pouring down at her.

Officer Eisling normally wouldn't have let the man just run off like that, but normally she wouldn't have come out here on her own. Normally she wouldn't have played it so dumb, normally... Well, shit, "normal" just didn't apply to this day, and her mind was so addled by Mukikel's words that it barely registered to her when the man went off. She just drove forward, started looking for the tree and trying to remember where in the truck her siphon was stored.

Mukikel's plan (inasmuch as she had one) was not for Brenda to actually be a major part of the attack. Her real hope was that the Earthbound would either stupidly kill the trooper, bringing all kinds of mundane hassles down upon it, or cleverly deal with the trooper, which would still distract it from the three demons flanking it. She had overestimated how many people would be at the compound, but since she was best at controlling people, that meant she'd overestimated how useful she'd be in the fight.

She didn't pause to consider any of that, however. She was being mauled by a pack of dogs. They barked and snapped as they tore into flesh far sweeter than any they'd tasted before. They fought to get at her meatiest limbs, but none of their snarls were as hate-charged as her own as she howled back at them. It was the same dark evocation she'd used to disable Blackie, and while the dogs couldn't understand the spiritual depths of the blasphemies she showed them, the physical pain communicated quite clearly. They yelped and whined and fled.

She panted and fluttered a wing, only to realize it was snapped like a twig. She made a low hissing sound and stood, starting to walk forward instead of flying.

The sun was hidden as Shadrannat flung a handful of seeds at the ground—as it happened, pumpkin seeds. She scattered them in an arc, and the vines barely had time to surge to life before the mudslide oozed into one side and the zombies started to crawl and clatter around the other. She flapped back, retreating from the pincer movement.

There was a moment when she felt it—felt the shift of power into one stumbling corpse, so intense it was like a stab of pain or a shiver of pleasure—and then that body detonated, leaving a crater and a hole in her vegetable wall. Unripe pumpkin rind rained briefly down.

She was buzzing orders at the vines, telling them how to grow into the living dirt, telling them how to bind it, and now it was the force of growing things matched against the strength of falling granite. It was wrestling free, and she had only one second to think, plan, then there was that feeling of impending power once more, it was going to be a good trick…

Step One: Ramp up the momentum on the ticking zombie bomb. Instead of stumbling a couple of feet around the barrier before turning to her, it lurched forward and slid about ten feet to her left.

Step Two: Command the vines to expend all their strength and grow right, pulling the stone that way.

Step Three: Jump back, out of blast radius, as Avitu's detonating zombie destroyed Avitu's animate mud.

The last two zombies—Who was buried out here, anyhow?—were too slow to catch her, too slow to even escape the remaining vines as they wound around their tibias and fibulas. Bone was weak. Avitu could leave them to struggle helplessly against the plants, or she could destroy the plants by sacrificing her pawns. Whatever.

It made Shadrannat smile. Only a little hurt, she flew aloft and forward.

Buniel wasn't doing nearly as well. He'd just started to feel the Tree's presence when Avitu reached out to the dirt right in front of him and awakened it. It stood up, forming into a living wall, under his front axle. At top speed, he went airborne and landed on the roof.

Luckily, Buniel had a split second before impact, and he used it to change shape. As a living column of fire instead of a sack of bones and blood, he was far more crush-resistant. It still hurt—a lot—but he stayed conscious, pulled himself out of the wrecked jeep and started healing himself as he charged for the tree. His mud monster was right behind him.

But it was Officer Brenda Eisling who reached Avitu first. She pulled up her truck, parked it and hit the lever that revealed the gas cap. Then she calmly got out and started siphoning gas from the tank into a two-gallon plastic container.

Avitu wasn't exactly sure how to deal with Eisling. On one hand, the woman was clearly a menace. On the other hand, her priesthood seemed very clear on the idea that simply disposing of her would cause trouble. The best thing, it seemed, would be for her to leave unharmed and *then* cease to be a problem.

A breeze blew from Avitu's branches, and though she felt nothing, Brenda suddenly had a tumor in her brain. (Making it a brain tumor instead of lung or ovarian cancer had been Grant's suggestion. He felt the brain lesion would provide an excuse for any odd things the trooper might say.)

Another little gust gave Brenda narcolepsy. Without a word, she folded onto the ground and slept. As she fell, she knocked over her gas can. Petrol gurgled out, soaking her clothes and the sand.

In his own vehicle, Teddy pulled up and stared as Mukikel came into view. He wondered if he should try to stop this… thing? But Lance! Lance was in trouble; Lance had already *seen* it.

"Avitu," he whispered, "what should I do?"

But his Goddess was too busy consulting with others, too busy trying to understand the concept of the modern state police force, and she could not advise him.

"YOU," the apparition hissed at him. "GO... EAST. DIG UNDER THE... FENCE. THEN KEEP... WALKING."

Like Blackie, he was not compelled. But Avitu had told him that was where Lance was going, so he decided discretion was the better part of valor.

After all, if Lance and I both die, then only Blackie and Tim have the sacred blood, and Tim's is so weak, he thought. He didn't even want to think about Tim Grady trying to procreate.

Right after not thinking about that, he saw Blackie, huddled in the sand weeping. The dogs were around him, licking his face and whining. Teddy slowed, thought about helping his fellow priest, but Lance was so young, and the fence was electrified...

He told himself he'd pick up Blackie on the way back.

As the Devourer saw the Tree, the first drops of rain began to fall.

Here goes nothing, she thought, but somehow it was Jennifer's words that came out of Shadrannat's mouth.

"REEEMEMBER MEEEE, BIIIITCH?"

A crushing wall of wind slammed into her, whisking her down toward the ground, but she was ready for it. She'd fought her share of Scourges and the trick was to go with it, to put on the brakes a second before touchdown, then root yourself and throw the machete...

Her blade hit wood with incredible force—she'd tweaked its momentum until it had the inertia of a V-6 engine instead of a five-pound piece of steel. It sank in to the hilt, but did little apparent damage.

After all, this wasn't a person she'd skewered. It was a tree that had stood for over two thousand years.

Lightning stabbed down and Shadrannat smelled ozone as she dodged, barely in time, and then her voice buzzed forth once more, calling out to seeds.

In this case, the six pumpkin seeds wedged in the handle of her hard-hurtled machete.

They burst forth, blind and wriggling and questing for dirt. They found it quick enough—she'd thrown low, by the pine tree's base, and now her six vegetable servants were digging down deep, looking for Avitu's roots, pulling it up, pulling it out of the soil.

Mouthless, Avitu could not scream, but deafening thunder cracked as she called lightning to her own base, a fat forked flame that turned the attacking vines to ash and melted the machete. The hot steel slag kissed flames to life on the wood as it ran down. Her own might burned her, exposed her heartwood core, severed a third of her roots, but saved the rest of them...

And distracted her long enough for Shadrannat to get close. A lumberjack swing buried her second machete three inches deep in the dense, ancient pine, and the last of her seeds fell as she drew breath to raise them...

But the seeds and the weapon and the demon herself flew backward at Avitu's command, the wind she called down ripped needles from her branches and swept out, strong enough to push even mighty Shadrannat, let alone those pumpkin seeds, they were scattered and gone and the butterfly warrior was pinned to the ground, flat on her back, an easy target for the lightning's next stroke.

Then Mukikel staggered into view.

"MAD AND HATED ASHARU," she shrieked, "I CONDEMN THEE IN LUCIFER'S NAME!"

Her words, her weapons, were hell-poisoned and vile, gnawing the tree like worms in the wood, corrupting and corroding not only the matter, but the energy that made it whole, attacking the life (or half-life) of Avitu bound within it. The winds howled, the lightning crashed and Overlord Mukikel fell to the desert, unmoving.

The Devourer screamed her commander's name and ran— the wind was now too strong, she couldn't fly. She ran to her friend, heedless of the next electrical bolt...

A third voice joined the fray, and it spoke combustion's language.

Still looking over his shoulder at his stony pursuer, Buniel spoke and ignited the gasoline. Brenda had no time to scream, no air to shriek with as she burst into flames, all that air was sucked away by greedy fire trying to reach those branches, trying to eel between the raindrops and get the wood that was usually so desert-dry. He spoke and the smoldering body of Avitu, embers lying next to red-hot steel, awoke again and burned.

The Tree's soil servant rolled over Buniel and engulfed him, but then it broke apart into dust.

The ozone-scent warning of impending lightning formed around Shadrannat and Mukikel, but then dispersed.

The truck burned. Officer Brenda Eisling burned. The Tree burned. But the demon Avitu could no longer feel the soil around her roots or the wind around her branches.

Buniel staggered over to his fellow soldiers, his form of fire guttering out like a match in the rain. He licked the bruised and swollen lips of Bailey Sanger's shape and stopped.

"Oh," he said, and his tone made Shadrannat—now, apparently, just plain Jennifer Arliss—look up, look away from her leader and friend. It made her ignore the ringing of thunder in her ears.

"Charles is invoking me," Buniel said. "Mitch has been taken."

A thousand miles away, in Calgary, the Morningstar sipped a double malt scotch and spied on the three warriors of "Lucifer's Army.'"

He was concentrating very hard on four things. He could do that.

Part of him was watching the desert donnybrook, coolly assessing the tactical choices taken by each side. He thought Shadrannat showed quite a bit of combative flair—the other three, less so. Avitu in particular, he felt, should have been more braced for a counterstrike—or pre-emptive strike. Had he known she was so weak... but there was always something more pressing, more urgent, more dangerous. Now, of course, there was no point in getting personally involved. Better to wait and watch how things played out.

That was the second topic on his mind—Avitu's future, particularly as it related to Usiel the Reaper. That pattern was tricky to read, thanks to Gaviel and Sabriel scuttling around in it like rogue spiders. It would be interesting.

The third topic concerned him a great deal, because he wasn't sure why it was on his mind.

It was a memory, and Lucifer was not a creature normally given to nostalgia.

But still, he kept thinking about John. John had been a theologian and a monk and a priest hundreds of years ago. Before Lucifer gave up faith. Back when the Adversary was still interested in finding keen minds with strong spirits, the better to bend them to his service.

John wasn't John the Baptist or John the Gospel-writer or any of the popes who took that name. He was from a comfortable monastery, he was pudgy and soft and wore some jewels. He looked unremarkable, but his mind was the equal of

Erasmus or Duns Scotus or even Thomas Aquinas. Had Lucifer not dealt with his works, this John might have changed the course of Christian thought.

Lucifer had revealed himself and tempted John, and John had refused him, which was interesting all by itself. Rather than master and slave, they'd become… well, never friends, but wary colleagues. Lucifer even told him about the man in the desert.

"It's much as it sounds in the Bible," the Morningstar told John. "A rabbi fasting in the wilderness. I offered him food, and he refused. I offered him protection, and he refused. I offered him mastery, and he refused. A good man, I suppose. Wise and compassionate and full of integrity. But God? How could he have been God? I *know* God. Or knew Him, at least. And in the presence of your Messiah, I did not feel Him."

"He was truly man?"

"Yes."

"If he was also truly God, could he not have hidden that from you?"

"Why would he?" Lucifer asked, though he had instantly thought of a legion of reasons.

John just shrugged and then said, "In what you've told me of your war, you speak of the Lord assaulting the world."

"Yes."

"Does that seem like the sort of thing He would do?"

"No."

John nodded, then asked, "What can an infinite being sacrifice?"

"An infinite being can sacrifice endlessly."

"Or can it sacrifice its infinity?"

Lucifer thought about it. He felt a chill.

"No…" he whispered.

"What if that shudder in the world—which maddened the skies, as you said, and threw all into chaos, as you said, and brought death into the world… what if that was God becoming mortal?"

Lucifer said nothing.

"What if God so loved the world that he would stop being God to save it?"

"Old man, you make no sense."

"Given the choice between infinite virtue and infinite power, could a being of unbounded goodness make any choice, save to—"

John never finished his thought, because the Devil killed him.

Then Lucifer had killed everyone John had talked with in the past year.

Then he'd burned the monastery to the ground and breathed a vicious plague into the land, so that the women and men of the region would have something to think about besides philosophy.

But still, John's thought lived on in him. What if?

"What if God is dead?" Lucifer whispered to himself, "and can live again only through human choice?"

The thought made him shudder.

The fourth thing on his mind was the destiny of his would-be followers, the so-called Luciferans. Usiel's words had made the Adversary uneasy. Could he condemn them? If God was in His Heaven, He had bound the Reaper to Hell for just such sweeping judgments. But lead them? Could he forgive himself for that?

Especially if God had sacrificed Himself?

Lucifer frowned and sipped and watched. Being the enemy of God was troublesome, but not as frightening as having no God to fear.

I will judge the Luciferans by these Luciferans, he thought, watching Mukikel and Shadrannat and Buniel. *And I will judge the fallen…*

A smile creased his features, which were middle-aged today, handsome, a little feminine.

Charles Rodriguez, had he seen that smile, would have called it compassionate and sad and gentle.

Had Mitch Berger been there to see it, he would have described it as mirthless and cold and utterly without pity.

Who better than God's servant, loyal even through his chastisement? I shall judge the fallen by Usiel.

Chapter Nine

Five days after Avitu burned, Gabe McKenzie kept watching a video tape. He'd actually brought it home, though it showed him nothing, and his five-year-old Samsung VHS player wasn't going to reveal anything that could hide from the FBI's Image Enhancement Lab. He would learn nothing, and he knew he would learn nothing. But he still watched.

So did Mrs. McKenzie.

It was a black-and-white surveillance tape from the jail where Tim Grady was held, while various agencies and offices tried to decide which of his trials to schedule first.

Grady's cell was tiny. The camera had a distorted image (though he'd seen it "unstretched" by a video processing program) because its bubble lens permitted every inch of the room to be seen, with the exception of perhaps the five square inches occupied by the camera and the wall directly behind it.

It wasn't an exciting tape. Grady sat. Seconds ticked by on a gray digital clock at the bottom of the image. 17:25:02. 17:25:03. 17:25:04.

"Here it is," Gabe said as 17:25:05 came up. Grady hadn't even twitched.

The screen went blank for a moment, a little rolling hiccup in the tape, and then the Hollywood Ice Pick was gone.

17:25:12.

"Did someone cut power to the building?" Mrs. McKenzie asked. The baby started to snuffle and make little mewling noises.

"Nope. And no one entered the cell—the hall cameras work fine and show that, and so do the guard station cameras and the guard logs. Besides, all the cameras have battery backups."

"Could someone have..." she trailed off, because the baby was starting to cry in earnest. With a casual glance down, she hiked her shirt up to nurse it.

"The wall behind it's solid. The camera is tamper-evident. There's no space large enough for a man to get through, other than this corridor, nothing that's adjacent to Grady's room except for other rooms, and they're all blocked by six inches of concrete. The walls are unharmed. He didn't go down the hall. The alarm got sounded two minutes after... after this. He couldn't have gotten far. They've turned the facility upside-down."

"Into thin air," she murmured.

For a moment they were silent. Gabe rewound the tape and watched it again.

"Maybe May will turn up, even with him gone," she said.

He said nothing.

"You think she's dead, don't you?" Mrs. McKenzie said softly. "You're hoping for remains."

Gabe shrugged. "Seeing this... anything's possible."

The phone rang. Gabe was tired, but he got up. His wife heard his side of the conversation.

"McKenzie. Yeah. Yeah?"

She could hear him perk up, hear the interest in his voice. "When? What, both of them? Are they still there?" A pause. "Damn it!"

He was quiet, listening, for a long time. He gave his wife and child a look, and she felt a sinking sensation. His expression wasn't happy.

"Let me talk it over with... yeah... well, hold on." He put his hand over the receiver, licked his lips.

"Go," she said. He blinked.

"How did—"

"You're not the only one in this house who can figure things out. Where are they? Never mind. When you're off the phone. If you think it'll help you find her, go."

"Yeah," he said into the phone. "I can go to Las Vegas. Tomorrow?" He glanced at his wife. "Yeah, all right. Yeah. You too." He sighed. "The big break. Sure. This case has 'big break' written all over it."

He hung up the phone.

"Mitch Berger checked into a hospital last week. Emergency room. Apparently he was close by when a gas station exploded."

"Mitch? He was..."

"The guard on duty the night Grady escaped. The guy who disappeared. And guess who rode with Berger in the ambulance?"

"I'll say Noah Wallace."

"Bzzt. It was Grady's other missing guard, Charles Rodriguez."

"So you're going to Las Vegas?"

"Looks that way."

The baby had quieted. Its throat worked steadily, and its eyes were closed.

"I'm very, very sorry," he said.

She sighed.

"Gabe," she said. "I love you for being the kind of man who'll go to these lengths for May Carter."

He nodded and gave her a little smile. It was sad, not happy.

"I love you for being the kind of wife who'll put up with me going to those lengths."

"You better go pack."

Grant Dagley's trip to Las Vegas was fraught with considerably more difficulty.

Avitu invoked him as soon as she was assaulted, and she fell silent when the tree burned. He allowed himself to hope — allowed it long enough to finish the bourbon in his glove compartment and huff himself dizzy. When he had a good fume-goof going, he decided to invoke her. After all, if she didn't answer... well, he was free once and for all, right? Free forever! Free to kill the son of that chicken-fried cunt O'Hanlon, free to lock up Tim Grady without fear of reprisal — or, for that matter, kill the crazy bastard for "resisting arrest." Shit, they'd give him a goddamn medal if he nailed the Ice Pick. His State's Attorney problems would just up and disappear...

The euphoria was good and solid as he hopefully said, "Avitu?"

GRANT DAGLEY.

It all came crashing down.

It kept crashing, too.

She wanted him to leave Illinois. Leave! Just up and... and leave! After he'd spent thirty lousy years carving himself a place, he was king of the mountain, and she was asking him to just abandon it, pull up stakes and haul ass for Las Vegas!

He resisted.

She explained that her compound in Nevada needed him, needed his expertise in security and law-enforcement.

He countered by talking about East Saint Louis. It was going so well, it was ripe to fall for her, he said.

Things had changed. There was no point in reaching for more when you can't hold what you have. Once Las Vegas was secure, perhaps he could return to Illinois, but she needed him there as soon as possible.

He proposed some alternate solutions. She ate part of his soul. He bought a plane ticket as soon as he could gasp into the phone again.

It got worse.

"Don't you worry, Grant," Gaviel the Devil said, pulling into Dagley's driveway with his fancy goddamn convertible. "I've got a friend here who's going to make this fugitive business far simpler. Sabriel? Let's go inside and give the sheriff a new face, would you?"

The woman in the back glowered at them both as she got out. "You're awful fucking free with my power," she said, as she crossed the threshold into Dagley's home.

(Grant had not let anyone into his house, other than a few meter readers and one time an exterminator, since his wife had died. It wasn't a weird house—no Ed Gein chamber of murder trophies, just a disorganized bachelor place. But he didn't like other people coming there. Now there was that smug shit Gaviel, and some skank with a bad attitude, and this sad sack slacker with a nervous expression and druggie eyes.)

"We could have a fascinating discussion about power and the possession thereof," Gaviel said, his lip curling. "You say it's your power." He turned to the long-haired man and said, "Thomas, make her change Dagley's face. He should be hideous."

Grant was just getting it straight that Thomas was the guy and Sabriel was the girl when the drugrat turned to her and woodenly said, "Sabriel, change Dagley's face. He should be hideous."

Grant stepped back, getting the sofa between him and the woman, but Gaviel pointed out that getting him a new identity was Avitu's will, and he'd hate to have to tattle to her about this situation...

Dagley screamed. He'd let her touch him, but he still screamed when he felt the change.

"Oh pipe down," she said, annoyed, and he felt his voice become hoarse, choked off.

"This could, then, be Thomas's power," Gaviel said, pedantic, "since he can command the use of it. But Thomas can't resist my charms. Too bad, Sabriel—you could just command him to release you. If you knew the way. And if he hadn't abjured you against compelling him."

"On your advice, I'm sure."

"On my advice, yes. Is this, then, my power? It seems that way now, certainly. But even I'm just a tool in the hands of the Keeper, the Tree."

Grant, a grotesque Elephant Man, felt his face and wept. The sound was barely a kitten's mew.

"That's perhaps too much," Gaviel said, his voice suddenly bored. "I mean, we're not trying to sell him to a sideshow. Ugly, but not memorable." His eye gleamed. "Say, why not make him black?"

Hasmed the Scourge played the slots. He wandered from casino to casino, marking time, waiting for his old buddy. He played quarter slots for a while, figured out the game, got bored. Tina was getting to know her new private tutor. Roscoe was at a gym, catching up with some old acquaintances who'd known him as a boxer, hadn't known him as a shaking, pathetic wreck.

He'd found a place that was all slots—the sign outside said, "Where the Nickel Player is King!" It was depressing. He felt like being depressed.

He'd pissed away $30 and was shifting down to the penny slots when he realized someone was looking at him.

"Take a picture, ass-eyes," he growled. "It lasts longer."

The man turned and fled. Hasmed kept cooling his heels, waiting for Gaviel.

The watching man didn't return, but he told his friend Sal that he'd seen another demon. When Barney described him, Sal had gone to look for himself.

"Would you have owned slaves?"

"What?"

"If you'd lived in the old south," Sabriel said. "If you'd had the money, had a plantation. Would you have owned slaves? Flogged them? Raped them to get you more slaves?"

"No!" Thomas twisted in his seat, looking away from her.

They were at the airport, and everything had gotten complicated. Not in a dangerous way, or in an interesting way, but complicated in a boring way. Like income taxes.

Gaviel had felt that it would be simpler and more dignified for them to hire a private jet instead of going through all those airline security checkpoints, and he'd also felt that Dagley should pay for it. That meant that Sabriel had to undo all her work on him (Dagley had insisted, and it made it a lot easier to turn his numerous bank accounts into cash) and that meant the sheriff had to cancel his airline ticket (which had been coach, actually). Now Grant and Gaviel were trying to figure out if they could get Gaviel's sports car into the cargo hold.

Sabriel and Thomas waited, sitting in the cramped backseat of Gaviel's convertible.

"Why not?"

"Look, I know where you're going with this, and it's not the same."

"Because I'm not human? You think Scarlett O'Hara considered her slaves human?"

"It's not the same 'cause you'd kill me otherwise."

She snorted. "Yeah. Good pretext. And you're right, if you free me now—you're one dead stoner fuck. But you could have just bound me against harming you. You could have negotiated any particulars you wanted—the standard 'never harm me' business, sure, but service until you die? You needed that much control to be safe? Sorry, Thomas. I think it was Foghat that once said, 'That dog won't hunt.'"

"Look, Gaviel said—"

"Oh, Gaviel told you to enslave me. If he told you to jump off a bridge… well, I know the answer to that one. You don't even remember him bossing you around in Dagley's home, do you?"

"He didn't command me—"

"Sure, believe whatever you like."

"Stop interrupting me!"

She turned to him, opened her mouth and shut it, then turned a bright red. He could hear her gritting her teeth.

"As you wish," she whispered.

"It's like that thing, you know? About having a tiger by the tail? You can't hold on and you can't let go. That's why I did this—you think I had a lot of choice? After you, damn, you tortured me and uglied me up and threatened to kill me by eating my soul an' shit? Come on! Why should I feel bad about, you know, taking control of a clear an' present danger?"

"Raping a murderess is just as bad as raping a nun," she replied. "And that's where this is going, isn't it?"

"What?"

"Come on. We both know you're going to." She turned to him, her face unhappy but her posture provocative. "I can be anything you want. You know this. I'm under your command. I know this." She was an exotic beauty today, curvaceous and dusky with fat smooth hands and a choker necklace. Dark almond eyes looked at him, moist and miserable. She unbuttoned the top buttons of her shirt. "You're going to sculpt me into whatever sick punishment shape you want, and I'll crawl and debase myself, and we'll both know who the boss is then."

"Stop it!" he shouted. "Be quiet! Don't move. Don't do anything!"

She obeyed. He looked away, back, sighed hugely, exasperated and shaken.

"Jesus, I'm not gonna. Shit, just because every guy you meet… I mean… quit looking at me!"

She turned away.

"Stop being so pretty. Not… ugly, just… Just be ordinary."

She nodded and complied.

"In fact, be a guy. Can you be a guy? Be a normal-looking guy."

She was.

"All right."

They sat in silence for a while.

"You can talk again, if you want to."

"What does my master wish me to say?"

"Oh Jesus Christ!"

"'Oh Jesus Christ,'" she repeated.

"Be quiet again. Don't speak until you have something worthwhile to say."

They were silent until Gaviel came to get them. They didn't speak to each other all through the flight, either.

"Pamela, hey! How's it going?"

Pam Creed jumped and her hands fluttered up in front of her. Then she saw a familiar face and relaxed.

"Oh hi there… uh…"

"Sal."

"Sal…"

"Well, the last time we talked, I told you my name was Pete," he said, flashing a crooked grin. He'd followed her into the casino bar and stepped up beside her at the counter. "I was wondering if you could tell me the name of your boss."

"Wait, you said your name was…"

"Yeah, I lied about that. Hey, you're a martini drinker, right? Dewey, could you… Thanks. An' two Millers for me an' Barney here," he said, with a gesture behind her. The bartender left, and Pam turned to see the man at her back. Her eyes got wide.

"You!"

"We're not going to hurt you," Barney said, his hands in front of him, trying to be soothing.

"Speak for yourself," Sal told him pleasantly, then laughed. "Just kidding, Pam, sheesh. Don't be so uptight. Where's Gwyn these days, huh?"

"You didn't hear?"

"Nuh uh."

"She's… gone."

"Gone? Gone how? 'Moved away' gone? 'Shallow grave' gone?"

"Just gone," she whispered.

Sal shrugged. "Yeah, well, I never liked her much. And she wasn't your boss, really, was she?"

"I don't know what—"

"The demon," Barney said, leaning in, his eyes turning fevered and very unpleasant. "You lay with her, didn't you? You have ground together and felt the intoxication of her vaginal secretions…"

"Barney, please! Cork the secretions, a'right?" He gave Pam a smile. "Just a name. That's all, huh? Say the name, and I'm outta yer hair."

"Look, I don't... I, I shouldn't..."

"It's like an irony, ain't it?" he said, conversationally, and his arm was around her, steering her away from the bottles and barstools, she pushed against it, but somehow she went with him because the alternative was making a scene and screaming and running. She'd look crazy, here where she worked she'd look crazy, and maybe she would have been willing to do it if she hadn't worried that she was crazy...

"You could call her," he said, leaning in, still smiling. "You could ask her help, yeah? But doing that, I find out the name. And that's all I want. So c'mon. You want help, don't you? You say that name, and I'm outta here. Badda-bing. Or..." he shrugged. "I dunno, I guess the alternative is, we make you want help more an' more. See?"

"You don't want her," Pam whispered. "You may think... but really, you don't. You don't understand. Gwyn was just... just the, the tip of the iceberg."

"I know, honey. I know. But I gotta talk to her. Really. My buddy here, he's pretty hard up, y'see?"

It was crazy, they were in public, but she had this helpless sinking feeling. She couldn't do anything to them until they did something. And once they did something, it would be too late to do anything. She was trapped.

She looked from one man to the other. One was feverish, mad. The other was icy sane, cheerful, merciless.

"Avitu," she said in a rush, "Help me, protect me, please, there are these two guys..."

And as swiftly as they arrived, Sal and Barney were gone.

"Langdon's dead," drawled the voice in Hasmed's mind. "An' that lil' twat Irene."

"Yeah yeah," the demon muttered into a dead phone receiver. "Tell me something important."

"The Savior's down."

"Down meaning down for the count, or down meaning what?"

"Down in Hell, boss. I put in the be-sure myself."

Hasmed breathed a sigh of relief.

"Yeah, an' you wanna hear somethin' funny?" Lee Boyer jr. asked. "The one chick left, Dez? She's gone all Rambo. I guess she didn' see the real Rabbadün or anything. Didn't know what she was really up against. Now she's buyin' all this shit that I'm from this secret government X-Files crap thing, hunting demons. She's dumb as a sack of potatoes but she's ready to go."

"Just one left," Hasmed said, licking his lips.

"Yeah, this Stone of whatever."

"Despair."

"In Guam? What the hell is he doing in Guam?"

"You'll find out, I bet."

"Yeah, I'll find out." Lee cackled. "You know what? This shit can be kinda fun."

"You need any more money?"

"Ask me again when we get to Guam."

Hasmed broke the communication and mentally resigned himself to losing his vassal. His feelings about it were mixed. On one hand, Boyer had really given away the store to him, and the guy was crazy enough to believe with a vengeance. But there was a queasy feeling Hasmed got. Drinking from Boyer's soul was like being halfway through a long chug from the milk bottle before you notice the grapey taste and realize it's turned.

He grunted and hung up and went back to the tables. Blackjack, today. He was losing.

Wherever the man with the awful scar and the sunglasses and the Cubs hat sat, players started folding, started getting up to leave. Some of them consciously decided that, in a city this full of sight and lights and gold-diggers, they just didn't want to look at him. For other players, it was subtler. Maybe they felt a queasy tinge of indigestion or weariness or an unaccountable chill. And it was nothing sudden and dramatic, but through perfectly casual movements, the area around him always seemed to get more and more empty, until the only people there were him and his dealer and maybe a waitress passing through.

One floor down and a hundred yards away, the opposite thing occurred. A man walked through the doors, and the crowds gathered near him. And once more, some consciously decided to follow the handsome stranger for a while. And some just felt unaccountably warm—not the dusty heat of the desert—but warm inside, like a glow of accomplishment even when they hadn't accomplished anything. Somehow, just his proximity made people feel wiser and stronger and sexier and more free. Men wanted to be near him. Women wanted to be underneath him.

As he walked up the steps and approached the lone blackjack player, the crowd folded back around him, almost like a matador flinging back his cape.

They sensed one another; they had for a quarter mile.

Hasmed finished his hand and turned to look at Gaviel.

Gaviel stopped, standing. He was perfectly at ease, and his face was blank.

Hasmed wanted to speak to him. More, he wanted to speak the True Language, the way wind talks to trees to make them move, the way light speaks to water and turns it into drifting clouds. He wanted to explain, and apologize, and explain why he didn't have to apologize.

"Old buddy," he said instead.

Gaviel embraced him. "My friend," he whispered. Sighs and coos came from Gaviel's admirers, who didn't know what had just happened but could tell it was something.

Hasmed wept.

"No offense, but fuggeddaboudit," Sal said, rolling his eyes, thinking *Sheesh, what is it with demons? You can't fuckin' talk to 'em without they think you wanna worship 'em.*

IF YOU DO NOT WANT A PACT, WHY HAVE YOU INVOKED ME?

"Does it have ta be the master-an'-servant thing? That's all I'm saying. I'm a businessman. I thought maybe you an' me could deal."

WHAT IS YOUR BUSINESS?

Let's say I deal in… hard-to-obtain goods, and services."

WHAT SERVICE ARE YOU OFFERING ME?

"Well, for one thing I can summon you outta Hell."

I AM ALREADY OUT OF HELL.

Sal bit his lip, almost started the Rebluhé, but then he figured that life was short—he might as well play balls out. "A'right, so the ship's sailed on that. What do you want?"

I AM INTERESTED IN SECURITY.

"Security, fuggeddaboudit, I'm yer man! Whatcha need, dogs? Guns? Motion detectors?"

WHAT CAN YOU DO AGAINST DEMONS? RABISU WHO CAN REND FLESH WITH A WORD? NAMARU, WHO CAN DO THE SAME TO MINDS? WHAT SECURITY CAN YOU OFFER AGAINST THOSE WHO SCULPT THE EARTH WITH NO TOOL BUT WILL, AND WHO COMMAND THE STORM AND THUNDER?

Sal thought hard. "There's only one thing that's good against them," he said. "Information."

There was a long pause.

YOU BEGIN TO INTEREST ME.

"Summoning, binding, all that jazz... that'd sure gum up the works for your Rabisu and Naramu, yeah? I got some contacts, some people who are just itching for names to screw around with. I can't promise that these punks are going to completely boss up your enemies, but it can't hurt, right?"

AND WHAT DO YOU WANT IN RETURN?

"Well, I've got a start on this whole 'demon ritual' shit, but what I'd like is sort of a second opinion. Someone to look over the answers on my homework, y'know?"

THAT IS A GREAT FAVOR YOU ASK.

"Oh please. You guys can, what, change people's shapes? Fly around the world in an eye-blink? Turn invisible and make people sick and I don't know what the hell else? I mean, looking over a ritual an' saying 'Here's where he pops out of the circle and eats your ass' doesn't sound like much next to rending a mind with a word. I may not be ten thousand years old, but I wasn't born yesterday."

Sal worried that he was sounding too arrogant, and his eyes flicked across the hotel room to where Barney was absorbed by a GameBoy and a bottle of gin.

"In fact," Sal said, "why don't I bring you a lil' somethin' to prove my goodwill?"

"He thought the Cubs were due," Hasmed said, shrugging.

"Someone should have explained to him that the World Series isn't a library," Gaviel replied.

Gaviel hadn't been able to get his convertible on the plane, so he was renting a Jaguar while a service driver brought his out over the highways. Dagley had rented another vehicle—a Ford Explorer, of course—and gone straight for the compound with Sabriel and Thomas. Gaviel had stayed back to pick up Hasmed and Tim Grady.

As the three of them drove, Grady sat still in the backseat, hulking and immobile, gazing out into the desert, barely blinking.

"I saw the dead," he said. "I saw everything dead."

The two demons ignored him. Periodically he'd say some random, kook thing. They just tuned it out.

"I hope you're right," Hasmed said, after a few miles of silence.

"Right about what?"

"About everything."

There was another pause.

"How much do you think she's changed?" Hasmed asked.

"Plenty."

"Like you an' me, I guess."

"Yes."

Hasmed watched mile markers and highway reflectors switch past. "It's kind of funny."

"Yes," Gaviel said, unsmiling.

"That I used to be her commander, I mean."

"That's what I meant, too."

They talked about their host bodies for a while.

"She was coming to get me," Tim Grady said.

They ignored him.

Then Gaviel sat up straighter in the driver's seat. "Do you feel that?"

Hasmed looked around, squinting. "Yeah."

"Who do you think?"

"Dunno."

They both peered out around them, trying to see the entity they sensed. Gaviel looked over his right shoulder briefly, then did a frowning double take. "Back there, I think."

Hasmed turned all the way around in the passenger seat. "Uh… yeah."

"You think it's an agent from your old boss?"

"I wouldn't think so. We'd see it if it was one of us. Probably nothing to see."

"One of the ghost-binders, then."

"Or one of their servants."

Gaviel shrugged. Hasmed kept staring until the sensation faded.

The ghost of Rosemary Nevins left the car and drifted along the side of the road, thinking about how they could feel but not see her. That could be unpleasant.

But on the plus side, she'd leaked news of Grady's escape to the papers, and now he was nationally famous. The movie about her murder was getting re-released on DVD.

As a mortal, she'd always craved attention. As a ghost, the craving was far more intense.

"How's he doing?" Blackie asked softly. He glanced up at his father, saw Teddy's red-rimmed eyes, and quickly looked away again.

They were in front of the cabin. Blackie was leaning against the wall by the door, keeping in the shade. Teddy stepped out of the door, closed it and sat on the stoop, shaking his head.

"It comes and goes. You have to understand, he… he isn't protected like I am. Or even you. That thing was… it was the first time he ever… experienced…" He sniffed, hard, and his voice showed how hard he was trying to control himself. "He hasn't accepted Avitu and... and that monster, that thing... seeing it unshielded..."

"Yeah."

"His consciousness," Teddy spat. "That creature has infected it. Aggravated the fever of mind. He seems fine for a while, hours on end, and then, for no reason, he gets up and he... he tries to go to the fence."

"The command will wear off, right?"

"Avitu can't heal it!" Teddy cried. "She can't... can't restore consciousness, it would be..." He shook his head and uttered a weird, despairing laugh. "It would be unconscionable."

"What if he did... what you did? Became, you know... a priest?"

"I don't think so. I think the damage is done. Besides, he won't."

"What do you mean, he won't?"

"I... tried to explain the Goddess to him. It..." Teddy licked his lips. "It didn't help. He said, 'You want to feed me to one of them.' That's what he thinks, that Avitu and, and what he saw... he thinks they're the same thing and that I... that me his father, he thinks I..."

Blackie crouched down and put his arm around Teddy's shoulders. "Look, I..."

"Like you," Teddy said suddenly, turning a sharp gaze on his oldest child. "You haven't accepted her either."

Blackie stood up, stepped back. "It's... you know it's hard for me. I don't get the dreams like you and ma... like you do."

"It's more important now than it has ever been," Teddy said, his eyes intent. "The death of the Tree... the physical tree, I mean... it has been hard for the Goddess. She has lost much of her power to work freely in the world. Now, her last and best tie is us, the priests of the blood! Tim has it, and the will to serve, but it's not strong in him like it is in me, like it was in... in your mother." Teddy paused, working his lips and his teeth against each other. "Like it is in you."

The younger man said nothing.

"Black Hawk, it's your destiny. You know it's your destiny, right?"

"You should call me Oscar," Blackie said, looking at a cloud of dust rising past the fence. Someone was coming.

Teddy sat in silence for a moment, staring down at the dust between his feet.

"How can I do this to my own son?" he asked.

"You're doing what you think is right."

Teddy lifted his head. He didn't immediately speak, but his posture changed. One moment, he was slumped in despair, but a new energy seemed to straighten his back, lower his shoulders, smooth the anxiety from his face.

"Lance needs to be sacrificed," he said.

"Wait," Blackie said.

"No, it's clear to me. Really, he's no good as a priest now, the… the curse, the madness has too strong a hold. He'll never accept… he could never comprehend how important it is, and it has to be voluntary, I can't make him a priest. And if he can never be a priest, why should he have to suffer?" Teddy stood and turned toward the door.

"No, let… let me do it," Blackie said.

Slowly, Teddy turned.

"It might be… you know, easier. For me. And for you. And I… I mean… it's time, isn't it? It's time I got off the fence and decided to go all the way. Do it. Become a priest." He swallowed. "Accept Avitu completely."

Teddy looked deep into his eyes and then embraced his son.

"We can do it tonight," he whispered.

Then a horn honked, and Blackie's eyes jerked open as he heard a familiar voice shout, "Hey! You guys wanna let us in here?"

Thomas couldn't help noticing the way the tall, swarthy guy kept staring at Dagley. He introduced himself as Oscar Black, said the guy with him was Teddy Mason—"the High Priest," a phrase that made Thomas giggle and earned him a quizzical look—and when the sheriff said his name was Grant Dagley, Black's face got even weirder. It wasn't like a proper expression—it was just a complete blankness. Almost like he was dead with his eyes open.

"You got a problem?" Dagley asked the guy.

"No, no, just... you're here because..."

"I serve at the pleasure of my master, Avitu," he said, and he didn't bother to hide his bitterness. "These two needed an escort, I guess, and I'm s'posta beef up security 'round here."

"That's right," Teddy said, glancing at Thomas and Sabriel. "I was told to expect them. You two are..."

"I'm Sabriel," she said, "And this is my master, the great sorcerer Thomas Ramone."

"Quit it," he said to her, glaring.

"Forgive me, master. Have I spoken out of turn?"

"Just don't... aw, forget it. Look, where should we take our stuff? Gaviel said we'd be staying out here."

"For the time being, I guess. We don't have very... you know, luxurious, mm, quarters. There's the other cabins, I guess..."

"My master and I can take one," Sabriel said, "and the sheriff can have the other."

Oscar Black whispered something in Teddy's ear.

"Oh," he said. "Well, put her... excuse us for a moment, will you?" He and Oscar had a brief huddle. "Oscar here is going to clear something out, and then we'll have it ready for you. Sorry for the delay."

Oscar hurried off, and Teddy made small talk—how was your flight? Uh huh. Hot enough for you? Yes, but it's a dry heat—until the other man returned, looking a little aggrieved.

"All ready?"

"Yeah, she's in the longhouse." Oscar picked up suitcases and started forward.

"Mr. Dagley? Do you want to go get settled first?"

Grant's eyes flicked to Sabriel, and then to Thomas. Tom noticed just a little sneer.

"Naw, I'd prefer to get cracking. Let's see what y'all got."

"Well, I guess I should start with the perimeter fence." Teddy paused, then turned to Mr. Black.

"After you drop off their luggage, take Thomas to the Tree."

Something about the way he said it made Thomas uneasy, but he couldn't have said what.

Mitch Berger was down to three pain pills.

He'd had them with him ever since that weird day when Shadrannat and Mukikel came for him. They were left over from his physical therapy, from getting his leg working partway right again. He'd gotten in the habit of carrying them. They were in a little canister on his key-chain, and he hadn't bothered to clean it out when he stopped using them.

He'd had eleven pills when he made his break from the hospital.

Escape wasn't hard. He'd been a nurse at a maximum security asylum, so he knew how security worked and how it failed. He knew that he was low-risk—burn victims who weren't crooks or kooks rarely took it upon themselves to get out of bed and flee. But he'd done just that.

He took his pain meds and stumbled out of bed and down the hall. He watched nurses and orderlies until he found their locker room, and then he let himself in and helped himself to a Polo shirt and some Haggar slacks.

The burns were mostly on his arms. He'd turned his head when Buniel cried out, so one ear and the side of his neck was scalded too. His clothing had protected his legs and his chest, but he'd instinctively flung up his arms, so they were burned pink and tender from the elbows down to the palms.

He knew the burns weren't that bad since they'd put him in the "stable" ward and were talking about releasing him the next morning.

Mitch did not want to go back to Mukikel and Shadrannat. Thanks, but no.

There had been all of sixty cents in the pants pocket, but it was enough to call a cab. He took the cab down to the strip and bailed out on the driver, who shouted at him but didn't give chase.

Mitch was sure the cabby would call the cops, so he had to move fast. He didn't want to use his credit cards—he knew the cops could track him through those, and with demons, shit, who could tell?

He walked to the bus station, where it took him about half an hour to find a pusher. He gave the man a sample of his pain meds (and took one himself—his arms felt like they were still on fire), and through a drug haze they negotiated: six pills for the price of a ticket to Austin.

Mitch sprawled in an uncomfortable bench—shit, it had to be uncomfortable if he could feel it through his drugs—and picked at the bandages on his arms and grew weary of the askance gazes of the other patrons. He sat and bit his lip and was certain that Mukikel and Shadrannat would walk in to reclaim him any minute.

But the bus came before them.

That had been five days ago, and nothing since then had felt as close. Until today, maybe. Mitch had a cousin in Austin, someone who was more physically close than emotionally close, but when Mitch showed up with burns on both arms and no cash, she was willing to put him up and not ask questions— or at least, take it gracefully when her questions went unanswered.

Now, Mitch was driving in her borrowed car. He was headed toward a small town, picked pretty much at random by the simple virtue of having a bank and being four hours away from Austin. He'd called his old landlord in LA, he'd called a friend there too, and arranged for the friend to get his mail from the landlord. Then he'd had his friend send the mail to a PO Box halfway to his bank-cashing town.

No one had jumped him when he got the checks, and they'd give him enough to live on for a couple of months—long enough to heal up his arms and get some under-the-counter job. If he could just cash them without getting caught.

What could go wrong?

The cabin was stripped down and utilitarian. Poured concrete floor, a row of cots and footlockers, no shades on the windows, sinks that produced no water.

"We're getting water later in the summer," Blackie—as Oscar—explained, "but for now we use the shower house. And the, uh, outhouses... we passed those on the way in."

"Like summer camp," Thomas muttered.

"I'm sorry it's kind of..." Blackie shrugged.

"So... when I 'see the Tree'..."

"Shall I come with you, master?" Sabriel asked.

"Quit calling me that, okay?"

"Forgive me."

"I think it's... uh, just supposed to be you alone," Oscar said.

"I would be remiss if I let my master go into peril without me," Sabriel said.

"I... ummm..."

"Or, you could invoke one of your other diabolical allies for advice, if you suspect mine," she said, her voice utterly docile and sweet.

Thomas glared at her and said, "Gaviel. The Tree wants me to go to it, uh, without Sabriel. You think I should? Yeah? You? Okay."

He shrugged.

"That's our... other guest?" Blackie asked, a crawling feeling in his gut. He'd gotten used to seeing Teddy invoke Avitu, and Tim... well, Tim was just so fucked up in every direction that invocations didn't stand out. But seeing this new guy do it, to some demon, and so casually...

Avitu and his dad seemed confident that these guys were all right, but Blackie had his doubts.

Especially when they showed up with Grant fucking Dagley in tow. Blackie had gone to the Las Vegas library and looked up where he was when his mother got raped. He'd gotten a librarian to help him find out who was the sheriff there, and he was surprised to see that their assailant was the man in charge—and that he was in the papers for a corruption investigation. (The corruption didn't surprise him, but he was pleased that someone was looking into it.) He mailed in an anonymous tip about Dagley's barn, and he followed the regional papers, but apparently Joan Pratt's team hadn't found his accusations credible.

And now… here he was. Out in the middle of nowhere, and the ass-wipe hadn't recognized Black Hawk O'Hanlon, thanks to the efforts of Las Vegas's finest unscrupulous plastic surgeons.

How easy could it be? Sure, the guy was a cop and armed, but he had no reason to suspect "Oscar Black."

Only… it didn't make sense, and he didn't like it, because the guy clearly knew all about Avitu.

"Huh." Thomas Ramone's voice brought Blackie back to the present. "I expected it to look… different."

"Well, up until last week, it did."

"What happened last week?" Cautiously, Thomas got closer, looked at the burned roots, the burst trunk and the blackened metal slag, solidified where it spilled between the tree and the sand.

"We had some uninvited guests."

"Shit."

"Yeah," Blackie said, thinking, You don't know the half of it. I'm the one who wound up burying a burned-up Nevada State Trooper in the middle of the desert.

Then he thought about Dagley again. Room for one more.

"So… do I…"

"Just go up and touch the Tree." He turned his head and said, "I don't mean any disrespect, Mr. Ramone, but… I mean, aren't you… familiar with all this?"

"What, 'cause I'm s'posta be some big bad-ass sorcerer?" Thomas snorted. "It's a long story but… um, short answer, no." He bit his lip. "So, what's gonna happen?"

"Well, she might just talk to you. Or she might take you somewhere."

"Huh?"

"She's got… other spaces. Part of her is in those other places." Blackie looked down at the ground and scratched his head. "It's kind of hard to explain."

"I bet."

"There's the Blue, it's... well, you can't really describe it."

"It's blue, though."

"Actually, it isn't. Or there's the clouds. That's almost normal, except you're in clouds. Or she could pull you down into the earth, but I think she only does that when she wants to... um... preserve you."

"Preserve?"

"It's like suspended animation. I was in it for a while, you don't even... don't even feel time pass."

Thomas just turned to him with a wide-eyed look of abject fear.

"I'm not sure I—"

And then the sorcerer vanished.

Blackie waited a little while, then went and checked to see how May was doing in the longhouse. She was a little freaked out at the two other potential sacrifices, and they were a little freaked out by her, so he did his best to calm everybody down. It didn't do much good.

When he came back to the Tree, the demon-binder was sitting on the ground, eyes wide, breathing heavily.

"You okay, Mr. Ramone?"

"I'm... aw fuck, what was that? I mean, dude, what was that?"

"The Blue, I'm guessing."

"People aren't s'posta see that! I mean, it's... it's wrong!" He looked like he was going to cry.

"My da— the High Priest says you get used to it. He looks forward to it, says it's starting to feel like... the natural way to think."

"Shit, I wish I was as high as your High fucking Priest."

Blackie suppressed a snort. From the ground, Thomas looked up at him with a speculative look and—it made Black

Hawk feel self-conscious and confused—the sorcerer looked weak and afraid, too.

"You wanna spark up a doob?" Thomas Ramone asked.

Blackie blinked. It took him a moment to believe what this stranger was offering.

"Yeah!" he said.

Gaviel honked the horn as he pulled up to the gate. He waited, while Hasmed drummed his fingers on the dashboard. Gaviel had gotten a bright silver Jag, and now it was covered with dust.

"I'll have to get that washed, tomorrow," Gaviel said.

"What's the point?" Hasmed asked. "You're just going to turn it in when your other car gets here."

"A car like this deserves to be clean. I'll get some beater for the commute out here, keep the convertible for town."

"You're not staying out here?"

"Tonight, yes, but I don't see any reason to spend most of my time in some wasteland dust-farm where they can't even get the fence open." He honked again.

"I guess it's up to Avitu, isn't it? Where we stay, that is." Hasmed said. Then he cocked his head. "Yeah? Well, c'n you send someone to let us in?" He waited.

All three of them waited.

"Fuck it," Hasmed said. "I'll open the damn thing."

As he unwound the chain, he had a weird flashback. It wasn't his own memory—it was one from his brain, Harvey's brain. It took Hasmed a moment to place it.

Harvey opened a fence like this, with a chain, the day he died.

He felt a strange chill, but he shook it off and returned to the car.

Hasmed didn't bother to re-attach the lock, so the fence was still open when Sal and Barney drove up twenty minutes later.

Out on the perimeter, Grant's rambling discourse on security was interrupted once more.

"Excuse me," Teddy apologized, "but Avitu is speaking to me."

"Again?" Grant rolled his eyes.

"What is it, my mistress?"

Teddy listened, and his face furrowed up.

"Blackie didn't go do that?"

He frowned.

"Well, I'll call him again. And maybe I should start heading back towards the gate, too. I guess. Yes." Another pause. "Of course. I'm sure it's nothing. No, he's obedient. In fact, he's going to join the priesthood tonight!" Teddy waited, listening, once more. "I obey."

"We have to go back?" Dagley asked.

"I'm afraid so. I tried to call Blackie's cell, but he didn't answer. I'm going to page him, but if he doesn't have his phone he might not have his pager, either. I'm sorry."

"This seems like a kind of grab-ass setup, if you don't mind me saying."

Irritation flicked across the High Priest's face. "We are a little disorganized, yes, but—"

"Well, don't expect to get real safe if you keep putting off security because you're 'disorganized.'"

"Things are under control."

"Okay. Still, I'm mighty glad I brought my guns. From now on, I want everyone armed when they're on the compound."

"I'll consider your suggestion," Teddy said. "Now, if you don't mind?"

After a moment's indecision, Black Hawk had ditched his pager and phone back in the cabin with Lance while Thomas got his stash from his luggage. Then the two of them had walked out into the grit, lathered up with sunscreen, and started toking.

At first, they just exchanged weed stories—first time, worst time, best bud, close calls. Thomas told him about getting arrested and actually being high when he went before the judge.

"I'm tellin' ya," Thomas said over Blackie's laughter, "If I hadn'a been stoned, the guy would have thrown the book at me. As it was, I guess I didn't seem guilty. Y'know? 'Cause he let me off with a warning."

"How did a guy like you ever get involved with demons?" Blackie asked the question before he even thought about it.

Thomas rolled onto his back and stared up at the cloudless sky for a moment.

"Well, I decided to break into this house. I was pretty sure the owner was gone for the night, 'cause her car wasn't there. But it turned out her car was just in the shop."

He told the story, and at first he made it funny, but as he went on it got less and less so. Blackie giggled less and listened more.

"Jesus," he said at one point.

When Thomas was finished, they were quiet for a while. Then Blackie told how he'd come to know the Tree. He left out quite a bit, of course—all his mother's murders, for one thing, his real name, that gas station clerk they beat up—and the outline that remained was enough to get Tom shaking his head in sympathy.

"That sucks," he said.

Then Blackie asked Tom how he'd come to master Sabriel, and Tom told him. By the time the joint was smoked past the smallest roach, and the THC buzz was wearing off, they were pals.

"An' just who are you?" Sal asked, his eyes narrow.

"I am a servant of Avitu," Tim said.

"Uh huh. I thought some guy named Thomas was gonna check this thing. Some kind of independent contractor."

Tim paused, like he was listening.

"Thomas is not available. I can do what you request."

"Okay. But don't fuck with me, you got it?"

Sal had been understandably dubious about the first "safe summoning" ritual Vodantu had dictated to him. He'd shown it to Dr. Roark, who'd been uneasy but excited, and who had eventually decided that it had a few "errors" in it. He'd gone back to the demon prince and said "nice try" and had gotten a "corrected" ritual that Roark seemed to think was "orthodox." He had both versions—the one she'd dinged and the green-lighted one—typed out and paper clipped. This "Tim" guy seemed like a retard to him, but he handed over the pages.

Tim gazed at them, his face blank. "This is wrong," he said, pointing.

Sal kept his poker face, but re-evaluated his assessment. Tim had found the same error as Roark, but he'd done it in seconds. The woman with the Ph.D. had taken an hour.

"This version is okay," Tim said presently.

"And by okay, you mean..."

"It will summon the Neberu you desire and bind him into a structure. He will be compelled to accede to any agreed-upon commands, most particularly the command that he never harm you, either directly or indirectly."

Sal cracked a big smile. "Pleasure doing business with you."

Tim's face displayed nothing. "What about the worshipper you promised?"

"He's in the car." But when they reached the vehicle, Barney was gone.

"Oh, that crazy little fuck," Sal snarled. He looked at Tim. Still no expression.

"I'm sorry 'bout this," Sal said. "I'll fix that little rat for you, I tol' him to wait inna car..."

Finding him wasn't hard: He'd left clear prints in the dust. He was standing in the doorway of a cabin, an expression of rapt joy on his face.

"Makiko," he breathed, gazing inside.

"Good grief," Sabriel said, wrinkling her nose in distaste and disbelief. "Did you really manage to find me after all this time?"

"I felt you," Barney said. "Once we got close, I felt it. I smelled your secretions."

She shook her head and clucked her tongue. "Wow, I really spanked your inner child, huh? Well sorry chump, but this window's closed for business."

"But you have to," Barney shrieked, and Sal wouldn't have thought the old bum could move so fast, lunging at her. Sal took a step toward him, but one of Tim's meaty hands held him back.

The mobster sized up the psychopath and did some mental math. "Look, pal," he said, but then he trailed off.

Barney had grabbed Sabriel by both shoulders, and she'd laughed. And then she'd... flowed... out of his grasp, like water spilling out of a glass, she dissolved and reformed as a slender little Japanese girl.

"This is what you want, isn't it? But why would I? Hm? You got money? Power? You have nothing, so you can't have me. So sorry." Again, that tinkling laugh. It was lovely. Barney made a few more grabs, getting more and more desperate.

"Would you serve Avitu for what you want?" Tim asked.

Barney turned to face him, eyes wide with desperate hope.

"Would you serve Avitu for the pleasure of this creature?"

"Yes! Forever!"

The changing woman started, and Sal had never seen such a look of perfect horror. He'd killed a helpless man with a power drill, and that guy hadn't looked this afraid.

"Don't," she whispered, but Tim spoke. That weird gobbly language, the one Sal had first heard from Hasmed. Tim Grady spoke the name Thomas had spoken at the pond, the name he'd called out over the salt and ice, and Sabriel's cry of despair was wedded to Barney's laugh of delight.

Sal stared, his skin crawling.

"I believe our business is concluded," Tim said.

It was the merest coincidence that Hasmed didn't see Sal going to his car, but Hasmed had other things on his mind. There'd been some crazied-up kid scrabbling at one of the cabin doors, and Gaviel had started to talk to him. Apparently the kid was named Lance.

Hasmed watched with little interest as Gaviel worked at untangling the kid's crossed wires, and then Lee had invoked him, desperate, pleading for help against the Stone of Despair. Hasmed had nothing to offer him but a quick death. He'd known that crazy milk-sucker would probably snuff it against the Stone, but he'd hoped Lee wouldn't reveal Hasmed's name at the end. But what could you do? Nothing. Nothing except drain away as much of the guy's soul as he could get before the Stone killed him. Damn shame, but he still had Paum and Tina.

Hasmed went out to the toilet while Gaviel kept talking to Lance.

"SO YOU SEE, YOU DON'T HAVE TO GO TO THE FENCE."

"No, I... I don't have to go to the fence."

"YOU DON'T HAVE TO KEEP WALKING EAST."

"I don't have to keep walking east." Lance chuckled and shook his head. "Man, yeah, that's kinda crazy."

"And you never saw an angel or a devil." Gaviel's voice was normal now, but the tones of command were still present—just hidden. "It was probably heat stroke."

"Yeah. I was running around with the dogs an' everything..." Lance trailed off, a small happy smile on his lips.

"So, what games have you got for that GameBoy?" Gaviel asked, but then the phone rang. He excused himself and answered it.

"Hello?"

"Hello, can I speak to... uh, who's this?"

"May I ask who's calling?"

"My name's Jim... Tompkins. I'm with the, uh, electric company? We've got a question, mm, about your bill out there."

"I'm afraid I don't know anything about that sort of thing."

"You don't even know who I'd send it to?"

"No, sorry."

"What about an address?"

"I'm not sure where they're having bills sent, but I can find out and have someone call you back. Mister... Thompson, was it?"

"Tompkins. Jim Tompkins. Why don't I give you my phone number and address?"

Gaviel wrote down the information and, at the caller's request, read it back. Then he politely said goodbye and hung up the phone.

At the other end of the line, a wide-eyed Gabe McKenzie did the same.

Gabe had been tracking Mitch Berger. He'd gotten the trail as far as the bus station from the Nevada clues—the cab driver had given the cops a good description, and a big guy with bandages all over his arms and neck stands out, even in Vegas. Then Berger's old landlord called in about the mail pickup. The LA bureau branch wouldn't do dick about finding the guy who got the mail, but it didn't matter once the checks got cashed. That sent up a flag and let Gabe eliminate all the east- and northbound buses from the station that night. One of the westbound busses went to Austin, and Mitch had a cousin there. When Gabe called her, she seemed nervous and cagey, and that was all Gabe needed to book a flight to Texas.

He'd only called Teddy Mason one last time in the spirit of tying up loose ends. He was shocked when he heard Noah Wallace answer the phone. It rattled him a little, but he kept the guy on the line, he taped the call and played it back against his old tapes of Wallace's interview, and damn it, it was him.

Gabe left the office without a word to anyone and went to a public library. He needed to think, he needed quiet, and he needed to review his notes.

An hour later, he came back to the office, cancelled his flight to Austin and started pulling strings for a raid.

In the lands of death, the Reaper of Souls flexed his wings and called his scythe.

"Sabriel," he whispered. "Is it time?"

Presently, the sun began to sink.

Thomas had come back from the desert with a terrible sunburn, he'd walked into his cabin and been shocked at what he found—shocked and disgusted. He'd ejected Barney with a series of shoves, slaps and kicks, and then listened, horrified, as Sabriel explained what had happened.

"You gave her my Name," Sabriel said, "and now I'm her slave as much as yours."

"Look, I didn't... I didn't just give it to her, I was, it was that Blue, that place, I couldn't... it was like she could read my mind! I mean, how was I s'posta..."

"You couldn't," Sabriel said, her voice leaden. "You're powerless against her. Just as you're powerless against Gaviel. Just as I'm powerless against all of you."

Her back was slumped, and matted black hair hung down in front of her eyes.

"Sabriel, I'm... shit, I'm so sorry..."

"You don't have to apologize to me," she said. "Slaves don't get apologies."

Teddy had chewed out Blackie, long and hard. In fact, he was louder and angrier with his bastard son than he'd ever been with his lawful one—more vicious and abusive than he'd ever been with anyone in his life. All the anger and resentment he'd held inside, all the horror at his wife's death, all the guilt that he felt for sleeping with her murderer… it all came spewing out, and once it started he couldn't seem to stop it.

The two of them argued so loudly and long that Teddy was in no mood to listen to Lance talk about his new friend. He ignored it, dismissed it as a lucid moment that would soon pass. The only thing that finished the shouting match was when Blackie started building a bonfire for the ceremony.

"Maybe when you're fully pledged to the goddess, you'll be more responsible," Teddy said, unbuttoning his shirt.

"Sure, whatever." Blackie kept shoving logs. Then he stopped. "What are you doing?"

"We should be naked for the ritual."

Blackie sighed. "Look, I know that's how it is in the dreams, but do you mind if I keep my clothes on? I mean, this is going to be hard enough without…"

"Fine! Shit, you are the most conscious person I know!"

Blackie recognized his father's foulest insult.

Once Blackie bucked the nudity trend, Dagley tried to do so as well—but Avitu insisted. Gaviel slipped out of his clothes easily, folding them in a tidy pile on a tarp, like Tim and Teddy. Hasmed rolled his eyes, shook his head and remained clad. So did Thomas, and the pair from the first longhouse—once Blackie had sacrificed Lance, Teddy would take over and do them. Sabriel asked Thomas if she should strip or not, and he told her no.

May wandered out when the door was left unlocked. She took one look at Gaviel and curled into a ball, clutching her head and moaning.

Teddy felt a pang when he saw Dagley emerge from the cabin, carrying Lance. The boy was screaming, struggling, but Teddy knew it was all for the best. The voice of Avitu whispered within him and he didn't cry. Crying was conscious, crying was the curse…

"The wand," Blackie whispered. He couldn't be heard over the sounds of Lance's shrieks, but his gesture was clear. Teddy held out the slim piece of wood, sharp and holy, the sliver of Avitu's body that was used to give sacred release...

Naked and impassive, Tim sat on Lance and pinned his arms down. Dagley squatted by the boy's head like a toad, clamping his head still.

"It's okay, son," Teddy whispered in Lance's ear. "Soon you'll be better. Soon all the pain will be gone."

In the firelight, the burnt-out tree seemed to writhe and dance.

Biting his lip, Blackie lowered the wand toward his half-brother's face.

"Nooooooo!" Lance howled. "Dad, don't! Don't let him!"

Blackie stared. Everyone waited.

"Do it," Gaviel said. "You know you want to. Do it now." Perfuming his words were the strength and lure that had led generations to defy Heaven.

Hearing those tones, Black Hawk O'Hanlon visibly relaxed. He breathed out, his shoulders dropped, he breathed in again.

Then he stabbed Sheriff Grant Dagley in the eye.

"Take that, rape-o!"

All hell broke loose.

In the chaos, no one noticed the sound of approaching engines.

Dagley screamed and turned away, but Blackie got a hard boot into the sheriff's face before Dagley could get his arms up.

"Black Hawk! What are you doing?" Teddy shouted.

Gaviel started to snicker.

Tim bolted up and seized Blackie, pinning his arms and lifting him, but Black Hawk landed one last solid kick on Dagley's chin before Tim pulled him away.

Lance immediately stood and started to run. His father tried to grab him, but the boy was too scared, too quick, too greasy with the sweat of fear.

A gun went off.

Teddy turned at the sound and heard a second shot, he saw Tim staggering back and bleeding. Blackie was holding a small pistol, one of the several Dagley had brought, and Teddy wondered if that was why he'd wanted his clothing.

Then the anger came back. Blackie was everything wrong with his life, rolled up into one package. He hadn't wanted Blackie, hadn't wanted to fuck Joellen, hadn't wanted to have sexual dysfunction because of it for decades, and now Blackie was ruining his sacrifice too. He had the holy blood, his blood, but so did Tim. That sacred blood was running out on the ground.

Teddy held out a hand, called Avitu's wind, and the pistol nestled in Dagley's clothing whirred through the air to him.

Gaviel turned and calmly walked to the Tree.

"Let's renegotiate," he said. Then he disappeared.

Teddy had never fired a pistol in his life, but he was too close to miss, he aimed it right at his son's head but Blackie had his arm free and his gun was up too.

A Mexican standoff.

"You bastard!" Teddy shrieked.

"Your bastard!" Blackie shouted back. The two men glared, each holding a gun only inches from the other.

For a moment, there was just the crackle of fire, Dagley's muffled curses, Lance's receding screams and the faint echo of engines. Then another gunshot.

Teddy dropped, half his face blood and meat , and for a second Blackie wondered if he'd shot him — but no, the hole was in the side of his head.

Blackie felt a pistol barrel touch his temple. It was still hot. Suddenly, he could see Hasmed standing next to him, he could smell the cordite from the demon's gun.

"Be smart," Hasmed said. "Drop it."

Blackie dropped it.

Slowly, Grant unwound from his crouch, realizing that his face didn't hurt, realizing his eye was healed. With a snarl, he dove for his clothing, burrowing for the gun he still thought was there...

Tim was healed too, and he arose.

"Sabriel," Tim said clearly, "kill Hasmed."

"Nah," she replied.

Grady spoke again, repeating the Name he'd used before. She shrugged and raised her middle finger.

"What's... huh..." Thomas stammered, looking around.

"Thomas, sweetie, you might want to laugh now," she told him. "As for me, I think I'll start killing some priests." But then she, too, vanished.

"PUT YOUR HANDS UP! THIS IS THE FBI!"

"I KNEW YOU WOULD BETRAY ME!" Avitu shrieked. Her words, enraged and tormented, echoed through time, shadows and reflections reverberating to form her ultimate statement.

But since this was the Blue, the Godspace, they weren't just words. Here, expressing rage and getting revenge were the same thing. Her words were like chains or blades or flames, twisting in around Gaviel. Even that comparison couldn't do them justice. They were the words of an angel, more real than any chain or blade or flame.

"YOU'RE LYING," Gaviel responded. "IF YOU'D KNOWN, IT WOULD HAVE NEVER BEEN SO SIMPLE. YOU SUSPECTED, BUT I PLANNED FOR YOUR PETTY SUSPICION." And he did not merely speak the truth, his words were truth, the truth he was forcing upon her.

"YOUR PLANS ARE NOTHING AGAINST MY POWER," she answered. "ALL YOU HAVE DONE IS DELIVER YOURSELF TO ME."

That was her truth, her power. He didn't try to deny it. Instead, he chose to usurp it.

His voice crackled forth with phrases that were not mere patterns of sound in air, but waves in the fabric of reality. He spoke two syllables, the part of her Name that she had given to him. He spoke to seize her strength, but it was not enough, it was two parts in a multitude, she encircled him, growing.

And he kept on speaking, adding to those two syllables, others he had learned from Hasmed, forming a long and complex Name. Each separate idea turned her against herself, and each phrase containing them laid bare her secrets. Some of the concepts were wrong, some had changed over the centuries, but the core components were still true. She was, at heart, still a defender, she still sought to heal and help humanity, however twisted and strange her means had become. And so, the Name he had learned from Hasmed, the Name she had given her commander during the War, still had the power to bind and confine.

It was a lot. Backed by Gaviel's cunning, and his willingness to pare his thralls very thin, it was almost enough. But Gaviel's flawless confidence shook as he spoke his last word and realized it was not enough to destroy her. It wasn't even enough to stop her.

She would crush him in minutes instead of seconds, but the outcome was no longer in doubt. The Tree of Ignorance was just too strong.

Like so many, Gaviel had come to Las Vegas planning a gamble. Like most of them, he lost.

Sabriel was in the clouds. Avitu had tried to pull her down and imprison her in the earth, but Sabriel had navigated Avitu's secret courses before and slipped free during the Tree's distraction. She found herself in Jennifer Arliss's old prison.

She gazed at the frozen lightning, and up at the ground in the place of the sky. This moment of frozen time, a lightning-stroke stretched to infinity, was another place where Avitu hid her soul. Sabriel smiled, all alone, and spread her wings.

From a pocket, she produced a canister of yellow powder—mustard seed. She'd need it to make Avitu's binding pattern. She began to fly and spread the dust, weaving chains for the demon's soul.

Gaviel had told her Avitu would cave in quickly, so Sabriel was unprepared when the lightning reached out and struck her.

In Los Angeles, Stuart Flaubert spun his car onto the next exit ramp, prompting a cacophony of car horns as he fought to obey the urge to return to the Tree, immediately, at top speed. In Vegas, Pam Creed obeyed the same urge, leaping out of a hairdresser's chair to run for her car. But they didn't have the blood, they could not fully hold her.

Grant Dagley felt the power surge into him, and it was good. He left off the search for a weapon, for now he knew he was a weapon, and he turned to Blackie and struck the ground with his fist.

The earth leaped up and seized the young man. A wave of mud flowed up him, clamping on his legs and his thighs and his waist. Blackie raised his gun, fired, missed, and then the dirt was up over his arms, up to his neck, pinning him with the strength of soil, he was being buried alive.

Grant saw his pistol lying next to that dead wimp Teddy. He made the stone freeze and waddled over to get the gun.

"I'ma shove this in your mouth and shoot your goddamn head off," he said, quite matter-of-factly.

The greatest lurch of power, however, went to Tim Grady, the Hollywood Ice Pick, the last of Avitu's sacred bloodline to accept her holy priesthood. He faced the demon Hasmed and called the force of the storm.

Once a mighty angel of storms himself, Hasmed was nevertheless blasted back by a torrent of wind and lightning. He arose winged and awful, but Tim Grady could no longer feel awe. His poor broken mind could respond to only a few things, and one of those was the will of his owner, Avitu.

Two storm demons struggled, each trying to squeeze their power through the narrow aperture of a mortal body and spirit. But one had been back in the world for less than a year, and the other had gathered strength for centuries. Once her commander, Hasmed was now badly overmatched. Avitu flung him to the ground, and the ground reached up to seize him.

Then the wind became foul as the Reaper of Souls appeared. He said not a word but raised his scythe, aiming for the back of Grady's head.

"No!"

Usiel blinked as a ghost appeared before him, a naked woman with red hair blowing in the dust storm. "He's mine," Rosemary snarled. "He murdered me, and I own him!"

With an annoyed grunt, the Reaper swept his scythe through her, calling her into him. But that pause was enough, it was the time Tim needed to awaken the stone beneath Usiel's feet, time enough for Avitu to work through him and call the lightning. It was enough time for Grant to howl and blaspheme, his words shaking apart the connection between Usiel's potent spirit and the vulnerable flesh of Clive Keene, the mortal man whose body held the mightiest of Slayers. Avitu could feel the Reaper's strength, and she knew her only hope was to hold nothing back.

(With a pained, sudden cough, Stuart Flaubert pulled over. He could feel breath going in and out of his lungs, but it didn't seem to be doing him any good, he was still smothering.)

(Joeesha Murfee felt the same thing, but much harder and quicker. Less valuable to Avitu, her soul was burned up to fuel the demon's battle.)

Hasmed struggled, but Avitu was far too strong. Through her, through her priest, the winds that had been his life were rending him to pieces. He made to speak her Name, but this was not a pure space where thought and word were one. Here he needed breath and tongue and lips to speak, and his breath was stolen by the whirlwind, his mouth blocked by probing fingers of sand.

"DROP THE GUN AND PUT YOUR HANDS UP!" Special Agent Gabe McKenzie shouted through his bullhorn. He needed it to be heard above the shrieks of the air. His officers had found Lance and were proceeding toward the fire, pistols drawn and rifles ready, while Gabe aimed through the dust cloud at the naked gunman.

"*BAJA EL ARMA!*" he tried. Then, because some people only respond to rudeness, "*DROP THE GODDAMN GUN! TIRA LA CHINGADA PISTOLA!*"

And then, because he had no other choice, he put a bullet through Grant Dagley's back.

Sabriel dodged and fluttered, with Avitu's lightning reach only inches behind her. She had danced with this lightning before, but this time there were no hostages to use as shelter, this time each stroke was closer than the one before it.

And then the lightning was gone, winked out. For a moment, Sabriel was baffled. Then she looked up and around and saw the movement begin.

Time had come to Avitu's stolen moment. A sun that had stood for centuries began to roll once more.

Sabriel wondered how long she had to complete her pattern before the realm collapsed altogether.

Inside the cage of the Reaper's heart, Usiel spoke to Rosemary.

"She did it, you know," he told her. "He only murdered because of her hold over him. He is your enemy, but the demon is no less."

"He makes me real," Rosemary whined. "He keeps me alive!"

"No. You're not alive. You're not supposed to be real." The soil was hardening around him, he was trapped as hammers of lightning struck him once, twice. He drew on his beloved Glenda, but took only the little he dared. He did not have much time.

"YOU CAN CLING TO YOUR ABUSERS AND STRUGGLE TO STAY TRAPPED HERE. OR YOU CAN AVENGE YOURSELF, MAKE AN END TO IT, AND BE FREE. MY STRENGTH IS WANING, SO I'M GOING TO GIVE YOU YOUR CHOICE."

He exhaled her.

For a minute, Rosemary hesitated. Then she stepped in front of Tim Grady and said, "Look at me."

Tim Grady froze. The storm began to drop. A whimper escaped his throat.

"Yes," Rosemary said. "You remember me. And it's your fault. Because of you, a memory is all I am."

Great sobs of horror escaped the huge man's throat, and his piss struck the desert sand. Killer and victim locked eyes as she tried to show him, tried to make him understand.

Behind him, the Reaper of Souls broke free of the stony hold and raised his weapon of release.

"I'm sorry," Tim Grady whispered. His tears spattered on the dry ground. An instant later, his blood did too.

The strike team surrounded the fire and the Tree as the rending dust storm died out. Hasmed and Usiel felt the pressure of those human gazes, pressing them back into human shape.

Hasmed didn't want the hassles of being seen, so he wasn't seen. He picked up Tim Grady's severed head and started drawing Avitu's binding seal in the sand around the tree, muttering the incantation as he did. The police never looked at him, they just instinctively stepped out of his way.

Usiel, no longer a winged apparition of doom, but merely a tired-looking man, staggered over to the burned-out trunk and sagged against it. He made sure the ring on his hand pressed the blackened wood.

"PUT YOUR HANDS UP!" Gabe commanded. Usiel ignored him.

Sabriel completed her design, a yellow mirror of Hasmed's red rune.

In the space without space, Gaviel felt that inexorable pressure ease, and then collapse altogether. He didn't know what had happened, but he knew what he wanted. A thought, a word, a pattern—all were one as he bound this third facet of the great demoness.

Usiel was the last to act. He could feel Avitu being confined, and his role was to deliver the final stroke, to use his severing tool and lay her open. Once he split her wide, they would feed like pigs at a trough.

Even at that last moment, clinging to that blasted trunk, he wondered why he was doing it. Gaviel had lured him with promises of the richness of Avitu's soul and, when that wasn't enough, had goaded him by threatening Sabriel. Did Gaviel really have her Name? Would he really use it? Usiel still didn't know. In the end, he'd decided not to risk it.

Even as he'd made that decision, he'd heard Lucifer's words. "I can't let thousands wreak havoc because one might repent." Was Sabriel even worth saving? She'd gone along with Gaviel's plan willingly, even eagerly. Her vengeance on Avitu meant more to her than the chance of peace or recovery with Usiel.

In the end he made the cut.

Perhaps, like Lucifer, he felt that Avitu was a threat too grave to ignore. Or perhaps he reasoned that she was doomed anyhow, and he was as justified in benefiting from her death as anyone.

But most likely he did it because, like Gaviel, he wanted to. And that was what he did not want to face. He wanted to kill her and steal her power, and it was sweet, it was good. The consumption lured and fascinated him in a way even Sabriel could not, and the promise of more—so immediate, so real— drove him like no misty hint of salvation could.

Sabriel took the knowledge of storms, fighting Hasmed for pieces of it, but it was hers by right, the movement of water through wind and wind upon water. She took it, along with the sensations of a thousand years of bringing nourishing rain for generations of worshippers.

Gaviel sought the command of stone, greedily sucking in the right to shake the earth and form it to his will, as Avitu had to shield her tribe and smite their enemies.

Hasmed absorbed her skills with the flesh of men, the power that had saved countless infants through rude births, that had blessed her people with health through harsh winters, that had swept their rivals aside with reeking plague.

And Usiel, he took her feelings for humanity, her ability to look through their eyes and follow their movements and feel their sensations. With it came her horror at short years of grinding toil and fear and mortality, her despair, the helpless empathy that led her to declare war on consciousness, that led her to think men would be better off as mere beasts.

It was a rich meal, and they all savored each flavor from her past.

And then the unexpected happened.

"Are you okay there?" Gabe approached cautiously, gun still at the ready, creeping toward the man who was clutching the burned out trunk. Then he heard a soft cry and turned. Eyes wide, he realized he'd finally found May Carter.

The feasters found Avitu's deepest memory.

They had stripped her down, consumed her existence as a goddess, as a demon in Hell, as a warrior against God, and now, like a tiny pearl buried in the rotted flesh of a dead oyster, they found the angel she had been before the fall.

The purity gave them pause.

Could we save her? Hasmed wondered. *What would happen? All that rancid shit, the thousand years of pain, they're gone now, and this is what's left. Her last, best part. What happens if we back off now? Is she born again as an angel? Is there enough of her to salvage?*

Sabriel had similar thoughts, for even though she had told Usiel that her old self was dead—had believed it passionately— she now saw Avitu as she had been, as a newborn Angel of Life, untouched by bad choices and unstained by tragedy. She hesitated, and she tried to stop the others.

But Gaviel saw only the finest treasure of a creature who had defied him, who had bested him, who had stolen power and privilege he coveted. Avitu had wounded his pride, and that blinded him to any thought of mercy. He could not see how she could be saved, and even if he had, he would have said she did not deserve it. He plunged onward, plundering her last scrap of identity.

Usiel joined him. He knew it was wrong and cruel and heartless. But he could not resist.

Sabriel withdrew in disgust, returning to the physical world as a cloud of mist drifting among the guns and men and ashes. Hasmed, too, stepped away, shaking his head. Ignored, he walked back toward the cars.

When Gaviel had consumed the ultimate gasp of Avitu, he sank into the soil and waited, still grinning.

And Usiel drunk on the power of slaying a goddess, opened his eyes.

"Sir! Put your hands on your head."

"Very well," Usiel said, peeking over his shoulder.

One of the FBI men gasped and started clutching at his throat.

"O'Neil! What's wrong?" Gabe asked. O'Neil couldn't reply.

Usiel started to turn. "Face the tree!" Gabe shouted. With a shrug, the prisoner complied.

Another agent fell. This one had blood pouring out of his nose and mouth, and he couldn't seem to stop coughing.

"I'm ready for you to arrest me. If you dare," Usiel said. Gabe looked at him, at the two downed agents, and then a third fell, convulsing in the dust, heels kicking helplessly.

A thin fog of water vapor floated past the Reaper, and a voice echoed in his mind instead of his ear.

Usiel, please. Stop it.

"Very well, sweet Sabriel. For you." He turned, ignoring Gabe's brandished pistol, and snorted.

"Mortals." He shook his head in contempt. Then there was a gust of odious wind, and he was gone.

Epilogue

How does one punish a creature that has endured Hell? What torment could compare with the prison of the Almighty?

One can threaten with more of the same, but even some demons feel sympathy, and anyone freed from the Pit would think twice before returning anyone there. Especially someone whose previous service had been brave and intelligent.

"I am disappointed with you, Mukikel," Princess Nazathor said.

Her words were more than words. Her words conveyed a sense of sorrow and regret that a thousand human poets would need a thousand years to write. In those words was the weight of a ruined world.

Mukikel hung her head. She knew the Princess would not harm her, but hearing those words, she excoriated herself.

"Forgive me," she whispered.

There was a pause. Then Mukikel whispered again, and what came out was more than words. She spoke herself, naked and vulnerable, her True Name submitted freely as a gesture of repentance. Her words were the ultimate regret.

The Princess nodded, and the Autumn Overlord—still burned and aching—rose and departed.

"Can we talk about this now?"

Sabriel looked at Hasmed, who shrugged. "Sure," she replied.

"Okay," Thomas said. Then he stopped. "Okay," he said again.

The three of them had driven all night to get away from the compound, pausing only to stop at motels to steal new cars, and all-night service stations so that Hasmed could shoplift the other two some new shorts and T-shirts.

"So... okay... what happened?"

"Is this going to be like the time we rented The Usual Suspects and watched it while you were stoned?" Sabriel said. "'Cause if it is, I'm not even going to bother."

Dawn was breaking, and they'd pulled into a truck stop for gas and breakfast at Stuckey's.

"Let's start with when I... you know, the thing at the lake."

"All fake," Sabriel said.

"So all that stuff..."

"Big fake out."

"And that creepy fucker at the camp?"

"Barney?" She smiled. "It's just a piece of meat, Tommy. Though you were very noble."

"But why?"

"Because they figured Avitu would pry any Name you got out of your head," Hasmed said, spooning unflavored oatmeal into his mouth. "You wouldn't have a chance of fooling Avitu, so you had to believe the lie yourself in order to pass it on."

"So I was never really in control of you?"

"Not for a second," Sabriel said, a sweet smile on her face.

Thomas sat and digested that, along with part of an omelet.

"What about that Reaper guy? What was his thing?"

"Gaviel talked him into it."

Thomas nodded again, wondered briefly about the specifics but decided they didn't really matter.

"Okay, so... what about the eye-gouging?"

"Gaviel helped Mr. Black out with that," Sabriel said, nodding at Hasmed.

"Helped?"

"Gave him a little nudge. Like he used to nudge you all the time," Hasmed said. He poked at his side dish. "Fresh fruit my ass," he murmured.

"So he knew Black was gonna stick Dagley?"

"He probably didn't," Sabriel said. "He probably figured he'd sacrifice the boy."

"That would be a big distraction for the Tree," Hasmed said. "The original plan was for me or the Reaper to ice Black as soon as he got invested as a priest. He'd be real vulnerable then, and it'd be a good way to waste a lot of Avitu's power fast. But then Black got squirrelly, so we had to improvise."

Thomas stared down at his food. "So Gaviel would have just let him do it?"

"'Fraid so."

Tom pushed his plate away. "Pardon me." He went toward the bathroom.

The two demons ate in silence. "You want the rest of my biscuits and gravy?" Sabriel asked.

"No," Hasmed said. "That stuff is fucking disgusting."

"Yeah." She pushed it away. "I can't believe the Reaper... you know. At the end."

"Why not? He was jonesin' for a big juicy soul all along. Why else would he throw in with a motley group of assholes like us?"

"You're right. I guess I just expected better from him."

"The guy busted a multiple-murderer psychopath out of jail and you expected better?"

"Those were just mortals," Sabriel objected. "With... us... I guess I thought..."

"Yeah, well, we all had some rude awakenings."

"So you were..."

"With my old buddy? Shit yeah." Hasmed looked away, out at the sun rising over the highway. One finger rubbed the scar on his forehead.

"I think Gaviel's wounded a lot worse than I am," he said, "and I don't think he'll ever heal."

Sabriel nodded, and excused herself. On her way to the restroom, she met Thomas coming back.

"Thomas?" she asked. "When you thought you were my master, why didn't you take revenge?"

He shrugged. "I dunno."

"You can't do better than that?"

He frowned. "My first parole officer had this little sign on the wall in her office," he said. "She was the softy kind of one, the one who always wanted to talk, real nice, candy on the desk, wanted to be a social worker... and this sign, someone had made it for her. It was burned into a wood plaque, and it said, 'Hate won't save you. Hate won't help you. Hate won't even make you feel better.'" He shrugged. "I thought it was kinda gay, but... I can still remember it, I guess."

"Do you want out?"

"Out?"

"If you want, I'll release you from our pact."

Thomas blinked.

"Huh?"

"You wouldn't be able to change anymore, and I wouldn't take anything from you anymore." She looked down at her feet and twirled a strand of hair around her finger. "You want out?"

Thomas said yes. Later, he was surprised that he'd had to think about it. She nodded.

"Okay. It's done."

"Just like that?"

"Mm hm. Don't tell Harvey, okay?"

"Sure."

Then she was gone into the ladies' room.

Time passed.

Once the crime scene calmed down, Gaviel arose from his stony rest. An evidence technician just had time to register that a naked black man—holy crap, it was Noah Wallace!—was walking toward her when he spoke.

"HI," he said. "YOU SHOULD GIVE ME SOME CLOTHING AND A RIDE INTO TOWN. ALSO, SOME MONEY."

In a mountain cave, in the highland border between Turkey and Iraq, native Kurds prayed to their new god, their Death God, for the power to drive forth their oppressors.

"Usi-el! Usi-el! Usi-el!" they chanted. But their lord did not appear until they made their sacrifice.

The trials arising from the "Tree of Death" cult raid were a media spectacular. Grant Dagley was convicted of multiple murders after Oscar Black turned state's evidence and described what the National Enquirer dubbed Dagley's "Rape Barn." The next rape Dagley experienced was his own, in prison. He wasn't there long, though. Carrying Avitu's power without the priestly blood to protect him wasn't tenable for a mortal frame. He was sick a lot, and he died three weeks after the Nevada Attorney General finally acquiesced to the State of Illinois's request that Dagley face charges for the crimes he committed while wearing a badge before those committed as a cultist. Joan Pratt, who had already begun to raise money for a run to become Illinois Attorney General based on her longstanding investigation into the Dagley case, was removed from the role of chief prosecutor when Oscar Black's story of having left an anonymous call about Dagley's barn months earlier became public. Her replacement had just begun deposing Dagley's former deputies when the accused saved the Illinois taxpayer a great deal of money.

Oscar Black himself was judged one of the most fascinating people of the year. No one ever conclusively proved whether or not he was Black Hawk O'Hanlon, and then no one ever proved if Black Hawk O'Hanlon participated in any of his mother's crimes, or was (as Black claimed to be) essentially a helpless hostage along for the ride. Gabe McKenzie testified that when he got on the scene, Black had been encased in some kind of quick-set cement and had to be dug free—testimony that directly contradicted Lance Mason's tearful testimony that Black had saved his life at tremendous personal risk.

For years, crime buffs would spin elaborate theories connecting Lance Mason, Joellen O'Hanlon, Grant Dagley and the decapitated Hollywood Ice Pick. They tied them to dozens, then hundreds of unsolved murders and abductions. But none of them even came close to guessing the truth.

Gabe McKenzie had the unpleasant task of bringing May Carter home. A doctor who examined her guessed that the lobotomy was performed before the police even knew she was missing. McKenzie couldn't have saved her, no matter how quickly he'd found her.

It was cold comfort.

Mitch Berger was living in a slum in Mexico City, working as a day laborer when Shadrannat and Mukikel came for him.

They were not gentle.

Sal moved to St. Louis. There, he met a creature called the Stone of Despair, and they both got jobs working at the Gateway Arch.

The Reverend Matthew Wallace offered to perform the funeral rites for Leotis Grant and Renee DeVries. Both children had been mentored by his missing son Noah, and both had died— suddenly, inexplicably, painfully—on the same night. Matthew was the only one to connect their deaths, and he was the only one who thought there was some link to the FBI raid hundreds of miles away that same evening.

The Grants and DeVries declined. No one wanted to hear it. No one wanted to hear about devils.

More time passed.

Pam Creed, who had felt Avitu die, drove right past the compound when she saw the flashing lights, turned around and went home and took the curlers out of her hair. She went into therapy and got a job in a credit union and lived a marginal life for a while, until she killed herself.

Avitu's other surviving priest, Stuart Flaubert, didn't even last that long. He continued to try to practice her faith, got caught by the police and spent the remainder of his days in prison.

"The opera finishes at 10:00," Sabriel—today going by Irene Wasserstein—said, looking at a tiny and feverishly expensive watch. "Come a little early and wait for me."

"Yes ma'am," her loyal thrall Barney said, emerging from the limousine to open her door for her.

She stepped out of the car and was glorious.

Hasmed was going over Tina's latest skill worksheets with her when he felt the presence. He tried to get her out of the house, but the presence came up on him too fast.

They didn't even bother with the door. One minute it was just Tina and Hasmed, trying to rush out the back, and then the living room was full.

Sal Macellaio looked at him dully. He'd lost weight. Something else about him seemed absent too, but you couldn't say exactly what.

The Stone of Despair was there too.

In between them, the demon lord Vodantu took shape.

Tina screamed and hid her face from something that was all eyes and wings made of brushed steel. Its voice made the windows shake.

"HASMED," it said. "MY ERRANT SERVANT."

"Tina, run." Hasmed smashed out a window with his elbow, tried to hoist her through it but she was thrashing and fighting him. She was hysterical, and he knew she would never outrun the Stone anyway. Not if it wanted her.

"LET NO ONE SAY I AM NOT PATIENT AND FORGIVING. I WILL HOLD OUT ONE MORE CHANCE TO YOU. ONE MORE OPPORTUNITY TO RETURN TO MY FOLD. IF YOU BUT SLAY THE GIRL, YOU MAY SERVE ME ONCE MORE—THOUGH UNDER THE SUPERVISION OF SALVATORE, HERE."

"I won't."

Hasmed didn't keep guns in the house, but he knew they'd do little against Vodantu anyhow. He lashed out with wind instead, with a torrent of plague and pollution. He drained Paum into convulsions, hoping that it would somehow harm Vodantu, or even just slow it down.

But no.

Vodantu spoke again, and this time the name he gave Hasmed was no mere word, but that spirit's place in the universe.

"BY THY NAME I BIND THEE. CEASE YOUR INSOLENT RESISTANCE."

Hasmed could do nothing but obey. Tina had curled into a ball around his feet, sobbing.

Hasmed glared at Sal. "You must be real proud," he said.

"SLAY THE CHILD."

A trickle of blood seeped down from the mark on Hasmed's brow. "I won't," he said again.

"REMARKABLE. YOUR MISPLACED AFFECTION HAS WARPED EVEN YOUR NAME OUT OF TRUE. BUT WHY DO YOU DEFY ME? YOU KNOW HER FATE. YOU KNOW SHE'LL DIE SOME DAY. WHY RESIST THE INEVITABLE?"

Hasmed looked up, and a small smile quirked his mouth. "I can't believe I'm gonna die protecting a human. But, here we are."

"VERY NOBLE. VERY *FUTILE*. IS THAT WHAT YOU WANT AS YOUR FINAL STATEMENT?"

"How about this?" He threw back his shoulders, and spread out his wings. And this time, the light that flowed from his face was pure and unsullied. "MAYBE HUMAN LIFE HAS VALUE. MAYBE IT'S WORTH FIGHTING FOR. EVERY LAST SECOND."

Vodantu's mechanical voice ground through Hasmed's True Name again, and this time the command was, "DESTROY YOURSELF!"

Hasmed had no choice but to obey. His relationship to Tina was different, his connection to the world and humanity had changed drastically since he'd become free. But his connection to Vodantu he could not alter or sever.

There was a flare of light, and he was gone.

Then those baleful eyes turned themselves upon Tina Ciullo.

"AND WHAT SHALL WE DO WITH YOU?"

"Man," Thomas Ramone said as he entered his cramped, messy Louisiana apartment. "Work was all hassle today."

"Same here," Black Hawk O'Hanlon replied from the sofa. Two thirds of a Pabst six-pack was sitting on the orange crate they used as an end table. "Nothin' but piss and moan all day long." He tossed a beer to his roommate.

"An' the Honda's still pinging, even with premium gas."

"Maybe Saturday we can mess with it."

Tom cracked open the beer and sat on the couch. "Dude," he said, "I'm real sorry."

"What for?"

"Just wait a minute."

Seconds passed, and then Blackie grimaced and waved a hand in front of his nose. Tom laughed.

"Damn it!" Blackie said. "That's fuckin' rank! You have those burritos for lunch again?"

"Chili," Thomas said smugly. "You want me to light a match?"

"You light a match and the whole floor could blow! Shit!"

They were silent as Thomas's fart dissipated.

"So, anything on tonight?"

"*Silent Night, Deadly Night 2* starts at eight."

"Cool!"

They ate microwave pizza rolls and watched TV and were silently grateful to be free men.

About the Author

In the course of his life, Greg Stolze has had the glasses punched off his face by a police officer, has fallen in love, has ridden an elephant, has sat around with three blonde women discussing their underwear, has danced badly, has gotten drunk, has danced while drunk and has written novels. Only the writing, the love and the elephant were as exciting as you'd think.

Curious about other Crossroad Press books? Stop by our
website: http://crossroadpress.com
We offer quality writing
in digital, audio, and print formats.

Subscribe to our newsletter on the website homepage and
receive a free eBook.